DATE DUE		

COPY 2

FIC GOR c.2
Gorman, Edward
The first lady

L.C.
2010

★★★★★★★★★★★★★★★★★★★★★★★★★★★★★★★★

THE
FIRST
LADY

★★★★★★★★★★★★★★★★★★★★★★★★★★★★★★★★

Forge Books by E. J. Gorman

The First Lady
The Marilyn Tapes

✮✮✮✮✮✮✮✮✮✮✮✮✮✮✮✮✮✮✮✮✮✮✮✮✮✮✮✮✮✮✮

THE FIRST LADY

✮✮✮✮✮✮✮✮✮✮✮✮✮✮✮✮✮✮✮✮✮✮✮✮✮✮✮✮✮✮✮

E. J. GORMAN

A TOM DOHERTY ASSOCIATES BOOK
NEW YORK

There are three people I really need to
thank for helping me with this book—my
editor, Greg Cox, writer Larry Segriff,
and director Nathaniel Gutman.

THE FIRST LADY

Copyright © 1995 by E. J. Gorman

All rights reserved, including the right to reproduce this book, or
portions thereof, in any form.

This book is printed on acid-free paper.

A Forge Book
Published by Tom Doherty Associates, Inc.
175 Fifth Avenue
New York, N.Y. 10010

Forge® is a registered trademark of Tom Doherty Associates, Inc.

Design by Lynn Newmark

Library of Congress Cataloging-in-Publication Data

Gorman, Edward.
  The first lady / by E. J. Gorman.
    p.   cm.   C. 2
  "A Tom Doherty Associates book."
  ISBN 0–312–85777–2
    1. Presidents' spouses—United States—Fiction.   2. Women
detectives—United States—Fiction.   I. Title.
PS3557.O759F57   1995
813'.54—dc20   95–35369

First edition: December 1995

Printed in the United States of America

A NOTE TO THE READER

This book is a work of fiction. Its story and characters are products of my imagination. The setting is Washington, D.C., and certain locations, institutions, and public figures are mentioned, but the incidents depicted are entirely imaginary and fictional.

To Dean Koontz, whose talent
is exceeded only by his generosity.

I HAD A SUDDEN IMPULSE TO DRIVE [BY
MYSELF]. . . . I JUMPED BEHIND THE WHEEL
OF A CAR AND, MUCH TO THE DISCOMFORT
OF MY SECRET SERVICE DETAIL, DROVE
MYSELF AROUND TOWN. FOR SEVERAL
HOURS, I ENJOYED A MARVELOUS
SENSATION OF PERSONAL FREEDOM.

—FIRST LADY HILLARY CLINTON IN HER
   COLUMN *TALKING IT OVER*

While the most dangerous weapons of this century are thought to be nuclear bombs and warheads, the power of radio and television runs a close second. Hitler used radio, for example, as one of his primary tools for taking and maintaining his power. . . . While America has not produced a Hitler, it has produced a number of haters and bigots who have used electronic media to exploit the fears and resentments of the masses. The early electronic shamans were loud and crude; the modern variety generally uses mockery and code phrases to get their messages across.

—Del Weaver, "Shaman of the Airwaves," *Channel One*

I

★ ★

You are either one with righteous, one with
us [Christians], . . . or you are an enemy of God
Almighty . . . and one with the evil bankers of
Wall Street . . . and the dark people alien to
this nation.

—Radio Evangelist
Father Charles Coughlin, 1938

1

★ ★ ★ One moment the night shadows were empty. Then, suddenly, the man was there, staring up at the second-floor window of the expensive town house across the street.

Two silhouettes played against the drawn white curtains: a man and a woman.

The man in the shadows wore a black fedora and black raincoat. His collar was turned up against the light rain.

His breath was vapor.

His cheeks and nose were numb.

Late April, and it was still 38 degrees at night.

A new Mercedes sedan went by, splashing water in a rolling heavy wave against the curb. In this part of Washington, D.C., the prosperous part known as Foggy Bottom, you saw a new Mercedes every few minutes.

The woman in the window had once owned a new Mercedes. Back in Springfield, Illinois, it was, the year her husband first ran for the Senate.

He stared up at the window again.

He wondered if they were going to kiss. Perversely, for all the pain it would cause him, he wanted to see it.

But they disappointed him by moving away from the window entirely.

Cop car.

The man sensed it even before he saw it.

Cop car at the far end of the block.

Coming down here slowly but inexorably.

He certainly could not afford to be seen here. They'd put a flashlight beam on his face and—

Imagine the headlines that would make.

And wouldn't his enemies love it.

There was a small cheese boutique behind him. He stepped back into the darkened doorway just as the cop car drew closer.

His breath was coming in gasps. Scared. Couldn't help it. So much at stake here.

The cop car rolled right on by.

The pudgy cop riding shotgun didn't even look over in this direction. Probably headed toward the Kennedy Center a few blocks away. Tonight's symphony would just now be getting out.

He took up his position in the shadows of an oak tree. The town house window was still empty.

She was going to cheat him out of his show.

The brown government Ford came from the opposite direction. Even from here, he recognized the man immediately.

The man who helped her get away with all this.

The man in the Ford tapped his horn lightly and then sat back to wait for her to appear.

A few more cars came past headed in the direction of the Kennedy Center.

He moved back into the shadows of the doorway. Too easy for the man in the Ford to spot him in the passing headlights.

Then the front door of the town house opened at last, and she stood framed in the glowing light. She wore her usual disguise—wig and thick eyeglasses and bulky coat—but she could not hide her beauty.

At least not from the man in the shadows.

She turned to the town house owner and said something quickly. No kiss. No touching of any kind. And then she was hurrying down the steps toward the brown Ford.

As she opened the door and slid inside, he got a look at her in the interior light. She'd made herself look drab.

But that was her intention, of course. If she were homely, nobody would guess who she really was. Nobody would give her a second look.

She closed the door, casting the interior of the car into darkness.

She said something to the driver, who nodded and then pulled away from the curb.

It was going to be so lovely when it all came out. So much intrigue and mystery.

He could just imagine how the tabloid TV shows would handle it.

A woman who goes to meet her lover disguised as someone else . . . romantic intrigue behind the closed doors of fashionable Foggy Bottom.

But best of all was the real identity of the woman herself.

He wondered how many Americans knew that the First Lady of the United States was frequently seeing a very special friend of hers . . .

They might not know it right now . . . but they would know it soon enough.

Because the First Lady was about to become involved in a scandal that would shock not just America but the entire world.

He was going to make sure of it.

2

★ ★ ★ The First Lady of the United States said, "Tonight's the last time you'll have to do this, Dana."

Dana Hopper, friend and White House Secret Service agent, looked over at her and said, "I hope so, Claire. For your sake." He smiled, "Besides, I'm getting tired of looking at you in that ugly wig."

Claire laughed and it felt good. She hadn't been able to laugh for two weeks, not since David Hart had asked her for the $100,000 in cash. He called it a loan. She called it blackmail. Whatever it was, she'd paid it tonight and now it was over with.

"How'd it go?" Dana said. He was a tall but heavy man who'd served with the Marines in Vietnam. Like most Secret Service agents, he wore the kind of dark suits and conservative ties that were the pride of responsible funeral directors everywhere. He tried a new diet at least once a month.

Claire and Dana had a special bond. A year ago his seven-year-old daughter had died of an aneurysm and his wife, in a kind of crazed grief, had left Dana and gone back to her previous husband. Dana had gone through a very bad and shaky time. One day he started telling Claire about all this and found her a sympathetic listener. Claire herself was feeling alienated in those days: her husband always gone . . . and hints of an affair were being whispered of inside the Beltway. Then, following her accidental meeting with David Hart six months ago, she just naturally confided in Dana, as Dana had confided in her.

"He doesn't sound like a very nice guy," Dana said.

"He used to be. That's the funny thing. He used to be one of our best friends back in college. My husband really respected him and enjoyed him. But I guess all the failures he's had— Well, he's turned bitter and angry. God, it was so stupid of me to start seeing him—"

He looked over at her and smiled. "Hey, it's over."

"You really think so?"

"I really think so."

"Don't blackmailers always come back for more?"

"Yes, they do. But he's a registered lobbyist now and he can't afford a scandal any more than you can."

"I guess that's right."

"Plus, you just gave him $100,000 tax free. I'd think that'd tide him over for a while. Especially with his lobbying money."

She shook her head. She'd saved the money from writing magazine articles over the years. She'd been planning to use it for Deirdre's college. Two more years and Deirdre would be going to Princeton, where the President had gone.

"I sure hope you're right," she said. "I sure do."

At the White House, in the Oval Office, President Matt Hutton sat at his desk, rubbing his eyes. He needed a good strong jolt of regular coffee. The decaf just didn't cut it. The problem was, if he drank caffeine after six P.M., he couldn't sleep well.

He looked down at his cluttered desk. So much work to do to keep his promises to the Americans who had voted for him. Matt was a conservative Republican, one who believed that fifty years of Democratic influence had turned much of the country into a welfare state rife with crime and despair, a state that frequently enslaved (both physically and spiritually) the very people it claimed to be helping. There were too many taxes on enterprise and too many subsidies for everything from defense contractors to farmers. And there were far too many regulations on businesses. Lifting many of those regulations was the only hope most people had of seeing their paychecks increased because their bosses were now forced to compete with countries that paid their workers a third—or even a fourth—of what American workers earned. And income taxes were robbing Americans of their way of life. In less than fifteen years, America had slipped from first place to ninth in quality of life—and yet federal income taxes, adjusted for inflation, had gone up 14 percent.

The Democrats, of course, ever eager for big government, fought Hutton on every front.

But equally troublesome was the far right of his own party. Matt was a fiscal conservative who believed in staying out of peoples' intimate business. Abortion had to be a personal decision, he believed.

Homosexuals deserved the same rights—no more, no less—as anyone else, and discrimination against them was not right. Prayer in school was a bogus issue—if a child wanted to pray, let him or her bow his head and offer up a silent prayer. He believed in cutting government, cutting taxes—and staying out of peoples' personal lives. Like his friend Governor Weld of Massachusetts, he was essentially a libertarian.

These beliefs did not endear him to the religious right of his own party. In fact, he was being challenged in the upcoming presidential primary—by a far-right Republican senator.

The Republican moderates in both houses were trying to rally support for him, but as former Iowa representative Fred Grandy (himself a mainstream conservative) had noted, "The problem with moderates is that they are great at cocktail parties but lousy at coups. It's very difficult to find a militant moderate movement."

So now the President sat at his desk and rubbed his tired eyes and worried about wars on two front—trying to cut through all the excesses of previous Democratic administrations and concerned about the challenge in the upcoming primary.

"So you really think it's over?" Claire asked again.

Dana Hopper smiled. "I really think it's over. You've heard the last of Mr. Hart."

"I just hope the President doesn't find out what I've done. Giving David that money."

The President. There it was again. Calling him by the title all his aides used when addressing him . . .

They'd lost a child together in miscarriage, survived a horrible breast cancer scare, and endured the slings and arrows of five major political campaigns, everything from local alderman to mayor to the House of Representatives to the governorship. And all that while he'd never been anybody but good old Matthew Hutton. But during the past three years in the White House she'd caught herself every once in a while thinking of him not as good old Matt but as an abstract symbol known as The President.

"David has a lot of debts," Claire said, thinking again of the man she'd just left.

David had always been like that. Handsome, artistic, and snobbish in a curiously appealing way. Women always found themselves rather desperately seeking his approval—David was never without women and never *with* money. Even though his parents had been poor, they'd been spendthrifts, blowing their money rather than paying their bills or putting any away for future security. David had learned all their bad habits. If you didn't think so, ask any of his four ex-wives, or any of the three movie queens he'd lived off of at various stages during his Hollywood period.

She'd always considered him a friend—somebody who really did understand her, who valued her as a person—but now she knew better.

She'd run into David at the National Portrait Gallery seven months ago. He'd just arrived in Washington, having given up on Hollywood. She remembered thinking: he must have run out of fading movie queens to live with. But in the course of a one-hour conversation, she forgot all about David's cynical side, and let herself bask in his charm, quick wit and ability to convince you that he really was your soulmate.

Just what a First Lady, terrified that her husband really was having an affair, was in need of: attention.

She'd been reckless and foolish. Dana had helped smuggle her out of the White House in her disguise. She'd spend two hours or so at David's and then Dana, as now, would bring her back.

Six visits to David's.

Chaste visits.

Never more than a single glass of wine.

Never so much as even a kiss on the cheek.

All she'd wanted was laughter and companionship.

But she'd soon learned that David wanted more, much more. Like any self-respecting lady-killer, David was heavily into trophies. And what could be a bigger trophy than bedding the First Lady?

David had gotten insistent. He'd even tried one of the oldest and most laughable ploys: "You need to prove to yourself that you're still a beautiful and desirable woman, Claire."

Actually, she didn't. At forty-three, with a slender body, long coppery hair, and a freckled face that managed to suggest both little sister and sophisticated woman, Claire knew that she was no great beauty. But she also knew that men found her sexy in her quiet way.

She'd never once thought of going to bed with David.

She'd always been faithful and always planned to *be* faithful.

Once he understood that she was never going to go to bed with him, David changed directions. He started telling her about all the money he owed. She didn't have the heart to suggest that maybe he live a little more modestly. The town house alone leased for $8,500 a month. And there were respectable alternatives to Armani suits and custom-sewn shoes.

Two visits ago, he'd said it: "You know, I've got a friend who works on the *National Informer* here in Washington and if I ever really got desperate . . . well, all I'd need to do was hint that I knew somebody who was seeing the First Lady on the side and—"

She'd slapped him.

She couldn't recall slapping anybody since she was sixteen and Michael Bannion had forced his hand down inside her bra.

He had betrayed her, David had. Utterly.

She'd fled home, unable to confide even in Dana.

Her husband, the President, had misinterpreted the reason for her depression that night. He assumed that she was reacting to his months of stony silence as the jackals in town gossiped of his affair with a striking young congresswoman from Utah. He apologized for how he'd been treating her, and then he confessed that he had thought of having an affair with the young woman but had pulled back, afraid of the damage it would do his marriage. She could still see him against the window, the lights of the Washington Monument in the background, a tall, still-boyish man nimble of mind and body—still a great reader of very serious books and still a killer tennis player four days a week.

She'd had no doubt that he was telling her the truth.

She went to him and they held each other long into the night, and then they went with a quiet solemnity to their bed where they made love twice, the first time as a means of healing the identical wounds they shared, the second time for the pure bawdy pleasure of sex itself.

That night, she'd fallen in love with him again.

Deirdre, the daughter they both loved with almost embarrassing zeal, watched them both carefully at the breakfast table the next morning. She'd obviously sensed that they'd come together again because when she stood up from the table, she smiled mischievously and said, "I guess I'll leave you two lovebirds alone."

Four and a half wonderful weeks followed, some of the best times of Claire's entire married life.

And then it all ended with David's phone call and his demand of $100,000 cash.

The White House was coming in sight now, and, thanks to John Kennedy, the sight was beautiful. Kennedy had complained during his brief, melancholy tenure as President that the places surrounding the White House were an eyesore—dirty crumbling buildings selling cheap merchandise, or, even worse, vacant grassy lots. The Congress had responded to this complaint with promenades and parks plus new buildings that included several architectural masterpieces.

"You bought the President his birthday gift yet?"

"I still haven't figured out what to buy him."

"The kind of weather we've been having," Dana said, "maybe some long underwear."

"You know Frederic Remington?"

"The man who painted all the western scenes?"

"Right."

"The President's a big fan of his work. I saw an original Remington at a gallery last week. That's what I've got my eye on."

"I'm sure he'll love it," Dana said.

"Do you really think it's over, Dana?"

"With David?"

"Yes."

"Uh-huh. From what I know of him, he's an opportunist but he's not a high roller."

"High roller?"

"He's willing to take chances but only up to a point. I'm sure he understands that he's pushed you as far as he can."

"God, I was a fool to ever go over there."

"You were feeling lonely, Claire. And you had good reason. All that talk about Matt—excuse me, the President—having an affair. You needed a friend."

She smiled and touched his shoulder. "You're my real friend, Dana."

He looked over at her and smiled. "I never would have made it through Sarah's death without you, Claire. So we're more than even." Then he beamed even more. "And things are looking up for both of us. You've got your husband back—and that nice-looking secretary in Senator Kenyon's office has finally agreed to have dinner with me."

"Finally!" Claire said. "I thought I'd have to write you a letter of recommendation or something."

"Or have the President give her an official order to go out with me."

Then they reached the White House. She had been getting out by making up excuses about places she had to go—art gallery openings, children's hospitals, things like that—with Dana always accompanying her, covering for her. When they got near David's house, she always put the wig on.

Now she took it off.

She wanted to burn it.

Forget everything it had come to signify.

So foolish, she'd been; so foolish.

3

✶ ✶ ✶ They were having the tattoo argument.

It always went something like this: why couldn't a nice, normal sixteen-year-old girl have a tattoo when all her nice, normal friends had one? (Deirdre)

Honey, you're old enough to understand what's at stake here. If Knox Stansfield ever found out that my daughter had a tattoo, he'd put it on his radio show. (Matt)

I'm so sick of Knox Stansfield! I wish he'd die! (Deirdre)

Honey, look, a far-right conservative in my own party is going to challenge me in the presidential primary next month. He's going to say that I've gone Washington and that I'm not a real conservative anymore. And Knox Stansfield is helping him every way he can. So if they found out that my daughter had a tattoo— (Matt)

I'm sorry, Daddy. I just wish I could have a nice, normal life. Ever since you were elected President— (Deirdre)

Which was when Claire walked in, carrying her appointment book and a draft of a speech she was giving two days from now to the Washington Woman's Conference. She also carried a small manila envelope of some photographs she'd taken of the White House grounds. Fifteen years ago, Matt had bought her a 35mm Nikon for her birthday, and she'd been a photography buff every since.

"Not the tattoo argument again?" Claire smiled.

"The tattoo argument," Matt said, coming over to kiss her.

"Honey—" Claire started to say.

"I know, I know," Deirdre sighed dramatically. "Knox Stansfield."

Even mention of Stansfield's name put Claire in a tense, irritable mood. She thought back to their college days in the early seventies. The four of them—Stansfield, David Hart, Matt Hutton and Claire Delaney—had been the best of friends and just about the only political conservatives at the University of Illinois. Instead of books by Mao and Allen Ginsberg, they carried books by Ayn Rand and William F. Buckley. One other thing: Claire had been Knox Stansfield's lover then, not Matt's. Matt came later.

And now, years later, Knox Stansfield, through the reach and power of his ultraconservative radio talk show, was one of the most influential forces in American politics. And he had spent every day of Matt's White House tenure trying to destroy the President.

"I think we should boil him alive," Claire said, forcing herself to play the humorous little game that Deirdre loved so much.

"I say a guillotine," Deirdre said. She wore a buff blue sweater, jeans and a pair of fuzzy pink slippers. Her pigtails and freckles and braces gave her the timeless look of the classic girl-next-door, cute and appealing.

"I'd rather drop him out of a plane and listen to him scream all the way down," Matt said. He wore a blue V neck and white button-down shirt and tan slacks and a decade-old pair of cordovan loafers, his favorite shoes. Despite an increasingly noticeable little belly, he was still a striking man, his graying hair only adding to his air of authority. He was quickly learning the differences between being a senator, which he'd been for a term, and being the President. There was no more imperial presidency, for one thing. A President could make very few significant decisions on his own and govern effectively: given the increasingly combative clash between Congress and the White House, the President always needed a consensus if he wanted to hold on to his power. You could see this knowledge in some of the new wrinkles in his face.

"How about covering him with honey and inviting some grizzly bears in?" Deirdre said.

"That sounds pretty good to me, how about you?" Claire said to Matt.

He brought them together and held them tenderly. They were hardly an ideal family—the mythic "ideal" sitcom family that the far right insisted all Americans should be part of—but nobody could dispute their love for each other, nor the loyalty they felt.

Loyalty.

Images of David Hart came back to Claire.

She wanted to tell them, both of them, how foolish she'd been. Even though nothing had happened, even though she hadn't even *wanted* anything to happen, she'd fled to David for solace, and in so doing jeopardized Matt's political future.

One word to the press from David—

But Dana had said it was over.

David wouldn't be coming back for more.

All Claire could do was hope and pray that Dana was right.

Matt squeezed them tighter.

"I not only have one beautiful woman in my arms, I have two," he said.

"Yeah, take *that* Warren Beatty," Deirdre grinned.

"Warren Beatty?" Matt said in mock surprise. "Why would you think of some old coot like Warren Beatty?"

Deirdre giggled. She'd always loved it when her father got silly. When she was an infant, he could keep her laughing for half an hour at a time.

"All right, then," Deirdre said, "take *that* Harrison Ford."

"Now there's a guy I like," Matt said.

Claire glanced around the living room, savoring the moment. Deirdre was right. It was very difficult to live a nice, normal life in the White House. That's why Claire had fixed up the second floor to resemble a nice, normal all-American house. None of the Empire furniture of the Lincoln Sitting Room, or the gold damask draperies of the State Dining Room, or the thirty-six-lamp chandeliers of the Red Room.

No, the living room, like their two bedrooms, was a comfortable, informal arrangement of an upholstered couch and matching chairs, a large and splendid fireplace, a leather recliner favored by Matt, a twenty-seven-inch TV set packed with cable channels and soft-light table lamps that always lent a cozy glow to the place.

When you were in here, you could almost forget that you were First Lady and that your husband was President, with the power and authority to destroy a good share of the world if he felt the need. And you could even almost forget all the jackals that prowled the night just outside the White House fence, sniffing the air for the first smell of fresh blood.

"Well, I'd better go finish up my trig," Deirdre said wearily.

"I'll bring you in some cocoa if you want some," Claire said.

"That'd be great, Mom. Thanks."

Deirdre gave her an enthusiastic little peck on the cheek. Claire had been bringing Deirdre hot cocoa for years. It was a symbol that everything was fine in their lives. It had an almost religious significance to Claire and—given her anxiety about David coming back for more money sometime—she needed the comforting feel of routine.

She'd bring Deirdre hot cocoa.

And everything would be fine.

David Hart wouldn't come back and ask for more money.

And Knox Stansfield would quit bashing the President day in and day out.

If only she wished and prayed hard enough, these things would come true.

She was sure of it.

She went to get Deirdre's cocoa ready.

"Are you all right?" Matt asked after they had finished making love.

"Fine. Why?"

"You just seem a little—withdrawn, I guess."

"No, really, I'm fine."

The rain had started again.

Sometimes she liked to snuggle up in bed, listening to the rain. Made her feel like a lucky, privileged animal to be safe and dry when it was pouring outside.

But tonight the rain just made her feel lonely somehow, alienated from the man who lay next to her. The man she loved.

She knew why, of course.

He had told her about his near-tryst—he was caught up in the power of the office, he'd said, and somehow that had translated into the need to make new sexual conquests. And now she needed to tell him about her friendship with David.

But it wouldn't be easy.

After college, Matt and David had had a falling-out over a female friend of Matt's whom David had romanced and then dumped rather brutally. Matt had never forgiven him. And if he found out that his own wife had gone to David—

But she had to tell him. Sometime. Somehow.

She forced herself to think of happier times. When they'd first moved into the White House, they'd decided to make love in every bedroom in the venerable mansion. And so they had. That was only a few years ago but things had seemed so much saner back then—

"Honey?"

"Yes?" she said.

"You sure you're all right?"

"Fine."

"Is there anything you want to talk about?"

"Not that I can think of."

"I'm real tired but I don't want to go to sleep if there's something you want to say."

"No, I'm fine."

"Then I'm going to sleep."

She leaned over and kissed him on the mouth.

"I'll bet my breath is bad," he said.

"Mine is, too, probably."

"Huh-uh."

"Well, yours isn't, either."

He laughed. "See, that just proves we're wonderful people, doesn't it?"

He really could be very silly at times, and that was one of the reasons she loved him so much.

She lay awake for long hours there in the darkness, listening to her husband snore quietly and peacefully.

He was a little boy sometimes and that was another reason she loved him.

But then other night thoughts came, and she was unable to sleep.

Susan: her sister who had died of cancer at age nine. At fourteen, Claire had felt she needed to comfort both her parents and Susan. But she had seen her folks die right along with Susan—even though they would physically live another decade, their old passion and fervor were all gone—and so Claire felt she had failed all of them. She saw now, enshrined in a golden glow like an angel of old, Susan's tiny earnest face the night she died. Now, Claire reached out across time and space, across the bridge between life and death, to hold that face tenderly and to kiss Susan gently on the cheek.

Brad: her first boyfriend, the one she'd foolishly given herself to during her senior year in high school. She had never been an especially popular girl—"the pretty one who reads all the time" was the way she'd overheard one teacher describe her—and so she wasn't prepared for Brad's tricks and wiles. Only later was it clear to her that he'd simply been searching for another maidenhead. They slept together twice, and then he told her he was going back to his old girlfriend. Her pride required that she never cry about it—she wouldn't let herself, wouldn't give him the satisfaction even if he'd never know. Only years later, on her twenty-fifth birthday, slightly boiled on champagne, did she tell Matt, the only human being she'd ever told. And then she'd begun to sob uncontrollably and Matt had held her tenderly until she stopped and then put her in bed and stroked her hair and back until she fell asleep.

Then her thoughts turned, much against her will, back to David Hart.

She had this terrible sense that it hadn't ended with him; it had only begun. That this money tonight had only been a down payment . . .

She slept in troubled fits and starts, twice waking up cold from the icy sweat that covered her.

4

★ ★ ★ Off came the black fedora. The black raincoat.

He hung them on the hooks in the back entranceway and then moved up the three steps to the kitchen.

A year ago he'd had the entire place redecorated. Blue and white ceramic tiles here in the kitchen. A circular stainless steel hood. Floors and cabinets of matching buffed pine wood. Simple. Imposing. The way he liked things.

He poured himself a glass of chablis and continued on into the living room.

Again simple and imposing. French doors. Classically simple fireplace. Shiny, lacquered walls of dark brown. Sisal carpet and brass shell reading lamps. Small, elegant off-white couches. Built-in bookcases that matched the golden white of the fireplace mantel.

"Sir—"

He was about to sit down when he heard Clemmons, his servant, behind him.

"Yes, what is it?"

"Your shoes."

"My shoes?"

"I'm afraid they're tracking, sir."

He looked at the sisal carpet behind him. Muddy footprints.

"Damn."

"Yes, sir."

"Well, clean it up for God's sake."

"Yes, sir."

The lean and proper black man, dressed as always in a dark, funereal double-breasted suit and glowing white shirt, backed out of the room.

Never knew what the bastard was thinking.

Had long planned to fire him.

Always sensed he was secretly smirking.

"I'll be in the den, Clemmons," he called out, though he wasn't sure where Clemmons was, or if Clemmons could hear him.

Then he took off his shoes, found a section of this morning's newspaper.

The den. Thunder. Lightning bright and jagged against the glass in the French doors. Rain hissing like writhing snakes.

Muddy footprints.

Should be a lesson to him.

If he was going to try to do something this complicated and this clever, then he had damned well better start taking care of the little details.

He should have checked the soles of his shoes the moment he reached the back entranceway.

He glanced at the ticking grandfather clock in the corner. A good time to call.

He picked up the receiver. Dialed.

Three, four rings.

"I need to see you tomorrow," he said when David Hart's voice came on.

A deep sigh. "I don't want any part of it. I've told you that."

"Look, jerk, you seem to be forgetting a certain bank note I signed a while back."

Pause. "I'm not ungrateful."

"Don't tell me you're not ungrateful. I ask you to do me a single favor and you say no."

"You really are good at this, you know. Browbeating people, I mean."

"Then you'll do it?"

Another pause. "I want to think about it some more."

"I'll pay off your bank note and pay you $150,000."

"Are you kidding?"

"I am absolutely not kidding."

"The note *and* the cash?"

"The note and the cash."

"Right away?"

"As soon as it's done."

"Wow."

"Now there's a word I don't hear much anymore. Thank God."

"What time did you want to see me tomorrow night?"

"We have to be careful."

"Careful?"

"Of course. I don't want to be seen walking in your front door."

"There's a back entrance."

"I know there is. I sent Clemmons over to check it out last night."

"Good old Clemmons. Everybody should have a colored man to do his bidding." He was still a liberal and a pontifical one at that.

"I didn't create this world, David. I merely play by its rules."

"You're being damned generous."

"Yes," he said, laughing. "I am, aren't I? I'll be there at eight o'clock. Promptly."

He hung up before Hart could say anything else.

He couldn't take much of Hart and he'd reached his limit for to-night.

5

Dear First Lady,
  I told my teacher that I thought you were real pretty but she said I shouldn't say that in my letter so I won't.
                                                        Sincerely,
                                                        Michael Daly, Age 8

★ ★ ★ "Another groupie." Jane Douglas's laugh only made her all the more lovely. Jane was Claire's chief of staff. They worked together in the East Wing of the White House five days a week.

"Where were they when I needed them back in grade school?" Claire said.

The role of the First Lady had expanded greatly in recent years. Now she was expected to be a full-time public relations person for the White House, pushing its agenda and giving literally dozens of speeches a year. To help her in all this Congress had established a First Lady fund, which meant a staff of sixteen working out of the East Wing, plus three speechwriters who worked on retainer.

But Jane Douglas was special. She had been Claire's best friend since seventh grade. They'd stayed in touch after college, Jane coming east to work in public relations, eventually starting her own prestigious firm. Jane had always been the more beautiful of the two and, despite a few shameful moments of jealousy, Claire had never had any trouble with that. Men were instantly wooed by the large dark eyes and wry, erotic mouth and classic French look of her nose and chin. Jane's mother had been a Paris model before coming to the States after World War II. Jane had stayed in public relations, surrendering two marriages to the task of establishing and maintaining her own firm. But when Claire called and asked Jane to help her in the White House—

One more thing about Jane. Despite the silken gloss of body and manner, despite all the poise and self-confidence, she had never gotten over her limp.

At age six, she had been struck by a car and left lame in her right leg. There had been a series of operations, to be sure, but none had succeeded. By the time medical technique had become sophisticated enough to help her, it was too late. Jane was crippled for life.

Only when you watched her walk across a room filled with people did you have any sense of Jane's embarrassment. Then the lovely dark eyes looked very different: no more poise, no more self-confidence. She was once again a little girl sad because she was not the equal of the other little girls.

"Sounds like a good marriage prospect to me," Jane said. She took the letter from Michael Daly, Age 8, and slipped it into the jacket pocket of her navy blue double-breasted suit.

"You're starting to think of marriage again?" Claire said gently. Jane didn't like to be pushed on the subject of her single status. "I'm glad."

"Third time's a charm."

"Anybody in mind?"

Jane grinned. Patted her pocket. "Sure. Michael Daly, Age 8."

They worked nonstop right up till noon in the large, sunny office with the yellow curtains, built-in bookcases and handsome, silver-framed portraits of the six most recent First Ladies covering the west wall.

"As long as I can stay in my own hotel," Claire said when Jane showed her an invitation from a group of farm wives in Ohio.

For all the bad press she'd received, Nancy Reagan had changed the job of First Lady from a simply ceremonial one to one that was efficient and responsive to public needs. Mrs. Reagan had always graciously acknowledged that Rosalynn Carter had done all the groundwork in streamlining the First Lady's office.

A First Lady's schedule was such that appointments had to be made as far as a year in advance. Invitations often included the promise to find sleeping quarters for the First Lady. While "home cooking" and "bed-and-breakfast atmosphere" might *sound* good, what this too often meant was heavy, grease-soggy meals and a mattress and box springs that should have been thrown out twenty years earlier.

Claire had learned the hard way to choose restaurants and lodging for herself.

"This could be a tough one," Jane said.

"I know. Matt's still in trouble with farmers."

"He spoke the ultimate no-no."

Claire frowned. "But we won't have farm subsidies forever. They should be able to understand that."

Jane smiled. "They're in favor of losing farm subsidies, Claire—as long as they happen three or four generations from now."

Americans wanted a balanced budget without making any sacrifices. Everybody was on the welfare dole, even if they chose not to see it that way. The generals at the Pentagon got to double-dip on their retirement funds; the big businessman got tax breaks that amounted to kickbacks from the federal government; and the gangs terrorizing the good hard-working people of their neighborhoods often got their meals from food stamps and welfare checks.

"How about we pencil it in and I'll call and make sure they agree to everything first?"

"I'd appreciate it."

Jane nodded and wrote herself a note on a tiny yellow sticky.

"You know, I'll bet we could afford bigger stickies if you wanted them."

Jane laughed. "Let me think about that for a while. The thought actually never occurred to me."

Just as Jane finished writing on both sides of the sticky, a chunky man in a gray suit appeared carrying a large paper sack that he set on Jane's desk.

"Morning, Earle," Claire said. "I'm afraid to guess what you've got in that sack."

"This got pushed back and didn't get brought up," Earle said.

He nodded to the two women and left.

Claire stood up, appealing in her black watch plaid jumper and white cotton turtleneck sweater, her copper-colored hair shining from her morning shampoo.

She went over to the bag and peeked inside.

"Fan mail from some flounder, no doubt," she said, mimicking the voice of her all-time favorite cartoon character, Bullwinkle.

"No doubt," Jane said.

Claire reached down inside and started taking out handfuls of envelopes.

There were always one or two that attracted her immediate attention. A charming misspelling by a kid—The Wite Hows—or a particularly attractive envelope: some were as beautifully designed as fine artwork.

"Anything special?" Jane said from her desk.

"Not so far."

Claire continued looking inside the sack for any piece of mail that grabbed her attention.

"You're like a little kid with one of those surprise bags where you get to stick your hand in and pick your own gift," Jane said.

"I was always trying that at the state fair, but the most I ever got was one of those things that gave you a black eye when you looked inside."

Jane got to work on the phone.

She was more efficient and competent than anyone Claire had ever known.

Some said cold and even a bit ruthless.

But Claire disagreed. She knew why Jane was this way and didn't blame her at all.

By being super-competent, Jane hoped to discourage pity. Poor woman. That limp and all. Jane wanted none of that.

Claire found the first interesting envelope.

Ms. Stacy Norwalk
1037 Fuller Avenue
Trabucod Canyon, CA 92679

        Ms. Claire Hutton
        The White House
        Washington, D.C.

Your Horoscope Enclosed

"This should be good," Claire said, explaining the contents of the envelope to Jane.

Jane was in the middle of dialing her next call. "Hey, don't open that till I get done here, all right? I love stuff like that."

Claire smiled. Jane had a real passion for occult matters.

"I'll hold off till Swami gets off the phone."

"Smart-ass."

Claire laughed. "That's me, all right."

As Jane spoke with a news producer at CBS in New York about a possible story involving the First Lady, Claire returned to searching through the mail sack.

        Her Majesty Queen Claire
        The White House
        Washington, D.C.

The Secret Service checked out every piece of crank mail. It was sometimes difficult to decide which was a serious threat and which was just a joke.

The sarcasm of the "Her Majesty" intrigued her, though. Sometimes, crank mail provided some lighthearted moments at the dinner table.

She took the envelope out and opened it up.

As her eyes scanned the three typed lines on the plain white paper inside, she must have rocked back on her heels or sighed sharply because Jane looked up at her, looking very concerned.

Claire read the lines once again, a sick feeling starting up from her stomach and spreading up into her chest and throat.

> You whore
> I know what you do
> at night with David
> Hart

6

★ ★ ★ Bobby LaFontaine had served two terms in prison, one for armed robbery, a second for attempted murder. Both involved drug deals gone wrong. During his second term, in Joliet, Bobby's cellmate was a serious reader who introduced Bobby to the world of ideas. Bobby had no interest in ideas for themselves but he knew that when you could throw the right words around—two of Bobby's favorites were "elucidate" and "ennui"—you could impress the hell out of the right people.

And that's how Bobby was spending his days in Joliet—impressing the hell out of people and beating up as many colored guys as he could get his hands on, a gang of them having beaten him up during his first week there—when the Rev. Hugh Goodhew, rich and famous TV evangelist, brought his TV revival show *God's Hour* to the prison.

If you judged a TV ministry just by real estate holdings, Reverend Hugh Goodhew was certainly the most prosperous. He had not one, not two, but three "monuments to God", as he called them—vast spires that suggested both Gothic cathedrals and modern office buildings—in Dallas, Los Angeles and Washington, D.C. In the basements of all three were boutiques that sold *God's Hour* vitamins and "medicinals," *God's Hour* religious relics (the Shroud of Turin must be one massive piece of cloth, as one wag had observed, because so far Goodhew had sold about six hundred yards of it) and *God's Hour* audio- and videotapes on everything from being a good Christian to improving your sex life.

According to *Time* magazine, Reverend Goodhew's annual income was in excess of two hundred million dollars. Tax free, of course.

Unlike his evangelistic competitors who liked to stay in their cathedrals to produce their TV shows, Reverend Goodhew liked to "travel" his show.

For example, he did a show from a rodeo ("God's Buckaroos!"), a show from a WWF wrestling tournament ("Put the Devil in an Airplane Spin!") and a show from a home-shopping channel ("Use Your Credit Card to Get Some of God's Great Love While It's on Sale!"). And now he was at a prison ("Throw Open the Prison Bars of Your Soul!").

Reverend Goodhew was accompanied to Joliet by his usual entourage: the six Satan Begone singers; the twelve-man Living in Christ orchestra; and the one, the only sixteen-year-old Jenny Goodhew, his eye-poppingly gorgeous daughter, a girl who inspired lust in every heterosexual male (and many nonheterosexual females) in the U.S. of A.

Seven years before his prison gig, Reverend Goodhew's wife Irene had died a long and grim death from cancer. She was with him on the show each week, and the sicker she looked, the more the donations poured in. Cynics claimed that he was using his own wife's sad and protracted death to grub up more money. He naturally took great offense to all this. But he kept bringing her on. He had secretly hoped that she would actually expire right on the air—in the chair where they had her sort of propped up—but she missed her cue by ten minutes and died backstage.

So the slogan Let's Raise Money for Dying Irene became Let's Raise Money So That Jenny Can Grow Up Straight and Strong.

That was when Jenny became a major part of the show. She appeared on every single *God's Hour*, and the money came in by truckload, boatload, planeload.

She sang, but not especially well, and read the Bible, but not especially movingly, and she played the piano, but not especially ably.

What she did do was look great. Even at twelve there had been a hint of the erotic in the smile and dazzling blue eyes, and by fourteen she was inspiring dreams of jailbait around the world. The thing was, her daddy dressed her up real good and real pure in white high-necked dresses that fell well below her knees. And very proper behavior: she never spoke unless spoken to and never tried to take the spotlight from her daddy. She didn't need to try.

Reverend Goodhew brought Jenny to Joliet with him and the place went crazy. If this was the reward for being God-fearing, the Lord was indeed going to be blessed with a motherload of salvationed souls.

Before the show was put on in the cafeteria—lights hung, cable laid, an impromptu stage rigged up—Reverend Goodhew asked if there was an especially well-spoken inmate who might be brought up to the stage during the course of the show as it was being taped. The warden naturally suggested Bobby LaFontaine. That little pecker knew words that probably even dictionary writers hadn't heard of before.

Bobby was one fine actor. Put him in a part and he could do it wonderfully.

The part he played that day was the remorseful criminal. He went up on stage and received the Lord and ended up on his knees with the Reverend Goodhew and all six of the Satan Begone singers gathered around him bearing witness to Bobby's tearful conversion.

Even some of the cons were conned. Goddamn Bobby anyway; he done went and found the Lord, the little rat.

Rival TV ministers often envied Goodhew his Bobby. It didn't hurt that Bobby had the sweet freckled face of an altar boy. A made-for-television face it was. And it didn't hurt that Jenny kept sneaking somewhat ambiguous looks at him, either. Bobby always had a good sense of when a woman's pussy was getting in a pout over him—but dare he hope that Jenny was pouting over him now?

The viewing audience around the world was so taken with Bobby's story—largely made up, especially the part about living in the sewer system of Chicago and killing rats with his bare hands so he could have something to eat—that donations that Sunday tripled.

The Reverend knew he had something in Bobby and so he started a petition to have the parole board let Bobby out early. It took a year and a half to get it done, but Bobby was sprung and became a regular on *God's Hour*. Every week it was the same rap: who knows better about degradation and shame than an ex-con? They loved him. The Reverend's accountants figured that when Bobby was on a show, donations went up a minimum of 6 percent.

Bobby was apprised of how the show worked, of course, how everybody who had even the briefest contact with *God's Hour* was put on the computer and how the computer could hunt you down no matter where you lived and coerce you into giving your "gift." People dying of cancer gave because they desperately hoped that Reverend Goodhew indeed had the power to bribe God; lonely and forgotten widows gave 25 or even 50 percent of their Social Security checks because Reverend Goodhew seemed to be speaking just to them; and good-hearted but profoundly confused young couples sent gifts because they wanted some sense of order and purpose and meaning in their lives, and their local churches just didn't seem to have the theatrical flash and flair of the Reverend Goodhew. Sometimes *God's Hour* received more than five thousand "love envelopes" a day.

And then there was the Prayer Umbrella, an invention of a competing TV minister. The Prayer Umbrella worked this way: You sent this minister X number of dollars and he mentally constructed a Prayer Umbrella over your house—an umbrella helped repel physical disease and the wiles of Satan. The Prayer Umbrella was the ultimate con—you couldn't see it, touch it, taste it, smell it—and yet it was there if you *believed* it was there. Reverend Goodhew was relentlessly jealous of the Prayer Umbrella because there wasn't any postage involved—they sent you cash and you sent them nothing in return—and you didn't guarantee that the Prayer Umbrella would work, you simply suggested it *might*. Reverend Goodhew charged Bobby LaFontaine with coming up with a better scheme, and whenever he had any thinking time, Bobby tried to dream up his own version. So far his efforts had been pretty lame: the Prayer Tent, the Prayer Missile (sending God's love exploding into your house) and the Prayer Dome. Bobby's stomach always got tight whenever Reverend Goodhew said, "How you coming on that Prayer Umbrella deal, Bobby?"

Bobby had one other use to the Reverend. He became a kind of unofficial troubleshooter. Anybody got out of line in any way, the Reverend put Bobby on him. Who better to quell a problem than a street kid who was as verbal as he was physical? Bobby rarely had to punch people. His demeanor was enough to scare them back to Jesus and the path of righteousness, especially if this was one of the assistant ministers who was bopping somebody else in the church. The networks were always trying to get something on the Reverend and so his people had to be clean clean clean. And Bobby became the enforcer.

Bobby was so scrupulous about his job that he even declined sweet innocent Jenny's lustful passes. Bobby wanted a long run with *God's Hour* and bopping the Reverend's daughter was not a good idea at all.

Bobby learned the God business and loved it. Tax free, who wouldn't love it?

One other thing about Bobby: in prison he'd learned all about electronic bugging. He had every major room in the Reverend Goodhew's headquarters bugged and he could tell you everything that went on and everything that was said. Not even the Reverend knew as much about his operation as Bobby did.

There was one fact, especially, that Reverend Goodhew did not know: that his preciously guarded daughter was screwing the hell out of Knox Stansfield.

There was some fuss on the set. Senator Jack Wagner was getting ready for his taped interview, which would be broadcast tonight. Talk about a central-casting candidate. Hitler would have been positively orgasmic about this blond-haired, blue-eyed representative of everything that was right and true about the American way.

Wagner was the far-right conservative who was challenging President Hutton in the primaries. He was the hand-picked candidate of both Reverend Goodhew and Knox Stansfield.

And speaking of Stansfield—

Bobby's stomach tightened.

Stansfield had just walked on the set. There was more excitement and turmoil over him than there had been for Wagner.

Stansfield walked across the huge stage with the giant electric letters GOD'S HOUR flashing out into the darkened seats where the audience sat.

He was a sleek, handsome bastard, Bobby LaFontaine had to give him that. And he was very good on the radio. Guy could whip a crowd of nuns into a lynch mob.

In fact, right up until yesterday morning, Bobby had been pretty much of a Knox Stansfield fan. But last night there'd been a board of directors meeting and Reverend Goodhew had brought up the subject of nominating Bobby LaFontaine. Everybody but Knox had been for it. "Wrong image," Knox said. "It's fine to have him on TV and all. But not on the board. Leaves us open to too much criticism. Attempted murder is a pretty stiff rap." And that had been enough to make the other members have second thoughts.

Bobby had heard all this on his handy-dandy walkie-talkie. He'd wired the board room six months ago.

And now that hypocrite bastard was walking toward him, hand out, saying, "Hey, Bobby. How's it going?"

Going to be going just fine, Bobby thought, once I get some recordings of you pumping sweet little Jenny. Then things'll be going just fine.

"It's going great," Bobby LaFontaine said, ever the actor. He even mustered up a smile. "It's going just great."

And he reached out and gave Knox's hand a manly grasp.

7

★ ★ ★ "We have some as small as a lipstick case."

"Really?"

"Absolutely."

"And the tape is clear, when you view it?"

"Well, it's not going to win any Academy Awards for cinematography." The man had shaved his head and wore a forest green shirt with epaulets. The way he held himself, the walls filled with both guns and security devices, told of his deep and abiding esteem for all things military.

Robert Clemmons was running one of his more important errands for his boss. Even given some of the strange things Clemmons had done for him over the years, this one was a rather bizarre request. And ominous. Definitely ominous.

"But you can see things clearly?" Clemmons asked.

"Pretty clearly. Enough to do the job, anyway."

"I want it small but it has to produce a pretty clear piece of tape."

"Well, we've got a three-by-five."

"And that's better than the lipstick-sized one?"

"Better in terms of picture, definitely."

"Is there any way I could see some tape the three-by-five made?"

The man started openly studying Clemmons.

The man obviously didn't get many African Americans in here. The customers at high-end security stores like this one, over here not too far from Dupont Circle, were mostly upper-class whites.

But clearly the man sensed something about Clemmons. Education. Intelligence. Pride.

"Sure," the man said. "C'mon in the back."

The back of the store, behind the curtains, looked pretty much like any other repair shop. Cameras, locks, guns and other security-related devices were broken down in various stages and scattered across tables and workbenches. A reedy man with a bad cough, a rubber apron and quick, nimble fingers was taking apart an outsize padlock.

"In here," the man with epaulets said.

A lot of spooks probably hang out in here, Clemmons thought. He'd known one of the first black CIA agents, and the man had been a nut for James Bondian stealth devices.

Clemmons followed the man into the room.

A monitor was set on an ancient desk. A VCR was plugged in. "We've made a transfer to VHS tape already."

"I see."

"Makes it a hell of a lot easier on the eyes."

"I'll bet."

The man smiled. "If seeing bare ladies bothers you, my friend, I'd look the other way."

Clemmons laughed. "It hasn't so far in my life."

"Good."

A hotel room. Two naked women. One white. One black.

Neither woman was in her prime, but then, the older Clemmons got, the more appreciative he was of the fiftyish female body. He'd grown to positively love love handles. And in a certain soft light, cellulite didn't look half bad at all.

Then he finally got around to noticing the quality of the videotape itself.

A little dark. A little out of focus.

But identities and action were unmistakable.

"This was a three-by-five camera?" Clemmons asked.

"Right."

"Where was it placed?"

"See how it's angled down?"

"Right."

"Top shelf of a seven-foot bookcase."

"Any trouble to install?"

"I could show you in under fifteen minutes."

"And you'd guarantee that it'd work?"

"Long as you follow my instructions."

Clemmons's dark face grew studious for a moment. He'd never been handsome, but women, black and white alike, had always found his grave and considered manner attractive. He was a man who knew what he was doing but didn't have to peacock around to demonstrate it.

"This is what I'm looking for," Clemmons said, nodding toward the screen. "The three-by-five."

White woman pushed black woman slowly back on the bed, her long white thigh working up between the black woman's parted thighs.

These women obviously knew what they were doing.

8

★ ★ ★ That afternoon, the temperature back up into the mid-sixties, David Hart went for a walk around Georgetown.

He was trying to forget the late night phone call he'd received.

With the $100,000 he'd gotten from Claire, he was determined to start a new life. He had been born with the looks and manner and soul of a great artist. All that God had forgotten to give him was the talent. So he'd had to develop a different talent—the ability to be charming while *talking* about art, giving his vast and endless *opinions* about art. No matter that he didn't actually know all that much about the subject; no matter that he changed his mind about a given artist every time he read the Art section of *Time* or *Newsweek*. In time, of course, he became what all such people become: a critic. He had even had a show on PBS for a season. And in the meantime, David did what he always did for money: performed as a paid companion for older women, recently dumped women, women never lucky or plucky enough to get themselves a handsome, rakish and amusing man. He considered himself to be not unlike a rental car. You could rent a Ford or you could rent a Buick or you could rent a Lincoln Towncar. He was the Towncar. You got what you paid for. Chicago, Las Vegas, Hollywood, New York and now Washington, D.C. David had blessed each of these cities with his charms.

But then a funny thing had happened to him over the past two or three months: he got tired of being David Hart.

No more long stares at himself in the mirror.

No more jaunty whistling as he took the front steps of his town house two at a time, on his way to the latest conquest.

No more walking through art galleries and silently posing for the women who were watching him.

He was forty-two years old and he wanted to be a guy.

A regular guy.

Marriage, kids, maybe even working on the family car every once in awhile.

All this had become important to him—he was absolutely convinced this was not a whim—after he'd started seeing Claire Hutton.

Claire was still everything she'd been back in college when the four of them—Claire, Matt, Knox Stansfield and himself—had been elite campus intellectuals. (Or so they'd fancied themselves, anyway). Back then she'd been honest, kind, wry, tender and genuinely concerned about other people. And being First Lady hadn't changed her.

Maybe Claire, by her very presence in his town house, had shamed him into seeing himself for what he was.

And that was when David Hart had come up with the idea only David Hart could:

He wanted to start a brand new life for himself, right? Right.

He wanted to find the straight and narrow and walk it for the rest of his days, right? Right.

He wanted to be the kind of man he could admire and respect and feel good about, right? Right.

Well, there was only one way he knew of being able to turn over a new leaf to a high-minded and moral life: he had to blackmail Claire to the tune of $100,000.

This would give him a little spending green as he went out in the world in search of his masculinity and honor.

1. Claire had plenty of money.
2. Claire would someday look back on this and realize that she had not really been paying shakedown money, she had simply been investing in the salvation of a man's very soul.
3. Claire had plenty of money.

He walked, enjoying the day.

You could tell he felt different about himself already.

Gone was the jaunty stride, the eye searching for females.

He was a serious, sober, practical sort of guy now.

He walked.

God, he loved Foggy Bottom.

Tudor Place, with its splendid Federal architecture; the Department of State, a building so vast it spanned four blocks; and the imposing, spectacular Kennedy Center. The American flag snapping in the wind;

the Hall of Nations where all flags flew; the huge bronze bust of President Kennedy himself.

Even if he didn't quite understand the verities of architecture—though of course he *pretended* to—he did have a real love of it.

Standing here now, the front of the Kennedy Center made him feel a real part of history, and for a moment he felt overcome by thoughts and notions he rarely had.

Honor.

Courage.

Self-esteem.

No, by God, he couldn't do what his late-night caller had hinted at last night.

This was a new David Hart.

And the new David Hart was a good and true and decent man.

David Hart had a heart full of resolve and a pocketful of cash.

David Hart was New and Improved.

David Hart needed to find a phone.

Fast.

"I can't do it."

"Do you realize that I'm about to go on the air?"

"I can't do it.

"I'm about to go on the air and be carried *live* over five hundred radio stations and you call me *now*?"

"I can't do it."

"Do you realize how *difficult* it is to do a live radio show without any script?"

"I'm a new man."

"And you call me *now* and completely mess up the peace of mind I need to go on the air?"

"I'm sorry if I screwed you up but I won't do it, whatever it is."

"We'll talk about it tonight, when I come over to your place."

"You're not coming over to my place."

"Of course I'm coming over to your place. We made an appointment."

"I'm breaking the appointment."

"Of course you're not. Listen. I'm going to have something messengered over to your place in about an hour. You look it over and then tell me you want to break our appointment."

"You bastard."

"I have to go, David. I have to get into my mind-set for my radio show."

"You don't seem to understand, Knox. I'm a new man."

Knox Stansfield laughed, hard and cold. "You've become a new man at least once a year since we were back in college, David. You just go home and read through the little gift I'm sending you. Then we'll see each other tonight."

He hung up.

A new man, David thought, swearing at the pay-phone receiver as he slammed it back on to its cradle.

I'm a new man.

Really.

I am.

Really.

9

★ ★ ★ Penetration.

Oh God.

Ecstasy.

Wanted to just start wailing away.

But had to go slow.

Had to last for two hours.

Pacing.

That was the trick.

Pacing.

Never felt so good—so vital, so self-aware, so *living*—as when he was on the air.

"You hear how much the Pentagon budget for military shoes has gone up since President Hutton started allowing gays in the military? Well, don't be surprised. Ballet slippers cost a lot more than combat boots."

Always lead with a joke.

Good guy.

No malice.

Not now, anyway.

The heavy stuff came later.

But a little sentimentality never hurt.

"You know what I did last week? I climbed up to the dusty old attic—don't you just love attics? I sure do—and you know what I found? Some pictures of my grandfather taken on VJ Day. The end of

World War II."

Lower the voice.

Intimate.

Even suggest some tears in the old throat.

"Now I know people of my generation—you remember us, we're the generation that bought all that marijuana but never inhaled any of it—we're not supposed to get choked up by seeing pictures like that. . . . But you know what? When I saw my grandad there in his Navy uniform kissing my grandmother, . . . I realized what a sacrifice his whole generation made. You know how many people *died* in that war just because of that sonofabitch Hitler?—and I make no apologies for using that kind of language when it comes to Herr Adolf—52 *million* people died. And it took the Yanks to finally put an end to it. It took the Yanks."

Which was a great and moving story except for the fact that (a) his grandparents, both sets, died before he was born; (b) neither grandfather had served in World War II; and (c) he did not have an attic.

Rush Limbaugh and other respectable commentators pretty much stuck to factual presentations of their opinions, . . . but that wasn't why you listened to Knox Stansfield. Oh, no: Stansfield gave you emotion; Stansfield gave you catharsis. Or as the good gray *Times* had noted: "Stansfield gives you a lurid soap opera about the machinations of democracy, none of it true in any factual way, but much of it true in a metaphorical way. This is how too many right-wingers choose to view their government."

This is how all this started: it was senior year at the U of Illinois. All the standard student activities were still going on in 1971. Demonstrations. Attacks on ROTC buildings. Sit-ins. Love-ins. Be-ins. Rampant drugs, rampant sex, rampant violence. And this theater major the four of them knew vaguely was putting on this series of skits about life on campus . . . and he said wouldn't it be fun to have some of you conservatives do a few bits . . . and Matt thought it would be fun, too . . . so the four of them got together and they came up with this news commentator parody who took these real outrageous positions on familiar issues . . . and they decided that Knox did the best job of portraying this guy, who was in fact much further to the right than any of them were.

And he was a great big hit. The hard-core Students for a Democratic Society members and the Yippies and the Black Panthers, they went absolutely crazy.

They took him seriously.

One black kid even tried to storm the stage.

Matt had to step in and grab him just before he reached Knox.

But a weird thing was happening.

For the first time he could ever recall, Knox Stansfield felt sort of good about himself. You have a mother who marries three times, each choice worse than the previous one; you have scarlet fever when you're a little kid and you never exactly feel real secure about being an all-around boy; and you cling desperately and jealously to Claire, the girl you love almost insanely . . . well, it felt good to no longer be Knox Stansfield.

That very night on the stage he became KNOX STANSFIELD.

The politics didn't matter—he could just as easily have taken up the Maoist cause. It was the *power* his words had over people . . .

Nothing much happened for several more years. KNOX STANS-FIELD made appearances at parties, and as a means of amusing women into bed, and occasionally doing guest appearances when ole Knox had had too much to drink . . .

But most of the time he was plain ole Knox Stansfield.

Working in a Manhattan ad agency.

Striking out with half the women he put the moves on.

Striking many of the men he dealt with as . . . strange. Not the kind of guy a real guy often found himself comfortable with.

Tried marriage but he wasn't any better at it than his mother had been.

Tried shacking up but that wasn't the answer, either.

Tried screwing his brains out with strangers and that was the worst of all—the loneliness afterward, the fact that he'd been so close to intimacy but that it had, as always, eluded him.

Then he met this wealthy guy at a party, guy who said he was going to buy himself a small Manhattan radio station and force-feed conservative ideas into the intellectual marketplace . . . and how would Knox like to have a half-hour show of his own a couple nights a week to interview conservative guests?

Cool.

Fun.

Maybe there were some conservative groupies.

Just ask Ted Kennedy about *liberal* groupies.

He took the guy up on the offer.

Bombed at first: too much Ayn Rand and *Atlas Shrugged* and his idealized version of the United States, where capitalism did eventually solve almost all the problems.

Guy was obviously thinking of replacing him when—

KNOX STANSFIELD suddenly appeared on the air one night and said, "You know it's not fair to label Governor Cuomo 'Mafia-connected' just because he's Italian, . . . but it seems you can't say it even if there is some real evidence that it *is* true . . . "

And then proceeded to read a couple of news stories that the liberal papers didn't seem real interested in carrying . . .

And then he gave this really treacly account of how Italian-Americans came to this country in the early 1800s and made a life for themselves . . .

And at midpoint in the tale (which he was spontaneously creating), he heard his voice fill and shake with tears and when he looked through the studio glass, he saw that the station owner and even the engineer were watching him through tear-filled eyes . . .

After that, KNOX STANSFIELD was on the air every night. Forget Ayn Rand and true conservative principles. They didn't matter.

What mattered was that some defenders of Cuomo's started picketing the station; and what mattered was that CNN picked up some video showing these hearty defenders; and what mattered was that some of Knox Stansfield's remarks about Cuomo made it on the air; and what mattered was—

Two months later he was working for the biggest talk-radio station in New York.

Six months after that, he went syndicated.

And by 1989, he was heard on more than six hundred radio stations around the country. *America Speaks* was now the name of his show, and God help you if you called in and said anything against this country. In the early days, Knox had used plants, paid-for people who'd call in and say really awful things about the capitalist system. And then America Spoke all right. His listeners would call in as wrathed-up as Knox himself. And say things like, If I ever got my hands on that last caller, Knox, why I'd . . .

And then Knox, now the voice of reason, would admonish: Now, let's remember one thing, people. This country of ours that we love so much is a democracy. That means that everybody gets a chance to take his or her turn at the microphone. Now personally, I think that last caller was a scumbag commie—yes, it may come as a shock to some of you that commies still exist but they're still out there and let's not kid ourselves—but just because he expresses himself doesn't mean we have the right to do him personal harm. That's called fascism, people—and that's what a lot of enemies of this show would have you believe *we* are, you and I, but we're not. We're good ordinary *decent* Americans trying to do what's right for this country is all. Right? I knew you'd see it my way. We'll be right back after this commercial.

MESSIAH OF THE YAHOOS
THE MASTER OF WHITE TRASH
THE PIED PIPER OF THE EXTREME RIGHT

And the more the headline writers, the liberals and the moderate Republicans bashed him, the better he did.

Even Limbaugh bashed him a few times.

Most people forgot (or chose to overlook) that Rush, for all his barbed comments, was actually a centrist Republican.

Not so Knox Stansfield.

Oh, no. Tune into his show for half an hour and you got the impression that the most evil man who had ever lived was not Adolph Hitler, Joseph Stalin or Pol Pot. No, the most evil man who had ever lived was the current President of the United States, Matthew Hutton . . .

1972: Christmas Eve. Dusk. The streets of the college town filled with Christmas carols from loudspeakers and the sounds of the merry, stout bells rung by streetcorner Santas. The scurry of last-minute shoppers, the darkening streets festive with red and green and blue lights . . .

He was hurrying down the street when he happened to glance in the front window of the favorite campus hangout, The Monkey's Paw, when he saw them.

Claire and Matt.

In a booth halfway back.

In profile.

She was crying gently into a handkerchief.

Matt was holding her hand.

He sank back from the window, utterly devoid of feeling for this moment. Coldness-numbness-death. That was the only way to explain what he felt. A banishment from all trust and love and hope.

Claire and Matt.

Matt and Claire.

God damn them for betraying him.

And then feeling came. Too much feeling. An avalanche, an overload of feeling.

He had very little recollection of the next few minutes.

Rushing inside—grabbing Claire, slapping her again and again—Matt grabbing him and throwing him up against the wall—a furious fistfight for the next few minutes—students pulling them off one another—Claire sobbing and sobbing and sobbing . . .

Three days later, Knox packed everything he owned into his Volvo sedan and left school. Wouldn't tell anybody, not even his mother, who was desperately worried about him, where he was going . . .

Mexican fishing village. A week. Two weeks. Who could remember? Tequila with the worm in the bottle; young girls whose vaginas needed washing-out before you had sex with them. But at least they were up for his ugliness. Lashed one of the little bitches to his bed and started whipping her with his belt. Her father came running in, shouting. But two hundred-dollar bills had silenced the man. The father even suggested putting a gag in the girl's mouth so they wouldn't hear her when she screamed. The screaming upset her mother terribly . . .

Once he'd drawn a little blood, he'd had no trouble with impotence at all.

Came up straight and hard.

Took her anally the first time.

She screamed even louder than when he'd used his belt on her.

He loved it.

. . . Six months later, he was finishing up his senior year of college in California.

By his count, he had called Claire more than six hundred times. She would not speak to him even once.

By his count, he had sent her more than a hundred bouquets of red roses. She did not acknowledge them in any way.

By his count, he had sent more than a dozen expensive pieces of jewelry. They were all returned.

He heard from her only once.

By letter.

Knox—

The last time we talked, you called me a slut and said that I'd betrayed you with Matt.

Knox, you really need to get some psychiatric help. You are not dealing with reality.

Knox, you and I broke up eleven months before you saw me with Matt that afternoon. I was crying because you'd sent me another threatening letter and because I was afraid of you.

Knox, have you forgotten how many times you had beaten me up? Did you forget breaking my arm? Blacking both of my eyes at different times? Pushing me down a flight of stairs? Pounding my head against a radiator until I was unconscious? You beat me up at least once a week for the entire sixteen months we lived together off campus, Knox. And I stuck it out because I loved you so much and because I hoped that you would eventually seek professional help. But you didn't. You just got worse. I was so much in love with you that I even wanted your baby, hoping that you would straighten up if we had a child. But you insisted on an abortion . . .

Knox, Matt was being my friend the day you saw us in The Monkey's Paw. You've never been able to understand how a man and a woman can be friends. He was deeply in love with Monica Hughes at that time. You've probably heard through the grapevine that Matt and I are going out now—but that was only after Monica dumped him for somebody else. Matt and I were both hurting (despite all the beatings you gave me, I was still in love with you) and we turned to each other out of friendship. We didn't even kiss for seven or eight months. It was more like brother and sister. So when you called me a slut . . .

I wish I could say that I was completely over you, Knox. I've done some reading on battered spouses and see now that I was in some ways addicted to you . . .

But please don't try to contact me in any way anymore. I want to get on with my life.

All I can do is pray that you finally seek professional help, Knox. For your sake and the sake of the women in your future.

Claire.

1973: Labor Day. His mother's Gulf Coast mansion. Lying in the den, listless, depressed, as he had been for long weeks now. His mother in the matching leather chair across from him.

"She was a whore, Knox. I wish you could see that."

"I treated her so well."

"I know you did, darling."

"I gave her everything."

"You gave her too much. Too much money, too much of yourself. You're a very sensitive and vulnerable young man, darling."

"I was so damned good to her."

"Coarse, darling. I never told you this but that was the very first thing I thought when you brought her back home with you that time. Very striking and very chic but sort of coarse, too. Didn't you say her father had a little grocery store?"

He nodded.

"Darling, I know you don't like to hear things like this, but you really should stick to your own kind. I know you hate the word, but it matters—breeding. One of our own, darling. That's what you need to think about."

"She's telling everybody lies about me."

"Your true friends will know not to believe her."

"She said I hit her."

"Oh, darling, doesn't that alone tell you what kind of coarse girl she is?"

Mother glanced at her watch. "Oh, dear, I'm late for the club and my bridge game. Why don't you get up and go somewhere, too? You shouldn't sulk anymore, darling. She's not worth it. She's really not."

Mother came over and kissed his forehead the way she used to when he was a little boy.

Then she was at the door. "For what it's worth, darling, you know very well that your father used to—well, hurt me sometimes. I just always assumed he wouldn't have hurt me if he hadn't loved me. It's just something men do—within reason, of course. I mean, you have to be careful, darling, if you're going to hurt your women. Don't hurt them too much. If you know what I mean."

Then she was gone.

1976: Soho. Rainy August night.

Naked. The two of them. On the bed. Darkness.

"Please don't touch me, Knox."

"Listen, Susan, I'm really sorry I—"

"You were sorry last time."

"But—"

"And the time before that—"

"But Susan—"

"One of these times you could kill me, Knox—"

"That's crazy, Susan—"

"You need help, Knox. Professional help."

"But—"

"And now I'll have another black eye for work tomorrow. Do you know how embarrassing that is? Always having some kind of bruise or scar from the man you live with— People always whispering and smirking behind her back and—"

"Bitch."

"Oh, great. Now you're calling me names."

"Not you, her."

"Oh, Knox, not Claire again."

"I never would have been like this—hurting you—if it hadn't been for her. That day I walked in and found her in bed with Matt, my best friend—"

He had told this story so many times, he now believed it. Utterly. Without question.

"I'm sure that was devastating, Knox. But are you sure you never hit Claire the way you hit me?"

"Never."

"Never even thought about it?"

"Never even thought about it."

"Then that's all the more reason to see a shrink and talk it through, Knox."

Then he told another story he now believed because he'd told it so many times. "I went to a shrink once when I was sixteen. And guess what?"

"What?"

"He came on to me."

"The shrink did?"

"Uh-huh."

"Oh, God, Knox. Really? You're not making this up?"

"Scout's honor. Right there. Middle of the afternoon. His own office. Came on to me."

"God, what a sleaze."

"So I guess you can see why I'm not real keen on shrinks."

"Oh, Knox, I'm so sorry."

"I won't hit you anymore, I promise."

"Knox, it's just you've said that so many times, it's—"

"Please just give me one more chance. Please—"

"Well—"

Three weeks later, he broke her nose.

Present day: Studio.

"Good afternoon, Knox."

"Good afternoon."

"I'm just calling to tell you that I think you get a little too personal about President Hutton sometimes."

"Well, I'm sorry you feel that way."

"The other day you implied that he hadn't always been faithful to his wife. How do you think his daughter feels when she hears things like that?"

"Would you mind if I asked you a question?"

Pause. The listener was obviously afraid he was being set up for something.

"This isn't any trick question."

"Uh, all right."

"Have you ever heard of the *New York Times*?"

"Sure."

"How about the *Los Angeles Times*?"

"Of course."

"And *Time* magazine?"

"Yes."

"And *Newsweek* magazine?"

"Sure."

"Well, all you liberals who are always calling in to complain about me picking on poor President Hutton should keep one thing in mind."

"What's that?"

"That before I ever uttered a word on the subject of whether or not the President had a mistress, all those newspapers and magazines I mentioned were carrying a story about it."

"But you also call him a drunk."

"Now that I resent. You cite me date and time when I called the President a so-called drunk and I'll send you $50,000 cash."

This was the sort of thing his listeners loved.

Silence.

"Can do you that, sir?"

"Huh?"

"Can you cite me the date and time when I called the President a drunk on this program?"

"Well—"

"I didn't think so. Good day to you, sir." Beat. "I sure hope my next call is from a real American."

"Good afternoon, Knox. I just want you to know that I *am* a real American."

"Good afternoon to you, sir."

"You're just being nice, Knox, because it's not in your nature to be mean."

"Thanks for saying that. I get cut down so often I'm beginning to wonder if I *am* really like my critics say."

The caller said, "You're not mean, Knox. But I am. And I say that President Hutton is a skirt chaser and a drunk."

"Well, well," Knox Stansfield smiled. "Sounds like this is going to be a real interesting afternoon now, doesn't it?"

"And I'll go you one step better on the subject of the ATF."

"Oh, yeah?"

"Yeah. You said we should refuse to hand over our weapons if they come on our property and try to confiscate them?"

"Right. That's what I said."

"Well, any ATF agent comes on my property, Knox, you know what I'm gonna do? I'm going to pump six bullets into his face!"

A real interesting afternoon, indeed.

10

★ ★ ★ On the radio, Knox Stansfield said: "You may be surprised. President Hutton may be the first sitting president to lose in a primary in this century. Maybe there's some justice after all. Maybe his cowardice and his lies have finally caught up with him."

Deirdre knew where the studio was.

She could just drive over there someday.

When he wasn't expecting it.

God, she'd had the fantasy so often.

Him sitting smugly behind his microphone, the way she saw him in magazine photos sometimes.

And her walking into the studio. A gun in her hand. And him looking up.

And her firing.

Once. Twice. Three times.

Do you have any idea how much pain you've caused my parents? she'd say as she watched his dying body slump over in the chair.

Do you?

"I'd better turn this off," said the Secret Service agent who was driving her home from school. "Your mother doesn't want you to listen to him."

Knox Stansfield became a rock song.

"Better," the agent said.

"How old do you have to be to buy a gun in this town?" she said.

The agent smiled. "Thinking off bumping off Knox Stansfield?"

"Exactly."

The agent smiled.

David on the phone, twenty minutes after the broadcast:

"I can't do it, Knox."

"Listen to yourself, David. Do you enjoy sounding this way?"

"Knox, I can't do it. I just can't. She's too close a friend of mine."

"So good a friend you blackmailed her for $100,000?"

"How the hell did you find out about that?"

"I was in your apartment this morning."

"You sonofabitch."

"You're going to help me, David. You might as well get used to the thought."

"You have no right to go into my apartment."

"And you have no right to owe me money for as long as you have."

"Knox, please, listen—"

"You're whining again, David. It's really getting tiresome."

"I'm not a blackmailer."

"Right."

"I planned to pay the money back."

"Right. Just the way you paid me back."

"I am not a blackmailer."

"Whores can't afford to have pride, David. You should know that by now. Now enough of this. I'll see you tonight. And don't call me back, understand?" Beat. "Oh, Clemmons is going to stop by and install a very small video camera in your living room."

Before Hart could object, Stansfield slammed down the receiver.

11

★ ★ ★ Somebody whispered that a famous movie star had just up-chucked in the ladies' room.

The occasion was a state dinner for England's new prime minister and his wife.

The evening started out with a private cocktail party in the Yellow Oval Room and then shifted to the State Dining Room.

Strictly an A-list occasion: among movie stars, Robert Redford and Sharon Stone; among ambassadors, those from Germany, France, Russia and China; among distinguished Americans, six Nobel Prize winners in the sciences, as well as Luciano Pavarotti, who sang an aria.

Black tie, of course, the President looking stiff and uncomfortable as always in what he called his "monkey suit."

Claire wore a black Chanel number and a Wonderbra. Bosoms were back this fashion season and so, as always, she'd had to go out and buy herself one.

A state dinner was an ordeal, one she was happy to share with her friend and associate Jane, who looked lovely, as always, tonight.

The two divided the huge dining room in half, policing their sections regularly to make sure that the guests were all smiling and going through the motions of having a good time.

Occasionally, there were uncomfortable moments, as when the comedian Jackie Mason, seated next to the Israeli ambassador, announced that Israel no longer had any integrity. Or when one of the Redgrave sons told a visiting Irish Catholic prelate that Martin Luther should not only have broken away from the Church, he should also have assassinated the pope to prove he was serious.

As both Claire and Jane had learned early on, seating arrangements were critical. While there had never been anything resembling a real brawl at a state dinner, there had been some awfully tense situations. And there had been some truly bizarre moments, as when a prominent starlet had put her hand under the crisp white tablecloth and brought endless pleasure to a dashing young senator she'd hoped to impress.

And had indeed impressed.

Tonight was going pretty well. Both Claire and Matt really enjoyed the young comedian, Paul Lydon, who did such great impersonations of political figures from Matt ("The only thing *I'm* radical about, Mr. and Mrs. America, is being moderate") and Knox Stansfield ("Sure I hate the President and his wife; but I hate out of respect and admiration")—capturing both the mildness (some said blandness) of Matt and the unctuousness of Stansfield. He was particularly good with Stansfield; if you closed your eyes, you could really imagine it was Knox speaking.

Everybody at the dinner tonight loved Lydon and was sorry when his act was over. A couple of pop singers followed him to complete the evening's entertainment.

"What's wrong with the movie star?" Jane whispered to Claire during one of their brief meetings at the back of the dining room. Spread out before them, the dining room and its glittering guests resembled a painting from the past century, when men and women of the finest stripe lived out their lives at the castle balls given by kings and queens.

"Flu."

"Poor woman."

"She says she feels better now."

"I just keep thinking of how George Bush threw up on that Japanese ambassador's leg that time."

Claire smiled. "Maybe we'll get lucky and she'll throw up all over Senator Wagner. He's at her table."

Jane laughed. "Wouldn't that be wonderful? He couldn't blame us."

"No. But he'd try."

Senator Jack Wagner was the archconservative running against the President in the Republican primaries next month. They had invited him to this dinner to show that they weren't afraid of him.

Actually, they were very afraid of him, and with good reason. Republican primaries were notorious for bringing out the most extreme of voters. "The Hitler wing of the party," as Matt sometimes jokingly called them.

Claire looked over the room.

So far so good.

"Maybe I'm hallucinating," she said. "But things look under control."

"It was all that Prozac you took."

"Don't think I haven't thought about it."

Jane patted Claire's hand. "Everything's fine, Claire. Now we can both sit down and enjoy ourselves."

"Throw back a couple of boilermakers and enjoy ourselves," Claire said, laughing, referring to the wife of a prominent Democratic senator. The lady drank boilermakers and made no apologies for it.

"See you afterward and we'll compare notes," Jane said, looking so good in her blue gown and dramatically upswept hair that several famous men were staring at her.

"Thanks for being here," Claire said. "As usual, I wouldn't have made it without you."

"You'd do fine without me and you know it."

"Oh, sure I would," Claire said.

Then it was time to go back to her table and pretend that she devoutly enjoyed this sort of evening.

"God, the dinner looks great," Charlton Heston said.

Claire had always been a fan of his and liked him even more now that she'd gotten to know him. Sometimes he could seem a little humorless when he was discussing a political issue but he was a bright, kind and very witty man who never let his politics get in the way of his humanity.

Heston was on his feet, holding Claire's chair for her.

"Thanks, Chuck."

He nodded and seated himself.

Dinner was Columbia River salmon with lobster medallions, loin of veal with wild mushrooms, and zucchini boats filled with fresh vegetables. For dessert there would be honey ice cream with petits fours. Champagne was readily available at all times.

The waiters were just bringing the main course when Claire happened to notice the envelope lying next to her plate.

Hadn't noticed it before.

Felt an unmistakable chill when her eyes found it.

Shouldn't be there.

And how would it have gotten there, anyway?

Then she relaxed.

Maybe she really was in need of Prozac.

Talk about overreacting.

This was undoubtedly one of Matt's little jokes. He loved little jokes. He'd been especially jovial since making things up to Claire.

Matt.

That's who put the envelope here.

No reason to worry.

"Are you all right?" Chuck Heston said.

"I'm fine, thanks."

The others at the table were looking at her now. Two ambassadors and an opera singer and a baseball player named Kitchin. She followed no sports and had no idea why he was famous. Did he bat the ball or throw it?

She looked at her food. "Please," she said to everyone, "go ahead and eat."

They all nodded agreeably and proceeded to eat.

Nobody, apparently, had noticed the small white envelope. She let it sit for a time, ate her dinner.

The fish was delicious.

At one point, Matt caught her eye and smiled and waved. He was three tables away, with Cardinal O'Connor and Peter Jennings.

She smiled back.

He must be waiting for her to pick up the envelope. Probably a dirty limerick inside, or something like that.

But she didn't want to open it at the table.

She spent the next five minutes finishing her meal. Then she gracefully slid the envelope into her lap and said, "Excuse me. I'll be right back."

They all smiled and nodded.

Chuck Heston said, "You look great tonight, Claire. As always."

Claire nodded her thanks.

She waited until she was out of the dining room and on her way to the bathroom before opening up the envelope and reading its message.

I KNOW ABOUT YOU AND DAVID
HART, YOU WHORE.

She didn't return to the table for nearly twenty minutes. When she did, Chuck Heston noticed right away how pale and shaken she looked.

12

★ ★ ★ He had always given in to Knox Stansfield and this time was not going to be any different.

David Hart stood at the front window of the town house, looking out over Foggy Bottom. Sometimes, as tonight, he felt old and spent. An almost luxurious self-pity overcame him. Poor David. Nobody had ever understood him. Not really.

He had been forced to do cynical and cruel things but he was not himself cynical or cruel. That's what they didn't understand about him. He fancied himself still innocent at heart, a boy-man, really, rather than an adult—a boy-man far more sensitive than even his lady patrons seemed to understand.

A boy-man far too sensitive for the likes of Knox Stansfield.

He went back to the bar for some more brandy, and then returned to the window, the still-bare trees forlorn as his own heart.

He wanted peace of mind.

He wanted true love.

He wanted twice as much as Claire had given him.

That was one well he would definitely have to go back to. Oh, not right away. He would be as judicious as possible with the first hundred thousand. But inevitably he would run out of money and—

Or was he a rat?

Was this notion of his innocence nothing more than a shield to protect him from the real truth—that he was an unmitigated rat?

But, no.

He wasn't.

He checked his watch.

Knox was late.

When the phone rang, he just naturally assumed that it would be Stansfield.

He stepped across the room—taking satisfied note of his black turtleneck-and-designer jeans outfit reflected in the front window—and lifted the receiver.

"I really believed you, David."

Claire. In tears.

"Things have changed."

"Oh, don't give me your lost-little-boy act, David. Save it for those old ladies you always squire around."

"Are we going to get personal now?"

"You're damned right we're going to get personal. I'll be there in an hour and a half and you'd damned well better be waiting for me."

She said no more.

She slammed the phone down.

Knox Stansfield slid into the back seat of his limo. He had given this whole operation three dry runs. He would have ten minutes to get in and out of David Hart's. Ten minutes or his entire plan would crumble.

To Clemmons, he said, "There's an alley behind Hart's. Use that. The back way." Nothing untoward there. Of the half-dozen times he'd visited Hart, he'd usually used the back way. He'd always known he would use Hart in some way and so wanted to be discreet in his dealings with him.

Clemmons eased the limo out into traffic.

Stansfield kept checking his watch.

Ten minutes. He would have ten minutes.

The President's daughter was trying hard not to believe she'd lost another friend.

Appealing as Deirdre was in many respects, she'd always found it hard to make and keep friends. She'd never been sure why.

And now she was having doubts about Heather Cowley, her best friend at St. Mark's, the private school Heather had attended for the past three years.

Heather had been acting weird lately. Spending less and less time with Deirdre. Even missing their sacred lunch hour a few times.

Deirdre had also noticed that Heather accepted fewer and fewer invitations? Tennis Saturday? Gotta study, Deirdre, sorry. A movie in the White House screening room? That's always fun, Deirdre, but I've got to do some crappy stuff with my folks? And so on.

Deirdre had called Heather half an hour ago.

In the good old days of just a few weeks ago, Heather would have called back right away.

But now she was obviously taking her time.

Deirdre lifted the receiver, thinking of calling Heather again.

But that would sound strange, wouldn't it, calling back right away?

So now all Deirdre could do was wait.

And wonder what she'd done to alienate Heather.

Had she inadvertently insulted her in some way?

But what could she possibly have said? Deirdre was always so careful of other people's feelings—and hoped they would be about hers.

She looked at the phone again.

So tempting to pick up and call.

But no—

She tried to get interested in her math.

Her father was so good at it. She must have inherited her mother's math genes. Her Mom was awful with math.

Deirdre's worst subject was math. Last year her parents had even gotten her a tutor.

The tutor hadn't helped.

Deirdre's final grade—after much intensive studying—was a C.

She stared at the phone again. Why didn't it ring?

Then she became aware of her bladder.

Size of a pea, her mother always said.

She pushed herself up, started off the bed.

Then heard something—

—something strange.

One thing people didn't understand about the White House was that it was actually pretty small.

Oh, sure, it was spread out quite a bit, and there were quite a few rooms in it, but the living quarters on the second floor were pretty tiny.

That's how Deirdre was able to hear her mother swearing and sobbing.

Neither of which was like her mother at all. Especially the swearing.

Deirdre, lying on her back on the bed, put down her math textbook and listened, feeling guilty that she would use her own mother's misfortune as an excuse to quit studying math.

She wondered what was wrong.

"You bastard!" her mother snapped. "You lying bastard!"

Deirdre had assumed that her mother was alone, but now she wondered.

Maybe her father and mother were both in their bedroom, and maybe they were having one of their battles.

They didn't fight very often but when they did—

They'd fought a lot about six months ago, when the press, led by Knox Stansfield, kept up the gossip and innuendo about Deirdre's father having an affair.

She'd really wanted to get a gun and go in and kill Knox Stansfield then.

God, it would have felt so good.

Just like Dirty Harry.

Blam-blam-blam-blam.

No more Knox Stansfield to torment her parents . . .

Sobs now.

Mother picking up the phone again.

Dialing.

But only three digits this time.

Which meant she was calling somebody here in the White House.

Deirdre got up and crept across the hall to the open door of her parents' bedroom.

Leaned against the doorframe. Listened.

"Dana. It's me. We need to go out again tonight." Beat. "It's urgent. It really is." Beat. "I'll have to make something up. I guess I can always say that I'm going to see Kendra." Kendra Lewis was a friend of her mother's, the alcoholic wife of a senator. Kendra was always falling off the wagon and Claire was always dashing over there to give her comfort and moral support.

Or so Deirdre had always believed.

But now she wondered.

If her mother was lying about tonight, how many other nights had she lied about?

"I'll be ready in half an hour." Beat. "Thank you, Dana. I really appreciate it."

"If I ask you a question, will you be honest, Heather?"

"Sure."

"How come you don't like me as much anymore?"

Hesitation. "Gee, why would you think a thing like that, Deirdre?"

"Because it's true."

"Gee, Deirdre, you're kind of putting me on the spot."

Deirdre had been about to go in and see what was wrong with her mother when the phone had finally rung.

Heather.

Now Deirdre almost wished that Heather hadn't called back. This was a very painful conversation.

"Did I hurt your feelings or something?"

"Deirdre, maybe we should talk about this some other time."

"You said you'd be honest, Heather."

Pause. "It's Knox Stansfield."

"Knox Stansfield? What's he got to do with it?"

"He's all you talk about. How much you hate him. How he just keeps on doing all these rotten things to your parents."

"But he does."

"I know he does, Deirdre, and I hate him, too. But—you're obsessed. You really are. And—well, it's just kind of boring talking about Knox Stansfield all the time."

"Oh."

"I know that hurt your feelings, Deirdre, and I'm sorry."

"It's all right."

"I don't want you to hate me, Deirdre."

"I don't hate you."

"Because I still like you, Deirdre. I really do."

"So you want to skip the swim meet tomorrow night?"

"Yeah, I guess I kind've do. But maybe we'll do something together some other time."

"Sure."

"I'd better go, Deirdre. I'm supposed to help my Mom."

"All right," Deirdre said and hung up.

By the time she got down to the hall, her mother was already aboard the elevator and going downstairs.

Deirdre got a brief glimpse of her.

Her mother, dressed in white sweater, tan suede car coat and tailored blue slacks, had tears in her eyes and was shaking her head over and over again.

Something was wrong.

Terribly wrong.

13

★ ★ ★ The knock came at the back door. Half an hour late.

Hart, cursing, resenting this whole business, went down the stairs off the kitchen to the dark landing below.

He got the light on and pulled back the small drape, and there stood Knox Stansfield looking like something out of a 1943 secret agent movie with Alan Ladd.

Black snap-brim fedora. Black trench coat, collar up. Black gloves.

Don't hit me any more. I can't take it. I'll tell you where the secret formula is and then you can blow up the world.

Hart opened the door. "You're late."

"Something came up."

"Right."

"Nice way to start our little session, David."

"You're late because you like to show people how powerful you are."

Hart turned around and led the way up the stairs.

"You want a drink?" he said over his shoulder.

"No, thanks. I need to get back as soon as possible. I just need you to show me how you've set the camera up."

"I didn't have to do anything. Your man did it all."

Stansfield laughed. "'My man.' I'm not sure Clemmons would appreciate that."

They passed through the kitchen and then into the living room.

Stansfield looked around, obviously impressed.

"You do live well, David," Stansfield said. "Being nice to all those senators' wives pays off."

"Getting a lecture on morality from you is sort of tough to take, Knox."

Stansfield laughed again. "You're very testy tonight, David."

Hart shook his head, looking miserable. "Maybe I'm sick of the way I've been living."

"You sound like a prime candidate for being born again, David."

Hart smirked. "I thought those were your people, Knox. All the religious nuts."

"I get very tired of that phrase, David. 'Religious nuts.' Liberals like you find it impossible to believe that somebody in this day and age might have deep spiritual values." He glanced around the room. "Now show me where the camera is and I'll be on my way."

Hart said, "Our debt is canceled?"

"You do this little favor for me and our debt is canceled."

Hart studied him a moment and said, "You're finally going to destroy them, aren't you, Knox?"

"You've always had a taste for melodrama, my friend. I'm not going to 'destroy' them, as you say; I'm merely going to expose them for the frauds they are."

That was always the spookiest part of dealing with Knox Stansfield these days. Realizing that he had truly begun to believe his own words.

Protector of the American Way.

"Nothing happened."

"So you say," Stansfield said.

"Nothing, Knox. No sex of any kind."

"She just gave you $100,000 because she liked you so much?"

Hart knew he was blushing. "I'm not proud of the way I made her pay me that money."

Knox Stansfield smiled. "You really are sounding born again, David. Now show me the camera."

"Very simple," Hart said, and pointed to an air-conditioning vent near the ceiling, just up from and to the right of a beautiful Degas print.

"In there?"

"In there."

"What's its range?"

Hart told him.

"Is it on now?" Stansfield said.

"No."

"How do you turn it on?"

Hart told him.

"Very nice," Stansfield said.

"She's coming here tonight. In a half hour or so."

"Oh?"

"She called a little while ago and was hysterical."

"The poor dear."

Hart said, "You've never forgiven her for dumping you, have you, Knox? God, man, you should've let that go a long time ago. Everybody gets dumped."

The smirk. "Even gigolos like you, David?"

"Even gigolos like me, Knox."

This was the first time that Hart noticed the way Knox's gloved hand moved around inside the right pocket of his black London Fog.

As if he were gripping something.

"You sure that camera isn't on now, David?"

"Positive, why?"

He couldn't take his eyes from Knox's right coat pocket.

Gripping something.

But what?

"Good. Because I certainly wouldn't want this to be on tape."

"Wouldn't want what to be on tape, Knox?"

"Oh, come on now, David. You're not stupid. Certainly you should've figured this out by now."

Hart was going to say, Figured what out by now, Knox?

But Knox didn't give him time.

Knox pulled his black gloved hand from his black coat pocket.

A black gun was in his black gloved hand.

A Ruger, to be specific.

"What the hell're you doing?" Hart said.

But the question was rhetorical.

It was perfectly clear what the hell Knox Stansfield was doing.

Or was about to do, anyway.

He shot David Hart three times in the chest.

He checked his watch. Eight minutes.

She had to be on time—

Had to be—

14

★ ★ ★ "I'm not sure this is a good idea, Claire."

"Neither am I."

"We could always turn around and go back."

"I need to talk to him."

"Why're you so sure those two messages you got have something to do with him?"

In the darkness of the Ford, Claire looked pale and solemn. "If he doesn't have something to do with them, Dana, then somebody else is involved. Somebody who can make my husband and me very vulnerable."

"I suppose he could have told somebody," the Secret Service agent said.

"Yes, and knowing how David likes to brag sometimes, I'm sure he embroidered the story a great deal."

Dana smiled. "He probably had you spending long, sunny weekends on the beaches of Brazil."

"I wouldn't be surprised."

He reached over and patted her hand. "It'll be fine, Claire. You just need to take some deep breaths and relax a little."

Foggy Bottom was alive, as usual, even though it was after ten P.M. on a weeknight. Washington was a party town and social status didn't matter. The political elite might have their elegant sit-down dinners, but every other group in the city had its own kind of meeting place.

Poor blacks, gays, reporters, cops, jocks and jock hangers-on . . . everybody had his or her special place.

Claire knew her special place.

Home. With her daughter and husband.

She felt cold and lonely, a stranger even to herself.

The real Claire Hutton didn't belong here or any place like it.

"Here you go."

She smiled. "You sound like a cabbie."

"That'll be twenty dollars, please."

She laughed. "I really appreciate this."

She took the wig from her purse and pulled it on.

"How do I look?"

"Ten years older and really ugly."

"Thank you."

"You had to ask."

"I really appreciate you trying to be funny and all, Dana."

"But it isn't working so why don't I just keep my mouth shut, right?"

"Something like that. No offense."

"Just keep calm. It's all going to be fine."

"I just wish I had your confidence."

Three minutes later, she stood at the front door of the town house, about to knock.

Dana had just pulled away from the curb.

A gentle breeze scented with apple blossoms filled her nostrils. Spring would be here soon. It was so nice after the rough raw winter.

She knocked.

No answer.

Knocked again.

And no answer again.

But this time something unexpected happened.

The front door, apparently under the pressure of her knuckles, eased open.

Darkness.

Very strange.

Why would all the lights be out? And why would the front door be unlocked?

"David."

One, two, three cars drove by fast on the street behind her.

"David."

Somewhere, distant, a police siren.

"David."

No answer.

She took a step inside.

And wanted to run away.

"David."

Heart hammering. A fine sweat on her forehead and arms. Something was wrong.

Another step inside.

"David, are you all right?"

The front door opened on the living room. The moonlight painted the room with silvery elegance; the angles of the fireplace mantel, the rounded back of the couch, the formal beauty of the French doors leading to the dining room.

But no David.

"David."

Another step inside.

Another.

A wild frantic sense of something seriously amiss now—

"David."

And then she saw his hand on the edge of the Persian rug, just beyond the glow of moonlight.

She rushed to him, then, without thinking of anything but his well-being.

"David!"

Saw him sprawled on the parquet floor, his white shirt soaked with blood.

Fine blue eyes wide open.

Staring. Dead.

Even though she knew it was no use, she bent to him to make certain that he was dead.

Bent and—

Later on, she would always come back to this point, try to reconstruct exactly what happened.

But the truth was, she had no idea. One moment she was bending over to examine David, and the next—

Darkness—

Cold, utter darkness.

15

★ ★ ★ Matt Hutton learned two things about the new prime minister of
England: he had terrible breath and he was a boob man.

The former was easy to learn. Prime Minister Cosgrove kept leaning toward Matt to whisper things to him.

The things he whispered invariably concerned the bosoms of various ladies here tonight.

At the moment, however, Hutton was having trouble focusing on
any of the evening's usual business, not even the persistent invective
Senator Gates was pushing into Hutton's right ear (the prime minister
had his left).

Gates was a plump, wattled, coarse old bastard who had never forgiven the CIA for lying to his pal Lyndon Johnson about the war in
Vietnam. Ever since then, Gates had dedicated his Senate career to
destroying the Agency. Tonight he was bitching about some new electronic spying equipment the Agency had spent $30.7 million on
without getting permission from Gates's Senate committee. Earlier this
evening, he had hinted that he might take the whole matter public.
Hutton had smiled and said, "Public? Are you kidding, Verlen? Dan
Rather had it on the news tonight." "Well, he didn't get it from me,"
Gates had huffed. "Of course not, Verlen. Of course not." Gates was
one of those liberals who hated all clandestine operations, even when
they were necessary, an attitude Matt found not only ridiculous but
dangerous. If it had been left to men like Gates, the Berlin Wall would
still be standing, and Moscow would still be the headquarters of the

international Communist party. The CIA made mistakes, and sometimes outrageous ones, but neither Gates nor the press often heard about all the good and important work the Agency did.

Gates was eighty-six and a walking testament to the need for term limits. He had enjoyed power so long that he had come to resemble, physically and spiritually, a corrupt Roman senator.

He got up and excused himself. He had terrible prostate problems and he seemed to waddle off to the men's room about every fifteen minutes.

Which is how Hutton had happened to notice Claire fleeing the dining room twenty minutes ago.

As President, of course, Hutton had to sit here and pretend that everything was just fine.

But he really couldn't concentrate.

Claire had been behaving erratically lately—sudden lapses into melancholy, then almost drunken periods of elation—and he had begun to worry that his rumored extramarital affair had done permanent damage to his beloved wife.

And she *was* beloved.

A few months in the White House and Matt Hutton had started to feel the special privileges that went with this most exalted of offices. Henry Kissinger was right: power *is* the ultimate aphrodisiac. And there was no power equal to that possessed by the President of the United States.

And this didn't just mean nuclear warheads or being head of the Republican party or being able to get somebody's cousin a cushy job in the federal bureaucracy.

This meant power on a personal level, too.

Hutton had been surprised to find how many women flirted with him. And flirted openly.

And so he'd given it a try, pulling back only at the last moment, when the story started appearing in gossip columns.

Poor Claire. Poor Deirdre.

How could he ever have done that to them?

Thank God, they'd been able to put their family life back together.

Or had they?

Where had Claire been rushing to twenty minutes ago?

And why had she looked so disturbed?

Just before Pavarotti was introduced, Matt walked quickly to the back of the dining room, smiling to his famous guests, nodding good evening to the various members of the White House serving staff. Presidents Nixon and Ford had set the highest standard for treating staffers well, as part of a family. Matt tried to keep that tradition going.

Marble hallway. A few quick words with one of his Secret Service agents about where the President was going. Then the elevator.

Two minutes later, he walked up to his daughter's room and knocked.

"Who is it?"

"The President of the United States."

"President Washington?"

"Very funny."

"*Entrez-vous.*"

She was lying on her bed, her math books and papers strewn all around her. In the light of her bed lamp, her long hair shone copper, just like her mother's. She wore pink pajamas that complemented the pink of the wallpaper and the pink of her gorgeous canopy bed.

"Hi."

"Do you like him?" she said.

"The new prime minister?"

"Yeah."

"Seems like a nice enough guy. A little left of center for me but then I'm probably a little right of center for him."

"Evens out."

"Right," he said, and then nodded to her newest poster. "Where'd you get that?"

"A girl at school made it for me."

The poster depicted a close-up of Knox Stansfield with an X drawn through his face.

"She's thinking about marketing it."

He came over and sat down next to her, taking her hand. "You shouldn't let him bother you that much."

"I can't help it, Daddy. I hate him."

"He's just a pest."

"Pests don't accuse you of embezzling money from your old law firm."

"He finally quit saying that."

"And pests don't accuse you of taking campaign money from Mafia guys."

"He quit saying that, too."

"And pests don't accuse you of having affairs."

At this one, he had to pause. His flirtation had not been public knowledge. Probably no more than two or three people in Washington had known that the President and his would-be paramour even worked together. Somebody very close to Matt had leaked the story to Knox Stansfield. And Stansfield has reported it without let up for three months. The primary season was coming up, and he was obviously using all his ammunition to ensure that the President would suffer some humiliating defeats. Now, Matt's old guilt overcame him:

he had been a faithful husband for nineteen years. But he'd come so close—

"You know what Dr. Solomon said, hon."

She sighed.

Matt and Claire had sent Deirdre to a shrink a few months back. Knox Stanfield's constant barbs had started causing her clinical depression. She'd felt impotent—unable to defend the honor of her family in any way. Some of the girls at school had started to be mean, too. Not everybody liked the idea of Matt being as conservative as he was, and this was reflected in the barbs of their children. Deirdre had stopped eating much at all, and sleep became impossible. So, a shrink. Fortunately, he hadn't been one of those Freudian racketeers who wanted to spend years (and tens of thousands of dollars) delving into her girlhood. He worked specifically on helping her deal with Knox Stansfield. He taught her ways of coping, and he gave her some mild antidepressants. Lately, and thank God, Deirdre had been more her old self.

"You're still listening to him, aren't you?" Matt said.

"Did John squeal on me?" John was one of the agents who drove her back and forth to school.

"John didn't say a word, but I know you."

"Yeah, I guess I do."

"Listen to him?"

"Uh-huh."

"Honey, why torture yourself that way? You know you're just going to be upset."

"Someday I'll get a gun and go over there and—"

He grabbed her arms tighter than he meant to, her freckled face reflecting her sudden pain.

"Hey. Listen to yourself. You're doing what all those creeps do to me."

"You mean the death threats?"

"Exactly."

The Secret Service estimated that Matt got six written death threats a week. Not so many as Bill Clinton, who had been so hated as President that written threats had become a form of sport.

"I'm sorry."

"Now never talk like that again."

"All right. I said I was sorry, Daddy."

"And please take down that poster."

"Oh, Daddy."

"Why give him so much prominence in your life?"

She stared up at the poster and shook her head. "I just can't believe that he used to be Mommy's boyfriend."

"I can't, either."

"Or that you used to be friends."

"I know. I think about that, too." But he was getting sucked into her game. "I want that poster taken down tonight, understand?"

"Understand."

He stood up. "By the way, where's your mother?"

Standing above her, watching her face, not expecting anything re-markable to happen in response to a simple question—he was surprised to see her avert her eyes. And surprised to hear her stammer.

"S–she went to her friend's."

"Lilly's?"

Shook her head. Silently. As if she couldn't speak.

What was she hiding from him, anyway?

He felt disturbed and angry and, curiously, afraid.

"Bonnie's?"

Again a head-shake.

"Then where the hell did she go?"

"Why are you swearing at me?"

They were both suddenly shouting at each other.

"Because I don't think you're telling me the truth."

"She went out."

"I know she went out. But where did she go."

"The alcoholic."

"Kendra?"

"Uh-huh."

"Why didn't you just say so?"

"I couldn't remember her name."

He took a deep breath, held it a long moment, let it out slowly. "I'm sorry I yelled."

She just watched him.

"Did you hear me?"

"Yes."

"Well. Don't I get a hug?"

And then she was off the bed and in his arms and holding him with the sweet, urgent, awkward grace of a little girl.

"Oh, Daddy, I'm sorry."

He held her longer, didn't want to let go. He realized there was a kind of desperation in the way he clung to her. And he wondered why.

He kept thinking of her face just a few minutes ago. She'd been purposely evasive, no doubt about it.

But what could she possibly be hiding from him about her mother?

The phone rang.

She spun away, grabbing the receiver. "Oh, hi, Heather." She cupped the mouthpiece with a small pink hand. "It's Heather."

He smiled. "I kind of guessed that when you said 'Hi, Heather.'"

She stuck her tongue out at him then held her face out for him to kiss it, which he promptly and dutifully did.

He left her to her phone.

All the way down in the elevator, all the way back into the dining room where Pavarotti was performing so brilliantly, he wondered just what the hell was going on with Claire these days.

16

★ ★ ★ Probably because of Jane's crippled leg, which had changed her whole life, Claire had always had nightmares about being paralyzed.

Trying to push herself up out of bed—

—only to find that her body parts would not do what she told them to.

Paralysis.

Complete.

Permanent.

As now.

Great pain traveled in an arc across the back of her skull. An icy sweat stood on her arms and face. Bile filled her throat.

The last thing she could remember was—

David Hart.

On the floor.

Dead.

She forced her eyes open.

David lay next to her, his handsome blue eyes still staring up at the ceiling.

By now, the smells were pretty bad. The wound. His bowels. His sweat and juices.

Had to get up.

Had to get out of here.

And that's when it happened.

She couldn't move. It was ridiculous but—

She couldn't move.

She gave herself up to her panic.

Who had killed David, and why?

Who had knocked her out and left her on the floor?

And why couldn't she move?

So ridiculous—

Her eyes moved down the front of David's blood-soaked shirt. He really was dead. She had to keep telling herself this. He really was dead.

Then she saw her own hand.

And the weapon in it.

She recognized the .45 at once as her gun, the one Matt had given to her when they'd moved to Washington, back when he had been a first-term congressman.

Her own gun. But that was impossible. How could her gun have gotten here?

Had to get out. Now. Had to.

This time, she was able to move. Clumsily, to be sure, slowly, too. But eventually she got to her feet on badly shaking legs.

The gun was still in her hand.

She wanted to fling it away somewhere.

Didn't ever want to see it again.

But she knew better. She gripped the weapon, as if it might leap from her hand.

She scanned the room, noticing only now that the living room lights were on.

The room had been dark.

Her assailant had turned on the lights. Why?

At first, she thought that her eyes were improperly registering what she saw on the dry bar at the far end of the living room.

A red high-heeled pump.

Very much like her own.

A single pump. Sitting on the bar.

She crossed the living room, her eyes flicking right and left for any more signs of disturbance. If only that bloody old corpse weren't lying on the floor, the handsome room would be just about perfect—

She was still three feet from the bar when she realized that this was indeed her red pump. For the Inaugural, Matt had had the pumps made for her to match her red ball gown. It was his very special gift.

What was it doing here?

Had to be careful. Didn't want to leave fingerprints.

She reached out and touched her fingers to the pump and then paused.

Eyes.

Somebody was watching her. She was sure of it. Could *feel* it. A part of her wanted to smile. Now how was that for a paranoid fantasy?

But she was sure somebody really was watching.

She turned abruptly, trying to startle anybody who might be lurking in the shadows.

But she was alone in the living room. Except, of course, for poor dead David.

Her eyes searched the room a final time. Nothing.

Why then the almost claustrophobic feeling of eyes on her?

She had to get out of here. Now.

She tucked the red shoe under her arm and walked quickly back across the living room.

When she reached the front door, she realized she still held the gun in her hand.

Her head was blindingly painful; she still felt nauseated.

Had to think clearly. Put the gun in your belt. Then use the corner of your car coat to open the doorknob without leaving fingerprints.

Hurry now; hurry.

She hurried.

She almost looked back at David but then stopped herself at the last moment.

This was no way to remember him, even if he had become a blackmailer at the end of his life.

She took the front steps of the town house two at a time and then dashed across the sidewalk to where Dana sat waiting.

She wondered if even good, trusting Dana would believe the incredible story she had to tell.

17

★ ★ ★ All the way down in the elevator, the President thought about Sullivan, the Democratic majority leader. Ever since Senator Wagner had announced that he would be running against the President in the primary, Sullivan had been hard to get along with. The President had proposed an important middle-class tax cut—one that favored neither the rich nor the poor but really did deliver a substantial cut to the middle class for once—and Sullivan had been shying away. Obviously, he was now going to come up with his own bill so that the Democrats could take all the credit for it in the autumn elections.

Then Matt's thoughts returned to Claire. He once again said a silent prayer that his recent dalliance hadn't destroyed his marriage. He wouldn't be able to face that. A few months of peacock vanity on his part (midlife crisis, if you wanted to get technical) and he lost the love of the only woman he'd ever really shared himself with—

But he had certainly humiliated her—the press had been murderous—and caused her abiding pain.

Now she was gone so many nights. To see Kendra, she said. But—

The elevator doors opened, and when he stepped out into the hall, he saw Jane coming back from the ladies' room.

He fell into step next to her, consciously slowing down to compensate for her crippled right leg.

Jane was beautiful in an emerald-colored strapless gown that seemed to set aflame her red hair and give a purity to her very white skin.

"Good evening, Mr. President."

"Evening, Jane. You look great."

"Thank you."

"Who's the lucky man tonight?"

He could see instantly that he'd embarrassed her. Claire believed that Jane's leg made her feel so bad about herself that she couldn't accept a compliment without feeling the person was being insincere.

"Bob Raines."

"From Senator Malcom's office?"

"Uh-huh."

"He seems like a great guy."

Jane smiled, looking more at ease now. "He is."

A few more steps. They were close to the dining room now.

Matt said, "Jane, have you noticed that Claire is acting kind of—funny—lately?"

"Funny?"

"Distant, I guess. Preoccupied is maybe a better way to say it."

Jane shook her gorgeous, tumbling hair. "Not lately I haven't. When you— Well, when you were in the press all the time, I noticed her withdraw, then. But lately she's seemed fine."

"When you were in the press all the time" was Jane's delicate way of saying *when you were humiliating your wife in public.* There was a hint of anger in her voice—loyalty to her best friend Claire—and he didn't blame her.

"Maybe I'm just imagining things, then."

Jane smiled. "Overwork, Mr. President."

"Well, I guess I'd have to admit to that, wouldn't I?"

He escorted her into the elegant dining room.

18

★ ★ ★ At this very moment, there were more than 25,000 registered lobbyists in Washington, D.C. This meant a ratio of roughly 45 lobby-ists to every member of the House and Senate. There were also more than 53,000 lawyers, a large number of whom aided and abetted the lobbyists. A reasonable person might conclude that this was not the government the Founding Fathers had had in mind.

But then nobody had ever said that Washington, D.C., was a rea-sonable town, a fact testified to this evening by the large number of liberals and moderates who had showed up to hear Knox Stansfield at the Mayflower Stouffer Hotel on Connecticut Avenue.

Clemmons, in one of his funereal dark suits that passed for livery in this town, stood in the back of the banquet room, tallying up just how many liberals had shown up tonight.

Thus far, he'd counted thirty-six. An outfit known as the Washing-ton, D.C., Better Government Bureau had sponsored Stansfield tonight and had invited all the members of Congress. The Better Government folks had needed a big-name draw because this was not a simple night of chat and chablis. The Better Government folks hoped to convince the Congress to give D.C. an additional quarter-billion dollars this year.

After he counted liberals, he counted conservatives—forty-three—and after that he counted blacks. Three. Most blacks would rather attend a Klan rally than hear a Knox Stansfield speech. While the commentator angrily denied that he was a racist, his rhetoric was implicitly anti-black. Clemmons had no illusion about his own race. Many members of this new inner-city generation seemed to be a mutant strain. Never had Clemmons seen such unnecessary or savage violence. Clemmons had grown up in Memphis, served in Vietnam and then moved to Washington, D.C. In all that time, he had never seen blacks treated worse than they were by some of today's inner-city kids.

But despite all this, Clemmons knew that they were still human beings, the black kids who roamed the streets today. Some of them needed to be killed (he believed ardently in capital punishment); some needed to be imprisoned; but most needed to be put in trade schools and drug rehab programs and be given one last chance to turn their lives around. He despised the hoary liberal notion of pity and welfare. But he still believed in trying to save souls through hard work, compassion and the mandatory use of Norplant as a means of slashing the illegitimacy rate by at least half.

But his boss . . .

Knox Stansfield's only solution to black violence was white violence. Cops coming in and shooting up the place, taking out large numbers of kids while they were doing so. Judging by the mail Knox received, a lot of Americans, white and black, agreed with him . . .

"Ladies and gentlemen . . . the most beloved *and* the most hated man in America . . . Knox Stansfield!"

And then suddenly there he was.

Standing ovation. Even the liberals.

Knox in his blue suit, crisp white shirt, dark gray-shot hair. Handsome in a professorial way, he was, until he started with his cutting remarks, anyway. Then he was more stand-up comic than professor.

Clemmons sometimes wondered if Knox really believed many of the things he said. He loved to shock and outrage people, and he loved to inspire cruel laughter.

Knox waved down the standing ovation, leaned into the microphone and said, "I would have been here sooner but President Hutton's motorcar tied up traffic. He was over at the unemployment office. Apparently, he read the same primary polls I did."

Appreciative laughter.

President Hutton's popularity was unquestionably waning. A lot of this was because of Clemmons's boss, of course. Knox had personally asked Senator Wagner to enter the primaries and challenge the President from the far right. Between Knox and the Reverend Hugh Goodhew's *God's Hour* TV show, Matthew Hutton had spent the past three months being denounced, stomped and castrated. Hints of everything from dishonesty to dalliances, from a bad marriage to an uncontrollable daughter were put forth, usually on Knox's show first, and then echoed later on *God's Hour.*

That's why all the liberals were here tonight.

They wanted to try to understand this man's appeal and power.

For fifty years, Clemmons thought, liberals had given the people what they thought they wanted. It was a trade: the liberals seized more and more power for the state, and the average citizen was given the illusion of a social safety net.

But all that changed in the nineties. Only the rich had safety nets, for one thing, and the people began to resent all the intrusions of the government. Waco, Texas, came to mind for many people. A religious cult saw most of its members slaughtered by government ineptitude in handling the situation. Stansfield had had little interest in the Waco killings—not "sexy" enough for his listeners.

No, Stansfield was mostly interested in assaulting the President frontally. Knox Stansfield hated Hutton and wanted to destroy him. The reason was simple enough. All you had to do was peek into Knox's den and see the photographs of Claire Hutton he kept around. Knox had a really sick thing for the President's wife, no doubt about it. Hutton could have gone on the counterattack, but in doing so he would have had to talk about his college days, when Knox and Hutton and Claire and David Hart had all been friends. And that was not a period that Hutton could afford to put under the public microscope . . .

More laughter, applause.

Clemmons came back to the Mayflower.

Knox was already breaking them up with his tart humor, most of which lit on the President.

Hard to believe that just half an hour ago, Knox had looked pale and deeply disturbed about something . . .

Clemmons had, as Knox requested, parked in the alley behind David Hart's town house. Also as Knox had requested, Clemmons kept the motor running. Knox liked the limo nice and warm. Clemmons had immediately turned the station from the "beautiful listening" that Knox liked to one of the local jazz stations. They'd been doing Dixieland tonight and Clemmons purely loved Dixieland.

And then suddenly, Knox had appeared, making a big show of being composed and normal.

But his sweaty face gave him away, and so did his trembling hands. And he could barely find his voice, spoke for a time in little more than whispers.

And the bar in back was opened, too. Knox rarely imbibed before a speech. But tonight he took down three quick scotches.

"Everything all right?" Clemmons had asked over the microphone.

"Of course. Why?"

"You just seem a little upset or something."

"It's your imagination. I'm fine."

But he wasn't fine. He was clearly upset. Clemmons wondered what had happened at Hart's. Hart had visited the mansion a few times. Clemmons had the impression that while Knox did business with Hart, he didn't especially like him.

"We're very low on scotch."

"I'll take care of it."

Clemmons had the sense that Knox wanted to say more but stopped himself.

Then: "I wasn't up there very long, was I?"

"No. Why?"

"I was just curious. Lost track of time, I guess."

"Fifteen minutes, maybe."

"Good. Fifteen minutes."

Clemmons checked the rear view and saw that his boss was smiling. Something about the "fifteen minutes" had made him happy.

Now Clemmons stood in the back of the Mayflower's banquet room and replayed that last bit of conversation in his mind.

The one about fifteen minutes.

Why would the boss make such a point of being up there only fifteen minutes?

Clemmons was a suspicious man, anyway.

Now he was even more suspicious than ever.

The car. Dana driving. Claire unable to concentrate. Moving away fast from David Hart's. Toward the White House.

"You don't look so good," Dana said.

"I'm not so good."

"You going to tell me what happened?"

"I need a few minutes. Just to think."

Dana reached over and patted her hand. "Tell me when you're ready to tell me. I can wait."

"Oh, God, Dana. It's so awful."

"Yes," he said, looking straight ahead. "I kind of figured it probably was."

They rode a few more minutes.

She wanted to keep on riding. Into the darkness. Somewhere far, far away. And never return. Never have to explain what she couldn't possibly explain about David dead on the floor—

She told Dana, then.

She saw his face tighten as he listened, saw his fingers grip the steering wheel so tight his knuckles went white.

"You're the only one I can turn to, Dana. Would you—look into it? See what you can find out about David? I can't just go in to Matt and tell him— Could you do your own investigation over the next couple of days?"

"Of course I will," he said. Then, "You realize you were set up, don't you?"

"Set up?"

He nodded somberly. "'Framed' is the right word, I think."

"Framed," she said, but it was a movie word, a mystery-novel word. "Framed," she whispered again. "Framed."

19

★ ★ ★ She went straight to the bathroom and stayed there for twenty minutes. She threw up, washed her face, threw up and washed her face again.

She brushed her teeth twice, brushed her hair three times, feared that she was going to throw up again.

She got out of her clothes, wrapped them up in a tight ball and then put them in the clothes hamper. She was well aware that her suit required dry cleaning. But by putting it in the clothes hamper she wouldn't have to deal with it. She was sure she had some of David's blood on the garment.

Then she was left with the gun.

The clean, cold, silver gun that had been used to kill David.

Her gun.

How in God's name had it gotten to David's apartment?

Put it away in the proper bureau drawer. That was the only thing she could think of to do. Put it away and try to forget all about it.

All she could do.

She stuffed the gun deep into the pocket of her robe and then went to see Deirdre.

"Are you starting your period, Mom?"

"Now that's a nice question."

"It's just you always get sentimental. You know, start talking about when I was a little kid and everything."

"Believe it or not, young lady, I think about you being a little kid a lot. Even when I'm not having my period. Which I'm not, by the way."

"I didn't mean to hurt your feelings."

She smiled and stroked Deirdre's hair.

Deirdre was lying on her bed in her pajamas, her long hair streaming out behind her.

"Dad was looking for you."

"He was?"

She wasn't sure why but Deirdre's words alarmed her. As if Matt might somehow suspect what had happened.

"Then he went back downstairs?"

"Uh-huh."

"Well, he'll be up soon enough."

"He seemed kind of worried about you."

"He did?"

"We both think you've been acting kind of weird lately."

"There's a vote of confidence."

"You just seemed kind of—distracted, I guess."

"It's just that I have so much to do."

"Yeah, and it probably doesn't help always having to run over to Kendra's all the time, either, does it?"

"She's my friend."

She couldn't use Kendra as an excuse anymore. One of these days, Matt might call Kendra's house and learn that Kendra was doing perfectly fine and that Claire hadn't been needed over there in a long time.

Deirdre yawned. "Boy, math really tires me out."

Claire smiled. "Or bores you."

Deirdre grinned. "Sssh. You're not supposed to tell anybody."

Claire bent down and kissed her and said good night.

Matt didn't come upstairs till well after midnight. He smelled lightly of gin.

He undressed in the dark, obviously assuming that his wife was asleep.

She wasn't.

She'd been keeping herself awake so that she could talk to him. Tell him everything. It was time now.

But it was easier to lie there, feigning sleep. Easier to lie there silently than to try and summon up words that would convey how foolish she'd been to visit David in his apartment—even though it had been innocent—and how dangerous and sad it had become now with David murdered.

The President was not a pajama man.

No matter how cold it got, he slept in his white jockey shorts, sans even a T-shirt.

He climbed into bed now and whispered, "Honey? Are you awake?"

But there was no answer.

"Honey?" Whispered again.

She should talk to him.

Tell him.

She parted her lips.

Darling, I need to talk to you.

That's what she should have said.

Instead she said—nothing.

A few minutes later, Matt had rolled away from her and was snoring.

20

★ ★ ★ Bobby LaFontaine happened to be in Reverend Goodhew's office when the call came. Bobby watched the taping of *God's Hour* earlier tonight and had taken notes on what he felt was wrong with the show. Reverend Goodhew generally claimed to be appreciative of Bobby's observations. The only time he'd balked was when Bobby had noted that the Reverend looked to be putting on a little weight. Bobby learned from this: it was fine to criticize every aspect of the show except for the Reverend himself. That was a definite no-no.

Just before the phone rang, Bobby decided to "scan" the various rooms, see if his listening devices picked anything up.

The phone rang.

Bobby LaFontaine swore. He'd just started having fun.

"Reverend Goodhew's."

"The Reverend please."

"I'm sorry. He's busy at the moment. May I take a message?"

Bobby LaFontaine was just thinking what kind of putz would call here this late at night, when he suddenly realized who he was talking to.

"Is this Bobby?"

"Yessir, Mr. Stansfield."

"Bobby, I want you to give the Reverend a very important message."

There it was. That tone again. As if Stansfield were addressing some kind of retard.

Oh, Bobby couldn't wait to play the Reverend some of the tapes he'd made out at the Motel Six. Indeed, indeed.

"If you tell me very slowly, I can probably remember it," Bobby LaFontaine said.

Long pause. "Are you being sarcastic, Bobby?"

"Not at all Mr. Stansfield."

Another pause. "I just don't know why Hugh keeps you around."

"What's the message, Mr. Stansfield?"

"The message is that we are about to receive some very good news about President Hutton."

"That's the message?"

"That's the message."

"Excuse me for saying this, Mr. Stansfield, but that don't make a whole hell of a lot of sense."

"I don't care to share the rest of the message with you, Bobby. That's why it 'don't' make any sense, as you say. You just have Hugh call me."

"All right, sir. I will."

"And he's not going to like it when I tell him that you were sarcastic with me again, Bobby."

"No, sir, I don't expect he will like it," Bobby LaFontaine said, and then hung up.

Good news about President Hutton.

Bobby sat himself down in the Reverend's own chair and wondered just what Knox Stansfield had been talking about.

11

★ ★

BY 1948, RADIO COMMENTATOR GERALD L. K. SMITH HAD WON HIMSELF A NATIONAL RADIO FOLLOWING RUNNING TO THE MILLIONS OF LISTENERS. THE FAVORITE TARGETS OF HIS SCORN CONTINUED TO BE NEGROES, WHOM HE REFERRED TO AS A "RACE OF CHILDREN" AND JEWS, WHOSE HANDS, HE SAID, "DRIPPED WITH THE BLOOD OF OUR SACRED LORD." HE ALSO ATTACKED IMMIGRANTS, CALLING THEM "ALIENS IN OUR CHRISTIAN NATION." ON NATIONAL RADIO, HE CALLED THE UNITED NATIONS "THE JEW-NITED NATIONS." HE USED THIS PHRASE FREQUENTLY. HIS LISTENERS APPARENTLY FOUND IT ENDLESSLY HILARIOUS.

21

TWO DAYS LATER

★ ★ ★ Henderson liked hookers, at least the kind produced in the D.C. area. They usually had some pretty good war stories to tell and the war stories usually involved congressmen.

"But he was p.c., you know," said the black lady with the spangled pink eyelids.

"What's p.c.?"

"You know, babe. Politically correct."

Henderson was a homicide cop and as such he should be on the far side of the bullpen working on his latest case. But he'd been coming back from the john when he heard the hooker say that she knew "a good story about a congressman." He just couldn't resist eavesdropping.

He leaned his short, stubby body forward, ears up, and tuned the lady in the same way he would tune in a radio station.

There. Perfect.

"So," Detective Jass said, "he asked you if he could wear your underwear?"

"Yeah. And my shoes."

"Your shoes? Your heels?"

"He has real dinky feet."

"I bet that ain't all he's got that's dinky."

"Actually, he's got a good size one."

"Surprises me."

"Seven inches, I'd say."

Jass's black face split into a grin as he looked up and winked at Henderson. "Seven inches, huh? About half of what I've got."

"Sure, babe," the hooker said.

"But I don't get this p.c. deal."

"The mink coat."

"What mink coat?"

"Well, there he is in my heels and my cut-out underwear and my heels and my teensy-tiny little bra and he says, 'I need something else, too.' So I look in the closet and all I can find is this old mink coat one of the other girls leaves there sometimes. I offer it to him but he won't take it. 'I'm an environmentalist and I don't believe in killing animals.' So I had to go find him a cloth coat to complete his ensemble. Can you believe that, a politically correct transvestite?"

"You aren't gonna tell me his name?"

"No way, babe. He gets booted outta office, I'll lose one of my best customers."

"You always told me the names before."

"Yeah, but I didn't have the investment in them that I have in this dude." She glanced at the expensive watch on her dainty little wrist. "Where's that rotten lawyer of mine, anyway?"

Story time was over.

Henderson drifted back to his desk.

The six homicide desks were empty, and with good reason. In the past four nights there had been eight murders and while two of them had been the usual sad frenzied bloodlettings of street gangs, two were murders of the more interesting kind.

Henderson had caught one of them, a dashing young man named David Hart. Thus far the surmise was that (a) one of Hart's many lovers had done him in or (b) somebody had managed to get through the rather sophisticated security system in his town house and waste him.

Henderson was still working on it.

He was just sitting down at his desk when the phone rang. In response, he felt an almost dizzying rush of adrenaline.

Maggie.

He was sure of it.

She'd made up her mind.

She wasn't going to leave him after all.

But it wasn't Maggie. It was the Commander down the hall.

"I need to see you for a little bit, Michael."

"Anything special?"

A deep—disturbingly deep—sigh. "Yeah, very special. Why don't you come down here?"

"All right."

What the hell was going on? Commander Craig sounded as if he'd just found out that his wife and two daughters had been found murdered.

He got up from the desk, and that's when he noticed it, lost among the various reports on blood and fiber and glass that had come from the Hart crime scene.

An envelope. A number ten.

Detective Michael Henderson
Sixth Precinct
Washington, D.C.

D.C. postmark. Single stamp. No return address. No other markings front or back. Hmmm. He was curious but there was no time for curiosity now. He dropped the envelope back on his desk.

First he had to find out what the hell was going on with the Commander.

"He's suing you and us," Commander Craig said, his black face scowling.

"For what?"

Commander Craig glanced down at the legal documents on his desk and read from them.

"He's suing for false arrest. He said you—and we—harassed him."

"That's a lie and you know it. He's suing me because I didn't bow and scrape enough. That jerk."

"Correction, my friend: that you *and* the department had some sort of vendetta against him."

"We didn't. I mean, God he used to beat her up twice a month. He was the most likely suspect. That's why I kept on him and built the case that way."

Commander Craig was a chunky former halfback who wore nice dark suits and a permanent look of discomfort. At fifty-three, he had a bad stomach and a bad prostate.

He reached now for the small prescription bottle of Bactrim on his neatly organized desk in his neatly organized Washington. "Guess how many men over age sixty have prostate cancer?"

Henderson wanted to talk about the lawsuit, of course, but he knew he'd have to answer Craig before they went on. Craig loved dis-seminating medical facts.

"I don't know."

"C'mon, guess."

"Twenty percent."

"Twenty percent? Man, don't you ever listen to the news?"

"All right, thirty percent."

"Thirty-eight percent. That's the new estimate, anyway. But you know why they aren't all bent out of shape about it?"

"Why?"

"Because it's usually so slow you can live your whole life with it. You'll die of something else first. By the way, you ever get that prostate exam I told you to? You sit down a lot and you have a lot of stress. You're a prime candidate for prostate problems."

"I haven't had time yet."

"I can get you an appointment with my urologist."

"Commander, could we get back to the lawsuit? I mean, this sounds serious."

The scowl was back as the Commander looked down at the legal papers again. "It wouldn't be serious if his name wasn't Richard Dayton, Jr., whose old man just happens to be one of the richest real estate men in the area."

"It'll get thrown out."

"Yeah, but not before he makes our life miserable." Commander Craig shook his head. "And that promotion you're up for, Michael— We'll have to put that aside for a while, I'm afraid."

Henderson lost it. "What? All because some rich boy who likes to beat up women says we harassed him? He's white, rich, Protestant and heterosexual. And now he wants to be a victim on top of it?"

"Michael, Michael, calm down." Commander Craig pointed down to his own groin. "The prostate really reacts to stress, remember."

But all Henderson could think about was what Maggie would say. He'd been counting on the promotion to buttress his argument that he really was going somewhere as a cop, that homicide detective was a noble and honorable and profitable calling.

But not now.

"Isn't that funeral this afternoon?"

"Yeah, I guess so," Henderson said, still angry.

"Better get ready for it, huh?"

Henderson nodded. "Sorry I'm being such a baby."

"You need to dump her, Michael."

His words shocked Henderson, and at first he wondered if he'd even heard them properly. "What?"

"It's a rotten thing to say, I know, especially to a guy you like as much as I like you. But Maggie— Man, she's messing up your whole life. She's in the fast lane with all her lawyer friends and— Well, you're a cop, Michael. Lawyers get the money *and* the glamour. We get the satisfaction of getting some real bad people off the streets—at least until the judges let 'em go a few hours later." He smiled sourly at his own humor. "She's killing you, my friend. You're always bustin' your hump to keep her happy. That isn't what marriage is supposed to be about." The famous scowl. "By the way, I know you're going to be pissed I said all this, but it's time, Michael. And maybe I should have said it a long time ago."

Henderson didn't know what to say. He just gave kind of a nod and then turned to walk away.

"Michael," Commander Craig said just as Henderson reached the door.

"Yeah?"

The Commander waved the legal papers at him. "I know you did the best job you could on the Dayton thing—but now you've got to be extra careful about getting the guilty party. Another big-time mistake like this—" The scowl again. He didn't have to finish his sentence.

He didn't even notice the envelope on his desk when he sat down.

He was living inside himself, a boil of anger and frustration and fear.

Dump her, the Commander had said.

But the Commander didn't know how it was to love the same girl since second grade, the same girl who would always be too beautiful, too smart and too ambitious for you. Somehow he had convinced her to marry him, promising a grand and golden life somewhere in a glowing future that neither one of them could quite see just yet. The first years hadn't been so bad. Maggie had become a cop's wife, one of a small circle of women who were every bit as tight and exclusive as their husbands. But then she decided to use her college degree to go back to night school and study law. And seven years later, she was a lawyer. And not hanging around with cops' wives anymore. In fact, finding cops and everything that went with them largely distasteful. She drank with lawyers and lobbyists and congressmen now, and didn't come home till one and two A.M. sometimes, and never really wanted to talk about what was going on with her or her life, and when she got angry all she could do was mock his cop life and how nickel-dime and mock-macho it all was, all this cop stuff, and she was tired of it. And all he could do was cling desperately to her, cling the way he had since they'd been in second grade and he'd walked her home through the smoky autumn afternoons, so totally enraptured that he had no other reality than her.

And he still didn't.

He noticed the envelope, examined it again. At one of the embassies a few months back there'd been a letter bomb delivered. These days, a guy had to think of things like that or he might be minus a few fingers.

He did what he should have done the first time he picked the envelope up. He patted it down carefully, almost tenderly. Felt flat. No suspicious bumps or lumps.

He slit it with his letter opener.

No boom. No KA-POW.

He extracted a single sheet of cheap white typing paper.

> David Hart and First Lady
> Claire Hutton were *very* good
> friends.
> A Concerned Citizen

Now just what the hell was that supposed to mean?

Every news account of Hart's death had noted that the President and his wife had been college friends of Hart's. They'd all gone to school with the radio commentator Knox Stansfield. The First Lady had even noted that she'd renewed their old friendship at some art gallery teas lately. The only thing that had surprised Henderson about all this was that the First Lady would want to be publicly associated with a guy who was essentially a gigolo. Hart had played the bored-wife circuit and played it well enough to afford a fancy town house and a fancy sportscar. Not exactly the kind of guy the White House would usually want to be associated with.

He studied the note again.

He was sure there'd be no fingerprints on it, nothing that could be profitably analyzed in the lab.

Political, Henderson thought.

This is meant to stir up trouble. Some Democrat seeing an opening to damage the President. The Republicans would do the same thing if the situation were reversed. That was one of the reasons Henderson hadn't voted the last two elections. He knew what both sides were like.

He put the letter back into its envelope and dropped the envelope into his in-box.

Then it was time to go to the funeral.

22

★ ★ ★ They would come face to face with Knox Stansfield and there would be some terrible scene.

This was the notion that had kept Claire awake most of the night.

Now, as she stood next to Max and Deirdre at graveside, the thirty or so black-clad mourners listening to the minister say the last words as the burial tent flapped in the wind, she could not keep herself from staring across the sun-dappled coffin at the familiar face of Knox Stansfield.

In his black suit and white shirt and black tie, he looked as handsome as ever. Even the ten extra pounds he'd gained in the past few years only served to lend him a certain authority that some stout men had.

His eyes met hers.

Claire quickly looked away.

All the terrible things he'd said about her husband over the past two years. Inexcusable.

Then she realized that Deirdre was glaring at Stansfield.

"Honey, please," Claire whispered.

"I can't control myself," Deirdre said. "I hate him."

But she finally averted her eyes back to the minister. A soft breeze blew through the funeral tent, sweet with the promise of summer.

Claire glanced at Matt, neat and impressive in his dark gray suit. Though his head was bowed as the minister finished, Claire suspected that he, too, had been looking across at the mourners on the other side—at Knox Stansfield.

How much her life had changed in the past four days, since discovering the body of David in his town house. All she could hope was that Dana's private investigation turned up the real killer . . .

If only she'd been more appreciative of the life she'd had before David's death.

She had complained too much, valued too little . . .

Her eyes raised again.

Knox was staring at her openly.

Was that the hint of a smirk on his mouth?

And for the hundredth time in the past four days, she wondered if Knox had something to do with David's death.

But, no: ruthless as he could be, even Knox had scruples, a certain line he would never cross.

Didn't he?

There was a good oak on a good hill above the fresh gravesite.

Michael Henderson stood there with his binoculars.

He wanted to get a good look at the people who'd attended the graveside services.

Earlier, as they'd left the church, Henderson had snapped their photographs.

Now he wanted to see if any of them behaved oddly in any way.

Because most murders were committed by people the victim knew, cops just assumed that the murderer would frequently show up at the funeral.

This was a curious assortment: dowagers who had likely been David Hart's "patrons," three very attractive ladies in their mid-thirties whom Hart was undoubtedly bopping, a dozen or so nondescript men in suits whom he'd probably known through business, and the President and his wife and daughter, both of whom looked remarkably alike—really fresh and appealing without quite being beautiful.

And then the Secret Service agents, most of whom stayed back by the Presidential limo. And finally, Knox Stansfield. The guy, dashing in his black suit and black camel's hair topcoat, did not exactly look humble.

Henderson didn't see anything especially notable and half the time he had to force himself to pay attention.

He was thinking of Maggie and how she was going to leave him and how he wouldn't be able to cope.

How he wouldn't be able to cope at all.

There was a guy in the slam who'd taught Bobby LaFontaine a great deal about locks and security systems of all kinds.

Forty-five minutes before the funeral started, Bobby sat across from Knox Stansfield's posh home and watched as the colored chauffeur named Clemmons wheeled his master out of the drive in the shiny new Lincoln Towncar.

Bobby moved fast.

Never knew when something would go wrong and Clemmons or Stansfield would suddenly return to get something forgotten.

The first thing Bobby had to do was defeat the alarm system. It was a variation on the basic sensor setup. It took Bobby just under five minutes to shut it down.

Then came the door. This, ironically, took longer than the alarm system. He possessed a ring with forty-six keys on it and he had to try thirty-eight of them before he found the right one.

Inside, feeling that he was off his best time, he hauled ass, finally deciding that the best place to plant a bug was the hot tub that sat to the west of the swimming pool. Guy going to dick his broad, he would most likely do it in the hot tub.

There was a shelf maybe five feet high above the tiled area to the east of the hot tub.

He continued to work quickly, even though his eyes and nose were running. Damned swimming pool chlorine. Always played hell with his sinuses.

He tucked the bug in a crack between shelf and wall. Fit perfectly. He then put the pool brush and cleaning solution back. Nobody would ever spot this bug. Nobody.

On his way out, he paused just long enough to wonder what it would be like to sit in a hot tub with naked young Jenny rubbing her breasts against him and letting him feel the sweet warmth between her legs.

His sexual fantasy was spoiled somewhat because of the way he kept sneezing. Damned chlorine, anyway.

He got out of there.

The minister finished up by thanking everybody for coming today and saying that he was sure David was grateful for their love and loyalty.

Claire turned away from the coffin, trying to lead Deirdre and Matt back to the limousine so they wouldn't have to face Stansfield, when she felt Deirdre push past her.

Before there was time to stop her, Deirdre walked quickly around the end of the coffin and went straight to Knox Stansfield, who was setting a stylish black fedora on his head.

"I don't see how you can live with yourself and tell the lies you do about my father!"

Claire, momentarily paralyzed, could only shake her head in disbelief as she watched and heard her daughter confront Stansfield.

Matt was not paralyzed.

In moments, he was next to Deirdre, pulling her away.

"C'mon, now, Deirdre, that's enough."

All the mourners had stopped; were watching, fascinated.

"Quit telling lies about my father!" Deirdre shouted at Knox Stansfield.

Stansfield looked shocked, then amused.

This time, Matt's grip was harder. He pulled her away into Claire's waiting arms.

Claire had found her legs again, was moving toward Deirdre and her father.

Deirdre was already sobbing in rage and embarrassment over this moment.

Knox Stansfield smiled. "She's like her mother, Matt. Spunk. You should be proud."

"I apologize for her behavior, Knox."

And then Knox, clearly aware that he had an audience, put his hand out.

For a moment, Matt didn't move, obviously not knowing quite how to play this.

Claire watched anxiously as he struggled with his decision. Should he shake the hand of the man who ridiculed him day in and day out?

Matt's hand went out. The two men shook.

Having scored a nice public relations point with the audience, Knox tipped his stylish black fedora to both Claire and Deirdre.

"Good afternoon, ladies," he said. Then he looked at Deirdre and said, "I'm just doing my job, honey, just the way your father does his. It's nothing personal."

And then he was gone.

"I hate him! I hate him!" Deirdre sobbed into Claire's arms.

Matt came up and took Deirdre for the next minute or so, trying to quell her tears, soothe her rage and bitterness. Claire could never recall seeing her daughter this uncontrollable.

This was a different, and frightening, side to Deirdre, and only now was Claire able to see just how much her daughter truly loathed Knox Stansfield.

Terrifying.

A few minutes later, Claire and Matt helped Deirdre back to the limousine. The girl's entire body had gone slack, almost as if she'd gone into shock after the incident.

Claire was now afraid that Stansfield's assaults were causing serious damage to her daughter. Perhaps permanent damage.

She glanced over her shoulder just as she was getting into the limo.

Stansfield's black driver, a striking older man, was holding the door for his employer.

But then Knox paused, too, and looked back at Claire.

Even from this distance, she could see his famous impudent smirk.

Knox had obviously enjoyed his encounter with the President's daughter.

Only now did she realize that he would soon enough be talking about it on his radio show.

Knox Stansfield, speaking up for America.

And the President's spoiled daughter accosting him for simply telling the truth.

Poor Deirdre.

She'd wanted to hurt him.

But all she'd done was end up giving him a public relations bonanza.

Now what the hell was that all about? Henderson wondered.

He wished he'd had a microphone so he could've picked up that last little bit of business.

The girl was crying and both the President and his wife looked humiliated.

Then he thought of the anonymous letter he'd gotten back at the precinct.

About Claire Hutton and David Hart.

Could there really be anything to that?

The First Lady having an affair—and being involved in a murder?

23

★ ★ ★ There were some in Washington who argued that a president's chief of staff was more important than the President himself.

Matt's chief of staff was a former Bush Republican named Chad McElroy. Even in a vested suit and solid gold cufflinks, his rangy body suggested the Utah mountains where he'd grown up. He was a balding man with a boyish grin, a six-foot-two body that seemed twenty pounds underweight, and a pair of killer blue eyes that "Ted Bundy would have been proud to own," as the brilliant columnist Jack Germond had noted.

After coming back from the funeral and having a long talk with Deirdre, who decided to take a tranquilizer and lie down, Claire went downstairs to her office, where she found Jane working furiously at the computer. And Chad pacing nervously.

As always, Chad's smile might have given the untutored the idea that nothing could be sweeter than this very moment. But Claire knew better.

"We'll be right back," Chad said to Jane, taking Claire's arm and leading her down the hall, past the offices where the First Lady's staff worked.

There was a tiny mailroom with slots, a metal desk that had been banged up over the years, two folding chairs and a door that closed.

Chad got Claire seated and then went and closed the door and came back and seated himself.

Chad always got directly to the point. His schedule didn't allow for amenities.

"CNN's already got it on the air." he said.

"Deirdre and Knox?"

"Right."

"What the hell happened?"

"You know how she is about Knox."

"For Christ's sake, I told her not to listen to him."

That was another thing about Chad. He sometimes gave the impression that he ran the entire White House, including the President, and sometimes he did.

"I've told her, too."

"This is real bad news given the primaries coming up."

"I know that, Chad, but she's a young girl and it's natural for her to strike out against somebody who is constantly on her father's back."

"That sonofabitch. Somebody's going to nail him someday."

"It won't be soon enough for me."

Chad shook his head. "We didn't need this right now. You know what that bastard'll do with this on his show."

"Do you want me to keep her chained in the basement?"

He sighed. "I'm sorry, Claire. You know I love Deirdre."

"Actually, I *do* know you love her, Chad, or right now I'd be very mad at you."

"It's just these primaries—"

"I know."

He got up, walked over to the window, looked out at midafternoon Washington on a nice spring day that was still too cold by ten degrees.

"I'll write something for her," he said.

"I'm not sure what you mean."

"An apology. For the networks."

"I want to see it before it goes out. I don't want any groveling. She shouldn't have done it but Knox isn't exactly Mother Teresa."

"No groveling. I promise." He slid his chair back under the desk. "How's that stuff on the First Ladies coming?"

It felt good to laugh again. "God, I swear you would have made a great den mother, Chad."

"Just asking."

"It's coming along fine. Actually, it's very interesting."

"That'll be an important shot for us. Barbara Walters pulls in a huge audience these days."

"Plus she's nice. She's not going to ambush me the way Kathryn Ryan did."

"Kathryn Ryan's a bitch."

"Tell me about it. I was the one on the air, remember?"

"She never should have asked you about your personal life. She promised me she wouldn't."

"Next time have her write it in blood."

He leaned over and gave her a brotherly kiss on the forehead. "Don't worry. I will."

Not all Presidents had had First Ladies to serve as White House hostesses.

Zachary Taylor's wife hadn't wanted him to run for President and subsequently didn't want anything to do with the White House. Their daughter presided for her.

Grover Cleveland, a bachelor until his last year in office, brought in his sister as hostess.

The famous Dolly Madison stood in to help her friend Thomas Jefferson, and Andrew Johnson asked his daughter-in-law to be hostess when his invalid wife could no longer get around properly.

Claire got all this down on the computer in her usual frantic two-finger typing style. A big yellow Ticonderoga No. 2 sat pinched between her upper and lower teeth. A lick of wild auburn hair stuck out above her ear, where the pencil had previously resided.

Coming back from the offices down the hall, Jane said, "You look like a college freshman cramming for a test."

Claire smiled. "That's how I feel, too."

"You'll do fine."

"I'm just so nervous. I just keep thinking of all the people who'll be watching."

Jane went over to her desk and sat down. In her black watch plaid dress, her red hair upswept dramatically, she looked as lovely as ever.

Claire was about to compliment her friend but realized it was pointless. No matter how sincerely you praised Jane's looks, she felt you were exaggerating just to compensate for her crippled foot.

Claire had always hoped that somebody would come along and convince Jane of her genuine spiritual and intellectual worth (forget her beauty—all the woman had to do was look in the mirror), but it hadn't happened.

Claire said, "The producer wants to know what we've done differently in the White House?"

"Well, you've made it formal again."

"Well, formal compared to the Carters and the Clintons but informal compared to Nancy Reagan."

"The Duchess of Windsor was informal compared to Nancy Reagan," Jane joked. Then: "I forgot to ask how Deirdre's doing."

"I thought I'd go check on her when I wrap things up here."

"Fine. I can handle everything."

"You always do, Jane. You're wonderful."

For once, Jane handled a compliment with grace. "Yes, I am, aren't I?"

Claire stood up, feeling old and scared suddenly. A part of her was still in David Hart's apartment, finding him dead next to her on the floor. Things were so crazy now—

"I'll see you in the morning."

"Tell Deirdre everything'll be fine." Jane said.

"I will. And thanks."

Jane waved goodbye.

Five minutes later, Claire went upstairs to see how Deirdre was doing.

She was just passing the living room when the phone rang. She ducked in there and picked it up.

"Hello?"

"You weren't very nice to him."

"Who is this?"

"A friend of David's."

The voice had been electronically altered to a robotic, inhuman tone.

"You're going to get a gift soon."

"I'm going to hang up now."

"Even if you hang up, you're still going to get the gift."

"How did you get this number?"

White House numbers were private.

Whoever the caller was knew how to learn secrets, she had to give him that.

"Do you know what this is going to do to your husband's presidency when the press hears about it?"

Metallic ringing.

"Hears about what?"

"How you murdered David."

She slammed the phone and stood there trembling, trying to figure out if the voice reminded her of anyone.

Inside the metallic voice was a human one.

If only she could think—

So many things to think about.

So many things.

She hurried away to see Deirdre.

24

★ ★ ★ They were in Knox's hot tub.

Jenny had a way of wiggling backwards toward him until they made the connection, him all hard and suddenly up inside her, and her groaning in glee and desire.

Good thing her father the Reverend didn't know about this. He was just the kind of crazed bastard to go public with the story and bring them both down.

But then, that was part of the fun.

Taking chances with her old man.

"Oh, God, Knox, harder, harder," Jenny said.

She was the first female who'd ever let him know that his sexual powers were waning. She never complained, she never said anything specific, but he could tell that many times he never quite satisfied her.

She was cinched tight on him now and using her hips the way a hula girl might, with a rhythm so overpowering it was not without a comic touch.

He tried to make a joke of it. "I think I do pretty well for an old guy, don't you?" But Jenny said nothing. He wanted to believe that she was having too much fun to speak.

"You thinking about anything special?"

"Huh-uh," Knox said. "Just sort of relaxing."

"Oh."

They were still nude, still in the hot tub, but now Knox was worn out.

"You all right?" Knox said.

"Yeah. Fine."

"You don't sound fine."

"Well, I am."

"All right."

Pause. "I guess it still bothers me."

Those were the two things he didn't like about this relationship—that he wasn't sure he could satisfy her sexually much longer, and that she needed constant reassurance that he cared for her.

She was always picking little fights as a way he could prove his love.

"I guess I'm not sure what 'it' is."

"The other day."

"What about the other day?"

"When I went in your den."

"Oh. The pictures."

"Right. There were so many of them."

"They don't mean anything."

"You broke up all those years ago and you have all those pictures of her and they don't mean anything?"

He really didn't want to talk about this.

Claire was a subject that was still painful, even now.

"You still love her."

"Don't be silly."

"If you didn't love her, you wouldn't have all those photographs of her."

"That's what you think, huh?"

"That's what I think."

"What if I told you I had even more pictures of you than I have of her."

"You really do?"

"Sure. All those shots I took of you a few weeks ago."

"Yeah, but those are different."

"They are?"

"Sure. Those are sexy."

"I don't understand."

"Hers aren't sexy pictures. They're just regular pictures of back when you were in college together."

"So?"

"So regular pictures mean you love her. That they're about *her*, not just about sex."

"I'm beginning to see."

"You love her but you just want to have sex with me."

"You bet I want to have sex with you."

"I wish you'd tell me you loved me."

"I have told you, Jenny."

"But mean it, I mean. You haven't meant it."

"Of course I meant it. There are lots of different ways of loving somebody."

"But there aren't lots of different ways of loving somebody the way you love *her*."

And that got to him somehow.

He sat in his hot tub with this veritable nymph ready to do anything he asked . . . and he was suddenly saddened and burdened by a love he could never seem to rid himself of.

She wasn't even the same person any more, physically, mentally, spiritually.

She had changed, and changed utterly, and yet still he wanted her.

He lay his head back and closed his eyes and recalled perfectly—down to the smells filling his nose—what it had been like to hold her, how her mouth always tasted sweet of spearmint gum; how soft and erotic her thighs always felt beneath the denim of her jeans, how there was always just a hint of melancholy in those blue eyes of hers.

He heard her laughter, and her tears, saw her white buttocks in the early morning sun just as she was hopping out of bed and heading for the shower, and watched her sorrow whenever she talked about the little sister she'd lost.

God, couldn't she see that they should always have been together?

But she had elected to punish both of them—him and her. No matter what kind of life Matt had given her, it could never have been as good as the one Knox had planned for her.

Never.

But now he was angry.

Now he was going to pay her back for all the misery and loneliness she had caused him.

Bitch.

You're going to be sorry.

Very, very sorry.

"A penny for your thoughts, Knox." Jenny said. "You look really intense."

And every word was being picked up by the microphone Bobby LaFontaine had planted on the shelf nearby.

25

★ ★ ★ "Just who I was looking for—the two most beautiful women in the world."

President Matt Hutton came striding into his daughter's bedroom late that afternoon, his best public smile riding his handsome face, just a hint of apprehension in his eyes. Deirdre had not held up well under the media scrutiny that accompanied life in the White House. She was a bright and sensitive girl and couldn't stand to watch the mob frenzy that sometimes took over the press. She especially could not stand Knox Stansfield's insistent attacks and today she'd simply gone a little crazy.

"I'm sorry, Daddy. I just made things worse."

"Nonsense," Hutton lied. "This isn't a big thing at all."

He sat down on the edge of the bed with Claire and leaned over and gave Deirdre a kiss.

When he was finished, he leaned back to see what stuffed animal he'd knocked over. It was a long, purple snake with a bright red bowtie and big black horn-rimmed glasses. Deirdre had a stuffed-animal collection that ran into the dozens.

Matt held the snake up to his face and peered into it's hugh cartoon eyes. "Let's see if I can remember. Sandra the snake?"

Deirdre, in her best pink sleepshirt, giggled. "Sorry, Daddy. Sandra's the salamander. This is Sam. The snake."

"Don't worry, dear," Claire said fondly, taking his arm and giving him a quick kiss on the cheek. "I get them confused, too."

Deirdre smiled. "She thinks the dragon's name is David."

"And it's really—what?" Matt said.

"Daryl. David's the dodo bird."

"Ah."

"You people have to spend more time with my stuffed animals," Deirdre said. "This is really getting embarrassing."

And with a wave of her slender arm, she indicated all the stuffed animals lined up on the floor and along the baseboard directly across the room. Giraffes, donkeys, ravens, alligators, and a myriad of other pets—all with crossed eyes, buck teeth, huge noses or other comic physical flaws—sat looking at the First Family with Disneyish interest.

"Yes," Matt said to Claire, "we definitely have to spend more time with these folks."

"At least an hour a day," Claire said.

"Or two if we can spare it," Matt said.

Deirdre spread her arms and embraced both of them. Matt felt tears in his eyes. At moments like these, he was aware of how vulnerable they all were. He wondered, as he had wondered so many times lately, if wanting the presidency wasn't an unholy ambition. You subjected your family to so much emotional brutality. . .

"I love you both so much," Deirdre said. "And I'm really sorry I just sort of snapped this afternoon. I won't do it again. I promise."

They sat holding each other for long and tender minutes, until Deirdre started yawning, the tranquilizer finally starting to slow her down.

They tucked her into bed as they had when she was a little girl, and then went into the den for a drink, bourbon for Matt, a Diet Pepsi for Claire.

Matt stood by the window, looking out at the dying day. "It doesn't even look that impressive any more."

"What doesn't?"

"Washington."

"Oh?"

"I think I forgot why I came here."

"You came here to show people that there was an alternative to being a cynical, give-away Democrat and a ruthless, greedy Republican."

He turned back to her and smiled bitterly. "Oh, yes. Idealism. I guess I lost that during my first term in the House. I can't remember if that was when the NRA tried to get me kicked out because I voted for a five-day waiting period for handguns, or when the unions tried to get me kicked out because I voted for the right-to-work laws."

He came over and sat down next to her on the couch. The den was a long, narrow room with leather furnishings, built-in bookcases filled with expensive leather editions of the classics (except for a long shelf of Tom Clancy and the other techno-thriller writers Matt liked so much) and two large, mullioned windows that looked over a wide expanse of White House lawn, including the apple trees that were promising to blossom any day now.

"I guess it's not what we expected, is it?" Claire said quietly, patting his thigh gently.

He forced a laugh. "Not quite."

"And it's going to get worse. The funeral, I mean."

"He'll kill me with it, the bastard."

"And I know how he'll do it, too. He'll pretend to be very concerned about Deirdre but then wonder if the job isn't just too much for the Hutton family, the President and his wife included."

"God, I'd like to tell people how he talked you into having the abortion, and how he used to beat you up and—"

"That's a door we'd better not open, Matt, and you know it."

When Knox Stansfield had first started in on them during the last presidential election, they'd thought of countering his attacks with attacks of their own.

Knox was an old friend of theirs, bitter because he'd lost Claire to Matt—or that was the way he perceived it, anyway. They would also mention the abortion and the beatings he inflicted on Claire and the KNOX STANSFIELD persona he'd invented as a party gag.

But Matt's media consultants had advised against this. Like most people their age, back in the sixties, the Huttons had smoked the occasional joint, made the occasional inflammatory statement, lived with people not their spouses.

The media consultants had said, sure, they could probably do some damage to Knox, but in so doing they'd also do damage to themselves.

Checkmate.

Matt said, "He still loves you."

"Oh, come on."

"I saw him watching you at the funeral. He hates you—but he still loves you, too."

"After all these years that's—"

"Impossible? Not with Knox, honey. He really believes that you two were fated to live happily ever after. He really does."

She slid her arm around him, tilted his face to hers and gave him a very passionate kiss.

"That's the happily ever after I want," she said.

"We're going to beat that bastard yet," Matt said.

"Yes. Yes, we are."

And then Claire gave him another kiss, this one even more passionate than the first.

A few minutes later they drifted from the den to their bedroom.

Afterward, they lay in bed, dusk creating a netherworld in the window, holding each other tenderly, Matt trying to rid his mind of Knox Stansfield, Claire trying to forget about David Hart.

She wanted to tell him everything now. Everything about David, including finding him dead. But she knew how devastated he would be. She'd check with Dana tomorrow. Maybe there would be good news—

26

★ ★ ★ At one time, there had been talk of having children, of buying a house in the suburbs, of having that life that Detective Michael Henderson—if not Maggie—had always dreamed of.

But there were only two constants in their lives—moving from one newly fashionable apartment house to another, and breaking up.

One bitter night, Michael had sat down at the kitchen table and thought back through the long, tumultuous years of their marriage.

Maggie had fallen in love with other men at least four times.

Been unfaithful at least twenty times.

Walked out on him over thirty times.

And cut him off from sex for long periods perhaps eight or nine times.

He could not calculate how many times she'd told him she no longer loved him, wanted him out of her life, resented him, found him boring, hated everything about their relationship.

His friends only smiled sadly now when he told them that he thought his relationship with Maggie was on track.

He'd try to break away and then she'd promise it would be different this time and he'd come trotting back, convincing himself that the breakup had somehow been *his* fault, anyway . . .

He was the drunk who couldn't give up drink.

The fat person who couldn't give up candy.

He couldn't give up Maggie.

He had seen seven different shrinks over the years—ten if you counted police shrinks—and they'd all gotten around to concluding that he was in a bad relationship and that she didn't love him and that she would never love him, at least not the way Michael needed and wanted and deserved to be loved.

He always had some rationalization to keep him from seeing how compulsive and hopeless his behavior was.

—If only he lost a little weight, she'd be faithful to him. The reason she was unfaithful was that the extra weight made him seem older. He lost twenty pounds. And kept if off, too. She kept right on being unfaithful.

—If only he made a little more money, she'd be faithful to him. He started consulting at night with security companies, teaching them how to set up first-rate security teams, and nearly doubled his police salary. She kept right on being unfaithful.

—If only he could—

He was going to get the promotion.

Screw the false-arrest suit.

He was *going* to get that promotion.

And then she was going to settle down.

At long last.

Be wife, companion, maybe even mother.

And the marriage that always should have been would finally *be*.

Finally.

She still wasn't home at 9:00 P.M.

The vast apartment was dark, empty.

He sat with a scotch and water on the end of the three-seat living room sofa covered in hand-sewn leather.

He'd called her office so many times tonight, he could feel the people on the other end groaning every time they picked up the phone.

It's only that poor stupid bastard Henderson.

He was sure that was how they talked about him.

Poor, stupid, *pathetic* bastard.

He knew she'd slept with at least a couple of them.

He was always uncomfortable at office parties, knowing that at least a couple of the lawyers were probably looking at him with that mixture of pity and contempt one reserved for cuckolds.

He picked up the phone.

Held the receiver several inches from his ear.

The street offered the only faint light; the white curtains playing in the breeze through the open window like mischievous ghosts.

The dial tone was loud and strange in the silence.

He wondered if he was losing his mind.

Somehow he was paralyzed.

Couldn't bring himself to set the receiver back on its cradle, yet couldn't bring himself to dial her number.

He set the phone back.

Almost immediately, it rang.

He picked up.

"Hello," he said.

"Hi."

"Where are you?"

"Work."

She was, as was frequently the case, lying.

"Oh."

"I'll be a little late."

"You already are a little late."

"You know what I mean. *Later*, I guess."

"Where are you?"

"God, Michael, you should clean out your ears. I already told you. I'm at work."

"I've called work. You're not there."

Silence.

"You're saying you don't believe me?"

"I'm saying I don't believe you."

"How about if I go get Roger and bring him to the phone and have him *testify* that I'm here."

"Do it."

"Are you serious?"

"Yes. Go get Roger."

Silence.

"He's in the men's room. When he comes back, I'll bring him."

Silence.

"I don't want to come home tonight if we're just going to argue."

"I don't want to argue, either."

"You could have fooled me."

Now it was his turn to be silent. Then: "He sued us."

"Oh, great. There goes your promotion."

"No way. I already checked with Commander Craig." He lied with chilling ease; he was becoming more and more like her every day. "He said there'd be no problem."

"I don't believe that. A high-profile lawsuit like that against you just when they're considering a promotion—"

She was picking his argument apart.

No way he'd get a promotion now.

Not until the lawsuit started to fade.

Now what was he going to say to her?

And then he saw it—out of desperation summoned it up from memory—and said: "I'll be getting a promotion anyway."

"Why?"

"The case I'm working on."

"What case?"

"I'm onto something nobody knows about."

"What is it?"

"I can't even tell you."

"I thought husbands and wives were supposed to share things."

"Why don't you come home, then, and we'll do a little sharing?"

"I—can't right now. It's real busy here."

The sound of a door opening in the background.

"Is that Roger?"

"No, it's—Brad."

"Brad who? You don't have a Brad in the office."

"He—started yesterday."

So that's who she was with tonight.

Some guy named Brad.

But the pain of it all was momentarily blunted by the thought he'd had just a moment ago.

What if there really was some connection between the First Lady and David Hart's murder?

And what if he was the homicide detective who broke the case?

"I'll see you a little later, then."

"Right. Later. Bye, Michael."

Imagine that, Henderson thought as he hung up in the gloom and shadow of his empty living room.

Imagine the First Lady being a suspect in a murder case.

The press would be worldwide and it would make every other police investigation in history seem minor by comparison.

Michael Henderson just might be on to something after all.

27

★ ★ ★ Taking Knox Stansfield's goblet of wine and splashing it in his face. The impulse wasn't always easy for Clemmons to resist.

Stansfield was on the telephone in his den and had just finished pantomiming that he wanted some wine. Burgundy was what he usually sipped at this time of night, imported directly from the French vineyards of a winemaker who had been a notorious Nazi collaborator. Fitting somehow, Clemmons thought.

As he poured the wine into a beautifully shaped crystal goblet, he saw himself reflected in the window.

Sometimes he forgot how old he was, and how old he'd started to look, what with the slumping shoulders and the little tumor of a pot-belly nicely hidden behind the jacket of his expensive coat.

He was one black man whose dreams were going to come true, or so he'd thought back in 1958 when he finished his stint in the Army and came back to Washington.

Take some night school courses. Get his degree. Get a good job in government. But then Dad had taken sick, and Mom, and there were his brother and sister to raise . . . and then one day he found himself at an employment agency accepting a position as a chauffeur.

He did not find it demeaning. That wasn't the point. Being a chauffeur was no different from working in a supermarket or a factory.

Nor was it that he was working for white people. He was not a foolish man. He knew that there was good and bad among the whites just as there was good and bad among the blacks.

No, his problem was simply that his dream had died. He was sixty-one years old now and much of his life was over and he had long ago silently ceded his dream to a younger black man, the coming generation, or the one after it.

But this was not what bothered him tonight. No, his problem tonight was that he was now in the employ of a murderer.

Simple enough to go to the police and name Knox Stansfield as the man who had killed David Hart.

But once Clemmons did that, Knox would then tell the district attorney about Clemmons's nephew Randy.

Clemmons had taken the seventeen-year-old for a few months after Randy's mother had simply given up on him. If it wasn't gangs, it was drugs, or stealing. Randy stole everything. He broke into houses, cars, stores. Didn't matter to him.

Clemmons spent two hopeless and hapless months trying to change the boy. One day, he even took Randy to work with him, showed him that being a chauffeur wasn't so bad, that the pay was actually good (Stansfield like to brag about how much he paid his hired black man) and that the working conditions were pretty cushy, everything considered.

Randy got into Knox's bedroom and stole a watch valued at more than $7,000.

Stansfield didn't miss the watch for several days, but then he exploded and accused Randy of taking it.

Clemmons told Randy to give it back, but Randy had already fenced the watch and blown the proceeds on drugs.

Stansfield surprised Clemmons by not going to the police. Instead, he said, "Now you owe me one. I did some checking on the nephew of yours. If I called a friend of mine in the D.A.'s office, that nephew of yours would go to the slammer for sure. With his previous record, he'd do four or five years." The icy Stansfield smile. "Now you owe me, Clemmons, and someday I'll collect—or I'll turn your nephew over to the law."

All this had happened six, seven weeks ago.

Now if Clemmons went to the police with his suspicions and those suspicions weren't believed—

Clemmons would be out of a job.

Randy would be in prison.

Randy's mother would never forgive Clemmons.

And maybe he was wrong . . .

That was the other thing.

Maybe he was wrong.

At most Stansfield had been in David Hart's town house for fifteen minutes. Was that sufficient time to kill a man?

Just walk right in and kill him and turn around and come back and use your chauffeur as your alibi?

Could even Stansfield be that cold and cunning?

Stansfield laughed. "That's how her mother used to be. Very explosive. Always giving you those little speeches of hers."

Deirdre Hutton. Stansfield had been on the phone all night with his best friends—a far-right senator and some far-right magazine editors—gloating over the public relations windfall that the Hutton family had handed him at graveside.

He would have to be careful, of course, of how he played it. He'd have to wrap his glee in Concern for Deirdre Hutton. But he'd run this particular little drama for weeks. And his listeners would love it.

Stansfield glanced at the tolling grandfather clock in the corner, then said, "I've got to get things ready for the broadcast tomorrow, Reed. I'd better cut this short." Beat. "Great talking to you, too, Good night."

As his boss hung up, Clemmons set the wine on the desk.

Knox, in a crisp white shirt, blue V-neck sweater and chinos, sat back and stared at Clemmons and said, "You've been acting kind of funny today."

"Guess I have a cold coming on or something." He didn't meet Stansfield's gaze.

"Or maybe you still think I killed David Hart."

Clemmons shook his head. "No, sir."

"Maybe you're not sure. But maybe you've still got doubts."

Clemmons said nothing.

"Would you do me the courtesy of looking at me when I'm speaking to you?"

Clemmons turned and looked at him. "Yes, sir."

"I worry about you."

"Yes, sir."

"I doubt you believe me but I do. The thing with Randy—"

Clemmons nodded.

"I thought that showed you I was a friend of yours."

"Yes, sir. I appreciate that."

"I could have sent him to prison."

"Yes, sir."

Stansfield stared very hard at Clemmons now. "In fact, I could simply pick up this phone and—"

"Yes, sir."

"If something happened that made me angry."

"Yes, sir."

Would he be threatening Clemmons this way if he weren't guilty?

"You do me favors and I do you favors."

"Yes, sir."

"Because we're more than employee and employer."

"Yes, sir."

"And that's the way it should be, don't you think?"

"Yes, sir."

"Then we're in agreement?"

"Yes, sir."

Stansfield smiled and picked up his wine glass. "Good. Then I can enjoy myself while I'm going over my notes for tomorrow. You may as well go home now."

Clemmons nodded.

He was more certain than ever that Knox Stansfield had killed David Hart—but what could he do about it?

And who would believe him? He goes to the police and the press—and then Stansfield says that Clemmons is just angry about Randy stealing the watch and Stansfield threatening legal action.

You could say all you wanted about these being more liberal times, and black people having many more rights, but when you came right down to it . . .

Clemmons left.

Five minutes later, he was in his rattling old sedan, pulling away from the mansion.

All Clemmons could see was his sister's sad and bitter face. She'd had no breaks in life whatsoever, one of those put-upon women who endure life rather than enjoy it.

He just couldn't send her son to prison.

He just couldn't.

28

★ ★ ★ "Oh, no, I enjoy sitting in motel rooms alone."

"I just can't get away."

"Of course."

"Next week, I promise."

It was a nice room on the second floor of a nice motel that overlooked the moonlit Potomac.

Jane met her lover here two or three times a month. There would be a time, or so he often promised, when he'd be free of his obligations and they wouldn't have to sneak around any more.

Dinner in good restaurants.

An evening at Kennedy Center.

Weekends together.

He was doing this as much for her sake as his, he usually said. As the First Lady's secretary, scandal and controversy had to be avoided at all costs.

Neither of them could afford to have their relationship revealed. Not yet.

"I've been thinking of you all night."

"I'll bet," Jane said.

"God, I hate when you sound like that."

"Do you know how lonely and isolated I feel right now?"

"Darling, there isn't anything I can do about it. There really isn't."

"I like it when you call me that."

"'Darling'?"

"Umm-hmm."

"Darling, darling, darling. How's that?"

"Wonderful. Oh, I wish we could be together."

"We will be. Soon. I promise."

"Say it once more."

"Darling."

"Oh, I love you so much."

"Me, too. G'night for now."

A few minutes later, having put her coat on again, she stood at the window looking out on the Potomac. She imagined what it would be like to be with him on one of those fine fancy boats you saw in the summer, just drifting off, nowhere in particular to go, just being together.

Then she flicked off the lights and left the room.

As she walked to her car, she passed a young couple. They were laughing and hanging on each other. She felt an irrational jealousy.

And then she saw how the young woman—a very pretty young woman—was watching Jane.

Crippled Jane.

So awkward, dragging her foot when she walked.

And then the old shame was on her once more, and she felt the way she'd always felt since the car had hit her: a freak, somebody meant to live in secret and in shadow.

Too many drunks, he thought, carefully climbing the stairs to his apartment.

Michael Henderson felt every ounce of bourbon he'd recklessly consumed in the past three hours.

Too many drinks and wondering bitterly where his wife was and admitting to himself that he'd been lying to her over the phone.

She was right: he wasn't going to get a promotion, not with a prominent false-arrest suit splashed all over the papers.

And he was wrong: the mysterious letter linking David Hart's murder and the First Lady had to be from some crank. It wasn't going to turn him into supercop. It wasn't going to do anything except make him defensive when she brought it up the next time she was reminding him what a failure he was.

The apartment: rain on the midnight wind, chill in the big, dark, empty rooms.

He went into the kitchen and managed to microwave himself a cup of instant coffee without spilling more than half of it on the floor.

He didn't bother to clean it up.

Screw it.

He was getting angry and mean.

This was going to be a late one.

He imagined her in somebody else's bed, naked and gentle and soft, and a terrible sickness came over him.

He sat on the couch, setting the coffee on a glass-and-chrome end table, and put his hands in his face and wept.

He loved her.

He didn't want to love her.

But he couldn't help himself.

No matter what she did, no matter what she said, he'd find some reason to take her back.

Since second grade it had been like this. Second grade.

His sobs were eventually lost in the gentle rain that came then, and the cool clean breeze balmed him, and eventually silenced his tears.

He would find some way to keep her. He always did. There had to be some way.

He slumped back against the couch. That was when he noticed it. Like a beacon in the corner. The fierce red light on the phone machine. Blinking. A message.

He wondered what excuse she'd have now.

He almost didn't want to pick it up.

Why listen to more of her lies?

They'd only make him angrier.

He stood up and started for the phone machine but instead turned abruptly to the right and went into the bathroom and peed and then washed his face.

In the mirror he saw a shockingly aged face looking back at him. Golden boy in high school and college. All the girls loved him. They couldn't have known, and neither could he, that his face would show all these lines and creases at his relatively young age.

He pulled back from the mirror and tottered back into the darkness of the apartment.

Red. Phone machine. Blinking.

He might as well get it over with.

She'd be a few hours late. They worked so hard—careful to emphasize that she was in a *group* of people—and now they were just stopping by to have a few drinks.

He could write her scenarios for her. All she had to do was ask.

He bent over, rewound the tape, punched the play button.

"Good evening. I hope you're back at the crime scene looking for the clue that can tie you-know-who to the murder of David Hart. It's there. I promise. All you have to do is look." The male voice—if it *was* a male voice—spoke through some kind of voice-altering device, one that robbed tones and patterns of gender.

He rewound.

Played it again.

The crime scene, the voice said.

The clue that can tie the First Lady to the murder, the voice said.

And he felt a stupid exhilaration. Couldn't help himself.

What if this *wasn't* just somebody playing with him?

What if this was somebody who *knew* that there was a connection?

What if he became the detective to put the case together? Then how would all of her fancy-ass lawyer friends look?

There would be a book deal, a movie deal, guest appearances. This was the era of celebrity cops, wasn't it? It was childish—foolish—to think this way but he couldn't help it.

Maybe after all these years, he'd finally figured out a way to turn his wife into the woman he'd always wanted her to be.

He went out and microwaved himself another cup of coffee. This time he didn't spill a drop of it.

"Can't sleep?"

"Guess not."

"Want some company?"

"You think I could say no to the President of the United States?" Claire said.

They were both in robes—Claire in red, Matt in blue—in the kitchen area where the staff prepared their meals. The refrigerator hummed and the Mr. Coffee machine bubbled. The sounds were lonely in the silence.

"Decaf?" Matt said.

"Uh-huh."

"Mind if I have a sip of yours?"

She smiled and touched his hand fondly. "I'll sell you your own cup for a dime."

"It used to be a nickel."

"Everything used to be a nickel."

He put his hand on hers. Looked at her a long moment. "You going to tell me?"

"Tell you what?"

"You know."

"I guess I don't."

"What's bothering you."

"Oh."

"'Oh.' That's all you're going to say on the subject?"

She wanted to tell him, of course.

Say it and get it over with and then he'd know and maybe he'd have some good ideas for dealing with the situation.

I used to go up to David's apartment sometimes, she'd say. You know, I got so lonely when I thought you were having an affair. I was so confused.

There.

That was the way to say it.

So simple. And Matt would understand. He always did.

But somehow the words wouldn't come out.

"It's the funeral, isn't it?"

He was making it easy for her.

"Yes, I guess it is. I'm worried about Deirdre." And she was. "She just can't seem to deal with her anger about Knox."

"She's young. She can't put any distance on it."

She shook her head. "I guess I can't either. How I ever put up with him—"

"Youthful indiscretion. That's the phrase you want." He turned his chair out from the table and patted his lap. "Want to sit down?"

She laughed at the absurdity of it. "I'd break your legs."

"Oh, come on now, that isn't saying much for my machismo."

"Are you serious?"

"Sure. Remember how you used to sit in my lap and we'd neck until we absolutely couldn't take it any more."

"It's been years."

"It'll be fun." He patted his lap again and grinned slyly.

Without another thought, she stood up, walked over to him, sat down.

"I'm breaking your legs, aren't I?"

"What gave you that idea?"

"The way your face got so red."

"Foolish girl."

And then he took her face to his and kissed her and in the center of his lap she could feel him getting excited.

And suddenly she was excited, too.

This was what she needed.

An escape. And what better one than twenty minutes of sex with Matt?

Soon enough, his hand was inside her robe, thumb and forefinger finding her nipple, as her legs parted and his other hand found the rich warm gift she had waiting for him.

29

✶ ✶ ✶ Sammi Lee Baxter's life sounded like the lyrics of a country-western song. There was her first pregnancy at fourteen—her cousin in the Quonset hut where their two families lived; her second pregnancy at seventeen—the high school quarterback who only liked her (she learned too late) for "your, you know, jugs." The first child died (and there was nothing funny in it) when her uncle backed over the two-year-old in the driveway, and the other boy went on to become a thief who incurred his first felony when he was eleven years old. During and after all this, Sammi Lee was variously a stripper, a hooker and a "divorce tart" for an investigative agency in Nashville, hired to find out if men were being faithful. If they could resist the wiles of Sammi Lee then you could bet that they could resist the wiles of just about anybody.

At the moment, her fifteen-year-old was in reform school, she was collecting unemployment, and she was a regular at the *God's Hour* tapings, which was where Bobby LaFontaine, who frequently trawled the audience for likely babes, had met her.

He'd been balling her for three months now and she was starting to irritate him profoundly, something all women did to him eventually.

"You think we could stop doing this?"

"Washing you, you mean?"

"Yeah."

"Some guys like it."

"Johns, maybe."

"It's a good way to get guys in the mood, washing them with nice warm soap and water."

"I get in the mood right away, anyway."

She didn't say anything.

He wondered if she was holding something back. Bobby LaFontaine could be one paranoid sonofabitch.

"I get in the mood right away, anyway, right?"

"Right."

"How come you didn't say 'right' right away?"

"How come I didn't say 'right' right away?"

"That's what I said, lover."

"Because I was swallowing, I guess. You know, my gum."

"I thought I told you not to do that. Swallow your gum."

"Jeez, Bobby, I forgot. That was all."

"I don't have no trouble getting in the mood, do I?"

"No, Bobby, not you."

"So don't wash me anymore."

"All right, Bobby. I'm sorry. I really am."

They were in her bed with the two velvet paintings on the wall, one of Jesus, one of Elvis. The two men bore an eerie resemblance to each other, at least in the eyes of this particular artist.

At least she wasn't playing her country-western tapes. She had a story to go with every singer—this singer had been in prison; another singer had been treated for alcoholism; still another had been sued for paternity—all of which she saw playing into their records, which was why she saw country-western as truly tragic music . . . music that reflected her own life, too.

It was eleven fifteen in the A.M., as Bobby cutely liked to say. He'd already been here an hour and he was already starting to feel kind of claustrophobic.

He needed to give himself an excuse to get out of here.

"You want pancakes and sausages tonight?"

"Tonight?"

"Yeah, I mean, you haven't been by for dinner in nearly a week."

"Not tonight, babe. Sorry."

"Oh."

"Don't pout. I hate that."

"I'm not poutin', lover. I'm just sad is all."

"Sad? What you got to be sad about?"

He wanted to say, how could a lady possibly be sad when she had somebody like Bobby in her life? But modesty prevented him from saying it.

What could he do that would give him an excuse to get out of this place? Back to the office didn't work because she knew he pretty much came and went as he wanted to.

Something else.

"You know that rose on my butt?"

"Yeah."

She was referring to the tattoo he despised. His momma had told him that tattoos were the sign of a cheap and low-down woman and he had never forgotten her admonition. Sammi Lee had tattoos everywhere except inside her twat.

"Anyway, it's fading."

"Good."

"Don't you care no more?"

"Sure I care."

"Well, look at it when I roll over then."

He sighed. Had to play along. He hadn't quite gotten tired of her sexually—even though he was tired of her in every other way—so he didn't want to end it completely quite yet.

She rolled over and he made the mistake of touching her.

"I knew I could get you interested," she said.

He was just starting to kiss her when he thought of a good excuse to leave as soon as they were done. The microphone he'd planted at Knox Stansfield's place: about time he checked on the tape, see if it had yet yielded up any bounty.

"You're the greatest," Sammi Lee said as he took her in his arms.

"I appreciate you saying that," Bobby said and grinned, "especially since it's the truth."

30

★ ★ ★ "You know how old she is?"

"Which one?" Claire said.

"The one doing the cancan."

"No. How old?"

"Ninety-two."

"My Lord."

"You should see her do the twist," the old man with the clacking dentures said.

Claire laughed. "I can imagine."

A group of elderly citizens had come to Washington to ask the President for more stringent laws governing nursing homes. Claire was here in the President's stead.

The lobbyists representing this morning's group had rented a large party room in a motel and were now staging a floor show for the First Lady.

She had seen a dog that sang, a parrot that could almost say her name, a harmonica player who played while standing on his hands, several patriotic tableaux, and four men with very white hair who had put their pleas to the President in the form of a rap song.

The hardest part of her job was to continuously applaud.

Now she was applauding for six elderly ladies in cancan outfits who were doing an extremely animated dance, gleefully showing their bottoms to the ecstatic crowd, and sort of urging the crowd on to request an encore.

"Aren't they great?" the old man next to her clacked.

"Great!" Claire said.

"You suppose you can talk to that husband of yours for us?"

"I certainly will."

They were shouting at each other, of course. Had to. You couldn't hear anything above the cancan music.

She didn't need much convincing to want to help them, Claire didn't. Their horror stories were truly horrific. The treatment of the elderly in too many nursing homes was abominable.

But the nursing-home owners had a powerful lobby and had long stood in the way of any meaningful reform. As usual, the two sides had polarized. The Republicans didn't want any oversight at all—in the name of keeping the government out of private business—while the Democrats wanted to micromanage every aspect of the industry.

That's where a moderate conservative like Matt was supposed to come in. Find a middle ground. But in his two years in office they'd sadly learned—as they'd suspected during his time in Congress—that the zealots on both sides got all the attention, and thus all the power.

The old woman was sobbing as she stood next to the microphone and talked about being beaten by a sadistic nurse.

"I even offered her money not to beat me no more," the old lady, who stood maybe five feet and weighed maybe eighty pounds, said in a shaky voice. Her wrinkled blue sweater and wrinkled gray skirt only underscored her wan, sad state. She had been beautiful once and was now a wilted flower.

"I appreciate you sharing your story with us," Claire said.

As the President's representative to many of these functions, Claire frequently found herself bored. Who wouldn't? Many of the meetings were intended to sell her on something she didn't feel was good for the country—as when a large union tried to enlist her support for requiring all employees in certain defense-related industries to unionize, or when the cotton manufacturers wanted her husband to support higher tariffs on foreign cotton. Scratch a free-enterpriser and you'd find a protectionist Democrat if it was his industry being tweaked.

"We really appreciate you coming here this morning," the old woman said just before she stepped away from the microphone.

Some of the lobbyists spoke next and they were not nearly as compelling as the people they represented.

They had learned all the proper "power" phrases, all the innuendo that hinted at blackmail, all the innuendo that hinted at big political payoffs for the President if only he'd join with them. And so on.

After a few minutes of this, Claire found her mind returning to late last night, after she and Matt had made love.

She'd almost told him then.

Almost. But then he'd gotten a late-night call from McElroy, his chief of staff, on some pending legislation. He'd sounded frazzled, whipped, as he'd slammed down the phone. "I don't need any more bad news!" he'd shouted at McElroy.

Today she would tell him. This afternoon.

Earlier today, Claire had scheduled an appointment with Dr. Solomon for Deirdre. Solomon was a psychotherapist Deirdre seemed to like and trust. Following the incident at the grave yesterday, it was important that Deirdre start seeing him again on a regular basis.

Matt would spend most of the afternoon in the Oval Office. They were bringing consultants in to discuss the upcoming primary.

But afterward they'd have some time alone and then Claire could tell him. Everything. He deserved to know. Especially the part about her giving David the money.

She had to tell Matt. Had to.

"And now," the chief lobbyist, beaming like a proud choirmaster, gathered all the performers around him—even the parrot who couldn't quite pronounce Claire's name—and said, "Now we'll sing 'God Bless America' to our new friend the First Lady."

The old man next to her broke out into applause, even though the song hadn't been sung yet.

His dentures clacked even when he wasn't talking.

31

★ ★ ★ "Damn."

Bobby LaFontaine had a good deal of bugging equipment set up in the spare bedroom of his modest house in Falls Church. He was home now, just getting his wind back after going two rounds with Sammi Lee in her big, sagging double bed.

And he was very frustrated.

Here he'd had the drop mike all set up near Knox Stansfield's hot tub—here he'd gotten several hours of very clear tape laid down (mostly Stansfield talking to his colored man from the other room)—and just when it started to get interesting—

Just when he heard Jenny's voice for the first time—

Something happened with transmission.

Bobby knew this wasn't all that uncommon. Bugs frequently failed to work and had to be replaced—

Her words were so garbled he couldn't tell anything she was saying. Or Knox, for that matter.

He'd have to go over there again. Check the drop mike. Make sure everything was all right there. If it was, then the transmission itself was at fault and there wouldn't be anything he could do about it. Hard-wiring a microphone to a recorder was the best way to do it, of course (instead of beaming a radio signal the way he was doing), but he didn't exactly feel like running thirty, forty miles of cable to pick up Stansfield's hot tub.

He went down to the basement to his supplies and his worktable and picked up another drop mike—silver, and about the size of a nickel—and then climbed back up the stairs, winded.

He thought again, in his paranoid way, about how Sammi had hesitated before saying he didn't have any problem getting it hard.

Was he losing his powers?

Guy in prison had told him that a man had only so many ounces of his precious bodily fluids—he compared it to a pint of whiskey, a man's fluids—and when you ran out, you ran out.

Had Bobby humped all his precious fluids away? Was that why Sammi Lee had hesitated? Was that why he was winded now coming up the stairs?

He tried not to think about it. There were so many women he wanted to screw.

He dropped the microphone in his pocket and forced himself to concentrate on Stansfield's colored man, Clemmons being his name.

He sure hoped that Clemmons had some business out of the house today.

He sure did.

Just what the hell was he looking for? That's what Detective Michael Henderson asked himself after he'd been in David Hart's town house for an hour.

He had a hangover, for one thing, so he wasn't in the most patient of moods, and, for another, his argument with his wife—she'd finally rolled in around three A.M.—had been notably vicious.

He'd gone through two rooms so far. The living room and the bedroom. There was a den and a spare bedroom that was used for storing boxes. Those he hadn't checked out.

He knew what he wanted to do but he kept talking himself out of it.

The phone company hadn't cut off service yet.

He could just walk over to it, pick it up and phone her at work.

Say: Hi, Maggie. I sure wish we hadn't argued last night. I feel rotten about it. I really do.

And they'd squabble some more and she'd say maybe it was time they split up again only this time for good, and then he'd say: It was my fault last night, Maggie. It really was. All you did was go out and have a little fun after a hard day's work and then I go and blow up at you. I'm really sorry.

And she'd say: Oh, I love you so much, Michael. I really do. I'll try and be better about getting in late and stuff. I really will.

Tonight they'd make steaks and have some good wine and make love all night on the water bed. Things'd be all right for a week or so.

He'd buy her little gifts and she'd get all sentimental about how long they'd been together and then—

Then she'd change.

It was like she became a vampire or something.

This different person back in his life suddenly. Angry, demanding, ruthless.

She terrified him, this other person, cowed him into absolute obedience.

He looked at the phone now.

So easy to go over and pick it up and call her.

All my fault, babe. Sorry.

He started across the room and then stopped.

No.

God, didn't he have even the smallest amount of self-respect left? Didn't he?

He took in a deep breath and held it until he felt the worst of the anxiety leave his chest.

Might as well resume his treasure hunt.

That was the way he was going to keep Maggie.

Not by calling her up and pleading his case. He'd done that too many times.

No, now he really needed to impress her with something, like tying the First Lady to the murder of David Hart.

Then Maggie'd be impressed.

Oh, yes.

He went into the spare room and resumed his treasure hunt, last night's words on the phone machine still playing in his ears:

"You can tie her to the murder of David Hart. It's there. I promise."

He was going to find it, whatever it was—he absolutely believed the caller was telling the truth now—and then his life was going to change forever.

Claire found Dana on the first floor of the White House.

"Anything?"

He shook his head. "A few leads. David knew some pretty sleazy people. But nothing solid yet. I'm still working on it." He paused. "I think you'd better let the President and McElroy know everything you can tell them."

Bitterness filled her throat. She'd hoped that Dana would be able to work a miracle—

She sighed, realized that she was trembling. "I know. I'll talk to Matt as soon as I can."

Defeated, she went back upstairs.

32

★ ★ ★ Presidential chief of staff Chad McElroy was contemplating
suicide.

This was not necessarily anything to get nervous about. McElroy
contemplated suicide at least three times a day—on the good days.

Early in the administration, so as to better serve his friend the President, McElroy had written out for himself a code of conduct, one he
hoped would ensure against the excesses and failings of the chiefs who
had come before.

1. Keep a list of the twelve hottest issues on your desk at all
times.
2. Don't intellectualize when speaking to the President. You
don't need to impress him—you need to inform him.
3. Take 15 minute walk 3 x a day for high energy.
4. Know when to speak up and when to be quiet.
5. Learn to read what the President really wants even if he can't
read himself.
6. Be on equally good terms with the congressional leaders of
both parties—one working lunch a week with each of them.
7. Limit all lobbyists (no matter how much they contributed to
the campaign) to fifteen minutes with the President.
8. Learn how to endure being disliked even by your friends
when you have to say no to them.

You didn't get to see the President without going through McElroy's office. Period. That simple. So he had to decide who was worthy, who was not; who would bring the President real information on a given issue, and who would merely and uselessly spout a party line. The press was not fond of McElroy (devious, they said); nor were the Democrats, nor was the zealot wing of their own party, the Republicans. All this criticism meant only one thing to McElroy—that he was pissing everybody off equally and was therefore doing his job reasonably well.

No, these were not the reasons he was considering suicide. That had to do with the three pages of fax material on his desk: the latest private poll results from the first state where the President was being challenged.

Not good.

The President was slipping a little every day.

McElroy would have to schedule a three-day trip to Iowa now whether he wanted to or not. The Christian Coalition had virtually taken over the Republican convention out there, and this boded even less well for the President. The Democrats were gleeful, of course. They wanted to see the President weakened in the primaries. They didn't much give a damn that the specter of Christian fundamentalism was threatening to tear America apart with the same kind of divisiveness plaguing Ireland. Business as usual; damn the welfare of the country (though welfare was probably not a word you wanted to use loosely around the Democrats).

He reached in his upper right hand drawer for his Tums.

The past three months, he'd had a lot of acid problems. His wife—who was hypochondriacal enough for both of them and who attributed all discomfort and pain to some form of incipient cancer—got him to a doctor who ran a few tests and found that the stress of McElroy's job was doing in his stomach. The doctor gave him three different prescriptions and then told him to back these up with some over-the-counter medicine.

He took three Tums and started looking at the faxes again. The combination of Knox Stansfield and the Reverend Goodhew's *God's Hour* were starting to take their toll. In the general election, they could only swing 8 to 10 percent of the vote, but in a small primary state such as Iowa they could be decisive.

Had to get the President out there, and fast.

The phone rang.

"Yes?"

From the outer office, his secretary said, "Mr. Byrne's on line one and he sounds very upset about something."

Byrne ran the President's reelection committee. Ever since Watergate had given such committees a bad name, they'd gone by loftier names. This year it was the MAKE AMERICA GREAT Committee, a name that usually sent McElroy to his Tums again.

He picked up.

"Sonofabitch."

"Well, thank you," McElroy said.

"Not you. Stansfield. Are you listening to him?"

"Not unless I have to."

"You have to. Listen and call me back. He's into a commercial break right now. You've got sixty seconds."

"Talk to you soon."

Only when Byrne hung up did the import of his call strike McElroy. Byrne's nickname was "The Ice Man" because he never got upset. Just fixed you with those steely baby blues of his until *you* got upset.

What could possibly have undone him this way?

McElroy opened his second left drawer, lifted out his small portable radio. It was tuned to Stansfield already. He monitored the show as much as he could stand, which wasn't much.

Stansfield was peddling something that increased your energy and virility, something he didn't need, the man being a legendary lady-killer.

Then he was out of break and saying: "Remember what I said at the top of the show about a possible link between the murder of one David Hart and the First Lady? Well, you heard it here first, gang. This program has it on good authority that a very highly placed Washington, D.C., homicide detective is exploring that very matter even as we speak.

"Now right here I'd better fess up. David Hart was a friend of mine, a member of the little conservative club the president and his wife and I had back in our college days. The sad thing about his murder last week was that he was just starting to turn his life around.

"I know this because over the past year, ever since he'd moved to the Washington, D.C., area, I've been helping him out with 'loans.' At least that's what he preferred to call them. I knew I'd never see the money again and I didn't care.

"I know liberals love to paint me as this really terrible, hard-hearted guy who lives to smother babies and beat up mothers . . . but I've been known to be a loyal friend, too. And I was a loyal friend to David Hart.

"Now, as you might expect, David Hart confided in me, told me different things going on in his life. I'm not going to go into detail here—not until I've had a chance to talk to the homicide detective in charge of this case—but let me say that he recently saw the First Lady, too.

"Now don't get me wrong. Don't start screaming at me that I'm persecuting somebody through innuendo and hearsay. I'm not.

"I don't know anything about the nature of their relationship, I don't even know if there *was* a relationship as such.

"I just know that David saw her on a couple of private occasions. And I also know—as of a few hours ago—that a homicide detective *is* looking into the possibility that the First Lady might be able to shed some light on this terrible murder.

"Didn't I tell you that this was going to be an extra-special install- ment of your favorite show? Did I let you down? I think not.

"We'll be back right after this message."

"Bastard," McElroy said into his phone forty-two seconds later.

"I told you," Byrne said.

"That sleazy bastard has already practically convicted her."

"Come on now. Let's be fair. Didn't you hear him say that he 'didn't want to persecute anybody through innuendo and hearsay'?"

"Bastard."

"You know anything about this, McElroy?"

"Nothing."

"You ever meet this Hart?"

"No."

"I can't imagine Claire screwing around on the President, can you?"

"I learned a long time ago not to be shocked by anything anybody does."

"Man, you really are a cynic."

"I've been around political people too long," McElroy said. "I know that they're capable of the same irrational and self-destructive acts as the rest of the population."

"This could kill us in Iowa."

"Tell me about it. First the President is rumored to be having an affair—and now his wife is not only implicated in some kind of re- lationship but murder? This could be all over for us."

McElroy felt a genuine chill trace the line of his spine. He was still in shock of some kind. If he hadn't been, he would already have been smashing things on his desk. When situations went over the top, McElroy frequently went with them. He was a yeller and a thrower and a smasher.

"What're you going to do now?" Byrne said.

"What the hell do you think?" McElroy said. "Go in and tell the President what Stansfield just said."

33

★ ★ ★ "You don't sleep very well even with the medication I give you, Deirdre?"

"Not all the time, I don't."

"You're taking warm milk and doing the relaxation exercises, too?"

Deirdre nodded. "I'm doing everything you said to, Dr. Solomon."

"It's still our old friend Knox Stansfield?"

Deirdre said, "My best friend doesn't want to hang around with me anymore."

"Maybe you're just imagining that."

"She told me that."

"Oh? When?"

Deirdre told him all about her conversation with Heather.

"Maybe she was just in a bad mood, Deirdre. Things like that—"

Deirdre shook her head. "No, she's right. Knox really has become an obsession with me."

Dr. Solomon's office resembled an elegant living room, a wide picture window overlooking the Potomac, two deep blue fabric-covered couches facing one another, two walls covered with Matisse and Picasso, a Persian rug of considerable vintage and exquisite condition, and enough Victorian knickknacks to delight the most enthusiastic antiques collector.

Dr. Solomon laughed. "You have good reason not to like him, Deirdre. It's not as if you're being completely irrational."

Dr. Solomon was twenty pounds overweight but somehow this only added to his regal and imposing stature. He was given to dark, vested suits, conservative ties and heavy black horn-rimmed glasses.

He changed the subject temporarily.

"How's school?"

"Fine."

"Getting along with your folks?"

"Good. I mean, now that Daddy— Well, you know, after the thing with the woman died down in the press."

"That's another question."

"What?"

"How're you dealing with having the Secret Service and the press around you constantly? That was getting to be a real problem."

"There are two Secret Service agents waiting for me in your reception area."

"So I noticed."

"The press, I just avoid." Her face tightened. "Except for Knox."

"That was going to be my next question."

"What?"

"About Stansfield."

"He still gets to me. I can't help it. All he does is try and destroy my parents with his lies."

"You should quit listening to him."

"Even when I don't listen to him, I see how he gets my folks upset."

"Is that why you confronted him at the funeral?"

"Sure."

"Do you think you did the right thing, expressing it that way?"

She shook her head. She wore a plaid jumper and a white blouse and the combination made her look even younger than usual.

"No. I shouldn't have done it. I just made things worse for my Dad. I'll bet that's all that Stansfield is talking about on his show today. I hate him. I can't help it."

"But you can help confronting him."

She hesitated. "I shouldn't have done it."

"I'm not trying to make you feel guilty."

"I know."

"I'm just trying to point out the practical implications of what you did."

"I gave him something new to use against my Dad, didn't I?"

"I'd have to say, yes, you did."

"You're really a neat guy."

"Why, thank you. And you're really a neat girl."

"I thought you'd really chew me out."

"I'm trying to help you. Not make you feel worse."

"My mom pretends she isn't upset but I know she is. She's been kind of strange lately, anyway."

"Strange?"

"Yeah. Like something's really bothering her but she won't say what."

"Has your father noticed it, too?"

"I think so. I catch him kind of looking at her funny, you know, like he's trying to see inside her mind or something."

"Maybe she's just concerned about you."

"Maybe."

"So tell me, if you saw Knox Stansfield again, what do you think you'd do?"

She giggled. "Shoot him?"

"Well," he smiled, "I'm glad to see we're making some progress here."

"I'd just look the other way and walk away."

"Good."

"Because nobody should have that kind of control over me. He just upsets me so much that I don't—" She paused. "See, I'm getting all wound up over him again."

"You don't have to. You can control it, Deirdre."

"I know I can. And I will."

"That'll make your folks very happy."

"Yes," she said, feeling sentimental about her mother and father. "And that's what I want—for them to be happy. They have to put up with so much abuse. And they're such good people. They really are."

Dr. Solomon nodded and smiled.

Things seemed very well in hand.

34

★ ★ ★ Two minutes after Knox Stansfield concluded his broadcast for the day, Claire rose from her chair in the office, walked over to the window and looked out on Pennsylvania Avenue. She used to think the White House was a safe haven. But not after all the attempts on Bill Clinton's life.

She didn't want to cry.

Moments after the broadcast was over, Jane had hurriedly picked up a brochure she was working on and said she needed to go get some copies made down the hall.

Claire didn't want to be in tears when she returned.

She turned away from the window and walked back to her desk, and dialed Matt's number.

Matt's killer-efficient secretary answered.

"Is the President available, Meg?"

"Not right now, Mrs. Hutton. Mr. McElroy is with him right now."

"I'll try a little later, then."

"I'll tell him you called."

"Thanks, Meg."

If Meg had heard the broadcast, her voice didn't let on. But then Meg was a steely pro. She knew how to cover such things.

Claire was back at the window, watching a group of sightseers looking at one of the small gardens that rarely got mentioned in White House publicity, when Jane said behind her, "Are you doing all right?"

"I'm doing fine."

Claire might have been more convincing if she'd turned to face Jane when she said this.

"CBS called already and wondered if we had a statement."

"Oh."

Silence.

Claire heard Jane sit down in her chair.

"Claire."

"Yes?"

Still not turning around.

Foolish.

Really needed to turn around.

Face Jane. Jane was not only her press secretary, she was also her best friend. If she couldn't face Jane, whom could she face?

"Claire, I really think you need to talk to the President."

"I know."

She turned around, then.

Fast. Get it over with.

"I have a call in to him."

Walked over to her desk. Sat down.

"I just want to say something, Jane."

As usual, Jane looked working-girl gorgeous. Lovely red hair upswept dramatically. Fitted gray double-breasted suit. Perfect face.

"All right," Jane said.

"I didn't have anything to do with David's death."

"Claire, you don't—"

"I just wanted to make it clear."

"But Claire, you couldn't possibly think—" Then she did a most unlikely thing, Jane did. She smiled. "Claire Hutton, murderess? No way, Claire. That thought wouldn't cross my mind in a million years."

"I appreciate that."

"But we do have to coordinate a story for the press."

"I know. McElroy is with Matt right now. God, he's going to be taking ten Tums a minute." She allowed herself a sigh. "I just keep thinking of the primary. This—"

"Don't make any predictions yet, Claire. That's one of the cardinal rules of public relations. Deal with the immediate problems one at a time. Don't start borrowing trouble—"

"I know but—"

"And consider the source. Just because Stansfield *says* there's a Washington, D.C., detective trying to link you to the murder, that doesn't necessarily mean it's true."

"But there's something you haven't brought up yet."

"What?"

Claire paused. "I did go up there."

"To David's?"

"Yes."

"I see."

Jane was trying to hide the impact Claire's words had on her.

"Nothing happened," Claire said. "I mean, no sex. It was innocent. I— It was when the press was hinting that Matt was having an affair. I just used David as—an escape, I guess."

Jane watched, nodded.

"There's one other thing. I may as well tell you now."

"What?"

"I paid him money."

"Money?"

"$100,000."

"You mean you loaned him $100,000?"

"That's what it was supposed to be—but I knew I'd never get it back. I mean, a 'loan' is how I thought of it to myself. But it was actually—blackmail."

"Oh, Claire."

"I really thought he was my friend."

The tears started.

"Then he said he'd go to the tabloids if I didn't pay him the money—"

She couldn't help it any longer.

Began to weep.

And then Jane was up, beautiful Jane, dragging her crippled foot across the floor to Claire.

Jane held her tenderly, the way she would a child, rocking her gently, letting her cry.

"I just couldn't believe that anybody would betray me that way—" Claire said. She wanted to tell her about the night of the murder, how David had lured her over there—but somehow she simply couldn't. She knew she could trust Jane but she didn't want even one more person to know what had happened that night—

Then it was important to stop the tears, compose herself. "Thanks."

Jane smiled. "And you know what?"

"What?"

"I'm not even going to charge you $100,000 for doing that."

Claire laughed. Good old Jane. She always came through. Always.

Jane went back and sat down.

Her phone rang instantly.

"No. No, Pat. Just tell her I'm not available right now. Pat, I know she's Connie Chung and I know we're supposed to be friends but I just don't want to talk to her right now, all right?"

This was one of the first times that Claire had ever heard Jane get testy with anyone. Usually Jane was a master of poise and grace.

Her voice softened somewhat. "Tell her I'll phone her tomorrow." She hung up.

"Connie Chung."

"I heard."

"This is going to be very tough."

"I know. But I'm getting pissed off and that's going to help me."

Jane grinned. "My God, I can't believe you said that."

"'Pissed off?'"

"Right."

"I have my moments."

"Good. I'm glad you do."

Claire's friends always kidded her for being so clean-cut. Her parents had been proper people and Claire had learned their style well, perhaps too well.

Claire had just started to speak when the phone on her own desk rang. She picked up.

Meg, the President's secretary said, "He'd like to see you as soon as possible."

"I'll be there right away."

"Thank you."

Claire hung up and said, "Matt wants to see me."

Jane said, "Who could say no to the President of the United States?"

It was supposed to be a laugh line but neither of them so much as smiled.

35

★ ★ ★ They were waiting in ambush for Deirdre.

There were maybe twenty of them, some with microphones, some with video cams. Some were familiar from the tube; a few who called out to her even had accents.

Her first reaction, as she came down the back steps of Dr. Solomon's building, was disbelief.

"Why do they want to talk to me?" she asked one of the two dark-suited agents who walked next to her.

Nice pleasant day. One she should be enjoying.

And now this—

The other Secret Service agent was already on his walkie-talkie, obviously trying to find out what was going on.

The long, black, sleek car that had brought Deirdre to the doctor's started to pull up, an agent in the back seat opening the door so Deirdre could get inside quickly.

But the car was not fast enough to deter the press.

The reporters surged forward as one, several questions shouted at her at the same time.

The two agents tried to keep them away, but they were far outnumbered.

A woman, wielding a long microphone, pushed past a knot of other reporters and shouted, "Do you think you mother had anything to do with the murder?"

"Murder? What're you talking about?" Deirdre said as the agents gently prodded her closer to the waiting car.

"The murder of her lover—David Hart!" the woman shouted at her.

"Her lover! My mother has never had a lover!"

"Haven't you heard the news?" a male reporter snapped. "Your mother is being investigated for the murder of a man she was seeing."

"That's a lie!" Deirdre shouted.

They all looked grotesque to her. They had bulging eyes and spittle foamed at the corners of their mouths and they had huge blackheads and warts and they smelled like something long dead and kept in a dank, dark grave.

Ghouls is what they were.

The undead.

Back from the grave to make life miserable for decent, hardworking people like her parents.

"That's a lie!" she screamed at them.

And was well aware that they were pushing closer and closer for a better shot of her face.

She'd be on the network news, shouting angrily into the camera.

And would again bring embarrassment to her parents.

She glanced back beseechingly at Dr. Solomon's office. How safe and secure she had felt in there.

If only she could be in there now.

"Did you ever meet your mother's lover?" a different female reporter screeched at her.

An agent guided Deirdre into the car and piled in right after her.

"Get out of here fast," he said to the driver.

"They're lying! They're lying!" Deirdre said, starting to sob. "They're lying."

The agent next to her slid a paternal arm around her and held her as she wept.

The driver floored the big black car, nearly knocking down two reporters who refused to get out of the way.

36

✳ ✳ ✳ The kitchen, the bathroom, the basement.

The bedroom, the spare room, the den.

The living room, the laundry room, the back porch closet.

And not a thing. Not a single useful thing.

The homicide department had been here, the coroner had been here, the criminalists had been here and—nothing.

The guy on the phone had to be teasing him.

You'll find something to tie the First Lady to David Hart's murder. Oh, sure you will. Right.

Around four that afternoon, he took a break. He'd brought a quart of Diet Pepsi and a submarine sandwich, the first half of which he'd eaten at lunch time.

Now he ate the second half.

He sat at the kitchen table, size 12DDD loafers on the chair across from him, trying to relax.

Some bastard had decided to have a little fun with him and Detective Michael Henderson had been stupid enough to go along.

The phone rang.

He had this irrational thought: the guy was watching him through binoculars across the street and now that he saw that Henderson wasn't ever going to figure this out by himself, he'd call and give him a little help.

"Hello."

"Henderson, it's Belson at the station."

"Yeah, Belson, what can I do for you?"

"The Commander said I should call you and tell you."

"Tell me what?"

"About the radio show this afternoon."

Then Belson told him know Knox Stansfield had insisted that a Washington, D.C., homicide detective was about to implicate the First Lady in the murder of a friend of hers.

"This Hart guy," Belson said, "he knew the First Lady, right?"

"Right."

"Then it's you that Stansfield is talking about."

"Man, something's wrong here."

"Like what?"

Henderson started to tell him about the strange phone calls but then stopped himself.

"What's wrong? Some talk-show host starts talking about me on the radio? Are you kidding?"

Pause. "The Commander'd like to see you."

"About what?"

Belson lowered his voice. He must be in the bullpen where everybody can hear him, Henderson thought.

"He got this call."

"Oh, yeah?"

"Yeah. From the White House."

"You're kidding."

"That's what the Commander said. The White House."

"They think I leaked it to Stansfield or something?"

"That's what the Commissioner thinks."

"The Commissioner," Henderson said. "How'd he get into this?"

"He called right after the White House did."

"Oh, great."

"He *really* thinks you leaked this to Stansfield. He thinks most cops hate Matt Hutton."

"Well, he probably isn't wrong about that." Henderson pawed his face, sighed.

Not only was he getting jerked around by some stranger on the phone—led into all these pointless little games—now he had the police commissioner on his back.

"The Commander want to see me right away?"

"Yeah."

"Tell him an hour."

"The Commissioner'll probably be here by then, too."

"Oh, great."

"Oh, you got one other call, too."

"From who?"

"Your wife Maggie."

"Yeah?"

"Said to tell you she had to work late again tonight."

Henderson slammed the phone.

The end of the world couldn't be far away, Henderson thought. The whole frigging planet, the whole frigging *universe* might as well collapse in on itself.

At this point he wouldn't give much of a damn.

He was just walking into the living room to pick up his suit jacket when the phone rang.

More bad news.

Had to be.

He was on a roll, wasn't he?

He picked up. "Yeah?"

A second before the voice actually spoke, Henderson was aware of the *presence* of the reverb equipment that scrambled the words into something without gender.

"Are you getting discouraged, Detective Henderson?"

"I better not ever meet you, jerk."

"Been a long, hard day?"

"You bastard. I'd like to get my hands on you. You called Knox Stansfield, too, didn't you?

"Believe it or not, we're on the same side."

"Yeah, right."

"I wanted you to work for what you'll eventually find, Detective Henderson. I want you to appreciate it when you finally lay hands on it. It's going to make you a very important man. It's—"

But Henderson couldn't handle any more of this fruitcake's games.

He slammed the phone, went in and picked up his jacket, and let himself out of the apartment.

The phone started ringing when he got halfway down the front steps.

He didn't even look back. He just let it keep on ringing.

37

★ ★ ★ "That's the hell of it," said the President of the United States. "I do believe you."

"That nothing happened?"

"That nothing happened."

"Oh, darling," Claire said and came into his arms.

She had told him everything, including how she had awakened on David Hart's living room floor with her own gun in her hand.

The Oval Office was in exquisite order as usual, its somber dark furnishings lending a heavy dignity to the otherwise sunny room. An American flag stood to the left of the President's large, orderly desk. Two comfortable hand-carved chairs stood on either side of the desk like lonely sentries. The fireplace mantel was covered with framed photographs of some of Matt's presidential heroes: Teddy Roosevelt, FDR, Dwight Eisenhower and Jack Kennedy. Not all of his more conservative friends were happy with his choice of FDR and Kennedy, but so be it. Great leaders did not tidily fit this or that party agenda.

"It's my fault," he said as they finished their embrace. "Me and that damned flirtation I had. I humiliated my family and I'll never forgive myself for it."

"I should have known better than to trust David," Claire said as her part of the recrimination. "I should have know that he'd eventually graduate into a blackmailer. It was one of the few things he hadn't tried yet."

Matt poured them brandy and brought it back to the desk.

Their very first day in the White House, she'd insisted on getting a snapshot of him in the Oval Office. Everything from the Cuban Missile Crisis to the Gulf War had been decided here. She'd felt that this should be the first entry in her personal photo diary.

Now they were talking about some far less noble matters and she felt vaguely ashamed to be speaking of such things in a room that had played so important a role in the country's history.

"Somebody set you up."

"Of course," she said. "I realize that now."

"One of my political enemies."

She nodded. "What did McElroy say?"

"He wants to work on a statement for you to read to the press."

She felt sick, weak.

She imagined herself at a packed, sweaty press conference, the reporters descending on her like ravenous wolves.

The statement that McElroy prepared would be true in its way, but it would be true in the fashion of political self-defense. No mention would be made of the President's would-be affair, not of the money she gave Hart, nor of finding what appeared to be the murder weapon in her hand and carrying it away from the murder scene.

They wouldn't believe any of it. They would already be convinced that behind her suburban good looks and poise lurked a wanton. They would already be convinced that just as the President had had an affair, so had she. They would already be convinced that, for whatever reason, she had become enraged with her lover and killed him.

The nightly news and the political talk shows would feast on the story for months.

Even Michael Jackson, even O. J. Simpson would look like minor stories compared to the kind of relentless and fixated attention this story would get.

The First Lady.

With a dead lover.

And a White House trying desperately to cover up the real truth.

"For what it's worth," Matt said softly, "I told McElroy that I didn't want you facing the press alone."

"I have to."

"I told him I wanted to be there, but he said that that would look as if you were trying to hide behind me."

"It would."

"You don't deserve this, Claire." He made a bitter face. "Me and my damned ego. Thinking of straying at my age—"

"I didn't have to see David, honey. I mean, that was my own choice."

"I just wonder who the hell could be behind it."

"You know who I'm thinking of," she said.

He nodded. "My first choice, too. But Knox isn't crazy—or stupid. He'd never risk everything he has to get me this way. It would be just too big a risk."

"Then who—?"

They were silent a moment.

Then, "You'll have to see that cop, too."

"What cop?"

"According to McElroy," Matt said, "his name is Michael Henderson. He'll want to interview you."

"That's going to be very difficult."

"Gil Toolan will be there."

Gil Toolan. Their family lawyer.

Matt's intercom buzzed.

"Mr. McElroy, line two."

Matt picked up.

"Hello."

Listened.

Paled a little bit.

"You're sure?"

Matt looked over at her. "Just a minute." Cupped the phone. "Did you wear a wig when you went to David's?"

She nodded.

Back to McElroy. "Yes, she did." Beat. "All right, thanks."

He hung up.

"I'm sorry I forgot to tell you. About the wig, I mean."

Matt sighed. He looked as if he'd aged several years in the past few hours. "You know how the press'll play it up."

"God, this is a nightmare."

"McElroy said that NBC is going to run a composite drawing of what you looked like when you visited Hart's town house. In your wig and all."

"The scarlet woman."

"Exactly."

"I'm worried about Deirdre."

"Maybe you should talk to her."

"I'm planning to," Claire said. "As soon as she gets back from Dr. Solomon's."

"The press conference should be tomorrow morning, according to McElroy."

Claire smiled tensely. "I'll be there."

"I wish we could avoid it."

"Right now I'm worried about Deirdre and the primaries," Claire said. "I'll get through the press conference somehow."

She put her brandy snifter down and stood up.

Matt came from behind his desk and held her again.

She tucked her face into the crook of his neck and shoulder, the way she used to when they first started to go together. She liked the crisp, clean, masculine smell of his body and his cologne.

She held him more tightly than she had in years, instinctively afraid that something terrible was going to come between them now.

And then Matt seemed to think something similar because he drew her even closer, held her even tighter.

"The gun is what I'm worried about," she said. "Once I tell them about our gun being there—there'll be no way I can convince them that I didn't kill him. That's why—" She paused.

"Why what?"

"I don't know if I can tell them about the gun."

"You have to tell them about everything, honey. You really do. It's very important."

And she added one more thing quickly: "And I think there has to be somebody inside the White House helping in this—"

"On the staff? But who?"

She didn't know the answer to that. But then a curt knock came on the closed door of the Oval Office and she didn't have to worry about answering. At least not for the moment. Who didn't she trust? Who would betray them this way?

Matt excused himself and walked to the door.

Agent Bick. One of the Secret Service agents assigned to Deirdre. Slender, dark-suited, wary of eye, he was interchangeable with any number of other agents.

"I'm sorry to interrupt, Mr. President."

"Fine. What is it?"

"Your daughter," Bick said. "She's not doing very well at the moment—"

It was Claire who asked the next question, hurrying now to the door and Agent Bick. "What happened?"

"When we got out of Dr. Solomon's there were all these reporters waiting for Deirdre and she sort of went—"

But Claire didn't wait to hear the rest.

She rushed past Matt and Bick out into the hallway. "Is she up in her room?"

Agent Bick nodded.

Claire didn't bother with the elevator. She took the stairs leading to the second floor and her daughter Deirdre.

38

★ ★ ★ The colored guy hadn't come out yet.

Bobby LaFontaine had been parked across the street from the Knox Stansfield mansion for nearly an hour now and his butt was going to sleep.

Damned colored guys, anyway.

Guy was probably watching TV and stealing food from the refrigerator while Stansfield was on the air.

One thing he'd learned in prison, Bobby LaFontaine had, was you couldn't trust colored guys.

"I need to come see you, Carlotta," Clemmons said.

"How come?"

"You're my sister."

"Yeah, but you don't come see me 'less there's a good reason. This got anything to do with Randy?"

"I'd really rather talk about this in person."

An animal panic seized her. "This got somethin' to do with Randy, don't it?"

"I could be there in half an hour."

"He in some kind of trouble? Somethin' happen to him?"

"Think about it, Carlotta. If something happened to him, why would they call *me*?"

She relaxed a little. "Guess you're right."

"I just need to talk."

"You got anything to drink?"

"I could have."

"Scotch?"

"Maybe."

"J&B?"

"Your taste has improved."

"I ain't no drunk. I want you to know that."

"You can handle it, sister. You always could."

"Jes' I don't have the money for any good stuff very often and you workin' for that Klan man—"

He laughed. "He isn't exactly a Klansman."

"No, but he'll do till the real thing comes along."

"Guess I couldn't disagree with you there."

"When you leavin'?"

"Right now."

"And you're stoppin' by the liquor store?"

"Bet on it, sister."

She laughed again. "You bet I'll bet on it."

The colored guy came out ten minutes later. Instead of his usual dark suit, he wore a dark blue windbreaker, a yellow sport shirt and tan slacks.

He walked stiffly, seeming to simulate a kind of military posture. Colored guys were always putting on airs. Driving Caddies. Or squiring around white gals. Or trying to impress you with all the big words they knew.

This colored guy didn't have a Caddy, though.

A rattletrap was what he had, a six-year old buff blue rattletrap that he kept shined like an apple on a teacher's desk.

Had to give him that.

You didn't see many colored guys who took care of their cars or their person the way this dude did.

He pulled out of the gates, turned right, was gone.

Five minutes later, Bobby LaFontaine was letting himself in the back door.

Clemmons was ten minutes away before he thought to pat his hip and check his wallet.

Damn.

He'd left it in the little room he used for himself back at Stansfield's. He sometimes left his suits there and changed when he arrived in the mornings.

And sometimes, being a man who had a great deal on his mind, he forgot things.

He couldn't buy his sister a proper bottle of scotch without his credit cards.

He went up to the corner, turned around, and drove back to the mansion.

Bobby LaFontaine was so transfixed by what he found that he didn't hear Clemmons pull up in the driveway.

39

★ ★ ★ "Honey, please. You really need to take this."

"Isn't there something we can do, Mom? There has to be something we can do."

"The first thing you can do, honey, is take this tranquilizer."

"I just hate him so much."

"And then I'll give you an aspirin. You feel like you're running a little fever."

"I just wish something would happen to him. That he'd come down with a disease or something or—"

"You know you shouldn't say that, honey."

"I know, Mom, but the things he says about you and Dad—"

Late afternoon and they were in Deirdre's pink bedroom with all the cute stuffed animals watching them. Or seeming to watch them, anyway. Claire had always noticed a truly weird phenomenon. Whenever Deirdre was sad, her animals tended to look sad, too. Claire obviously knew this couldn't be true and yet— Even the alligator with the big hungry grin looked kind of dour right at the moment.

"Here."

Deirdre was propped up in bed, already in pink pajamas and pink robe.

Claire wished the occasion were different—that Deirdre simply had a bad headcold or something—because she enjoyed taking care of her daughter this way. Brought back a lot of memories of when Deirdre had been a little girl.

Deirdre took the Xanax.

"Will this make me sleepy?"

"They make me sleepy," Claire said.

"Maybe that's what I need."

"I know it's what you need."

Then the aspirin.

Once swallow and Deirdre took it down.

"You should have seen them, Mom. They were like animals."

"I'm sorry you had to go through that, honey."

She took Deirdre in her arms and held her. This brought back more memories of Deirdre's childhood. She loved being gently rocked, then and now.

"You should've heard the things they said about you."

"This will pass, Deirdre. It really will."

Deirdre eased herself away so she could look into her mother's face.

"You're having a press conference, aren't you?"

"Yes, I guess I am."

"And you'll just have to sit there and be polite and listen to them scream dirty questions at you, won't you?"

Claire tried a tiny smile. "I guess I will."

"It's his fault."

"Honey, please—"

"This is what he wants."

"Deirdre, listen—"

"In his own sick way, he's still in love with you, and because he can't have you, he wants to destroy you *and* your family."

Claire pressed Deirdre back against the headboard.

"Why don't you just relax, honey? That's why I gave you the tranquilizer, remember?"

"You know what I'm saying is true, Mom. That he wants to destroy our family."

"Maybe you're right."

"You know I'm right."

"He wants Dad to lose the primary and get you in trouble with the police."

"Well, he's not going to. The truth will come out. It really will."

"It doesn't always, Mom. Look at Frank."

Congressman Frank Devlin had been a good friend. He'd infuriated a lobbyist, caused the man to look bad in front of the textile industry, and the lobbyist had gone to great lengths to destroy him. Frank had lost a wife in a car accident and was a bachelor again, albeit a sad one, and one who drank too much. He picked up a young woman one night only to learn too late that the girl had been planted on him by the lobbyist. The woman had called the police, telling them that Frank had forced himself on her. She'd hinted at charges of rape. No charges were ever filed, but the story made its way to the press (the lobbyist was sure of that) and in the next election, the honest young congressman was dumped by the voters. A candidate already in the lobbyist's pocket won the election easily.

"But in this case the truth *will* come out," Claire said, uneasy with her daughter's cynicism. Eight years as the daughter of a congressman had left Deirdre pretty much a normal girl. But that changed quickly with the move into the White House. Deirdre quickly learned that the truth itself didn't matter. It was the *perception* of truth that counted. You could destroy somebody by whispering lies about them, so that when he finally spoke the truth in defense of himself, he was perceived as a liar. This was a daily event when you were President of the United States, especially when you were (as Matt defined himself) "a radical moderate on the common sense ticket."

Deirdre yawned.

Claire and Deirdre shared a real susceptibility to medicines. They kicked in right away. Claire was the same way with alcohol. Two drinks and she was semidrunk. She'd always been the ultimate cheap date.

"I'm sorry about today," Claire said. Then, "How about a blanket?"

"I've got a robe on."

"Why don't I get you a nice big comforter, just in case?"

Deirdre grinned. "I like it when you play mom. It makes me feel all nice and secure. Even when I don't want the damned comforter."

They compromised on a plain blanket, and Claire didn't spread it over Deirdre's entire body, only across her legs.

"There."

"I love you, Mom."

"I love you, too, hon."

"Will you wake me for dinner?"

"I'd rather let you sleep."

"Oh, really?"

"Really."

"But I've got so much studying."

"I think we can put that off for a little while. You need a good long nap."

"I am getting sleepy."

"Good."

Claire kissed her a final time and then walked over to the door.

"I'll see you in a little while."

Deirdre nodded.

She was already sinking into sleep.

* * *

Claire looked at the debris of pink slips cluttering her desk.

Jane said, "It's been crazy."

"They want to interview me, I take it?" Claire said, nodding to the pink slips.

"Right."

"Well, he's getting his way."

"Knox Stansfield?"

"Right."

"Should I cancel your appointments for the next few days?"

"No," Claire said, suddenly very angry. "That's just what that bastard wants me to start doing—hiding out from the public, isolating myself, and I won't do it." Her jaws locked angrily. "I'm going to fight back and—you know what, Jane? I'm going to beat the bastard. I don't know how yet. But I'm going to."

Then she sat down and got to work on the statement she would read to the press tomorrow. Let McElroy put his spin on it if he wanted to—but the words were going to be her own.

40

★ ★ ★ Tampons in three sizes; string bikinis in four sizes; clogs in two sizes; sunglasses in a dozen styles.

All this was in a room just off Knox Stansfield's swimming pool. Obviously—in addition to the towels, suntan lotions and various toiletries you'd expect to find in a place like this—Stansfield kept a regular drugstore for his ladies.

Bobby LaFontaine had to admit a certain respect for any lady-killer who operated this smoothly. Even one who'd blackballed him from the board of directors six months ago.

Bobby was standing there admiring it when he heard the back door open.

Damn.

Somebody coming in.

Bobby moved silently to one corner of the small room.

Waited.

His breath coming now in harsh, nervous gasps.

Clemmons was surprised the maid wasn't here yet.

He let himself in the back door and went up the three steps to the kitchen. Through the windows he could see the swimming pool, nice and blue against the aqua tiles.

He had always promised himself that he'd someday take a swim in the pool. So far as he knew, Stansfield had never had a single black body in that clean blue water. And probably never would have, either, at the rate Clemmons was going.

Clemmons had just started to walk through the kitchen to his small dressing room when he heard the distant sound of something dropping on the floor.

His eyes followed the sound to one of the rooms off the swimming pool.

He couldn't be sure, but that's where the sound seemed to be coming from.

Something was wrong.

He was sure of it.

He did not hesitate now.

He walked through the kitchen, but then, instead of entering the dressing room, he went toward the hallway leading to the den.

Stansfield kept a gun in his desk drawer.

At the moment, Clemmons, an expert marksman, felt the need of a gun.

Bobby LaFontaine glared at the shoe box with a new pair of Reeboks in it.

He'd accidentally brushed the box off the chair as he'd passed it, and now it was on the floor.

The way Bobby LaFontaine was glaring at the box, however, an on-looker might think that the box had picked itself up and *flung* itself to the floor.

Bobby wanted to plunge a butcher knife into the box.

Or empty a revolver into it.

But now he had to move. Hide. Somebody else was in the house and they'd likely heard the box drop and now they'd likely come down and check to see what was going on.

The room was narrow and blue and held nothing more than the stuff Stansfield kept on hand for his chicks. Oh, yeah: and the massage table.

Footsteps now, on the tile.

Coming closer, closer.

Fast.

Bobby LaFontaine's ass was grass if he couldn't find a place to hide.

Another glance around. No place to hide. Absolutely no place.

Boxed in.

The footsteps again: louder, closer, faster.

A final glance around, this time stopping at a small pile of blankets sitting on a chair.

The poor darlings were probably all shivery and goose-bumpy when they came out of the water.

Needed some blankies.

And that's when Bobby got his idea.

How about throwing a blanket over the massage table? If both ends of the blanket touched the floor, he'd have himself a hiding place.

The footsteps.

Closer, closer.

Faster, faster.

Bobby bolted for the blankets, picked up a mauve cotton one and draped it quickly over the table.

Didn't touch the floor on either side.

Damn.

Had to hurry.

The next blanket was an amber color and felt heavier.

Footsteps.

Closer.

Faster.

Almost here now.

This blanket just had to—

He threw the blanket over the table.

It touched.

Both sides.

The Lord Be Praised.

The Lord Is My Shepherd.

Sometimes Bobby LaFontaine, especially when everything was going his way, felt positively *religious*.

He crawled beneath the massage table.

And waited.

He didn't want to look foolish, Clemmons didn't.

What if something had accidentally fallen off on the floor?

Get a couple of squad cars out here—a minimum of two when the citizen was as important as Stansfield—and the press would inevitably follow.

He could see the story now, hear the snickers.

Stansfield's colored man gets all weirded out because he hears a noise and so he gets the Army out here.

No, better to take Stansfield's gun and check this out himself.

His eyes scanned both sides of the pool as he quickly moved down the tiles.

The smell of chlorine stung his eyes.

He reached the end of the pool.

The door to the dressing room stood closed.

If somebody was here, the dressing room was the only place he could possibly hide.

Clemmons stared at the door a moment.

What if there was some crack-crazed thief on the other side? One of those mutant punks who'd kill you for twenty-five cents?

Maybe he should call the cops.

Maybe he should risk the scorn.

He walked up to the door.

Put his hand on the knob.

Turned the knob to the right.

Bobby LaFontaine was going to get nailed. He could feel it.

Somebody was at the door now.

Coming in.

He was going to get nailed and Reverend Goodhew was going to kick him right out of the church.

Where the hell are you when I really need you, Lord?

One, two, three steps into the dressing room.

Everything looked orderly and familiar except for—

A blanket had been haphazardly rolled up and tossed atop a small stack of blankets.

Clemmons knew now somebody was in here.

But where?

The closet door was open.

He walked over.

He was trembling.

He eased the door open even further.

He was trembling even more now.

He looked inside.

Everything in perfect order. And nobody hiding in there. No place *to* hide.

His trembling decreased.

It was the colored guy, Bobby LaFontaine saw, peering out around the corner of the blanket.

What the hell was he doing back here?

Bobby LaFontaine felt betrayed, as if the two of them had had some kind of *pact* or something and the colored guy had broken his word.

The colored guy was leaning over, peering into the closet now and Bobby LaFontaine realized that this was the only chance he'd have for escape.

Now.

Clemmons was just starting to turn away from the closet, face the room again, when he heard a noise behind him.

He turned just in time to see somebody pick up the massage table, blanket and all, and charge Clemmons with it.

Clemmons had time to squeeze off one shot before the table slammed into his upper torso and head.

In the confusion and panic, the gun fell from Clemmons's hand.

Then the table was pulled back and the person behind it—Clemmons wished he could get a look at the sonofabitch—came charging at him again.

This time the edge of the table caught Clemmons right on the temple and that was all it took.

Light became dark.

His mouth filled with curses.

He was not exactly unconscious but then he was not exactly conscious, either.

For a third time, with Clemmons only half aware of it, the table came charging again.

This time Clemmons was knocked to the floor.

The intruder, whoever he was, then hurled the entire table on top of Clemmons, the blanket flying free and entangling Clemmons's whole head.

Then—footsteps.

Running away—fast.

It was kind of ballsy but then Bobby was that kind of guy.

The colored guy might well be on his feet by now and coming after Bobby but Bobby needed to take the chance anyway.

He grabbed a chair, scrambled up to the shelf above the Jacuzzi where he'd planted the first microphone, and then did a quick exchange.

The old one for the new one.

He just hoped it was the microphone queering the pickup. He would hate for all this work to be for nothing.

"Hey!" the colored guy shouted.

He was still in the dressing room, must still be trying to get the table and blanket off him.

Now Bobby LaFontaine really had to haul ass.

After securing the new microphone, he jumped down and started running to the back of the place.

Then he was outside and on the drive.

And running.

Running real hard and real fast.

41

★ ★ ★ Henderson felt like a kid being kept after school.

He sat at his desk in the detective squad room watching a long bar of spring sunlight angle across his desk like a message from God.

Three times Henderson had been summoned to the Commander's office, only to be told that the Commissioner was in there and he was still talking with the Commander and would Henderson, like a good little boy, go back to his desk and wait?

His phone rang. He picked up. He said, "Yes, sir." He hung up.

But he didn't move.

What was the hurry?

He would just walk back to the Commander's office and be told to wait a little while longer.

What was the hurry?

Five minutes later, the Commissioner was asking him, "A mysterious caller told you this?"

"Yessir," Henderson said.

"How long have you been a cop?"

"Nearly twel—"

"A rhetorical question, Henderson," the Commissioner said. "What I was really asking was, Are you stupid enough to fall for some obvious ploy like this?"

"Obvious ploy?"

"Yes. Obvious ploy, Henderson. The President of the United States is a political job, Henderson. Meaning that he has enemies. Meaning that at any given time there are hundreds, perhaps thousands, of people, who want to destroy the President. Right?"

"Yessir. I mean, I guess so."

"You guess so?"

"I mean, I don't follow politics real close. Sorry."

The Police Commissioner was, of course, a lawyer. He had once been a municipal judge. He was a man of snowy hair, trim belly, impeccable taste that ran to conservative Brooks Brothers rather than flashier Armani. A generational preference, one assumed. He was also the Mayor's first cousin and was ruthless in protecting the man who sat at the head of the city council.

"How many times has he called you?" Commissioner Parker said.

"Uh, three."

"And he's told you what exactly?"

"I thought I told you that, sir."

"You did but I want to hear it again."

"He said that somewhere in Hart's town house is something that will link the First Lady to Hart's murder."

"Aren't you curious why you'd get a call like that?"

Henderson shrugged. "I figure it's somebody who knows something but doesn't want to get involved."

Henderson looked over at the Commander, who had been silent after their first few idle words. The Commander chose to avert his eyes quickly.

"Did it ever occur to you that you're being used?"

"Sure."

"But you went ahead with it, anyway?"

"Went ahead with what?"

"Calling Knox Stansfield and telling him that you were working on a possible link between the murder and the First Lady?"

"I didn't call Knox Stansfield, sir."

"You didn't?"

"No, sir."

Parker looked at the Commander. Some kind of telepathic message was passed, but Henderson wasn't sure what it was.

Parker sat on the edge of the Commander's desk. He leaned closer to where Henderson sat and said, "Are you willing to take a polygraph?"

"Yes, sir."

"Good." Parker got up and started pacing.

"Did you know that the President is in an upcoming primary?"

"I guess so, sir."

"He's fighting for his political life."

"Yessir."

"Well, what would happen if some unscrupulous sonofabitch decided to plant the story in the press that the First Lady had something to do with a murder? Wouldn't that sort of destroy the President's chances? And understand me here, Henderson, I'm a Democrat. I hate Republicans. But I also want to be fair to the President."

"I see what you're saying, sir. About me being used."

Parker came back and put his bony ass on the edge of the desk again.

"And then just imagine, Henderson, how this department, and how the city officials would look if the press decided that we'd played along in smearing the President. You know what we'd look like then?"

"Yessir. I can imagine, sir."

"That's why I'm taking you off the case."

Dayton had said it so quickly that it almost didn't register on Henderson but then he said, "What, sir?"

"Taking you off the case."

"But why?"

Dayton again glanced at the Commander. Another inscrutable telepathic message.

Then back to Henderson: "Your name has been all over the papers lately."

"Yessir."

"A major lawsuit. False arrest. Harassment."

"Yessir."

"So people are starting to form an opinion about you."

"They are, sir?"

"Sure. People want to believe the worst things they hear about cops because they basically think we're a bunch of lazy, stupid, crooked, violent thugs. Isn't that right, Commander?"

The Commander smiled: "Those are the only kind of cops I want in my department."

To Henderson: "So, as the Commissioner, it's my duty to make sure that a cop who has already got a bad public relations problem doesn't get a worse one."

"But, sir, isn't there at least the possibility that the First Lady might actually have killed—"

The Commander nodded. "Yes, of course there's that possibility. But you're tainted, Henderson. All the press can see is this guy who's accused of false arrest and harassment—and now they think he's playing footsie with Knox Stansfield trying to bring down the President. You see my predicament, Henderson?"

"Yes, I do, sir, but—"

"A rock and a hard place."

"Yessir."

"A goddamned rock and a goddamned hard place."

"Yessir, but—"

"So the Commander here says he's going to reassign you."

But at the moment Henderson wasn't hearing so good. Fame and glory and sweet green cash— Earlier today, it had all looked so simple. THE MAN WHO BROUGHT IN THE FIRST LADY. The book deal, the movie deal— Maggie'd stay with him forever. Proud of her husband for the very first time. And satisfied, too. Content. A good and loyal mate. At long last.

But now—

"Are you all right, Henderson?"

"Yessir."

"You don't look real good."

"Yessir."

"Why don't you knock off for the day? I'm sure the Commander won't mind."

Henderson nodded and stood up on unsteady legs.

Fame and glory— Fading now like the cheers in a football stadium as dusk fell and the fans went home—

Fading—

"I hope you understand that there's nothing personal in this," the Commissioner said.

"Yessir," Henderson said. "I mean, no, sir. Nothing personal."

"Nice seeing you again, Henderson."

"Yessir."

And then he was gone.

42

★ ★ ★ In the old days, it was a slum but it didn't look like a slum. Not then.

But that was a long time ago, back when Clemmons still had dreams of college and a nice cushy white-collar job somewhere in the government.

Now the old neighborhood even looked like a slum.

As he pulled up to his sister's place, Clemmons was still wondering who'd broken into Stansfield's house, and what he'd been looking for. He'd left a painful calling card: Clemmons's head still hurt from being smashed by the table. He'd called Stansfield and told him all this. Stansfield had been busy but sounded angry about the break-in. He'd told Clemmons not to call the police.

Climbing out of the car, he watched as some youngsters tossed a football back and forth on the empty street. His first thought was that he'd been a boy very much like them. But no, that wasn't true. A black man had had very little opportunity when Sam was growing up in this dusky neighborhood, but at least he'd been relatively free of the hard drugs and violence that lurked behind every tree, and down every alleyway, for blocks and blocks.

Clemmons watched the kids a moment, none older than ten, and was happy to hear the exuberance and innocence in their voices.

Still some hope for this particular group of kids. But hope was fading fast. Unless they had the right kind of parents, or a very dedicated teacher the way Clemmons had, then they'd slide into the easy ways of the ghetto. Gangs and guns. And soon enough there'd be prison or death.

He walked up to his sister's place, a tiny stucco house with cracks like cancers every few feet on the side walls. The front porch tilted far to the left and two of the four front windows had duct tape over the breaks. Even from here, he could hear the rap music that Randy loved so much—loud, grating, threatening.

Clemmons knocked.

Randy opened up, sullen as soon as he saw it was his uncle.

In the family, Clemmons was considered to be both an odd duck and a man who felt himself to be better than the average black. Clemmons had never married. He'd gotten his heart broken over a lovely young black girl thirty years ago and he'd never taken a serious chance since then. He enjoyed sex and got his fill of it, but he never again wanted to feel the helplessness and jealousy and humiliation of being heartbroken. He dressed well, he spoke well, he was always courteous. To his generation of blacks, Clemmons represented a modest success. To Randy's generation of blacks, Clemmons was a Tom, a man too eager to take the little the white man chose to offer.

"Yo," Randy said.

"Your mom home?"

"She said you'd be by. She's in the can."

"You could always say, 'She'll be right out.'"

"Aw, man this is my crib, all right? Don't gimme none of your lectures."

Randy was, as usual, playing the bad man. He was shirtless, revealing strong arms and chest, and a joint was dangling from the corner of his mouth.

Randy flung himself on the couch, turned the rap music up even louder, obviously knowing it would irritate his uncle.

"You dig Snoop, man?"

"Guess I'm not sure who he is."

"He's cool, man. He takes nothing from white folks. Nothing at all."

Randy's usual coded message: my uncle the white man's sucker.

"Isn't he the guy who killed somebody?"

"That's what whitey says. I say he was framed." Then he grinned. "How's Benito?"

That's how Randy had always referred to Stansfield. Benito, for Mussolini.

"All right, I guess."

"He didn't have to call the cops on me."

"You stole his watch."

"All the money that fascist bastard's got, why should he care about one watch?"

"Because it belonged to him."

The grin again, insolent: "You look a little whiter every time I see you, you know that, man?"

Henderson had five quick drinks and decided that the receptionist at his wife's law firm was lying to him when she said that Maggie was in a conference all this time.

Conference. Right. Probably in the supply room with her skirt up over her hips and taking it back door from one of the esteemed counselors of law.

Then he was out of the bar and in his car.

He'd show the bitch she couldn't hide behind any goddamned receptionist.

He'd show her.

He headed straight for Maggie's law office.

Clemmons was ashamed of himself.

He sat on the edge of the frayed couch, his body language saying that he would never quite be comfortable in this house, wishing that his sister dressed a little better (worn flannel shirt, aqua stretch pants so tight they only emphasized her heaviness, big bare feet), spoke a little better (she had never learned proper English, even though he'd encouraged her to take night school courses and finish her high school diploma) and fussed about the house a little more. She'd just knocked a magazine to the floor when she'd put her feet up on the coffee table. And she'd made no effort to pick the magazine up. Clemmons had to hold himself back from diving for the magazine and putting it up where it belonged.

He was ashamed of himself.

She was his sister and he should have loved her unconditionally, not giving a damn about aqua stretch pants or magazines on the floor.

But a part of him felt hard, cold. He had promised himself as a boy that he would escape the ghetto, that he would make a world for himself that was clean, orderly, literate and safe.

Well, he had that little world now and he was utterly isolated.

He had that little world and he was so smug about it that he sat here silently putting his sister down because she had not escaped the ghetto.

"What's that?" he said, hearing a noise from the rear of the house.

She smiled. "Washing machine. Damned thing sounds like it's going to come tearin' right through that wall, doesn't it?"

"Yes, it does."

She had a sip of the J&B she'd poured them (he'd secretly wiped a lipstick stain from the glass she'd given him) and then said, "Somethin' smell bad?"

"Smell bad?"

"Yeah. The way your face is kind of scrunched up."

"I guess I wasn't aware that my face *was* scrunched up."

A slow, sad smile. "You don't much like comin' here, do you, Sam?"

"Oh, come on, now. Don't get in one of those moods."

"You've changed, my man. You're like one of them white people Mom always used to work for—the ones that was always pushin' her around."

"Am I pushin' you around?"

"Not in no physical way, you're not. But you look like somebody just sat you down in a mound of dog shit."

"Poetic."

"I always was poetic, Sam." The sad smile. "Maybe I'll hire me my own housekeeper if the gov'ment ever gives people on AFDC more money."

"Believe it or not, I'm very happy to see you."

She had some more whiskey. "You and Randy have a good talk?"

"Uh-huh."

"He knows you don't like him much."

Clemmons began to squirm. Sometimes all his sister wanted to do was argue. It was her way of castigating him for being uppity. Today was apparently going to be one of those days.

"I like him fine. I just wish he'd do something with his life."

"He ain't no worse than any other boy his age."

"He's got two felony charges against him already."

"He don't shoot nobody. A lot of boys down here, they kill people. He don't kill nobody."

"Maybe he could go back and finish high school."

"They hassle kids like him. The white teachers, I mean. He gets in a little trouble like he done and they won't leave him be. Pick pick pick, all day long."

He decided that now would be a good time to say what he'd come to say. "I've got to go to the police on a matter that may get Randy in trouble."

Her face froze. "What you talkin' about?"

"My boss, Stansfield, he did something I think I should report to the police."

"What's that got to do with Randy?" Angry, protective.

"Nothing directly. But when Stansfield finds out that I did it, he'll tell the police that Randy took his watch. It's just the kind of guy he is."

"Then don't do it."

"Don't tell the police about Stansfield?"

"Right. Randy'd go to prison, they ever find out he took that watch."

"This is very important," Clemmons said.

She was up on her feet suddenly, a big woman, enraged now, standing over him and sloshing her glass so that scotch whiskey glistened all over her hand and arm.

"Yeah, well my son is very important to me! You understand that, you cold-fish bastard! You ain't got no child so you don't understand! But you ever turn Randy in like that, I'll kill you with my own hands! You understand me! I'll slit your throat myself!"

And then she did the worst thing of all, she went back to her chair and collapsed in it, and began sobbing.

And gave her brother a glimpse of how desperately, how all-consumingly, she loved her son Randy.

Bitch wasn't at any of the bars where she usually went. He saw some of the lawyers from her firm in a couple of them, though. They had their smirks all ready for him, as if they knew some terrible secret about him.

Henderson wanted to smash their smug faces in.

Then he remembered some other bars, and tried those. Still nothing.

On the very distant chance that she might have gone home, he tried their number a few times but—nothing.

Her going home was a ridiculous idea.

She was out somewhere and somebody was putting it to her.
Bitch.

He needed her now. His whole world had collapsed. Any future he had in the department had officially ended when the Commissioner had taken him off the case today.

Oh, he'd get his vacations and his occasional citations and at retirement time there'd be a small sentimental ceremony and a nice pension.

But Maggie would be long gone by then.

Maggie—

Bitch.

He was going to find her and find her now and drag her home where she belonged.

"Please don't get him in no trouble."

Clemmons knelt next to the chair in which she sat, and looked at her with eyes that now saw all her sorrow, all her misery, all her grief—years in the ghetto from which she'd never been able to escape, raising Randy as well as she could.

Easy for Clemmons, the outsider, to judge her harshly. To say that she should have been stronger, smarter, wiser—when all he was saying was that she should have been more like *me*.

As if he were somebody to emulate.

A lonely man drifting down the years into old age and death, with only his sense of decorum for company.

Well, he wasn't exactly a prize, either.

And he had no right to judge her.

Nor no right to risk putting her only son in jail.

He took her hand and held it for a long time, a work-coarsened hand now damp with the tears she'd wiped from her face, and from somewhere in the past came a song he used to sing her, and now he hummed it aloud, sitting there in the shabby living room with his sister whom he'd forgotten to love for so many years now.

And hearing the tune, she smiled.

And took him in her arms and held him, loving brother and sister once again after so long a time.

Loving brother and sister.

No way he could go to the police now. No way.

43

★ ★ ★ McElroy said, "I think you should talk to him. I mean, I've already suggested that but now I'm suggesting it again."

"Our lawyer will be there, right?" Matt said.

McElroy nodded. "Of course."

"We could fight it," Matt said.

"I don't want to fight it," Claire said, getting up from her chair to go look at the waning day through the windows overlooking the Rose Garden. Sometimes the Oval Office seemed almost eerily detached from the rest of the White House, as if it were a capsule floating in space.

"If we fight it, we just look as if we have something to hide," Claire said.

"I'm not sure," Matt said. "I used to be a prosecuting attorney, don't forget. I know how cops work. They can get you to say things you don't want to."

"I'll tell them the truth," Claire said. "That I didn't kill him. And I didn't."

McElroy said, "For what it's worth, they're as nervous as we are."

"Really?" Matt said.

"Absolutely. It's not every day they ask questions of the First Lady. The police commissioner himself is coming along to make sure that everything stays civilized."

Claire felt tired suddenly, and came back and sat down in the chair. "In half an hour?"

"That's what the Commissioner would like," McElroy said. He'd spoken with the Commissioner forty-five minutes ago.

"This'll get out," Claire said.

"To the press?" Matt said.

She nodded.

"Let it get out," Matt said with an air of defiance. "We don't have anything to hide."

His words stirred Claire. Matt was right. Nothing to hide and therefore nothing to fear.

"Tell them I'll see them."

"All right," McElroy said. "A half-hour okay?"

"A half-hour is fine."

"Great."

McElroy said, "See you in a while."

Then went away to call the Commissioner back.

"I'm scared," Claire said as soon as McElroy had closed the door behind him.

"Yes," said the President of the United States. "So am I."

Henderson found her in a bar near the National Portrait Gallery. Her lipstick-red Saab was hard to miss.

The bar was crowded with thirtyish, people, most of them, whose clothes and attitude bespoke an arrogance that Henderson found oppressive.

He pushed his way to the back of the place, where booths lined both walls.

These were his impressions: a sad Anita Baker song on the jukebox; a blond woman he at first mistook for Maggie giving a long, body-pressing kiss to a man in an Army officer's uniform; a man sitting in a booth patting a sumptuous young waitress on her elegant bottom; a pair of young men hustling a pair of even younger girls.

And then he saw her.

And went a little crazy.

And then she saw him.

And got a little scared.

She was sitting in the furthest booth back, a handsome man with graying hair next to her. She had her hand placed atop the man's hand on the booth table.

When she saw Henderson, she jerked her hand away.

She whispered something to the graying man.

He sat up straight, moved over toward the wall so that their bodies were no longer touching. Even from here, Henderson saw that the man's hands were trembling as he lit a cigarette.

Henderson could contain himself no longer.

The bar fell away, as did all its occupants.

There was just Maggie in her svelte dark dress and gorgeous tumbling blond hair and insolent erotic smile.

He walked over to the booth.

"C'mon," he said. "We're going home."

"David Armstrong, this is my husband."

"Did you hear me, Maggie? We're going home."

David Armstrong said, "Perhaps I'd better leave, Maggie."

He looked scared. He should have been scared.

Maggie leaned toward David and lowered her voice. "You're making a scene, Michael. You have no right to do this to me."

That's when he cleared the table of its drinks and empty glasses by sweeping his arm across it. Glass shattered, fell in glistening shards to the floor.

Maggie screamed; Armstrong looked as if he wanted to crawl up the wall backwards.

Michael grabbed her arm, ripped her out of the booth and to her feet.

Somebody unplugged the jukebox.

There was just silence now, and people standing around watching, fascinated and fearful in equal parts.

Whoever this guy was, he was a frigging lunatic. No doubt about it.

He pulled Maggie to him, "We're walking out of here together, you understand me?"

Maggie's beautiful green eyes searched the room for help. Anybody. Please.

And then the two men stepped forward. They wore suits but their big blunt bodies were not meant for suits. They'd played a little football in their earlier years, and they'd served a little time, and now they worked for this place as waiters and, when need be, bouncers.

They came up on either side of Henderson, and one of them grabbed Henderson's wrist and eased Henderson's hand from Maggie's.

"Why don't we go have a nice talk?" the first one said.

"I'm a cop."

"Yeah, well, we're not impressed," the second one said.

The first one said, "You go sit down, lady."

Henderson said, "You stay right here."

But obviously Maggie saw her chance for freedom and was going to take it.

She started to walk away.

Henderson's hand shot out to grab her.

The second one snatched his wrist and turned Henderson's arm inward on itself in a hammerlock.

Henderson was almost blinded with pain.

The jukebox came back on again.

"You see the back door, that's where we're headed my friend." The second one, having said this, marched Henderson straight back to a door that sat beneath a red glowing exit sign.

They pushed the door open and shoved Henderson outside.

"What kind of place you think this is?" the second one said.

The first one: "We have a respectable place in there."

"And you come and grab a woman and knock all the drinks on the floor. You know what that does to our business? People start talking about us like we're some kind of low-rent place. Then they start going somewhere else."

"*Capisci?*"

"She's my wife."

"So what?" the first one said. "You think you're the only guy whose wife ever balled somebody else on the side?"

The second one: "You never got a little tail on the side yourself?"

"No."

"Then you're a moron," the first said. "Washington D.C., the ratio is more than two to one, women to men, and you never got yourself some strange pussy? Then you really are a moron."

He was sobering up now and it was all rushing at him—the scene he'd made inside, Maggie's frightened and embarrassed face, the glasses shattering to the floor, the faces staring, staring at him—

And now the alley. Hint of rain. Smell of car oil. Stench of garbage in nearby dumpsters.

His name was Michael Henderson and he'd just made a drunken fool of himself and probably alienated his wife forever. He felt as if he were two people—the sober Michael and the drunken Michael. He had no control at all over the drunken one.

He turned away from the two bouncers abruptly and vomited.

"Sure glad I had dinner already," the first one said, listening to Henderson upchuck.

"Sure glad he didn't barf all over my new suit, anyway," the second one said.

When Henderson walked back to them in the moonlight alley, he said, "I just want to go home."

"Good. Because that's where we want you to go."

"I made a jerk of myself in there, didn't I?" Henderson said.

"You sure did, pal," the second one said.

"Can't I go in and apologize to my wife?"

"You just get the hell out of here," the first one said.

"And fast," the second one said.

So Michael Henderson got the hell out of there. And fast.

44

★ ★ ★ "So you've seen this before?"

"Of course."

"It's your shoe?"

"Yes, it's my shoe. My initials are in it."

"When was the last time you wore these shoes?"

"I still don't understand where you got it. That shoe, I mean."

"Mrs. Hutton—"

"Please, just call me, Claire."

"All right, Claire. When was the last time you wore these shoes?"

"Well, a few months ago, I'd guess."

"Do you have a lot of shoes?"

Claire tried to joke. "Well, I'm not exactly Imelda Marcos, but I have a dozen pairs or so. Of dress shoes, I mean."

"So some you wear more often than others?"

"Oh, yes. Some I hardly ever wear."

"How about these?"

Commander Delbert Craig and the Police Commissioner sat in the First Lady's office along with McElroy and Gil Toolan, the Hutton family lawyer. Matt had decided it would be best if he were here.

The Commander, a smooth, polished middle-aged black man, conducted the interview. Claire sat behind her desk. The Commander sat directly across from her, holding up a single red pump. The heel was missing.

"I don't wear them that often," Claire said. "But I don't understand where you got that shoe."

Gil Toolan said, "Yes, Commander, where did the shoe come from?"

Command Craig looked first at Toolan and then at Claire. "We found this shoe in David Hart's apartment."

The Commissioner leaned forward in his chair and said, "All we're asking, Claire, is that you tell us about your relationship with David Hart." A glance at Gil Toolan. "If that meets with your attorney's approval, that is."

Before Toolan, a plump, balding man in a brown suit could speak, she said, "I don't have anything to hide, Gil. I want to tell them everything."

Gil said, "I'm not sure I'd advise you to—"

"I want to, Gil," Claire said. "I want to."

The dark apartment: a rain-speckled wind blowing through the open veranda door. An ache, a pain so deep and so vital that Henderson could think of nothing more than taking himself to the veranda, nine stories up, and casting himself off.

Maggie wouldn't care.

Not any more. If she ever had.

But at least the pain would be over.

He had barely closed the door behind him, barely stepped inside, when the phone began ringing.

As always, his first ridiculous thought was: Maggie. Wanting to make up. Sorry she's treated me so badly all these years.

Wouldn't he ever give up his foolish and humiliating hope?

Didn't he know by now that she would never change?

Grimly sober—wishing he still had drunkenness to protect him—he went over to the phone in the darkness and lifted the receiver.

"Hello."

"Get the hell off my line," Henderson said.

Genderless, as always; echoing metallically.

"I have something for you, Detective Henderson."

"It's a little late."

"In fact, I have two things for you."

"I'm hanging up now. I'm sick of your games."

"I know what happened to you today, Detective Henderson, and I'm very sorry. I really am. Taking you off the case that way. They had no right."

Who was this guy? How could he possibly know about the case?

"I'm sorry you didn't find the camera on your own."

"What camera?"

"I thought you might be interested again, Detective Henderson."

"What camera are you talking about?"

"The one in the air conditioning duct. Just inside the grate."

"In Hart's apartment?"

"Correct. In the living room."

"A video camera?"

"Correct again, Detective Henderson."

"Where's the video?"

"Until this evening, I had it."

"Where is it now?"

"Go look in the den in your desk, Detective Henderson."

"Is this another one of your games?"

"Go look in your desk, Detective Henderson. And then you decide if it's another one of my 'games,' as you call them."

Henderson went to check his desk.

"Let me understand this exactly, Claire."

"All right."

"You gave Mr. Hart $100,000?"

"Yes."

"But you didn't consider it a blackmail payment?"

"No, I didn't Commander."

"You honestly believed that he would return the money to you someday?"

"I hoped he would. He said he was trying to change. You know, become a better person."

"And your $100,000 was going to help him?"

"Yes, it was."

The Commander looked over at Claire's lawyer. "Were you aware of this transaction, Mr. Toolan?"

"No, sir, I was not."

The Commander, it was obvious, did not want to take any chances with this interrogation. "Would you like to speak with your client for a few minutes in private?"

"I'd very much appreciate it," Toolan said.

Claire looked at the Commander and said, "We don't need a conference. I'm telling you the truth. I don't have anything to hide."

"Claire," Toolan said, "I really advise against you speaking this way."

"I just want everybody to know what happened. The real truth," Claire said.

"You don't have to speak to us right now," the Commissioner said. "You understand that, don't you, Claire?"

She nodded.

"But you want to?"

She nodded again.

Toolan looked at the Commissioner. "Very well."

"We should continue?"

Toolan nodded.

The Commander said, "I guess the next question I need to ask you, Claire, is do either you or your husband own a gun—and where it happens to be at the moment."

The gun. Claire felt her entire body tense. A headache started slicing across her forehead like heat lightning. The gun. Of course. She'd forgotten that she'd have to tell them about the gun.

And then she started to—but stopped.

"I guess I'm not sure what you're talking about."

"I asked if either you or your husband owned a gun, is what I'm talking about, Claire."

"I guess I'm not sure. Matt had one a long time ago. But I haven't seen it for years." She wanted to tell the truth but couldn't quite bring herself to look so guilty. "I mean it could be around here somewhere, I guess."

The Commander seemed to sense she was lying. "You're sure of that?"

The gun was safely upstairs in the drawer. Nobody would ever find it. To even mention it would incriminate herself.

Waking up on the floor with the gun in her hand. David next to her, dead. Disoriented. . . . She'd been so disoriented.

The Commander said, "You're sure you don't have a gun."

"Not anymore. My husband got rid of it."

But the Commander still seemed to doubt her story. He kept pushing, pushing. "When did he get rid of it, do you remember?"

"A year or two at least," she said.

She wanted so badly to tell the truth. But if she did, her story would destroy her husband. They would never believe that the gun had been stolen from the White House.

"A year or two? You're sure of that?"

Gil Toolan watched her closely. He seemed to know she was lying, too.

"Yes," Claire said. "A year or two."

45

★ ★ ★ Bobby had seen it all before, but he still never tired of it—the Reverend wheedling, prying, extracting all that beautiful tax-free money from his viewers.

God's Hour was at the point in the show where Reverend Goodhew, having given his sermon and his first two pitches for "Love Envelopes," sat in the living-room set and talked to his guests, tonight's segment featuring both Knox Stansfield and Senator Jack Wagner.

Just before this there'd been a six-minute bit where Bobby LaFontaine, all got up in a hip tough-guy leather jacket and skin-tight slacks, had talked to some fifteen-year-old black gang members about how *God's Hour* had changed their lives. The four members were actually would-be actors from a local high school. But *God's Hour* audiences loved conversion stories, and Bobby LaFontaine, "God's Favorite Ex-Convict" as Reverend Goodhew liked to call him, . . . well, Bobby always managed to get choked up at the end of each segment when the gang kids dedicated their lives to God and, well, . . . who could resist sending a Love Envelope when even God's favorite ex-con had some tears in his eyes.

Reverend Goodhew, white mane of hair proud atop the long New England Puritan face, sat in his easy chair, his unlit pipe sitting comfortably in his right hand and said, "The entire nation says a prayer that the First Lady isn't involved in this terrible, sordid murder." And he shook his head as if contemplating something horrible.

"I couldn't agree more," said Senator Jack Wagner. An aging foot-ball star, Wagner had the slick charm of a big-time college coach about him. The red-dyed hair was a bit ludicrous but he was big and strap-ping and formidable and when he got going, he sounded like a man rounding up a lynch mob. All in the name of the Lord, you under-stand.

Now, as a way of rubbing Claire Hutton's presumed guilt in the faces of the audience, Goodhew, Wagner, and Knox spent the entire eight-minute segment denouncing the media for jumping to conclu-sions.

Bobby watched all this with cynical glee. If there was a hell, these three would inhabit its lower depths.

"The only reason I brought it up on my show," Knox Stansfield said, "was because I thought it was my civic duty. I knew that the Washington press wouldn't give the matter any attention unless I forced them to."

Senator Wagner nodded. "Thank God for your show, Knox—right, audience?"

The audience didn't need an applause sign for this one. They genu-inely loved Knox Stansfield's show. Every half-truth, every lie, every piece of character-smashing innuendo. . . . It was their kind of show.

And in some ways, you couldn't blame them. The liberal press had lied to them for decades, either by omission or commission, protecting their own, dashing the ones they considered infidels. Barry Goldwater, a bright and decent man, had been treated as a joke and a pariah. And the same was true with all with responsible conservative voices every-where. If you weren't part of the Big Government crowd, then you were a hick, a yahoo or a fascist . . .

And so when somebody finally did come along it was a rabble-rouser because only a rabble-rouser could summon up enough public wrath to threaten the liberal press establishment. Maybe he didn't tell the truth, the whole truth and nothing but the truth, but at least he told part of the truth part of the time, which was more than the liberal press could say sometimes. They weren't devils, these liberal journalists, but they had an agenda just as Knox Stansfield had an agenda . . . and some-times they fudged stories that would make their icons look bad.

And so there had to be an alternative, and now there was . . .

Ladies and gentlemen . . . Knox Stansfield.

Stansfield said: "I feel very bad about all this. I even wonder if I *should* have broken the story on my show. I have my differences with the President—that's well known—but I certainly didn't want to bring down the White House or anything like that."

Yeah, right, Bobby LaFontaine thought as he watched the melo-drama.

Reverend Goodhew said: "Now you see—you see—the press is always calling this man ruthless. But did you hear what our friend Knox just said? Did you hear it, audience?"

This time the applause sign lit up.

The audience members clapped their asses off.

"Did you hear what our friend Knox just did, Senator?"

"I certainly did, Reverend. He extended a Christian hand to the First Lady. He said that whatever happened—even if she should happen to be involved in this tragic murder, even if she did sin and take a lover outside the bonds of her marriage—he said that in the name of the Christian God we all love and revere . . . he said he forgave her."

Another flashing applause sign.

The audience clapped till their hands bled.

"That's the kind of President you'll make, too, isn't it, Senator Wagner? Tough but forgiving. Christian but enlightened. You know, the liberals always try to paint us conservative Christians as people without mercy or charity. But they're wrong. It's just that we do what the Lord taught us to do—to despise the sin but not the sinner."

At some point in this weekly segment, the Reverend always spoke directly to the camera.

Now was the moment.

"I don't like to think of things like this. . . . I don't even like to consider the *possibility* that this kind of thing could be true, . . . but's let's just suppose that the First Lady of the country—the First Lady who is supposed to set an example of purity and Christian dedication to people around the world—let's just suppose that her carnal appetite was such that she fell into the arms of a lover. And that she then became so ashamed and so frightened of what she'd done—knowing that this, if it were ever made public, would destroy her husband's presidency—let's suppose that she then sinned against the Fifth Commandment . . . and took another life."

The camera panned the audience's faces: young, old, prosperous, poor, white, black, yellow. On each face there was a yearning for the kind of bliss that only Reverend Goodhew seemed able to deliver—the bliss of self-righteousness and condemnation, the bliss of casting another soul into the deep and irretrievable fires of hell.

But it was wrong to stereotype all fundamentalists as intolerant rubes—just as it was wrong to stereotype all liberals as naive do-gooders. At least half the audience tonight was made up of people who had real and legitimate fears—the son who was taking drugs, the spouse who had just been diagnosed with cancer, the plant or office that had just been shut down, displacing dozens, perhaps hundreds, of people from their jobs. These people needed solace and comfort and re-assurance. Their only mistake was that they were looking for it in the godless palace of a cynical and sinister TV minister who preached the same intolerance and hatred and wrath that the Bible said would be taught by the Anti-christ . . .

"Shouldn't we pray for the sinner now, . . . if she indeed committed that sin?"

The applause sign.

But this time the clapping was decidedly less.

Who wanted to save the First Lady's soul? She was probably screwing the colored boys and fags she was always championing. She never showed the humility a proper woman should show. She'd spoken up on the right to have an abortion; she'd spoken up on the right to express your own sexual preference; and she'd even spoken up on school prayer, saying that if you wanted to pray silently, fine, but that community prayer in school violated the separation of church and state.

No, they didn't clap very loud for the First Lady at all. And why should they? She was all that was unholy, and in all probability she had murdered the man whom she'd been sleeping with on the side.

"I can hear the Christian love in the sound of your applause," Reverend Goodhew said. "Can't you two men hear it?"

Stansfield and Wagner nodded somberly.

"Christian love! Christian love! If we can just get enough Love Envelopes, folks, we can conquer the entire world—and not with bombs, not with bayonets, not with tanks—but with Christian love! So please remember that, will you, the next time you open your checkbook? Make a place for God in your monthly budget and He'll make a place for you in His. That's how He works. He's got a big debit and credit book up there, and He keeps track of who really loves Him and who only pretends to love Him."

Then the Reverend was on his feet and the organ was booming "Onward Christian Soldiers" and Stansfield and Wagner were on their feet, too, along with the audience.

By the time the fourth chorus had been finished, the Reverend was weeping openly.

Bobby LaFontaine thought he might throw up.

After the show, walking to their respective limos, Senator Jack Wagner said to Knox Stansfield, "That bitch is going to get hers. You wait and see. Murder one. You can bet on that."

All Stansfield could do was sadly shake his head. "She's really a pretty decent woman, deep down. She must've just got caught up in it and couldn't find a way out. She really is a decent woman."

"And you're a decent guy, Knox," the Senator said fondly. "I just wish more people understood that."

Then they were in their respective limos, and driving away.

46

★ ★ ★ "I talked to Gil, honey. He said that everything went fine."

Claire had just come from the shower and was slipping into bed. She was halfway through the new Stephen King novel and hoped to get even deeper into it tonight. She needed one of those great vacations that a long King novel usually gave her.

Matt was doing his push-ups in front of the bureau and talking while he exercised. He could do a hundred of them (and a hundred sit-ups) without breathing hard.

"I had an easy time of it tonight," Claire said, tugging the red silk top of her pajamas down. She'd always preferred sleeping in men's pajamas. "Tomorrow morning will be the hard part."

"Just tell them the truth. The way you did tonight."

"Is that what Gil said I did, tell them the truth?"

Matt paused on push-up 79, staying in place. He looked up at her over the edge of their canopied double bed. "Well, you did tell the police the truth tonight, didn't you?"

"Pretty much."

Matt was suddenly on his feet, walking over to the bed. "What the hell's 'pretty much' supposed to mean?"

"I told them everything except the part about the gun—our gun—being there."

"Oh, Claire, you never should've—"

"—lied. I know. And I regret it, but—"

"Oh, Claire," Matt said again.

She knew enough to leave him alone at times like this. He did not want to talk, be talked to, or be touched in any way.

He walked around to his side of the bed and crawled in. He was working on the new Tom Clancy. He hefted it, propped himself up against the backboard, and started reading.

He read maybe half a page, then said, "Did you tell Gil?"

"That I lied?"

"Right."

"No."

"In the morning, call him and tell him. First thing."

"I was scared."

"I'm aware of that. But lying—"

"I'm sorry I'm not perfect," she said and then propped herself up against the backboard.

"I never said I expected you to be perfect."

"I was scared. Can't I be scared once in a while?"

"Maybe I shouldn't have said anything."

"Maybe you shouldn't."

"I'm not trying to make things rougher for you, darling."

"Well, that's how it feels."

She looked over at him, tenderly touched his arm. "I really was scared."

He leaned over and kissed her. "I know you were. And I know that talking about the gun— Well, it was really incriminating. I might have fudged the truth a little myself."

"I'm innocent."

"I know you are."

"That's why I got so nervous, I guess. I sensed that the Commander— I sensed he didn't necessarily think I was innocent."

"How about the Commissioner?"

"You know him. He'd be nice to Charles Manson if he thought Manson was your friend."

"I'm sure the Commander doesn't think you're guilty."

"You should've seen him watching me—"

"You're being paranoid—"

"You should've seen him, Matt. He really does think I'm guilty."

Matt laughed. "Well, I'll offer him an ambassadorship somewhere exotic. That should change his mind."

She frowned. "This isn't funny, Matt."

He got very serious, then, and she saw that his playfulness had simply been meant to cover his anxiety.

"You goddamned right it isn't funny," he said. "It's terrifying is what it is."

47

★ ★ ★ One thing Deirdre hated about heavy tranquilizers was the hangover they gave her. She was too sensitive to medication for most of it to help her much—there was always a downside to the "cures" the doctors prescribed.

She woke up around ten in the shadows of her bedroom and trying to figure out what she was hearing.

At first, she thought it was the cooing of a pigeon. They'd once had a house that was a virtual pigeon orphanage, and she'd gotten used to the sad bleating sound they often made.

But no . . . this wasn't a pigeon . . .

And then, finally, she recognized it for what it was.

Her mother.

In her bedroom.

Crying.

Her mother's tears did not come in torrents or dramatic spasms. Rather they came in reluctant little bursts, as if she was trying very hard *not* to cry.

Deirdre slipped out of bed without turning on the light, went into the bathroom, put her warm bottom to the cold surface of the toilet seat, peed, washed her hands and then came back and put her ear to the wall.

The crying was faint, now.

In fact, when the winds came up, she could no longer hear it.

Words: male voice. Her father. Comforting.

Something must have happened tonight.

Something to do with the murder case.

An icy rage coursed through her as the image of Knox Stansfield filled her mind: sleek, handsome, ironic.

Bastard.

She lay down again, still somewhat groggy from the tranquilizer, picked up the remote control and turned on the TV.

The Late News was just starting.

Handsome announcer: "Recognize this? It's a religious TV show called *God's Hour*, and tonight, all in the name of praying for First Lady Claire Hutton's soul, three prominent Americans accused Mrs. Hutton of being not only an adulteress but a murderer as well."

Then she saw the three despised men sitting on the set of *God's Hour:* Reverend Goodhew, Senator Wagner and Knox Stansfield.

The station played a long sound bite. It was just as the announcer had characterized it: under the guise of wishing the best for Claire Hutton, they repeated over and over the charges that Stansfield had raised against her on his show.

Deirdre found herself making a gun of her thumb and finger.

She aimed directly at a close-up of Stansfield.

Bam.

Bam.

Bam.

Dead.

And then, as she continued to watch, she knew what she had to do. So obvious. Should have thought of it earlier.

What she'd do to make Knox Stansfield tell the truth.

She knew just where the family gun was kept.

She knew just how to use it, too. Her father had always felt that it was important for Claire and Deirdre to know how to defend themselves.

Then she said, no.

No: doing something like that—

No, impossible.

She could never do it.

But then, as she watched more of the excerpt, and the three men became even more hypocritically unctuous—then she knew that she could do it.

And would do it.

Get the gun and—

The end of Knox Stansfield.

Two and a half years he had been making her family's life hell—day-in, day-out assaults on their integrity, intelligence and morals—and now he obviously meant to destroy them completely.

Put her mother in prison or in an insane asylum.

Force her father to flee from politics.

That's what he thought, anyway.

But he was wrong.

Because tomorrow she would have the gun and—

—tomorrow, she would have the gun.

Henderson looked at the video six times before he allowed himself the luxury of believing that it was real.

Really the First Lady.

Really holding the murder weapon in her hand.

Really standing in plain sight in the dead man's apartment.

So his fine, creepy friend hadn't been playing games after all.

As the videotape was rewinding, Henderson looked through his disorganized Rolodex for the Commissioner's home phone number.

He dialed.

"Hey, idiot," he said when the Commissioner answered.

"Who is this?"

"The best detective you've got on the force is who it is."

"I still don't—"

"Henderson, you jerk. The one you took off the case this morning because I'm so incompetent?"

"Do you realize what time it is?"

"I don't care."

"As of right now, you're on suspension. I'm going to give you the benefit of the doubt and assume you're drunk. If you were sober, I'd fire you on the spot."

"I am sober, Commissioner. But before you fire me, you better listen to what I have to say."

"Not at this time of night and not under these circumstances."

"I want a promotion to commander."

"What?"

"You heard me. After I show you what I've got, I want a promotion to commander."

"What the hell are you talking about?"

"What I'm talking about, ace, is incontrovertible proof that Claire Hutton iced David Hart."

Long pause.

Henderson could hear the Commissioner muttering something to his wife.

"Where are you?"

"My apartment," Henderson said.

"Do you know where I live?"

"Yeah. A place I can't afford."

"This better be serious, Henderson."

"I'm serious about wanting a commandership."

"You ever heard of Civil Service, Henderson? You think I can just make somebody a commander?"

"There're ways."

"We'll talk about that after I see what you've got."

"You have a VCR?"

"Of course." Beat. Henderson's meaning sinking in. "You mean you've got something on tape?"

"Yes."

"God, tell me about it."

"I'd rather show it to you."

"I hope the hell you know what you're doing. This is very danger-ous—"

"Put on some coffee. I'll be there in half an hour."

"I sure hope you're not going to waste my time. Not at this time of night."

"You just have the coffee ready, Commissioner. I'll take care of everything else."

Commander Michael Henderson.

He liked the sound of it.

Hell, he *loved* the sound of it.

And so would Maggie.

Once and for all, she was going to be his again.

He hauled ass over to the Commissioner's place.

The Late News was just finishing up and so was Knox Stansfield.

Motel along the Potomac. Room 284.

Been between the sheets the past hour. He'd come twice already and now it was her turn to experience ecstasy.

He could tell she was about to come because the long muscles in her thighs went rigid.

Her entire body, her entire *being* shuddered in anticipation of how good this was going to be.

Faster.

Now her entire body went rigid and then—

She shook for the next three minutes, a new spasm coursing through her every thirty seconds or so. Almost as a joke, he touched the tip of his finger to her magic button again and she went insane with pleasure that was also virtually pain.

She cried out as if he'd stabbed her.

"Oh, God," Jane Douglas—Claire Hutton's best friend and Knox Stansfield's co-conspirator—cried out again.

"Oh, God, it was wonderful!"

* * *

She kept waking up, Deirdre did, and thinking about tomorrow.
And the gun.
And what she was going to do to Knox Stansfield.
She wished morning would come.
She was eager. Eager.

48

★ ★ ★ Through the windows of the State Dining Room, where the First Lady's press conference was being held, you could smell the white lilies from a nearby garden. This was a lovely soft day for working in the garden, for walking through the park, for taking a kite to a hill and watching it fly like a great bright bird.

It was not a day for sitting rigidly and nervously in a wooden arm-chair while more than two hundred reporters, sixty still cameras, and four network cameras watched you carefully for even the slightest sign of lying. It was one in the afternoon and Claire Hutton wanted to be anywhere in the world but here.

Sitting beneath a portrait of a somber Abraham Lincoln, dressed in a royal blue suit with a white silk scarf at her neck, Claire tried her best to appear relaxed and pleasant.

Q. Mrs. Hutton, it's true that you knew David Hart in college, correct?

A. Yes. He was our friend.

Q. "Our" being—

A. "Our" being my husband and I.

Q. And Knox Stansfield?

A. Yes. And Knox Stansfield.

Next reporter:

Q. Did you ever date Hart when you were in college?

A. No. As I said, we were just friends.

Q. But you apparently kept in contact with him all these years.

A. We lost contact completely. I just met him again six months ago at a gallery opening here in Washington.

Next reporter:

Q. There are reports circulating that you wore a disguise whenever you visited Hart at his town house. Is that true?

A. Yes.

Q. If your visits were as innocent as you've claimed, why did you need to wear a disguise?

A. Because I didn't want anybody to get the wrong idea. You have to be very careful of appearances when you're in the public eye. Looking back, I shouldn't ever have gone to visit David there.

Q. You didn't want people getting what "wrong idea," Mrs. Hutton?

A. That there was anything wrong going on.

Next reporter:

Q. Were you aware that your friend Hart frequently supported himself by squiring around older, very wealthy women?

A. David wasn't a perfect human being. But then none of us are, are we?

(Reporters laugh)

Next reporter:

Q. Why didn't you phone the police when you found Mr. Hart's body lying on his living room floor?

A. Very simple. I got scared and panicked. I'd also been struck very hard on the head. I thought of how much damage all this would do to my husband. *(Pause)* It was a very stupid thing to do. I owe my husband and the American people an apology for how I handled myself in that situation. I like to think I'm stronger than that. Usually, anyway.

Q. A Los Angeles radio station is carrying the story today that you refused to cooperate with the police yesterday.

A. I've heard that and it's not true. I'd invite you to ask the police commissioner how cooperative I was. I spent more than two hours with him.

Q. Was your lawyer with you?

A. Yes, he was.

Q. Doesn't that give the appearance that you're guilty—that you need to have your lawyer with you?

A. Not at all. I'm told that's common practice in criminal investigations.

Next reporter:

Q. Do you consider yourself a suspect in this murder case?

A. I don't because I know I didn't have anything to do with it, but you'd have to ask the police about that, I guess.

Q. Do you think you're receiving any special treatment because you're First Lady?

A. *(Smiles)* On the contrary. I don't think that most people in similar circumstances would have to hold a news conference with two hundred reporters.

(Reporters laugh)

Next reporter:

Q. Do you absolutely deny that you had anything to do with the murder of David Hart?

A. I absolutely deny it.

Q. Are you aware of a CNN–*Time* magazine poll taken last night where 53 percent of the people interviewed said that they suspected you had something to do with the murder?

A. No, I wasn't aware of that.

Next reporter:

Q. Do you own a gun, Mrs. Hutton?

A. No, I don't. Not personally.

Q. Does the President own a gun?

A. Yes, I asked him the other day. He said he does.

Q. You weren't sure?

A. I—hadn't seen it for a long time.

(Claire visibly uncomfortable now)

Q. If you were to be indicted for murder in this case, Mrs Hutton, do you think the President owes it to the American people to step down?

(A rumble of shock at such a bold question. All eyes fixed on Claire now.)

St. Ivy's School For Girls was founded in 1803 by a man named Richard Everson, who may have been the world's first male feminist, not so unlikely a role when you consider that he was the father of eight daughters.

Everson, who had inherited a great deal of money from his father's Virginia plantation, created a school whose first goal was to move young women into the political process. At the ripe age of sixty-three, Everson had concluded that while men and women were basically equal in intelligence, women possessed more common sense. And common sense was in short supply in all political systems, especially the United States'.

Everson failed utterly.

Not for another century, with the rise of the suffragettes and the appearance of his great-great-granddaughter, did St. Ivy's produce a political figure of significance: she was a trial lawyer who later became a district attorney and, in the 1920s, ran for Congress.

The girls who attended St. Ivy's were well aware of its rich and compelling history. The first term paper that Deirdre Hutton had ever written for class here, in fact, dealt with a St. Ivy's graduate who was the first woman to ever get a conviction against a member of the KKK in Louisiana.

At the moment, however, Deirdre was thinking of other things. She was thinking of how she was going to escape from St. Ivy's without her omnipresent Secret Service agents spotting her.

Getting the gun had been a real problem. Her father had checked it the other night—he'd wanted to know if it had been fired—and then hidden it in one of his drawers. The search had taken some time.

It now dwelt safely inside her purse.

Getting out of St. Ivy's, however . . .

"Hi, Mr. Knowles."

"Good afternoon, Deirdre."

Mr. Knowles, one of the history teachers and the lacrosse coach, said, "Shouldn't you be in class?"

Deirdre frowned. "Upset stomach. That's why I'm going to the bathroom."

"Oh, I'm sorry. That darn flu bug going around."

She moved on past him.

Once inside the girls' john, she scanned the bottoms of the stalls. No shoes. The stalls were empty.

Good.

She went quickly to the window, opened it up.

God, what a great day. The first real day of spring.

She wanted to enjoy it but she couldn't.

There was too much to do.

"Oh, no," Deirdre said as she tried to push up the window.

St. Ivy's buildings were old. God knew how many coats of paint had been applied to the windows over the years, and getting them to move up and down on their tracks was no easy feat.

Deirdre decided to pretend she was bench-pressing it, the way she'd once tried to bench-press 150 pounds. Her forearms and shoulders had been sore for a week.

She needed to get beneath this window—

Get her shoulder into it—

The door opened behind her.

"Hi, Deirdre."

Deirdre spun around.

Stacy James.

"Hi, Stace."

"You all right?" Stacy was a plump but pretty girl wearing a white blouse and a blue suede skirt.

"Sure. Why?"

"Your face."

"My face?" Deirdre said. "What about it?"

"It's all sweaty and red."

"Oh."

"Like you were exercising or something."

"No, I'm fine."

"Oh. Good."

Stacy didn't look or sound as if she believed Deirdre. She went in and closed the stall door and made a lot of noise peeing.

Deirdre hung out at the sink, pretending to wash her face.

Stacy joined her in the mirror.

"You hear about Marcia Reynolds?"

"Huh-uh."

"Preggers."

"You're kidding."

"Her parents are taking her somewhere in New Hampshire for an abortion next weekend."

"Why New Hampshire?"

Stacy shrugged. "You know how parents are."

"God. Pregnant." The thought was almost inconceivable to Deirdre. She felt so young—

Then she remembered the gun in her purse.

Well, not *that* young.

Not anymore.

"I better get back to class. You coming?" Stacy said.

"I've got to take a couple of pills. Then I'm coming back."

Stacy gave her a long look. "You sure you're all right?"

"I'm fine."

"You're weird sometimes."

"Well, at least it's only sometimes." Deirdre tried to make a joke of it.

"Yeah," Stacy said, sounding most suspicious and unsatisfied, and then walked out of the john.

Q. If you were to be indicted in this case, Mrs. Hutton, do you think the President owes it to the American people to step down?

A. *(After a pause)* Well, first of all, I don't think I'm going to be indicted because I didn't commit the murder. And secondly, the people elected my husband President, not me. Whatever happens to me shouldn't affect his presidency.

Next reporter:

Mrs. Hutton, we're told that your daughter Deirdre has been under psychiatric care almost continuously since you moved into the White House.

A. She sees a psychotherapist sometimes. But not "continuously." She sees him once in a while.

Q. We hear that she has a particular problem with Knox Stansfield.

A. Living in the White House is very difficult. *(Pause)* It's not easy hearing someone you love torn apart and ridiculed every day.

Q. How is she doing presently?

A. She has her ups and downs. *(Pause)* Deirdre has a very well-developed ethical sense. She believes in honor and integrity and fair play. And you don't always get those things when you're in the White House. We're very honored to be here, believe me—but there are also some very stressful times. *(Smiles)* Like now.

Next reporter:

Q. I'd like to return to the subject of David Hart's personal life, Mrs. Hutton. You said that you knew he wasn't a saint—but did you also know that he took cocaine?

A. No, I didn't know that.

Q. I just wondered if the American people wouldn't find it a little hypocritical—your husband spending so much time trying to put drug dealers behind bars—and then you having a very intimate friend who used drugs himself.

A. He wasn't an "intimate" friend.

Q. Well, you spent a great deal of time alone with him.

A. Not a "great deal." I think your choice of words is misleading.

Q. Well, you spent time alone with him in his town house.

A. *(Smiling)* What you mean to say is that we were unchaperoned. *(General laughter)*

Next reporter:

Q. I'd like to return to the matter of the murder weapon.

A. All right.

Q. You say that the President owns a gun.

A. Yes.

Q. Do you know what kind of gun it is?

A. A .45, I believe. It was his gun when he was in the Army.

Q. Have you ever fired that gun?

A. Yes, I have.

Q. Are you a good shot?

A. I don't know about "good." I'm competent.

Q. As far as you know, where was the gun the night of the murder?

A. I can't say for sure.

Q. But you assume it was where your husband normally keeps it?
A. Yes.
Q. And you assume it wasn't involved in the murder?
A. Yes.

The gun. Always coming back to the gun. And so far, she'd been forced to tell three lies about it.

How many more lies would she have to tell before this was all over?

The next reporter stood up.

"Freeze it."

"Right there?"

"Right there."

The Commander punched the VCR to Pause and then stood back from the monitor so that both the Commissioner and Michael Henderson could see the screen.

Neither Henderson nor the Commissioner had been to sleep. After reviewing the tape over and over again last night, they'd agreed to shower and change clothes at their respective homes, then meet at the Commander's office around eleven A.M.

"I don't know what we're waiting for," Henderson said.

"You don't, huh?" the Commander said. "You think we can just breeze right over to the White House and bust the First Lady like she's some ex-con or something?"

"She's the First Lady," the Commissioner said.

"I know she's the First Lady. But she's also guilty of murder," Henderson said.

He was thinking book deal and movie deal. He wanted to get it all rolling. As yet, he hadn't been able to find Maggie and tell her. But when he did—

"Well, she does have the gun in her hand," the Commander said. "No doubt about that."

"This whole hidden camera thing bothers me," the Commissioner said. "The murder isn't on camera—but the body is."

"There's some evidence that Hart crawled some distance after being shot," Henderson said. "He could have been out of camera range."

The Commissioner said, "Why would Hart have a hidden camera in the first place?"

"He probably used it to shake down some of the old ladies he was balling," Henderson said. "He was a pretty accomplished gigolo. He just went a little high-tech is all."

"I agree with Henderson," the Commander said.

He was about to say more but there was a knock on his door. He made a face, stood up, went to answer it.

He listened to a few words that neither Henderson nor the Commissioner picked up and then he said, "I told you, Webster, handle it for me. I can't baby-sit you all the time."

He slammed the door.

"It's like running a nursery sometimes." he said, dropping back into his chair. "Now, where were we?"

The Commissioner said, "I was hoping that was the D.A. He'll have to call the shot on this one."

But Henderson wouldn't be dissuaded.

"We were talking about arresting the First Lady," Henderson said. "We have the motive—blackmail. We have the opportunity—she admits she was there. And now we have the proof—the videotape."

Then—another knock.

The Commissioner said, "I'll get it" and then walked to the door.

The district attorney was named Richard Alexander. He was black, gray-haired and dapper in the way of the successful trial lawyer he had once been. "I sure hope this is important, Commissioner. I had to cancel lunch with the Mayor."

The Commissioner laughed. "Maybe I did you a favor."

The District Attorney smiled. "Yeah. Maybe you did at that."

"You know the Commander," the Commissioner said. "And this is Homicide Detective Michael Henderson."

The two men shook hands.

"Henderson here is our star cop at the moment," the Commissioner said.

"Oh? Does that mean you're going to tell me now why you were so secretive over the phone?" the District Attorney said.

"I don't trust phones," the Commissioner said. "I think the press taps them."

"Now there's a real paranoid," the District Attorney said.

"Henderson here," the Commissioner said, "has a piece of videotape of the First Lady."

"That's what this is about? The First Lady?" the District Attorney said.

"Right," the Commander said.

"God, I just wish this would all go away," the District Attorney said.

"Wait till you see the videotape," Henderson said.

"Well, let's take a look at it, then," the District Attorney said.

So they showed it to him and all he said was, "Let me see that again." And they ran it back for him and when it was over all he said was, "Let me see that again."

Only after his third viewing did the District Attorney speak at any length. He said: "We'll have to arrest the frigging First Lady of the frigging United States of America for frigging murder one." And then he said, shaking his head as if trying to awaken from a bad dream: "Holy shit. The First Lady of the United States actually iced that sonofabitch."

Q. I'd like to ask you some more questions about the nature of your relationship with David Hart.

A. We were just friends.

Q. So you deny categorically the story on one of the networks this morning that you had actually been seeing him for a much longer time than you've been indicating?

A. I deny that categorically.

Q. You also categorically deny that you were ever lovers?

A. I answered that question a little earlier. The answer is the same. We were never lovers.

Q. In any sense of the word?

A. In any sense of the word.

Next reporter:

Q. Mrs. Hutton, how did the President react when you told him about finding David Hart's body?

A. He was shocked.

Q. He didn't suggest going to the police?

A. By then the police were already involved.

Q. Was that when you called your family attorney?

A. Yes.

Q. Do you think you would have come forward about finding the body if the police hadn't been tipped off about you and Hart?

A. I believe I would have, yes.

Q. You seem hesitant, Mrs. Hutton.

A. *(Very nervously)* Yes, I would have come forward.

Q. You say you would have, Mrs. Hutton—but the fact is that you didn't. Isn't that right, Mrs. Hutton?

A. *(Pause. Quietly:)* Yes, the fact is that I didn't.

"You're kidding," the Mayor said on the other end of the line.

"I wish I was kidding," the Commissioner said.

"She's holding a gun?"

"She's holding a gun."

"And the body's right behind her?"

"The body's right behind her."

"Holy shit."

"That's what I said."

"I'm not even sure we can arrest the First Lady. Constitutionally, I mean."

"I'm pretty sure we can."

"Isn't that like arresting the President?"

"I've got somebody working on that right now but I don't think so."

"This is frigging unbelievable."

"Tell me about it."

"Where did this Henderson get this tape?"

"He says he doesn't know."

"What kind of story is that?"

"I'm only telling you what he told me."

"You think we should charge her?"

"I don't think we have a lot of choice. And it isn't just the tape. There are a lot of other things, too."

"The goddamn First Lady?"

"The goddamn First Lady. If we don't act pretty soon, the press'll be all over us for not doing our job. If we had this much on anybody else, we'd have a charge by now."

"Oh, man, I play golf with the President."

"I know you do."

"Lemme think about it a little while. You get a decision on the constitutionality of it, let me know."

"I will."

"The First Lady," the Mayor said miserably.

"I know," the Commissioner said. "I know."

Sprained her ankle. That was Deirdre's first thought when she dropped from the second-floor bathroom window to the roof of the garage below.

Sprained her ankle.

Pain radiated in hot waves up the calf of her right leg.

From here, she could see the entire northern edge of the campus. This roof covered the various maintenance vehicles that the staff at St. Ivy's used.

She had to crouch down so that nobody would see her. The grounds of St. Ivy spread out before her. She saw the back gates standing open. That was where she needed to go. She could get a cab into the city. She had the gun. . . . She was ready . . .

She put weight on her ankle, preparing herself for blinding pain.

Not so bad.

She took a step.

She had not sprained her ankle. She was sure of it. She'd simply landed wrong on the ball of her foot, turning her ankle slightly in the process.

Another step, another.

Not so bad at all.

She had to move fast, now.

Up here, anybody walking around the campus could easily see her. She needed to drop from the side of this roof on to the dumpster. And then scurry to the gate . . .

Hurry . . .

She walked to the edge of the roof.

Looked down.

In theory it had all seemed so easy, safe.

But the angled lid of the dumpster looked further away than she'd imagined.

She worried about *really* spraining her ankle this time.

Then she thought of Knox Stansfield and she wasn't afraid anymore.

Somebody had to stop him, make him pay for what he'd done.

She closed her eyes even more tightly, and jumped.

A metallic sound as her 103 pounds collided with the lid; windmilling her left arm to stay upright.

Her ankle—

No pain.

She was all right.

No pain at all.

Now she really did have to hurry.

The Secret Service would be searching for her by now. Knocking on the bathroom door— Then sending another girl in to search for her—

Hurry Hurry

Q. Could the President have called the police?

A. He didn't know anything until the police were already involved.

Q. You realize there's been talk among some of the more right-wing people in your party that the President may have obstructed—

A. The President didn't obstruct anything. I'm completely responsible for anything that happened.

Next reporter:

Q. This is a follow-up question about the murder weapon. There's a report circulating that the police lab report says that the gun used was a .45 of the type common in the armed forces. Any comment?

A. No. Except to say that there are probably a lot of .45s like that.

Next reporter:

Q. Mrs. Hutton, you say that your relationship with Mr. Hart was absolutely innocent. But a lot of Americans find it troubling that a First Lady would put herself in those circumstances, even if it was innocent.

A. As I've said already, I made a very foolish mistake.

Q. Do you expect the American people to believe you that your relationship *was* innocent?

A. I hope they do. I'm telling the truth.

Q. Mrs. Hutton, would you be willing to submit to a polygraph test?

While her mother was finishing the last half-hour of her press conference, Deirdre was riding in the back seat of a cab. Her headscarf and dark glasses, a getup she fashioned based on several Audrey Hepburn movies, effectively disguised her identity.

Her ankle was fine now.

Her purse rode on her lap.

Only once had she checked to see that the gun was in there, and was all right.

The gun was fine, ready.

Just as she was fine, ready.

A. I'd be happy to submit to a polygraph test if I thought it was useful.

Next reporter:

Q. Last night on his *God's Hour* show, the Reverend Goodhew said a prayer for you and your husband. Do you think it was sincere?

(General laughter)

A. I hope it was. I seem to be in need of some prayers at the moment.

The cab pulled up in front of the four-story red brick building, the driver waiting patiently while the young woman searched through her purse. He was a skinny guy with an Adam's apple like a busted knuckle and several razor nicks on his pale white face.

"This is where Knox Stansfield broadcasts from," the driver said.

"Uh-huh."

"He cracks me up."

"Uh-huh." Still looking for the cab fare.

"He kicks them liberals in the butt, pardon my French."

"Uh-huh."

"'Bout time somebody did, the way I figure it anyway."

"Uh-huh. Here."

Seven crumpled ones. "Do you mind if I give you your tip in quarters?"

The cabbie laughed. "What'd you do, rob your piggy bank?"

Actually, that's just what she had done.

"Eight quarters."

"Eight quarters is fine by me, Miss. It all spends the same way, as they say."

"Here you go. And thank you."

"Thank you, Miss."

She got out of the cab and walked up to the red brick building and went inside.

Q. Mrs. Hutton, do you know if the police plan to talk to you again?

A. I'm not sure.

Q. Do you know if they're interviewing other people?

A. I'm sure they are.

Next reporter:

Q. Mrs. Hutton, there are stories circulating that you and the President and Mr. Hart were all part of a sex ring of some kind. Would you care to comment on that?

A. Aren't you embarrassed to ask a question like that?

(General laughter; even a little applause)

"Hey! Where're you going?"

The security guard had been getting a drink of water, bending his considerable girth over the fountain when he'd heard—

steps behind him—

and he looked up to see—

some young girl in a headscarf and dark shades—

tiptoeing past him down the empty corridor leading to the broadcast booth.

Then she'd started running.

Now he was chasing her.

And calling for her to stop.

But obviously she wasn't *going* to stop.

Who the hell was she and what the hell was she doing here?

She reached the broadcast booth well before he did and grabbed the doorknob and flung the door back with her left hand.

And that was when he noticed—

in her right hand—

the gun.

She had a frigging gun.

And she was headed into the broadcast booth where Knox was and that meant—

The guard didn't want to *think* about what that meant.

He was all instincts now, yanking his own weapon free of its holster.

Filling his hand with it.

Jerking his walkie-talkie free and shouting a mayday to anybody who happened to be tuned-in.

Little bitch was already in the broadcast booth now—

With Knox—

The guard ran and ran but it seemed to take forever to reach the door.

And look inside.

And wait for the gunshot—

The booming roaring gunshot . . .

Q. Mrs. Hutton, do you realize that the American people will never be able to see you quite the same way again . . . after this episode.

A. I realize that I've certainly disappointed a lot of people, including myself but I—

McElroy walked right up in front of the press, right up to where Claire sat, talking to the reporters.

He stopped, turned to the journalists and said, "I'm afraid we'll have to call this press conference to an end. Something has come up that the First Lady needs to take care of right away."

Claire was as mystified by all this as the reporters were. What did she need to take care of? And why so abrupt an end to the press conference? She found herself resenting McElroy's somewhat melodramatic manner. She thought she'd been doing reasonably well fielding the questions, but now—

McElroy came over.

"What's going on, Chad?" she said.

"I know you're mad about me interrupting," he said, already taking her arm and steering her out of the room. "But it's Deirdre."

"Deirdre! What about her?" Alarm seized; something had happened to Deirdre—

"She's in Knox Stansfield's broadcast booth. She has a gun on him and she's threatening to kill him if he doesn't tell the truth about you and Matt. C'mon, Claire, we've got to hurry!"

49

★ ★ ★ "I just want you to tell the truth."

"Deirdre, I think we need to calm down a little bit." Beat. "I'm not your enemy, Deirdre. I'm really not."

"You tell lies about my mom and dad."

"I just do my job, Deirdre. That's all. I never intentionally hurt anybody."

"You liar! You hurt people all the time and you take pleasure from it!"

Pause. The broadcast booth quiet now. A can of Diet Pepsi sitting next to Stansfield's elbow. A stack of tapes waiting to be erased by the wide flat degausser that stood next to them. And the microphone jutting from the console: the instrument of all his power.

"Deirdre. I want to say something to you."

"I just want you to tell people the truth."

"Deirdre, listen to me a minute. Please."

Silence.

"Deirdre, I don't think you'd shoot me on purpose but I'm afraid the gun may accidentally go off and— Would you please put the gun down? You're waving it around and—"

"Then you tell the truth. Now."

Claire heard all this on the way over to the studio. McElroy sat beside her in the back seat of the limousine. He had decided it would be better if the President didn't go over, if he stayed at the White House.

All Claire could think of was Deirdre.

She listened to her daughter on the radio and wondered how many millions and millions of other Americans were also listening. The news-vampires now had two great stories—the First Lady's implication in a murder and Deirdre Hutton's hijacking of the Knox Stansfield radio show.

All she wanted to do now was hold her daughter, comfort her. She'd had no idea that Deirdre had been driven this far by Stansfield's constant battering.

"We have to hurry," Claire said to the driver.

"In case you've just tuned in, this is Knox Stansfield coming to you live from the studios in Washington, D.C. President Hutton's daughter Deirdre is presently holding a gun and waving it around and demanding that I 'tell the American people the truth.'

"This is a very serious situation for everybody. I sincerely believe that my life is in danger, and I don't mind telling you that I'm afraid."

"Now I want you to tell them the truth."

"The truth about what, Deirdre?"

"The truth about my mother for one thing. She didn't have anything to do with David Hart's murder and you know it."

"Deirdre, I never said that your mother was implicated in that murder."

"You never said it but you implied it. That's how you work. You insinuate things so you don't have to prove them. Now tell the truth."

Claire was opening the limousine door even before the massive black vehicle had stopped completely.

A large crowd encircled the red brick building and frustrated police officers tried to keep the crowd from crushing them.

Two police officers steered Claire and McElroy through the people and into the building.

Some of the crowd cheered when they saw the First Lady; others booed.

Claire scarcely noticed. Deirdre was her only thought.

"Deirdre?"

"What?"

"Would you please put the gun down?"

"No." Then she smiled. "You're always saying that Americans have the right to bear arms. Well, I'm bearing my arms."

"That isn't what I mean when I say that."

"You think it's all right for people to carry around automatic weapons, so what's wrong with carrying around a little handgun?"

"You're distorting what I say, Deirdre."

"You distort things all the time!"

And that was when she struck him on the side of the jaw with the butt of the .45.

Struck him so hard that his head snapped back and a fissure of blood opened up on his jaw line.

Now he knew that he should be scared. That this wasn't just something he could milk for the biggest audience he'd ever had—maybe the biggest audience anybody had ever had.

Now he realized that Deirdre Hutton was insane and might very well kill him this afternoon.

They led Claire through a maze of hallways, deeper and deeper into the building.

Police officers were everywhere.

Terrified employees stood about in clusters.

McElroy kept a tight hand on her elbow, guiding her, supporting her, which she appreciated.

"You tell the people that my mother is innocent."

"I never said she wasn't Deirdre. I honestly didn't."

"You said she was being investigated."

"A lot of people are investigated without being guilty, Deirdre."

"You tell them."

"Deirdre—"

"Tell them!"

Beat.

He was sweating badly now, shaking.

He looked up and on the other side of the booth window saw the engineering staff and several cops watching them.

It seemed so ludicrous, all those people within feet of him, and none could help him.

All they could do was stand there and wait to see what the insane teenage girl with the gun was going to do next.

Then Deirdre put the gun directly to his temple.

"Tell them the truth."

"Deirdre—"

"Now!"

The sweat had turned icy now; the trembling working its way up from his fingers to his shoulders.

Swallowing was starting to get difficult. No saliva.

"Now," she said, jamming the gun harder against his head.

He didn't even notice the pain. He was beyond pain now. He vaguely sensed that he might foul himself.

Everything was starting to have the gauzy unreality of a nightmare.

The young girl. The gun.

"The truth, you bastard," she said.

And somehow, he found the words: "Deirdre wants me to tell you what she believes is the truth. Well, I'll tell you the truth. I don't know anything about the murder of David Hart—and I never said I did. Can't you understand that Deirdre? I never said I did!"

"You liar!" Deirdre said again.

Two things happened very quickly: the door to the broadcast booth eased open, and there stood Claire. And Deirdre brought the gun down against Knox Stansfield's head for a second time. This time, he let out a fierce cry of pain.

"Deirdre, honey, please let me help you."

Deirdre looked over at her mother but she didn't quite seem to recognize her, somehow. Then she said, "Mother, what're you doing here?"

"I want to help you, honey."

"He tells lies about you, Mother, and you know it."

"Deirdre, this won't solve anything. It really won't." Beat. "I'd like you to give me the gun, Deirdre."

All Knox Stansfield could do was sit in his chair and stare up at the two of them, a trickle of blood working down the side of his head from Deirdre's latest blow.

Then Deirdre slipped back into rage.

She grabbed Stansfield by the hair and slammed the gun into the side of his head once more.

"I want him to admit he was lying. I want him to admit that he hates you and Daddy! I want him to tell the truth for once. And if he doesn't—"

Claire took two steps into the broadcast booth.

"Deirdre—"

But Deirdre's gaze was fixed upon Stansfield. She seemed to see nothing else, feel nothing else.

She gritted her teeth, her face becoming a mask that made her almost unrecognizable to Claire.

"I just want him to tell the truth."

And she started to squeeze the trigger.

"Tell them you're a liar!"

She squeezed the trigger harder, harder.

"Tell them you're a—"

Now it was Stansfield's face that was a mask, covered with sleek sweat, lower lip trembling, eyes beseeching Claire to help him in some way.

"I just want to hear him say he's a liar!" Deirdre said.

Taking the trigger back, back—

And then Claire sprang.

In one motion, she grabbed Deirdre's arm, pushing the gun away from Stansfield, and at the same time, she pulled Deirdre to her and held her.

And Deirdre immediately began to sob.

"He isn't telling the truth, Mother; he isn't telling the truth."

All Claire could do was hold her. Hold her.

50

✳ ✳ ✳ Across town, the Police Commissioner said to the Mayor—maybe the only two people in the city not tuned to the Knox Stansfield show—"We don't have any choice, Mayor. Not with that videotape of her holding that gun in her hand."

"We're really going to charge the First Lady with murder?"

The Police Commissioner nodded somberly. "We're really going to charge the First Lady with murder."

III

****

"LOOK AROUND YOU. MAKE CERTAIN THAT YOUR
FRIENDS AND ACQUAINTANCES ARE *REAL* AMERICANS."

—RADIO HOST RICHARD BAXTER
LAUDING SENATOR JOSEPH MCCARTHY, 1954

51

★ ★ ★ Knox Stansfield, in his Jacuzzi, watched Tom Brokaw somberly say: ". . . relatively quiet day in the nation's capital following three of the most turbulent days in the nation's history. The President's teenage daughter, Deirdre, now in a mental hospital after holding radio personality Knox Stansfield hostage; rumors that the First Lady will be charged with the murder of her friend David Hart; and leaders in both houses wondering in increasingly loud voices if the President should step aside and let Vice President Sharon McCurdy take over—if the First Lady finds herself under formal murder charges. The only thing this crisis can be likened to is Watergate, when the entire United States government seemed on the verge of collapse."

Stansfield's mind started to drift as the anchor went into the day's other events. The comparison to Watergate was certainly apt. Virtually everybody in America was fixated on the First Lady Mystery, as one of the tabloids put it. This morning's *New York Post* showed a crazed-looking Claire Hutton (where did they find these pictures anyway) scowling out at readers, the headline blaring: DID SHE OR DIDN'T SHE?

As for Stansfield himself, his radio network had been able to demonstrate to advertisers that since Deirdre Hutton had broken into the studio, the Stansfield ratings had quadrupled—and were staying there, too. Deirdre had scared him, no doubt about that. But she'd also given him an advertising bonanza. Now, some of the blue-chip companies that had not wanted to be associated with him previously— General Motors,

Procter and Gamble, General Mills—now their agencies were all trying frantically to get on the show.

Amazing what a little hostage-crisis could do for your ratings.

He leaned his head back, enjoying the warm bubbling sensation of the water; closed his eyes.

He could pretty much relax, now. The police would take everything from here. The District Attorney certainly had everything he needed, including a videotape of the First Lady holding the murder weapon at the scene of the crime. Even the most sympathetic jury was bound to convict her.

Only one problem remained.

Without opening his eyes, Stansfield reached out and patted the tiles next to the Jacuzzi. A plain number ten envelope sat there, waiting.

Then he heard Clemmons walking from the other part of the house toward the pool area. He always went out the back way.

Stansfield sat up straight, snatching his glass of white wine as he did so. Wanted to look relaxed when he spoke to Clemmons. Looking relaxed was very important.

Clemmons came down the three steps into the pool area. As usual, his dark suit made him look even thinner and taller and more somber.

He carried his lunch each day in a brown bag that he used over and over until it was absolutely necessary to replace it. Clemmons's frugality had always amused Stansfield, and saddened him, too. Did Clemmons think he was actually going to become fiscally comfortable by using the same lunch bag over and over? There was something pathetic about it.

"Good night," Clemmons said, heading straight for the back door.

"Come over here a minute."

Clemmons allowed himself a rather obvious frown. There had been a lot of those lately, the obvious kind. Ever since—

Stansfield knew now that he'd made one miscalculation. His idea of using Clemmons as an alibi had been a bad one. In theory it had sounded so good. Have his own chauffeur testify that his boss had simply run up to Hart's town house for five minutes. Who could commit murder in five minutes? Perfect alibi.

Perfect.

Except Stansfield hadn't taken Clemmons's suspicious nature into account. Clemmons probably couldn't prove anything, but it was clear he sensed he'd been duped in some way.

Now Stansfield had to take care of that, win Clemmons over to his side.

"You've done your usual good job today, and I appreciate it," Stansfield said.

"Thank you, sir."

"You've been looking a little tired lately, though. Have you been feeling all right?"

"Feeling fine, sir."

Stansfield shook his head. "I know we don't always get along, Clemmons—we're both very strong-willed men—but I think we work well together."

"Yes, sir."

"That's one of the reasons I didn't press charges against your nephew."

"I appreciate that."

"I didn't want to see him go to prison—and that's exactly where he would have gone, you know, at his age."

"Yes, sir."

Stansfield gave Clemmons a big TV smile. "Oh, hell, I've never been very good at keeping a secret."

He reached over, picked up the envelope and held it up to Clemmons. "Here. Take it."

"What is it, sir?"

"I'd rather have you find out for yourself."

Clemmons stood up straight, opened the envelope carefully, then peered inside. "I don't understand, sir."

"It's yours."

"Mine? But why?"

"Call it a bonus."

"But $10,000—"

"And don't forget the airline tickets."

"London, but—"

"I want you to take some time off. Three weeks, in fact."

"But there's so much to do here—"

"Hey, I'm the boss, remember. And I'm ordering you to go to London for three weeks and enjoy yourself."

"But $10,000—"

"A bonus. Like I said."

Stansfield could see Clemmons weakening, and he felt enormous relief. The night before last, the night the First Lady had been formally charged with murder, Clemmons had come up to the Jacuzzi and said, "I don't appreciate the way you used me as an alibi. I don't think Claire Hutton killed him. I think you did." And Stansfield, who'd been pretty drunk at the time, had made the mistake of saying sarcastically: "Maybe I did do it, Clemmons. But you can't prove it and no jury in the world is going to convict me."

Now Stansfield said, "I want you to know something, Clemmons."

"Yes, sir?"

"About the other night— Well, you seem to think I had something to do with David Hart's murder. I didn't. I honestly didn't."

"Yes, sir."

"I just want you to know that. Since we're friends and all."

"Yes, sir."

"We are friends, aren't we, Clemmons?"

"Yes, sir."

But he was so hard to read. They said Orientals were inscrutable. Try uppity black chauffeurs some time.

"So you'll make plans for London?"

"All right. I appreciate it."

"And don't worry about things here. I'll take care of them."

"Thank you, sir."

"And tell that nephew of yours I said hello and no hard feelings, all right?"

"All right, sir." He waved the tickets in Stansfield's direction. "Thank you again, sir."

Outside, as he was climbing into his rattletrap of a sedan, Clemmons thought: now I know for sure the bastard killed Hart. I knew it the other night when he said I couldn't prove it. But now he's proved it for me. He just gave me a $10,000 bribe.

Clemmons drove off.

52

★ ★ ★ Claire never would have found the florist's bill if she hadn't accidentally knocked some papers off Jane's desk.

Late afternoon. Jane gone. Her phone buzzing constantly.

Claire decided to pick up, tell whomever that Jane would be back in the morning.

She'd leaned over Claire's desk, knocking a cluster of papers to the floor.

"That's right," Claire told the woman caller. "She'll be in around nine in the morning. Is there a message? All right, then. Around nine A.M."

She bent over to pick up the papers and saw that they were some of Jane's personal bills. She often wrote out checks over her lunch hour.

The top bill was from Metropolitan Florist in the amount of $82.63.

But the name near the bottom of the bill was what attracted her eye: Card enclosed with dozen roses reading:

> To Knox on his birthday.
> All my love,
> Jane

Knox.
Knox Stansfield.

Claire was overcome by a moment of anxiety that forced her down into Jane's chair.

Jane and Knox Stansfield.

Of course.

All along Claire had been wondering how somebody could have sneaked the murder weapon and her shoe from their living quarters.

Jane had access.

Often ate lunch up there.

Sometimes went to visit Deirdre.

Could easily have wandered around secretly and—

Oh. My. God.

Jane.

Her very best friend.

The screaming startled Claire.

She was just leaning over to kiss Deirdre goodnight, when somewhere down the hall a woman began shrieking.

Matt clutched Claire's arm. "It's all right. I'm sure everything is under control."

Claire still did not feel comfortable committing Deirdre to a mental hospital, but Matt and the doctors had urged her to.

St. Mallory's looked more like a small college than an asylum, four stone buildings camouflaged from the road by pine trees. Only the electrified iron fence and the bars on all the windows revealed the real nature of the place.

Claire visited twice a day. Thank God, the Judge had released Claire on Matt's recognizance.

Deirdre's room was dark except for the silver moonlight that cast everything into deep shadow. Two Secret Service agents stood at the door.

Deirdre had received her sedative for the evening and was already asleep.

Claire finished leaning over now and kissed her tenderly on the forehead. "Good night, honey. We'll see you tomorrow."

Claire had to fight the hot tears that filled her eyes. Everything had changed so abruptly. The Hutton family no longer *lived* in the White House; they hid out in it.

"I know she's involved in this somehow. God, Matt, she sent him flowers," She paused. "She's involved in it—with Knox."

They were in the limo, headed back to the White House. All around them, Washington sparkled in the great rolling night. She'd brought the subject up at dinner—about finding the florist bill and all—but Matt had been skeptical and still was.

"But your best friend. I just can't believe—"

"Matt, I know you think I'm being paranoid . . . but think about it a minute. Why else would she send him flowers—if she wasn't involved with him?"

"Maybe she did it to be nice to him. So he'd lay off you and me."

"Then she'd tell me about it if she had."

"Maybe not."

"Take my word for it. Jane tells me everything." Then she caught herself. "Except about her relationship with Knox, apparently." She stared out the window fighting the rage that overcame her every twenty minutes now. "God, I feel so betrayed."

"Be sure of what you're saying before you confront her." Matt was bundled up in a dark topcoat. His face showed the stress of the past few days, heavy dark rings beneath his eyes, an occasional twitch of his lips. Passing lights played strobically on his handsome face. He looked ten years older than he usually did.

"I'm going to follow her tonight."

"Oh, Claire, come on. You're not a detective."

"No, but I can follow Jane around without her knowing it. And I can't tell the police about her. They'll think I'm just making it up about her and Knox. The police already believe I did it and they're not going to change their minds. I'll have to change their minds for them." She took his hand. "Honey, we don't know who else is in on this. We know about Knox and Jane but—there could be others, you know."

For the first time, he seemed to see her logic.

"What about the Secret Service? They'll never let you go off like that. They'll be terrified that somebody will kidnap you."

She turned on the plump, plush limo seat and smiled at him. "Or they'll be afraid that I'll take off so I won't have to face standing trial. I'm sure they think I'm guilty, too—like seventy percent of America does."

"The poll today said only sixty-four percent did."

She smiled. "Now that's encouraging news."

"I don't want you to go, Claire. It could be dangerous. We don't know for sure what Knox is capable of doing."

She leaned over to him, holding his arm tight, kissing him on the strong line of his jaw. "Our whole world is collapsing around us, Matt. Somebody wants to destroy us. But I'm going to fight back, Matt. We owe it to ourselves—and to our daughter. Knox thinks he's won. But he hasn't. You can't leave the White House, but I can. And you have to let me do it, Matt."

There wasn't much of an argument he could mount against a woman as determined as Claire was.

He sighed, and nodded his silent assent.

*　*　*

Matt spent twenty minutes with the chief of the Secret Service, Richard Boyer.

At two different points Boyer threatened to go to the news media. He said he did not want to be responsible for the First Lady traveling around Washington, D.C., incognito.

But Matt ultimately won out by calling in an old debt. He'd stopped a drunk-driving charge from being pressed against Boyer, and helped get the man into an Alcoholics Anonymous group. Boyer had been dry for the past fourteen months.

So, just a few minutes after nine, Matt took the elevator up to the second-floor White House apartment and told Claire that she was free to go.

53

★ ★ ★ "Maybe I did do it, Clemmons. But you can't prove it and no jury in the world would convict me."

Rewind.

"Maybe I did do it, Clemmons. But you can't prove it and no jury in the world would convict me."

Rewind.

"Maybe I did do it, Clemmons. But you can't prove it and no jury in the world would convict me."

Bobby LaFontaine sat in front of his recording equipment, playing the same two sentences over and over. The untrained ear might think that Bobby was hearing a drunken Knox Stansfield obliquely boast about killing David Hart. Incorrect. What Bobby was really hearing was the sound of money. Lovely, lovely money. And lots of it.

Bobby had possessed the tape for two days and he still kept smiling about his luck. The whole deal had been to nail Stansfield for diddling Jenny, virgin daughter of Reverend Goodhew. Well, Bobby hadn't been able to do that—but he had been able to get Stansfield on a far more serious charge: murder.

Bobby had already decided to leave his ministerial calling. The whole thing had gotten a little boring. And there was definitely a glass ceiling in the organization. An ex-con could only get so far. There'd always be a Knox Stansfield there to keep you from getting on the board of directors.

Bobby had made a list the other day of who would pay the most for the tape:

Knox Stansfield
Reverend Goodhew
The Patriot's Network
Claire Hutton

Stansfield was the obvious choice but even given all his success, he had only so much money.

Reverend Goodhew had a lot of money and just might part with a good deal of it in order to have his hand on Knox Stansfield's throat. Knox could be a very willing servant and the good Reverend *was* a control freak.

The Patriot's Network. Knox represented more than half their annual gross income. If he went, he'd take them along with him.

There were certain problems with the first three, however. They were all ruthless. Every one of them would try to have him killed. It wouldn't be the money so much. It would just be the notion that some guy out there had something big time on them. Even if they had the tape, he'd be a threat to them.

Their inclination would be to ice him. Fast. And they knew the people to do it.

Over the past twenty-four hours, his focus had shifted to Claire Hutton. The police and the press had all but convicted her. She was desperate to clear her name. She had access to the two million he was asking. And she wouldn't try to have him killed.

The phone rang.

Bobby LaFontaine got up and crossed the big empty room he used for all his technical equipment and picked up.

"Uh-huh?"

"I've got something for you."

"This ain't what I need right now, babe."

"You sound all tensed up, lover."

"I am all tensed up,"

"About?"

"About nothing' I'm gonna tell you about."

Much as two million dollars sounded nice and easy, Bobby didn't kid himself. That kind of money was the big big leagues. And in the big leagues there was no margin for error. Bobby screwed up, Bobby could end up in prison for life, or dead. He had to be very, very careful.

"Why don't you come over and lemme relax you again?"

"I told ya. I'm busy."

It was funny about Sammi Lee. Sometimes that overlush body and that sweet smart mouth of hers were all he could think about. Other times, the very idea of her made him sick to his stomach. He'd never had a woman affect him like this and he couldn't understand it.

When he got the money, when it was nice and safe in a suitcase he'd be taking to Europe by boat, would he take her along?

Nah. No way.

"I got to go."

"You worry me, lover."

"Just lay off."

"You need takin' care of."

And then it struck him: maybe she was right.

Maybe he *did* need taking care of.

Maybe he was wound so tight he couldn't make a sound decision about who to bring the tape to.

"I couldn't stay all night."

"Oh, lover, I don't care if you stay just a couple of minutes. I got just one song I wanna play ya—"

"—no song—"

"—Reba McEntire—"

"—no song—"

"—and then I'm gonna kiss you like you ain't never been kissed before."

"No song," Bobby said.

"I think Reba's a poet," Sammi Lee said forty-one minutes later. "Don't you?"

Then she said, "You notice anything different tonight?"

"Huh-uh."

"Oh, c'mon, lover, open your eyes."

He looked around the room.

"Is that a new lamp?"

"No."

"Is that a new painting?"

"Elvis or Jesus?"

"Elvis."

"Nope."

"Is Jesus a new painting?"

"Nope."

"Aw, you know I hate stuff like this."

"C'mon, one more guess."

And then she spread her arms out wide and started laughing and turning around and around in circles.

What she did, see, was buy these transparent teddy nighties two sizes too small, so she was just bursting out of them. When she took them off, the lines from the material were as red and deep as rope burns.

You could see her nipples clearly and her pubic thatch clearly and sometimes her lips would get caught up in the material and you could see those clearly, too.

"C'mon, you mean to tell me you don't notice nothin' different about me?"

"Well—"

"That diet I tole you I was goin' on—"

"Well—"

"Well, feast your eyes, lover boy, because I've been doin' real good and I already lost a whole bunch of weight."

"You have?"

"Well, see for yourself."

"Well, I guess you have. Now can we talk about something else?"

"I lost three-quarters of a pound and in less than a week. For the first week that's a whole bunch."

"Yeah, I guess—" But his mind was drifting.

Who should he take the tapes to?

The big leagues. He had to be careful. Very careful.

And then Sammi Lee squealed and he thought somebody invisible had stabbed her or something.

"What's wrong?"

"That song!"

A new Reba had started.

Exactly what kind of name *was* Reba anyway.

"Oh," he said.

"She wrote this one herself and you just know it was sincere. From the heart, I mean."

"Uh-huh."

Then she was spinning around again and saying, "So don't you notice a lot of difference on my hips, lover?"

Bobby LaFontaine made his decision a little later that evening.

He was in Sammi Lee's bed and painting her toes the way she sometimes asked him to and he decided maybe this was some kind of sign.

Her toes.

Eenie-meenie-mini-mo.

That's how he was going to decide.

He'd play the game on her toes and whoever won, that's who he'd contact about the tapes.

He played the game sixteen times till it finally came out the way he wanted it to: he'd call the First Lady and offer her the tape.

54

★ ★ ★ Television had given Claire the notion that tailing somebody consisted of driving around a lot. What television didn't reveal was that tailing people also meant a lot of sitting.

Jane had been in the White Flint shopping mall for over an hour now. One hundred fifteen stores to choose from and Jane was apparently hitting each of them.

The only thing Claire had going for her was that the place was going to close up for the day in ten more minutes.

The waiting on the other end had been brief. Claire, in her wig and headscarf disguise, had wheeled over to Jane's place, parked, and then watched, a few minutes later, as the beautiful woman made her way down the front steps of her apartment house. The limp always slowed her down.

Then to the shopping mall.

And waiting.

"So who do you think would play me, in the movie, I mean?"

"Well, I think we're getting just a little ahead of ourselves here, Detective Henderson."

"I'm just kind of curious is all."

"Well—"

"You know who I could see?"

"Who?"

"Costner. Kevin Costner."

"Well—"

"Or maybe Alec Baldwin. People always say I look a little like him."

"Well, you see, there's one problem with those two, Michael—if I may call you Michael."

"Sure. I mean, please do."

"The problem is that they're not clients of ours and what we'd like to do is package the whole thing."

"'Package'?"

She nodded her gorgeous head.

They certainly had sent a seductress, the Raymond Sloane Agency, the biggest talent agency in North America.

True to Michael Henderson's fantasy, several agencies had called him the day the media had identified him as the man who'd discovered the videotape showing the First Lady and the murder weapon.

There had been so many calls to the station from talent vultures, in fact, that the Commander had gotten really pissed and told Henderson that they'd be screening his calls from now on, and not taking any that weren't strictly business.

So Henderson had had to make a decision quick. He called the *Washington Post* entertainment editor and ran through some of the agency names and that's how he'd found out that he should go with Raymond Sloane.

To hedge their bets, the agency had sent out this gorgeous lady in a $1,500 Armani suit and enough sex appeal to melt steel. She'd taken him to Dominque's downtown, bought him the best meal, told him all the best gossip about Hollywood, and now was getting down to business.

He had almost asked Maggie to come along but then decided, no, he'd save all this for a big surprise. Save it for when the deal was done. Then he'd tell her about his plans for getting them the honeymoon suite at the Canterbury Hotel—right before they flew off to the South Pacific for two weeks. And started their marriage all over again.

"'Package' just means that we draw all the principle players from our own agency roster."

"I see."

"You know, the star, the director, the writer. Maybe a couple of other actors."

"I see."

She laughed. "Don't look so glum, Michael. We have some of the biggest names in the business."

"Oh, like who?"

So she told him like who.

Meanwhile, out at the White Flint mall, Claire was just turning on her engine.

Just as the mall lights started going off, casting much of the vast exterior into darkness, Jane appeared, carrying a single tiny package.

An hour for a package that small.

Claire got kind of excited when she saw Jane get in her car and turn on the lights.

Claire touched her Nikon with the telephoto lens. As if for luck.

There was going to be some action again. Finally.

Claire felt that she was just about to learn something really useful. She knew it. She could feel it.

She started following Jane.

Henderson whistled. "Wow. You really do have some impressive clients."

"That's why packaging this won't be hard at all."

"So what do we do first?"

She smiled with dazzling teeth and started to speak, but he interrupted her.

"Can I ask you a question?"

"That's why I'm here, Michael."

Their waiter appeared. She smiled at him, shook her head, and he went away.

"You must've been an actress at one time?"

"Model, yes. Actress, no." She laughed. "If you saw the commercials I was in—the ones where I had to read lines?—you'd know what I'm saying. I was godawful."

"But you're so beautiful."

"Thank you. But there are fifty thousand of me in Hollywood, with five thousand more coming along every year."

"Wow."

"Wow is right. But wow doesn't make the car payments or pay the rent. So I went into the agency side of things and I'm having a great time."

"Well, great. 'Cause I'm having a wonderful time, too."

This was the first indication he had that he was getting bombed. Had to slow things down, way down. Had to be sharp.

He made eye contact with the waiter. The man was by his side in moments.

"I'd like a cup of coffee, please."

"Coffee. Of course. Regular or decaffeinated?"

"Regular."

"Thank you, sir."

"Thank you," Henderson said. And then, knowing he was being vulgar and not caring, he said: "So how much money are we talking about on a deal like this, anyway?"

That killer smile of hers again. "I thought you might get around to asking me that at some point."

This time it wasn't a shopping mall, it was a doughnut shop. In the gloom of the misty night, the place looked like the only human outpost in all of Washington.

Jane sat at the counter, daintily eating what appeared to be a cinnamon roll.

There were two men at the other end of the counter and they were transfixed by Jane, as what man wouldn't be when somebody so gorgeous just happens to drop into a workingman's doughnut shop?

Claire drummed her fingers on the steering wheel, picked up, set down, picked up, set down, picked up, set down her Nikon, and then thought of something else television didn't tell you about.

What happened when the person doing the tailing had to go to the bathroom?

"Could it be as much as a million?"
"Possibly."
"Possibly two million?"
"Possibly."
"God. Possibly three million?"
"Now that's starting to get unlikely."
"Three million is unlikely?"
"Three million is very unlikely."
"But two million."
"Two million is doable."
"And likely?"
"A million five, a million seven is probably more likely. But two is definitely doable. I mean, never say never."
"And this would be for—"
"For book rights, film and TV rights, audio rights, foreign rights. Though we'd want to negotiate a really good foreign deal because this is something the Brits and the Germans and the Italians would love."
"Are those big markets?"
"Huge. If you've got the right property."
"God. It's just incredible."
"Well, Michael, you've got an incredible story to tell. So why shouldn't you get an incredible sum of money to tell it? Did I tell you the deal we negotiated for Hillary Clinton's maid?"
"God? Hillary Clinton's maid? Really? How much?"
So she told him how much.

* * *

After leaving the doughnut shop, Jane sat in her car, making a call on her cellular phone.

Claire wondered who she was calling.

Claire was feeling a little better physically. She'd walked into the nearby alley ten minutes ago and relieved herself between two garages. Then she'd washed her hands on the mist-covered grass.

Now she was ready to go again.

Jane was still on the phone.

Even from across the street, Claire could see the stress lines in Jane's face.

Arguing. With somebody.

Maybe Knox. Probably Knox.

Then Jane hung up very quickly, snapped on her headlights, and took off.

Claire stayed half a block behind her.

"Would you excuse me a minute?" Henderson said.

"Of course."

"I just need to call my wife. Tell her about this."

"That's cute. Calling your wife. And sweet. Why aren't there any sweet guys like you in Hollywood?"

"Have you ever been married?"

"Five times."

"Oh."

"And not one of them was sweet. Not really sweet, anyway."

He found the pay phone, deposited the proper number of coins, and then dialed his own number.

After Maggie's voice was done telling everybody they were sorry they couldn't come to the phone right now and would the caller please wait for the beep, Henderson said: "Honey. It's very important that we sit down and have a talk. Something really incredible has happened. And it's going to turn our marriage around. It really is, honey. I can feel it. It really is. So sometime tomorrow when we're both sober and we've both had plenty of sleep—we really need to sit down and talk. You'll be asleep when I get home but I just wanted you to hear this message. Sweetheart, this is what I've been praying for. It's going to be better than it's ever been for us. It really is."

Not until he hung up did he realize that he was crying.

Now they were getting somewhere.

Twenty-seven minutes after leaving the doughnut shop, Jane pulled her shiny new car into the parking lot of a motel that overlooked the Potomac.

Now, Claire thought, they were definitely getting somewhere.

55

★ ★ ★ As she approached the motel, Jane started thinking about the eleventh-grade dance again, a subject that was always dangerous to contemplate.

The limp. That was the problem. Oh, she could dance well enough, but she looked funny doing it. Step one-two-three; one-two—it was on that second step that her entire body compensated for her limp and came down tugging to the right. Not exactly the step of a ballerina.

Which is why Jane had never gone to dances and did not want to go to the eleventh-grade dance.

Except she knew it was the only way she'd ever get to know David McLeod, the boy she'd had a crush on since ninth grade, the boy whose name appeared in her notebook more than three thousand times, as in:

David McLeod
David McLeod
David McLeod
David McLeod

Claire lined her up. Her best friend Claire knew all about her David McLeod thing and managed—since she and David were on the homecoming committee together—to mention her friend Jane. David said sure, of course.

So Claire and her boyfriend Rob and Jane and David all went to the dance. It was one of those nights when the girls were self-conscious about their low-cut dresses (didn't want all that Kleenex to pop up out of their bras) and all the boys were self-conscious about their rented tuxedos. They fancied that they looked cool—sort of like Sean Connery as James Bond—until they actually saw their reflections in the glass entrance doors of school. And then they felt kind of foolish. They looked, girls and boys alike, like little kids playing dress-up with Mom's and Dad's clothes.

The dance actually went O.K., David being not only handsome but dutiful as a date. Brought her punch, cookies, took her out on the side steps of the school where Jane had her first two puffs ever of marijuana, and even brought forth a pint bottle of bourbon. She didn't actually want to drink it, but drink it she did. She also didn't want to offend David. She had decided this evening that she was in love with him and that this was serious love. She wanted to spend her life with him. She knew it.

She danced once.

This was with only two songs to go, when the local disc jockey was winding up the night with ballads. He played four Bobby Vinton songs in a row, the one Jane danced to being "Roses Are Red," a song Jane had always found devastatingly sad. You would think that a girl who got straight A's in trig, English literature and philosophy would find Bobby Vinton lyrics a mite treacly but, no. Bobby Vinton songs broke her heart.

The nice thing was, David was so drunk by this time that he didn't even notice when the time came for her to limp. He just kept right on dancing. He held her very close. She could feel his erection against her belly and it thrilled her. He even put his hot mouth on her bare shoulder a few times, and she thrilled even more.

She decided, just as they were leaving the gym, that if he wanted her tonight, she'd give in.

It was the mid-sixties now and all her friends had long been making love. It was time for her, as a modern sort of girl, or so she liked to think of herself anyway, to became a "real woman," as that Gary Puckett and the Union Gap song said.

Directly after the dance, the four of them went to a restaurant for some food, but it was obvious that both couples wanted to be alone. They raced through their dinner and then said good night.

He took her in the backseat of his old man's Buick Electra, this big blue mother with fins like wings and an instrument panel like a spaceship's.

They were so intense that he put himself in her without even taking her panties off.

She felt great pain but was determined not to cry. She didn't want him to misunderstand. She didn't want him to think that she had regrets or anything like that.

He chewed her nipples so hard that it hurt.

Then it was over.

This was the part where she expected some of the soft warm Bobby Vinton words to come. But they didn't.

Instead he said, "My old man'll kill me if I get puke on his car," and pushed open the back door, and man, did he vomit.

All the booze.

All the food.

She'd never heard anybody be sick this way before. It was almost scary.

When he was finished, he didn't get back in the car. He leaned against the trunk, sipping whiskey from his flask again, smoking a cigarette, looking up at the stars.

He didn't ask her to join him.

But she did, finally.

"You all right?"

"I'm fine," he said. "How about you?"

"I'm fine, too." God, she wanted him just to hold her. Not even pledge his love or anything like that. Just hold her with a little tenderness.

All he offered her was the flask, which she declined.

"You want a cigarette?" he said.

"No, thanks."

"A joint?"

"No. I'm fine. Really."

He looked up at the stars some more. Summer was coming and tonight was a preview. Full moon shining on the fast, dark river below. The air sweet with rich black soil and blooming spring flowers. The breeze so soft it almost made you a little crazy, like sexual frenzy or something.

"I suppose I should take you home," he said.

"No hurry." Pause. "I enjoyed myself tonight."

"Yeah, it was good, wasn't it?"

He was sober now; sober in some terrible, almost frightening way. She wanted him to be the boy she'd been in the backseat with just a few minutes earlier. The boy who was all need.

"That's the first time I ever did it with anybody."

He turned to her now and smiled. "You're a sweet kid, you know that?"

"So are you."

He shook his head. "No, I'm not. I'm a jerk."

"A jerk? No, you're not."

He looked at her a long moment and then took a heavy hit on the flask.

"There's something I've got to tell you."

"All right." She knew he wasn't going to say any soft Bobby Vinton words. She knew what he was about to say would be terrible. He scared her now. He had this great power over her and he scared her.

"The reason I went out with you tonight—"

Then he stopped.

"Go ahead," she said, thinking that she had prepared herself for the worst.

"The reason I went out with you tonight was so I could get closer to Claire. I've been in love with her the last two years and I don't know what to do about it. She likes me as a friend, is all. I thought that maybe— Well, you know, she sees me making out with her best friend and all— Well, maybe she'd get a little jealous. Maybe she'd— Maybe she'd realize that she really does like me. You know, in a romantic way like me, I mean."

"Oh."

"So I'll bet now you think I'm a jerk."

"I guess I just wish you'd take me home."

"I'm really sorry, Jane."

"You can't help who you love. I know what that feels like."

"You do?"

"Sure."

"Are you in love with somebody?"

"Uh-huh."

"Who?"

"Oh, nobody you'd know."

"I'm sorry I puked. I'll bet that wasn't any fun to watch."

"It's all right."

"You think you would ever put a kind word in for me, with Claire I mean?"

"Sure."

"Tell her that I really like her. Don't tell her I 'love' her, just say that I really like her. If you see the difference, I mean."

"I see the difference."

"So would you do that?"

"First chance I get."

"I just don't think Rob's right for her. I think I am, though."

"You'd make a nice couple."

"You really mean that?"

"Sure."

"You're really a nice kid, you know that?"

Her pride was that she never cried over this. Not on the long and silent ride home, not in the shadowy loneliness of her bedroom, not in the shower next morning.

Not even when she called Claire next morning.

"So did you have a good time?"

"Yes, I did, except you know what?"

"What?"

"I think he likes you."

"David?"

"Yes."

"Oh, c'mon, Jane, there's your inferiority complex working again. He doesn't like me. He likes you."

"I don't think so." She paused. "In fact, he wanted me to tell you that."

"Tell me what?"

"That he likes you."

"You're kidding."

"Huh-uh."

"He actually *asked* you to ask me that?"

"Uh-huh."

"That rat," Claire said. "That stupid miserable rat."

This was the closest Jane ever came to crying over it—the moment when Claire called David a miserable rat—but she held on and didn't cry. Not at all.

And then all these years later, pulling into a motel along the Potomac, she thought of how many other times she'd been forced to live in the shadow of her friend Claire.

Claire *pretended* to be sorry about it, of course. But Claire didn't care. Not really. Good old Jane. Good old beautiful crippled Jane. That was how Claire thought of her.

Three summers later, Jane and Claire met a college sophomore named Matt Hutton. And Jane fell in love with him. And she sensed that Matt was in love with her, too. Until Claire started flirting with him, that is. Claire was the most subtle flirt Jane had ever known. Jane never came right out and said that she was in love with Matt. She couldn't have humiliated herself that way. But surely Claire knew. And didn't care. Claire dangled both Knox Stansfield and Matt Hutton on her string. And took up first with Knox—and then, when she was tired of Knox—with Matt.

Well, wouldn't Claire be surprised someday when she learned that Jane had been having a secret affair with Knox Stansfield almost since the Huttons had moved into the White House? She'd met Knox at a

Georgetown dinner party and had prepared to tear into him for all the abuse he'd put on the Huttons— And then, two nights later, she'd ended up in bed with him.

She pulled into a slot by the blue neon letters that read OFFICE in the fog.

All these years later.

56

★ ★ ★ Waiting again.

Jane had been upstairs for half an hour now. Apparently alone.

But what if the person had already been here when Jane arrived?

Waiting again. And indecision.

She kept picking up and setting down her camera. Had to do something. The waiting was awful.

She tried not to think of the things the press had been saying about her these past few days.

Some of them would be impossible ever to forgive or forget.

This wasn't the right-wing press, either. This was the mainstream press.

Headlights behind her.

She sank lower in her seat.

Brakes noisy in the mist. Headlights out. Engine dying. Car door opening and closing. Footsteps. Male.

This was better than just sitting here thinking of all the things that had been said about her. All that did was produce great bitterness, and a frustrated need to do something, prove them wrong.

Footsteps closer.

Approaching her car.

Then suddenly the figure was past. Tall blond man in suede car coat. Not Knox.

He carried an overnight bag.

She almost smiled.

A legitimate customer. What was he doing here, anyway?

Thoughts of Deirdre, the doctors reassuring her that her condition was not permanent, that this was depression due to all the stress. She would forever carry, like a wallet photo, an image of Deirdre's face against her hospital pillow—wan, sad.

A car. Behind her. Pulling in fast. Headlights out. Engine off. Footsteps.

She sank back down in the seat.

This customer had parked two rows over.

He walked quickly toward the office, then veered left. Now he was in profile, walking maybe five yards in front of her. He looked around anxiously but didn't seem to see her.

Knox.

He had on a kind of greatcoat with the steep collar full up, but she could still make out the shape of his handsome head.

Knox.

Definitely.

She brought her camera up fast, the telephoto lens looking like a weapon of some kind, and started snapping pictures.

He climbed the steps on the east side of the building leading to the second floor.

He walked six doors down. Knocked.

The door opened only part way, but even so, Jane was clearly seen.

Bingo.

Claire snapped several more pictures, both of them in the same frame.

As she started the car to head back to the White House, she tried not to feel ridiculously happy.

She didn't get any damning evidence tonight—after all, wasn't Jane free to have affairs with men of her choice, even if the men of her choice insisted on meeting at motels?—but she did feel that she'd taken positive action.

It was going to rattle them, anyway, Jane and Knox, when they found out she knew about them.

Claire worked until nearly two o'clock in the darkroom, busy with developer and printing paper and printing trays and printing tongs.

These didn't have to be masterpieces. They just needed to be clear and sharp.

When she was finished, when the photos were hanging on the wire, she looked at them with great pride.

She'd certainly taken more artistic photographs before, but none that had had this kind of emotional impact on her.

Jane and Knox.

If it hadn't been for Jane's florist bill fluttering to the floor that day, Claire never would have found out about them.

Jane and Knox.

Claire still felt sick with betrayal.

Somebody could pretend to be your friend, your *best* friend, and all the time be—

She was excited now.

Tomorrow, things would start to change. She felt sure of it.

57

★ ★ ★ "Do you ever feel sorry for her?"

"Oh, God, darling, please don't start that again."

"I'm just asking."

"Of course not. If I felt sorry for her—or for Matt—I wouldn't have done it. And you wouldn't have, either."

Shadow and silence; the motel room. Naked and warm beneath the covers.

"I saw another wedding dress I liked today."

"That's somewhere down the line. We have to be careful."

"I know. I just like to think about it."

Marriage. Knox knew that there was no way he could ever get rid of Jane now. They were married by the nature of what they'd done together. In a year, they would pretend to meet at some party, and then have a brief courtship, and then be married. Marriage wouldn't hurt his ratings, either. Americans wanted their heroes married. Confirmation of heterosexuality if nothing else.

She would not make a terrible wife. If she wasn't all he wanted in bed, she was at least eager. And if she was too chatty most of the time, at least her interest in politics gave them a common ground. He had no illusions that he would be faithful. But he would be careful. He would always have to be careful with her. She could always go to the law . . . Unless, somewhere in the future, an accident of some sort might be arranged. But that was nothing he need think about now. Now all he had to do was watch Claire and her family struggle through their daily soap opera on the nightly news.

"You know what you told me the other night? About your mother?"

"I really don't want to go through it again if you don't mind," Knox said. Women liked you to tell them little secrets about yourself. It humanized you to them.

"I'm just sorry it happened to you. You were so young."

"I'm not the only one it ever happened to, I'm sure."

"No, but I'm still sorry it happened. Walking in on your mother and another woman—"

He never should have told her.

It was a quick, cheap way of getting Jane to pity him, and thus feel closer to him, feel he was not so cold and distant after all.

She went on about it for some time, the tragedy, the trauma of it all, and the poor little boy who'd had to endure it.

Somewhere in the middle of it, he put one foot on the floor and began his slow but inexorable flight from the trapping musk and heat of her.

He never should have told her about his mother.

Never should have told her.

58

★ ★ ★ Breakfast was a slice of melon, Cream of Wheat and wheat toast for Claire; a slice of melon, Egg-Beaters and a slice of wheat toast for Matt. They shared two pieces of toast and strawberry jelly. They also shared a pot of steaming coffee.

They ate in a small breakfast nook that Claire had designed. She'd made a place for a fourteen-inch TV set they could both watch.

The morning news was on.

"What's on for this morning?" Claire said when the local anchor, who looked young enough to play college baseball, broke for a commercial.

"Meeting Senator Evans. You know how that goes."

Evans was a moderate from Oklahoma. Because he usually voted the way the President wanted him to, he showed up three times a year with a want list for his state, sort of like bringing your want list to Santa Claus. Some things Matt could help him with, some not.

"Then what?"

"Then McElroy has me meeting with some of the new Pentagon staffers. They don't seem to believe I'm a real American because I opposed the last two missile systems they wanted. And then I meet with Senator Michaels and try to explain to him that the Democrats can't have any more money because there isn't any more to be had. Anywhere. For anything. I'd like to see how these people run their own goddamned checking accounts. They must be overdrawn all the time."

He eyed her over the rim of his coffee cup. "And you leave your photos on Jane's desk."

"I'm way ahead of you. I've already done that."

"I still can't believe she'd do that to us."

"I can't either—but she did."

"But why? We've always been so damned nice to her."

Claire shrugged. She hadn't slept well and was tired. "Maybe that's the problem. Maybe she interpreted that as patronizing or something."

The youthful anchorman returned.

"There is news this morning that Washington, D.C., police have now verified that the gun the President's daughter brought to Knox Stansfield's radio studio is also the murder weapon used to kill David Hart, the friend of First Lady Claire Hutton."

Claire had expected this, but hearing it on TV was still a shock. "Is that four or five?" she said.

"Four or five what?"

She tried a smile. "Nails in my coffin."

Bobby LaFontaine spent most of the morning rehearsing what he was going to say to Claire Hutton on the phone.

He had to convince her right away that he was neither a crank nor somebody trying to entrap her further in the murder case.

Good morning, Madame President.

No, that was too much.

Good morning, First Lady.

No, that sounded too formal.

How the hell were you supposed to greet some broad who was married to the President?

Claire Hutton? Listen, babe, I'm going to tell you something you'll really want to hear.

A little too *in*formal.

He must have gone to the phone ten times in his apartment, and every time he'd stop himself to rehearse some new line.

When Claire walked into her office, she found a letter on her desk with "Claire" handwritten on the front of it.

She recognized the handwriting immediately as Jane's.

Claire read the note and then surprised herself by getting right to work.

She read and replied to three letters, made four phone calls, drank two cups of coffee, and answered three different questions from staffers.

Then she referred back to the note.

Dear Claire,
A picture tells a thousand words. At least this particular one
does. The one of Knox and me.
I've been seeing him for a little over a year. Met him at a
Georgetown cocktail party. I would have told you but I was
afraid you'd hate me.
I love him and I can't help it and I plan to stay with him.
I know you feel betrayed and I don't blame you.
I'm down seeing Milly in the mailroom. When I feel a little
stronger I'll come back upstairs and we can talk.
Love,
Jane

"She knows."
"Darling, I'm very, very busy getting ready for the show this after-
noon, so could you please be a little less cryptic? Who knows what?"
"Claire. About us."
Pause. "How the hell did she find out?"
"I don't know. But she left three photos on my desk this morn-
ing."
"Photos of what?"
"You and me at the motel last night."
"She *followed* us?"
"Apparently."
"I don't like this."
"There's no reason to panic, Knox. She doesn't know anything."
"She knows about us."
"But that's all."
"Where are you calling from, anyway?"
"The basement."
"Of the White House?"
"Yes."
"Why don't you use your mind once in a while?"
"I don't like it when you talk to me that way."
"Well, I can't help it. Calling from the White House. Not a real
bright idea, is it?"
She was startled to realize that Knox Stansfield was scared. She had
never seen him scared before. And until this moment could not have
pictured him scared.
"We'd better hang up now."
"It's going to be all right, Knox. I know it will."

"Thank you for your wisdom, O divine seer."
"Knox, please, it really makes me feel terrible when we fight."
"I'll talk to you later today."
"Knox, please, listen, I—"
He hung up.

59

★ ★ ★ "Hi."

"Hi."

"Did you see my letter?"

"Uh-huh."

"You probably hate me."

"I'm not sure yet."

"Is it all right if I sit down?"

"You worried I might trip you or something?"

"I wish you'd just be pissed and get it over with."

Jane came into the office, paused a moment and then walked over to her desk and sat down. This morning she wore a dark brown suit that gave her an autumnal elegance. That was the funny thing—Jane had never understood how much Claire envied her her looks.

Claire said, "I guess I am."

"Guess you are what?"

"Starting to get pissed."

"Good. That'll be easier to take."

Claire said, "Are you part of it?"

"Part of what?"

"You know. The murder."

"Knox didn't have anything to do with David's death. I know you don't believe that but it's the truth." Jane sat with her hands planted firmly on the top of her desk.

"I'm going to take those photos to the police," Claire said.

"Be my guest."

"You don't think they'll be suspicious?"

"No. They'll think that here's a very desperate woman. Someone trying to shift the blame from herself."

"I didn't kill him."

"That's what you say, anyway, Claire."

"And that means what exactly?"

"Exactly it means that I'll take your word for it but that you still could have done it."

Claire watched Jane for a long moment. "I guess I never realized until this morning that you hated me."

"I don't hate you."

"You don't seem to have any remorse for what you've done, Jane. You must hate me. You and Knox have nearly destroyed Deirdre."

Jane shook her head. "I didn't do anything to Deirdre, Claire, and neither did Knox."

Jane stood up. Picked up her purse. Slid the cover over the Royal electric typewriter she still preferred to a word processor. "Maybe I'd better be—"

And that was when the phone rang. There were three lines into the office. The first one was lit now.

Claire picked up. "Hello?"

"Is the, uh, President's wife there by any chance?"

"Who may I say is calling?"

"Uh, Bobby LaFontaine. From the *God's Hour* show."

As soon as he identified himself, Claire knew that this was somehow an important call. Why would the Reverend Goodhew's people be calling her if it wasn't important?

"I'll put her on the line, if you'll please hold a moment."

"Uh, sure."

Claire put Bobby LaFontaine on hold.

Jane said, "Is everything all right? You look kind of funny."

Claire said, "I'd appreciate it if you'd leave. I'll have your things boxed up and delivered to your apartment. I need to take this call."

"But—" But Jane obviously knew there was nothing more to say. "All right, Claire. I'll—talk to you again some time."

"Fine."

Jane took her purse and left.

Jane walked to the next office. It was empty. She wondered who was calling Claire. Claire looked awfully—strange.

Jane ducked into the office, went quickly to a phone, lifted the receiver while holding down the transmission button, and then slowly let the button rise so she could hear the conversation.

But there was no conversation.

The caller was apparently still on hold.

What was Claire doing, preparing herself in some way for this call? It must be quite important.

Jane thought she heard footsteps coming down the hall. Somebody would come in and find her overhearing Claire's phone call and—

But the footsteps went on past.

Jane remained on the phone.

Listening—

"This is Claire Hutton." She hoped Mr. LaFontaine, whoever he was, didn't recognize her as the same woman who'd answered the call.

"Uh, my name is Bobby LaFontaine."

He sounded very nervous.

"Yes, Mr. LaFontaine. How may I help you?"

"I guess it's more like, how can I help *you*."

"All right, then. How can you help *me*?"

"Uh, I know you didn't commit that murder."

"Oh? Why do you say that?"

"Well, the truth is, I've got something."

"I'm not sure what you're talking about, Mr. LaFontaine."

"Let's just say that it's something that would go a long way to proving who really killed that Hart guy."

"I need to ask you a question, Mr. LaFontaine."

"I figured you would."

"If you're with *God's Hour*, why are you trying to help me?"

"Let's just say that I'm moving on."

"I see."

"And that I want to do the right thing."

"I would really appreciate it if you *would* do the right thing."

"For a price."

"I see."

"You shouldn't act so surprised, Mrs. Hutton. I mean, there's a price for everything."

"There certainly seems to be, doesn't there?" Claire said.

"A million dollars is what I had in mind."

"I need to get off the phone now, Mr. LaFontaine."

"Wait a minute—are you crazy? You don't even know what I have."

"I guess I had hopes that you were somebody who wanted to help me. Actually, you're somebody who wants to make a lot of money."

"This tape could help clear you."

"What tape would that be, Mr. LaFontaine?"

"A tape of Knox Stansfield."

No doubt about it. Bobby LaFontaine, whoever he was, whatever he was all about, had just said the magic words.

As Jane listened, her entire body went numb and cold.

A tape of Knox Stansfield.

My God.

Bad enough that somebody from Reverend Goodhew's organization was going over to the other side.

But to implicate Knox—

"What about Knox Stansfield?" Claire said.

"You'll have to hear the tape."

"And in order to hear the tape—"

"You'll need to bring a million dollars in cash. I know you can raise it, Mrs. Hutton."

"Oh? And how do you know that?"

"You're rich. Your in-laws are, anyway."

"I see."

"This is very little money compared to what some other people would pay me."

"Then why don't you go to them with it?"

"I'd rather, uh, deal with you."

"Do you have the tape now?"

"Right here."

"I need to hear it."

"You mean right now?"

"I mean right now."

"But—"

"Right now or no deal."

"I don't think I should."

"If you don't, there'll be no million dollars."

"Cash? Small bills?"

"Cash and small bills if I think the tape sounds useful."

"Well—"

"I'm a busy woman, Mr. LaFontaine. Which is it going to be?"

"I guess I'll play you the tape. I need a couple of seconds here."

"Fine."

Jane gripped the phone so hard her knuckles were blanched white.

The numbness in her body had been replaced by trembling and an icy sweat.

She was terrified of what Bobby LaFontaine had on tape.

"Maybe I did kill Hart, Clemmons. But you can't prove it and no jury in the world would convict me."

Jane recognized the voice at once. Knox. Drunk. Boasting, as he often did after a few drinks.

The tape was every bit as incriminating as Bobby LaFontaine had indicated.

"Play it once more."

"Pretty heavy stuff, huh?" Bobby LaFontaine said.

"Please. Once more." Claire said.

The tape was rewound, sounding like a million chittering monkey voices.

Then: "Maybe I did kill Hart, Clemmons. But you can't prove it and no jury in the world is going to convict me."

"I need to hear it one more time," Claire said. Actually, she was trying to regain her composure. What she heard on the tape was not merely a group of words—but rather the good name of her family coming back to her. And her own dilemma resolved.

Chittering monkey voices, then: "Maybe I did kill Hart, Clemmons. But you can't prove it and no jury in the world is going to convict me."

Claire said, "Who is Clemmons?"

"His chauffeur and valet. This black guy."

"How did you get the tape, Mr. LaFontaine?"

"That I can't tell you. And it don't matter anyway, does it? I mean, it's the real thing and that's all you've got to worry about."

The vapors.

Jane had always wondered what it must feel like to be a heroine in one of those sexy antebellum romances she sometimes read. They were always getting "the vapors" and promptly collapsing to the floor.

Well, Jane was getting the vapors now, was literally afraid she was going to pass out.

"Where shall we meet, Mr. LaFontaine?"

He gave her an address.

"But the thing is, you have to bring the money."

"I understand," Claire said.

"Cash and small bills."

"Right."

"And you have to come alone."

"Fine."

"I'll need till four this afternoon."

"That will be fine. Let me give you that address again."

✷   ✷   ✷

Jane's fingers trembled as she wrote down Bobby LaFontaine's address. The writing looked as if it had been done during a roller coaster ride.

"I'll see you at four o'clock this afternoon, Mr. LaFontaine."
　"I'm looking forward to it, Mrs. Hutton."
　"So am I."

60

★ ★ ★ The President of the United States, sitting at his desk in the Oval Office, looked up to see his wife come hurrying in.

"Wow," he said, "is everything all right?"

"Maybe better than it's been in a long time." She had an almost giddy smile on her face. "But I need your help."

"Sure," he said. "What is it?"

"I need a million dollars in the next three hours—"

"A million dol—"

"In cash and small bills."

"My God, Claire," said the President. "Maybe you'd better tell me about this."

"You're right," Claire said, still smiling. "Maybe I'd better."

61

★ ★ ★ Bobby LaFontaine was cleaning up his apartment and it was ir-rational.

It's not like he was having some kind of date or something.

This broad, who just happened to be the First Lady of the United States, was coming over to buy *blackmail material* from him.

Who cares if the living room isn't straightened up or if the bed isn't made?

What's she going to do, give me demerits?

But what could it hurt if he did just a teensy-weensy bit of straight-ening and dusting of the living room?

He went into the hallway closet and got a towel—he never could find where the once-a-week illegal-alien cleaning woman kept the dust rags—and set to work in the living room.

"He found out," Knox Stansfield said.

"Found out what?"

"About the board of directors. Little jerk has probably got the entire place bugged. I told Goodhew he should get rid of that lowlife."

"Knox, you're not making sense."

"That's why Bobby LaFontaine hates me."

"You're still not making any sense."

"The board of directors. LaFontaine wanted to be on it and I black-balled him."

"When was this?"

"Six, seven months ago, I don't remember exactly."

"You think he had the place bugged?"

"Of course. That's mostly what he did for Goodhew when he was starting out. Bugging places. That's how Goodhew found out that one of his competitors—you remember that scumbag Ryerson?—was screwing this fourteen-year-old girl from the choir. Goodhew blackmailed him out of business, thanks to the tapes Bobby got for him."

"I'm afraid, Knox. I really am."

"I should have figured you'd panic."

"Thank you very much. I really needed to hear that." She was already tearing up.

"I'm sorry, darling. That wasn't very nice, was it?"

"No, it wasn't."

"We can handle this. We really can."

"How? She'll go over there and pay him the money and he'll give her the tape and—"

"Will you just listen to me for a minute?"

"All right."

"Just calm down a little."

"Please don't say 'calm down.' You know how I hate that."

"All right. I won't say it anymore."

"Thank you."

"Now listen . . ."

The next thing Bobby LaFontaine got out was the vacuum cleaner.

She was the First Lady, after all, not some bimbo who wanted to watch a little professional wrestling and get all felt up in the process.

A little vacuuming wouldn't hurt.

He vacuumed.

The President sat on one edge of the desk in the Oval Office, Claire on the other.

Both of them watched McElroy, who sat in the President's chair and yelled into the phone.

"I know a million dollars is a lot of money in cash, Ralph, but that's your problem. Now either you get it for me or I pull all our party's goddamn accounts out of your bank. And you've got one hour to do it."

McElroy slammed the phone. "Son of a bitch," he shouted at it. Then he looked at Claire and said, "Pardon my French."

Bobby LaFontaine walked past the dining room table and realized, for the very first time in the sixteen months he'd lived here, how *bare* it looked.

He tried to remember where the cleaning woman put the blue paper flowers that were supposed to go on the table.

And now that he was looking at the table, he saw that it could use a little polishing.

She dusted it, the cleaning lady did, but she never *polished*.

Bobby found a can of paste wax and a new towel and went to work.

"Now, do you understand that?"

"I wish you were going to be there, Knox."

"I can't afford to be there, darling. You know that."

"So I go up to his place—"

"—right—"

"—and I tell him just what you told me to tell him—"

"—right—"

"—and then I take the tape—"

"—right—"

"And I bring it to you—"

"—right—"

"And you handle it from there."

"Exactly."

"I'm scared."

"Bobby talks tough but he's a punk. He'll probably put the moves on you but he's harmless."

"God, he really will?"

"Uh-huh."

"Now I really don't want to go—"

"You'll be fine."

"Couldn't he have an extra copy of it, or something? The tape?"

"Not Bobby. This is a one-time score. He'll have to leave the country. Too much heat."

"I just hope he doesn't come on to me."

"You'll do fine, darling. You really will. Now I'll see you later, all right?"

"All right. I just—"

"You'll do fine. You'll do absolutely fine."

He hung up.

In prison Bobby had always managed to con his cellmate into cleaning the toilet.

Bobby had always considered such work (a) filthy, (b) undignified, and (c) strictly for women.

So what was he doing on his knees with his face maybe two feet from the toilet bowl?

Well, say the First Lady needed to take a pee or something—a not wholly unlikely turn of events, given how nervous she'd be—wouldn't he be embarrassed if the john was dirty?

He was a lot more nervous about this broad coming here than he'd realized.

Dusting. Polishing. Waxing. Scrubbing. Even vacuuming.

He wondered if he was having some kind of breakdown or something.

62

★ ★ ★ In the early afternoon, Clemmons went to the supermarket, the deli, the liquor store and the dry cleaners, doing his errands while Knox Stansfield was at the studio preparing for his radio show.

Clemmons had not slept well. Just before going to bed last night, he'd made the mistake of watching CNN. A panel of reporters had speculated on the fate of Claire Hutton. Not a single one of the reporters even hinted that they thought she might be innocent. Assuming her guilt, they talked about how President Hutton would have to handle the matter with his party and with the American people.

Afterward, he had gone into his bedroom, opened the top drawer and stared at the $10,000 Knox Stansfield had given him.

Bribe money. Hush money.

Stansfield had just assumed that Clemmons would be his alibi in the murder: No, sir, boss, Mistah Stansfield he sho 'nuff wasn't up there long enough to kill nobody, no sir he wasn't. But Clemmons hadn't gone along, at least not with the enthusiasm that Stansfield had hoped for.

So—the money.

Clemmons, leaving the dry cleaner's now, pictured the crisp green bills in the top drawer. A black man didn't often get to see that much cash. Hell, no man, black or white, often did.

It was his to spend. He might even be able to go back for more sometime, if he was sly enough.

All the way back to Stansfield's, Clemmons thought of different ways he might spend the cash. The vacation was out of the question.

He wasn't a vacation kind of guy.

But he could certainly buy a better car. Or fix up his bleak little house. Or just leave it in a bank account and take out his bank book every few days and just thumb through it. He thought of what his father would have said about his son having ten grand. He could picture the old man's grin now, looking like a kid when he smiled that way.

Wished the old man would have lived to see it.

Ten grand, Pop.

It would have been fun to take five hundred of it and just blow it on the old man. Nice steak dinner. Western movie (how the old man had loved westerns, especially with John Wayne). Buy him a new shirt and pants and shoes. And get him a few things for the house that had been empty since the missus had died of heart failure when Clemmons was nine years old . . .

Clemmons teared up. He'd loved the old bastard. Couldn't help it. The old man had been rough and tough in a lot of ways but he'd had humor about himself and he'd been a man of honor in all things. Honest in every matter, in every dealing.

Honest.

Clemmons tried not to think about that too hard.

To be honest would mean that his sister's heart would be broken and that his nephew would go to prison.

He wondered what the old man would have done.

He wished that heaven had a telephone line.

He wanted to call the old man up and ask his advice.

It was when he was hanging up the dry cleaning that he found the shirt again.

Stansfield always made the mistake of considering himself a genius. His pride was that nothing got by him.

But the shirt had gotten by him, the shirt he'd worn the night of the killing.

Apparently, Stansfield was under the impression that the shirt bore no signs of what he'd done. But he hadn't looked closely enough. A nice white button-down Van Heusen, it had tiny flecks of blood on the right cuff. The shirts he wanted dry cleaned, he always threw in a pile on the floor. The Van Heusen had not been put in the pile. Nor had the gray slacks he'd worn that night. Still there. Just as they'd been the night of the murder. He'd probably get around to having them dry cleaned after Claire Hutton was tried for the killing.

Clemmons rolled the walk-in closet door shut and went back downstairs.

He was thinking of the old man again.

He went into the den and dialed a familiar number.

"Hello?"

"It's me," he said to his sister.

"Can you hold on a minute? I've got some spaghetti boiling."

"Sure."

He usually called every few days. But he'd avoided calling lately because he was afraid of what he might say.

"There now. So how are you?"

"Fine. How're you?"

"Fine."

"Randy fine, too?"

"Oh, you know."

"He's not in any trouble is he?"

"No. No trouble. But—"

"But what?"

"You know. Those boys he hangs out with."

"How's he doing in school?"

"Well, he's going, anyway. Every day, I mean."

"Good." Beat. "This isn't right, you know that?"

She was angry instantly. "You can't make that judgment. He's my son and if you go to the police—"

And then she was crying, sobbing really.

He knew that she didn't think this was the right thing, either, that the best thing was to tell the truth, the way the old man would have done, but what could she do? You carried a child nine months, you gave him your milk and your blood, you saw him through endless days and nights of joy and fear and pain and wonderment, and you had a relationship with him you'd never have with nobody else. Not your father. Nor your brother. You'd take care of your son first. At all costs.

"He wouldn't last long in prison," she said. "He's not a tough boy or a mean boy and you know it."

"It's just—"

"I know what it is, brother. You think I don't think about that, too? I see that poor woman on TV, all them reporters screamin' questions at her— I don't like it, either, brother. But there ain't nothin' I can do about it, you know what I'm sayin', brother? Do you?"

A few moment later, they hung up.

Clemmons sank into a chair, miserable.

63

★ ★ ★ Bobby LaFontaine was cleaning the front window with Windex when somebody knocked timidly on his door.

There. The apartment was a showcase. The cleaning woman had never gotten it to sparkle this way.

He hoped the First Lady appreciated all the frigging work he'd done.

"Just a minute." he said.

He hurried the Windex and the towel into the bathroom, stuffed them in a narrow closet, and then returned to the living room and the front door.

She was very, very pretty—even sexy—the proper-looking woman in his doorway. But she wasn't the First Lady.

"Bobby?"

"Yeah."

"My name's Jane."

"I was expecting somebody else."

"I know you were. That's why I want to talk to you."

She wore a white turtleneck sweater and a blue jumper underneath a buff blue raincoat. She had the most gorgeous red hair Bobby had ever seen. And her shining brown eyes had an almost hypnotic effect on him.

"May I come in?"

"I really am expecting somebody."

"I just need ten minutes."

He looked at her some more. "What's it about, anyway?"

She smiled. And, God, her smile was devastating.

"It's about two million dollars."

"Huh?"

"Two million dollars. For you."

"For me?"

She nodded.

"Why would you give me two million dollars?"

"I really can't say any more. Not standing here in the hallway."

"Two million dollars?" Bobby said. "Why would you want to give me two million dollars?"

And then she said, with just a tiny hint that there might be another little gift to go along with the cash prize, "Why don't you invite me in and find out?"

It was only when he stood back and held the door for her that he realized she limped. It was like somebody painting a mustache on the Mona Lisa.

No sense in pushing hard anymore. The rest of the press was doing it for him. Now Knox could go on to talk about other things. Knox was playing it as part of the overall liberal-moderate conspiracy to discredit certain far-right leaders. His listeners loved conspiracy theories, a predilection shared by members of both the far left and far right.

At the moment, however, he was being nice about the First Lady.

This morning he hadn't exactly been thrilled with the material his staff had come up with for this afternoon's show—and he'd been even less happy with Jane's call about Bobby LaFontaine and his tape—so he'd skewered a few employees. Really tore into them. Which they needed every once in a while.

But he'd gone just the teensiest bit overboard.

Calling Shannon "fat ass," for example.

And Myrna "a dumb Polack."

And saying to Donald, "Afraid your fag friends won't like it if I get too tough on gay lib?"

Teensiest bit too far.

Which explained the caterers suddenly descending on the radio studio and serving gourmet hamburgers and fries to every member of the staff.

Knox's way of saying, Oops, sorry.

Knox's way of saying, Hey, we all get a little crazy now and then.

Knox's way of saying—

Screw it. The catered meal was all they were going to get. If he had any real guilt over his outburst, it had been expiated by the food.

He sat in the booth now, bulk-erasing tapes with his degausser, and wondering how Jane was doing.

There was a good chance Bobby *would* rape her. Kind of guy he was.

But Knox didn't care a long as he got the tape back.

He was overwhelmed suddenly with self-pity. He did not see himself as handsome, rich, powerful. Instead he saw himself as the little boy who could never quite please his mother. And the self-pity felt almost mortal.

Unloved. Misunderstood. In great and abiding psychic pain. That was Knox. Poor Knox.

He had not destroyed reputations out of malice, nor had he committed murder out of malice, either. Just something he needed to do, and people should understand and therefore forgive.

He was Knox Stansfield, after all.

He wondered if Bobby was screwing her.

Somehow the thought amused him. Prim Jane and a convict sleaze like Bobby. Maybe he could teach her a few new tricks. Lord knows she needed to learn some.

He looked up at the studio clock.

Where the hell was she?

"One million dollars." McElroy said.

The large brown leather briefcase sat on the President's desk, clasped and closed.

"This is what I take to him," Claire said.

"This is what you take to him," McElroy said.

"I just wish you weren't doing this," Matt said to Claire. "It scares me. The guy's a scumbag."

"But he has the tape," Claire said.

"He says he has the tape. This could be a trap of some kind."

Claire said, "I appreciate you worrying about me."

McElroy said, "He is a sleaze, Claire."

Claire smiled. "Then maybe he'll run for Congress. Be right at home."

"I'd be happy to follow you over there," McElroy said.

"I'll be fine. I really will."

She hefted the briefcase. "So this is what a million dollars feels like."

Matt said, "Do I get a kiss good-bye?"

She had a limp but she also had something else: a snub-nosed .38.

"This is kind of corny, isn't it? This gun, I mean?" Jane said, as she stepped into Bobby's apartment and closed the door behind her.

All Bobby could think of was that she was going to accidentally shoot him. The way her gun hand was twitching—

"God, Lady, you ever used a gun before?"

"Knox taught me how to shoot. On a target range, I mean."

"You're scaring me."

"That's what I'm trying to do."

"You said two million doll—"

"Yeah but I was thinking about that and this'll be a lot faster. This gun, I mean." Then she looked around his apartment. "Boy, this is really clean." She lowered the gun so that it was aimed directly at his heart. "I want the tape."

"You said two million dollars."

"I told you, I changed my mind."

"You wouldn't actually shoot me."

"I would, Mr. LaFontaine, I actually would."

She could see he was trying to get a sense of her, what she would and wouldn't do.

She had to ask herself: would she actually shoot him if it came right down to it? Nice Midwestern girl like herself? Pretty *sheltered* and shy Midwestern girl when you came right down to it.

Then she thought: If the police ever get that tape, they'll arrest Knox and me for sure.

"I will shoot you, Mr. LaFontaine."

"I don't think you will."

"You're really sweating."

"Huh?"

"Your face. It's all sweaty."

"Oh."

"And your left eye has a tic."

"I still don't think you'll shoot me. I still think you're bluffing."

"How high should I count to?"

"Huh?"

"Why don't I count to five? Then if you don't get me the tape, I shoot."

"You know what?"

"What, Mr LaFontaine?"

"Now *you're* sweating."

"No, I'm not."

"Honest. You are. Your forehead. And your upper lip."

"One."

"Go look in the mirror."

"Two."

"And your hand's all shaky."

"Three."

"You're just as scared as I am," Bobby LaFontaine said.

"Four."

"You won't do it."

"Five."

And that was when she shot him.

The briefcase sat next to her on the seat. Claire had the irrational fear that a cop was going to stop her for some kind of traffic violation and ask to look inside the briefcase. Then he'd start looking a little harder at her and see that she was wearing a wig and dark glasses just to disguise the fact that she was the First Lady—

All she could think of was the tape.

Once she got it, everything would be all right.

Deirdre would be all right. Matt's presidency would be all right. Life would be back to normal.

And Knox and Jane would be where they belonged: in prison.

Drive the speed limit. Make sure to signal. Watch for cross traffic at intersections.

She touched the briefcase beside her—as if it were a touchstone that could impart good luck.

Soon now, everything would be all right . . .

It was hard to tell who was more shocked—Jane or Bobby.

She'd shot him in the thigh and now he was rolling around on the nice gray carpeting.

She stood above him, holding the gun.

"You bitch. You shot me."

"I told you I was going to."

"That doesn't mean you had to do it."

Then he stared down at the bloodstains on the carpet.

"I worked my ass off cleaning this place up!"

"I want the tape."

"No way you're getting the tape. Not after you shot me."

"I'll shoot you again."

"No, you won't. You've got to get out of here and you know it. Somebody'll report that gunshot."

He grimaced. Clutched his leg. The pain.

She limped over to him and kicked him. Right in the wound. So squarely, in fact, that some of his blood got on the toe of her blue alligator pump. Red. Glistening.

He screamed. "You bitch!"

"The tape," she said. "I want the tape!"

Eight minutes later, as Claire pulled into the parking lot of Bobby La-Fontaine's apartment house, she saw a familiar automobile backing out of a parking space and then squealing away very quickly.

The car belonged to Jane.

Jane had been at Bobby LaFontaine's.

Bobby was in the bathroom, tearing open the fabric around his wound, when somebody started pounding on his front door.

Probably some neighbor wanting to know about the gunshot.

Bobby gritted his teeth—the pain was getting worse—and hobbled out into the apartment.

When the door opened up, Claire's gaze immediately fell to Bobby's right thigh and the bloody wound.

"Oh my God," Claire said. "She shot you."

"The bitch."

"Did she get the tape?"

"That bitch." His face was twisted with pain.

She grabbed him by the front of his shirt and shook him, hysterical. "DID SHE GET THE TAPE?"

"Yeah."

"Did you make a copy of it?"

"Huh-uh. I should've, shouldn't I?"

She shook him by his shirt again. "You didn't make a copy? YOU DIDN'T MAKE A COPY?"

She sounded as if she were going to sob.

Then, as if talking to herself, she said, "I've got to stop her before she gets to Knox. I've got to!"

Jane was still shaking. The whole right side of her body. It was kind of spooky, actually.

She'd already had to pull over to the curb a couple of times to settle herself down.

It was as if she'd lost total control of her reflexes, shaking this way.

She'd just take it nice and slow.

Ease her way back into traffic.

There. Just like that.

Nice and slow and—

That was when she noticed, as she was driving down the street at a leisurely 25 miles per hour, that somebody was zooming up right behind her.

And that was when she recognized, despite the wig and the dark glasses, that Claire was driving the car that was now riding her back bumper.

Claire had found her!

64

* * * Jane ran the red light.

Claire, who was maybe twenty yards behind her, wanted to run the same red light but a large panel truck coming through the intersection made her slam on her brakes.

Damn!

Jane had gotten away.

Claire had to find her. Had to.

Claire waited until the intersection was clear and then laid down some rubber. The light was still red. She didn't care.

Down the block, fast. Down a second block, fast. Scanning, looking—all the time scanning, looking.

No sign of Jane in her gray Volvo.

Down a third block, fast. Scanning—

There.

A block to the left. At a traffic light. Jane.

Red to green. The light changed. Jane drove on. Fast.

Claire raced down the block. Had to beat that light. Had to.

She approached the intersection. Jane was a block away again.

Had to speed up.

The intersection got closer, closer.

Approaching the intersection—

Squad car across the street. Cop in car. Watching.

Claire slammed on her brakes, skidding a little. She was barely able to stop the car from sliding into the intersection.

Heavy scowl from cop.

Jane. Driving away. Fast.

How long was this light going to stay red, anyway?

Cop still scowling at her.

Light turned green. She had to drive old-lady style so as not to irritate the cop. Nice and slow.

The cop scowled at her all the way.

When she reached the middle of the next block, she sped up again.

One block, two blocks, three blocks.

No sign of Jane.

Then she reached a highway overpass and saw below her, on the Capital Beltway, the gray Volvo. Jane.

She was headed to the George Washington Memorial Parkway.

This told Claire where she was going: Knox Stansfield's studio.

Claire floored the accelerator, reached the turn to the entrance ramp, and turned right, reaching the Beltway itself in seconds.

The fun was just starting.

Now she was going to catch Jane for sure.

For sure.

She entered the Beltway traveling 88 miles per hour.

Cellular phone:

"I got it."

"Fantastic! Where are you?"

"Headed for your studio!"

"We're going to have some celebration tonight, I can promise you that!"

"Claire's following me."

"What?"

"She saw me leaving Bobby LaFontaine's apartment house."

"That bitch. Can you lose her?"

"I think so."

"I'll see you in a little while, then."

"I love you, darling."

"I love you, too. Now lose her, do you understand me? Lose her!"

The next six miles on the Beltway would have given an Indy 500 driver pause.

Claire and Jane went bumper-to-bumper for three miles, then Jane veered suddenly to the right, taking an off-ramp at 72 miles per hour.

Claire stayed right with her.

As soon as Jane reached a street, she turned left, even though this was against a red light, and raced down a narrow street with no traffic.

Claire stayed within thirty feet of her the whole time.

Then Claire got even bolder, swinging out in the opposing lane and trying to force Jane to pull over.

At this point, they were going about 45.

Claire's car nudged Jane's. Jane had to fight hard, cursing, to keep control of her vehicle.

Jane spun the wheel so that her car tore into Claire's, knocking Claire a good five feet toward the opposite curb.

By this time, pedestrians were stopping to have a look at the demolition derby going on in the street.

Jane, giving it more gas, hitting 60 now, looked for only one thing: the on-ramp. She needed the opportunity to get away from Claire and these narrow streets weren't it. She needed the Beltway.

She didn't see the gasoline truck piling though the next intersection until it was almost too late.

She screamed, tightened her grip on the wheel, accelerated even more, and then angled her vehicle so that it would shoot through the intersection with only a foot or two separating it from the rear end of the gas truck.

Made it.

And then she saw the sign pointing to the on-ramp.

Seventy-six miles per hour.

Claire did not have the same luck.

Just as she approached the intersection, watching Jane slide through after the gasoline truck, she saw a second truck, a lumbering dinosaur of a moving van, enter the crossway.

All she could do was jam on her brakes and hope she could stop in time to avoid piling into the big van.

Jesus, Mary and Joseph.

Claire's car turned completely around when she slammed on the brakes, but it stopped in time to avoid colliding with the van, which went on through totally oblivious of Claire and how close she'd come to death.

Then Claire got her car pointed in the right direction, and resumed her pursuit of Jane.

She went three blocks without seeing any sign of Jane, then noticed the sign to the on-ramp and realized what had happened.

Claire turned left, entering the on-ramp at 88 miles per hour.

Six minutes later she spotted Jane, at which point she resumed some of her more spectacular driving stunts, weaving in and out of speeding cars, charging down straightaways, and then pulling up bumper-to-bumper behind Jane.

The next off-ramp was three miles away and it was all Jane could think of. Had to get there, had to get there, had to get there—

Claire saw Jane starting to ease ever-so-slightly leftward, favoring the upcoming exit ramp.

Claire prepared to follow.

She would not lose Jane this time.

Jane reached the ramp going 54.

Claire reached the ramp going 46.

Jane shot down the ramp to the stop sign at the end of the street and then shot straight on through.

Claire was about to follow her when she saw the Chevrolet sedan just reaching the intersection.

Claire had time to shoot on right ahead of it, but when she reached the middle of the intersection, her car went into a spin and before she could wheel the vehicle back around in the right direction, the engine died.

Right there.

Middle of the intersection.

Died.

Thank God, Jane thought, looking in her rearview for the fourth time in less than two minutes.

Thank God.

Now she could get to the studio.

Eight minutes later, Claire spotted Jane again.

On the street leading through Georgetown to Knox's studio.

Claire knew this was absolutely her last chance.

Two yellow lights, a red light and a curve sharp enough to send her up on the curb as she negotiated the almost angular curve—

People shouting. Pointing.

Somewhere—a siren. Above—a police helicopter dipping low like an angry metal bird.

But she couldn't lose her.

Had to get the tape.

With three blocks to go before Jane reached the studio, Claire caught up with her.

Bumper-to-bumper again.

Claire honking.

Slamming into her bumper.

Jane screaming and clinging tightly to the wheel.

And then—

Cop cars. Four of them. From nowhere. Blue lights flashing. Two of them forming a roadblock at the next corner.

Jane had made it through. That was the crazy and unfair thing about it all.

Jane had made it through.

The cops were concentrating on Claire.

Slamming on her brakes, she started sliding as her car slowed before crashing into the two-car roadblock.

She stopped no more than six feet from the police vehicles.

Jane drove straight to the studio, parked in the "private" spot next to Knox, and hurried inside.

Eight cop cars now.

Her car surrounded with cops holding guns.

"Get out of the car slowly with your hands up, lady," said one cop.

"I'm not resisting arrest, officer," Claire said through her open window.

"Look," said another cop. "It's the First Lady."

After Deirdre Hutton had held Knox at gunpoint, studio security became very tight.

Jane had to pass three different armed security officers before reaching the studio.

There were fifty-six minutes to go before air time.

Knox was looking through his notes for the show. When Jane knocked and waved the cassette tape at him, he broke into a boyish grin she didn't know he was capable of.

She opened the door and walked in.

Without a word, he got up and took her in his arms and kissed her.

"You know what I was wondering," he said, as he took the tape from her. He played a minute of the tape on a small cassette player not used for the air. Then he made a dramatic gesture, picked up the de-gausser and erased the tape in a few buzzing, throbbing moments.

"What?"

"Do you know Claire's car phone number?"

"Sure. Why?"

"Give it to me," he smiled. "I want to have a little fun."

Within five minutes, there were as many reporters as cops. Two of the local stations had dispatched mobile vans, one of them already linked up and broadcasting the fact that the First Lady—after having recently been charged with the murder of her very special friend—had just now been stopped for breaking at least a dozen traffic laws.

There were now at least a hundred onlookers. The cops had cleared the street as much as possible, but traffic was at a crawl. Everybody wanted a look, the way they did at a major traffic accident.

Word spread quickly that the First Lady was involved, and many of the onlookers were craning their necks, trying to catch a glimpse of her.

"You didn't have any special reason for breaking all those traffic laws?"

Claire sat in the back of a police cruiser. The two-way radio was crackling with codes she didn't understand.

"I was just in a hurry, I guess."

"You were clocked at 86 miles per hour. That's quite a hurry."

"I guess it is."

The balding uniformed officer looked as if he drank a lot of Pepto-Bismol in the course of a day. He'd probably drink several bottles today.

"So you're not going to tell me the truth?"

"What's the difference?" Claire said. "I broke the laws. That's all that matters."

"So there were no mitigating circumstances?"

"No. I guess not."

"You 'guess not'?"

"No. I mean N-O. No mitigating circumstances." What was the point of telling him about Jane and tape? The cop had already judged Claire as some kind of nutcase. She felt sure of it.

"You'll need a lawyer for this."

"I know."

"I'm going to impound your car and have somebody drive you to the White House."

"I appreciate that."

"And I'll need you to sign this."

"Sure."

He handed her a clipboard with some papers on it. He x-ed the line where she had to sign.

"There."

"Thank you."

She signed it.

"May I get my purse from the car?"

"Sure."

She'd left the car running at the curb.

She slid inside and started to grab her purse from the far side of the seat.

The cellular phone rang. She picked up.

"Hello?"

"You always did have a great phone voice, Claire."

Knox Stansfield.

"You bastard."

"Language like that from a First Lady? How unbecoming, Claire." He laughed. "I just wanted to let you know that I took care of the tape for you. I erased it all nice and clean so you can use it again if you want to. No sense wasting a brand new cassette like that, is there? Too bad Bobby wasn't bright enough to keep a copy, don't you think? Now you go back to the White House and wash that mouth of yours out with a little soap, all right? You've been a very naughty girl."

He hung up.

65

⋆ ⋆ ⋆ "Any more coffee, ma'am?"

"No, thanks, Ruth. I'm fine."

"I'll be saying good night, then."

"Yes, Ruth, good night."

And the President said, "Good night, Ruth."

After coming home—double the number of reporters at the White House gates, the sense of siege more palpable than ever—Claire had tried to take a nap, but it had been impossible. First because their lawyer had called and she'd had to help him write a statement to the police, and then—

She hadn't been able to resist turning on the news to see how the press was reporting her driving arrest.

ABC had a psychiatrist on, a beautiful, slick Park Avenue shrink, who hinted that the First Lady might well be going through a breakdown of some kind. "All the pressure—it must be crushing her," the shrink said with a certain quiet pleasure. "And then there's the whole question of guilt. If it turns out that she is guilty of the murder—well, that would only add to her confused mental state."

She'd turned the TV off and tried napping again but it had been no use.

She'd simply lain in bed watching the blue window turn gray with dusk. All she could think of was Deirdre. She felt a terrible isolation as she looked at the window—as if she had been accidentally left on a strange planet where people meant her only harm.

None of this could be happening to her . . .

Ruth, the housekeeper, called her for dinner just at seven, as always.

Matt had tried to laugh off the driving incident but she could see that it had deeply embarrassed him. He looked even older and more worn tonight.

Now, as Ruth left, he said, "We need to be getting to the hospital."

"Matt."

"What, dear?"

"I'm sorry I embarrassed you."

"You didn't embarrass me."

"I was just doing—"

"I know what you were doing, dear. But—why don't we leave it to the lawyers from now on?"

The words were terrible to her. "You mean just give up?"

He looked down at his hands on the long mahogany dining room table. When he raised his eyes, she saw only pity and fear in them. "There's going to be a trial, dear. Knox and Jane—they set this up very well. And you running around and—"

"—and getting stopped for traffic violations—"

"Well, dear, it doesn't help. I'm sorry."

How could she possibly disagree after this afternoon?

Leave it to the lawyers, yes.

Stand trial.

Give all the people who hated them the longest-running media circus of the season.

Have every aspect of their personal lives paraded before the cameras.

And maybe drive Deirdre into a mental hospital permanently.

All of it was horrible but—

But Matt was right. What choice was there?

Matt rose from the table. "I'll go wash up and then we can go see Deirdre." He paused and smiled sadly. "Is now a good time to tell you how much I love you?"

"Now is a wonderful time to tell me how much you love me. I appreciate it."

Inside the walls of stone and iron bars their daughter waited.

Claire checked with the head nurse to make sure that Deirdre was still not allowed to watch TV, Claire being afraid that the live coverage of her driving arrest would only have made things worse for Deirdre. The nurse assured Claire that Deirdre saw no TV.

Then the gray-haired woman, officious in a white pantsuit, shook her head somberly and said, "In fact, we're getting a little concerned that she doesn't make any of the usual patient demands."

"Oh?"

"By now, most patients would be asking for all sorts of privileges—including getting outside for at least a little while every day. But Deirdre spends most of her free time in her room, just staring out the window."

"The prescription drugs aren't helping?" Claire asked anxiously. Like many Americans, she secretly believed that there was a pill for everything. Just pop one down and you'd be fine.

Laughter. Claire looked over to see a group of six patients in pajamas and bathrobes watching Giggles, the new comedy cable channel.

"Oh, they're helping, Mrs. Hutton. I mean, she'd probably be in total withdrawal if she wasn't taking them. But they're not helping as much as we'd hoped."

"I see."

"Would you like to see Deirdre now?"

The room in shadows again. Pale wintry moonlight through the window casting silhouettes of iron bars across the bed. Deirdre awake. Staring.

But at what?

"Hi, honey," Claire said, leaning down to kiss Deirdre on the cheek. "How about a little light?"

"Hi, Mom and Dad. If you wouldn't mind, I'd just as soon leave the lights off."

Mom and Dad glancing nervously at each other.

Deirdre laughed quietly. "It's all right. I just have a little headache."

"We're just so glad to see you," Matt said.

He, too, kissed her cheek.

"I'm sorry I'm such a pain."

"A pain? Deirdre, what're you talking about?" Claire said.

"Well, you've got so much to worry about and then here I go and—"

She began weeping. Weeping in such a way that any kind of consoling was impossible.

Matt got on one side of the single bed, Claire on the other, and between them they just held her. And let her weep.

"Oh, honey," Claire said several times, not knowing what else to say.

Just held her. Rocked her as gently as she had when Deirdre was small. Just loved her.

And Matt did the same.

The duty nurse came along a few minutes later. When she saw that Deirdre was weeping, she said, "I had a bad night myself a while back, Deirdre. I starting thinking of all the Rocky and Bullwinkle shows I've missed since I started working this night shift—and it really got me down."

And Deirdre started laughing.

Still weeping and daubing at her nose and eyes with a little white handkerchief—but laughing, too.

"Your daughter's ashamed to admit it but she watches *Bullwinkle*, too. Soon as she gets her TV privileges, in fact, I'm going to take my dinner break with her and we're going to start watching *Bullwinkle* together. Right, Toots?"

Deirdre, weeping and laughing, nodded.

All the time she bantered with Deirdre, Ellen Katz worked efficiently at getting Deirdre to take her pills, sit up straight so Ellen could fluff her pillow and straighten the blankets, and clean up the top of the bureau next to the bed. And cast a knowing eye on Deirdre's daily charts.

Claire felt a great ebullience watching Deirdre respond to the nurse, knowing her first real hope that Deirdre was making a little progress in this place.

Deirdre said, "Ellen here is actually one of the patients, Mom and Dad. They just let her dress up and pretend she's a nurse."

"Yes," Ellen said, "and then later on, I change into a vampire."

"I thought it was a werewolf," Deirdre said.

"Oh, yeah," Ellen said. "I always get those two confused, don't I?"

And so it went for the next ten minutes.

By the time Ellen left, Deirdre was in a great mood. And Deirdre's parents were glowing.

On the way out, they saw Ellen sitting with the patients watching the Giggles channel.

They stopped to thank her for the care she'd so obviously lavished on their daughter.

As the President spoke with Ellen and the Secret Service agents stood patiently by, Claire noted that the comic on screen at the moment was Paul Lydon, the very clever young man who did such a good imitation of movie stars and political people—Matt and Knox Stansfield in particular.

Looking as much like an accountant as ever, Lydon stood on stage live at a comedy club saying, "Have you heard Knox Stansfield the last couple days?" And then he went into Knox's mannered, boastful style: "You know, just yesterday I had Reverend Goodhew call God up and ask Him if the First Lady actually killed David Hart—and you know what God said? He said—"

Claire wanted to hear the rest of it but she was called away by one of the agents. Matt had an Oval Office appointment at nine tonight and they had to hurry.

The TV audience, and everybody in the room, burst into laughter at Lydon's punchline. Claire looked longingly at the TV set, eager for

290 ★ E. J. GORMAN

a moment's diversion. She needed her own version of Rocky and Bull-winkle.

But it was time to go.

"I want to thank you again for being such a help to our daughter," Claire said to Ellen Katz. "We really appreciate it."

"My pleasure."

The women shook hands warmly.

Then it was time to go.

"Wow. What a woman."

"Ellen Katz?"

"Uh-huh," Matt said, sitting back as the limo started the long drive back to the White House.

"Thank God for her."

"You should have seen your face when Deirdre started laughing. You were absolutely glowing."

She leaned over and kissed him tenderly on the mouth, then they snuggled up, something they'd been forgetting to do lately.

She felt a moment's peace—the husky smells of Matt, the re-assuringly smooth ride of the limousine, the strobe effect of light and shadow as the vehicle passed in and out of the nimbus of street-lights.

Protected and optimistic.

Everything was going to be all right, after all.

She took Ellen Katz's success with Deirdre to be a portent.

But the optimism vanished suddenly when she saw the mobile TV vans parked out in front of the White House gates.

The press—ravenous for more scandal, starved for the grief of others.

The gates opened as if by magic and the limo shot up the asphalt lane to the White House.

The optimism was indeed all gone.

66

★ ★ ★ Claire went downstairs to her office. She sat in the darkness for a long time. She kept thinking of Jane. Sometimes she felt great rage, sometimes great sorrow. It was funny. She should hate Jane completely—and yet she couldn't quite. Ridiculous as it was, given Jane's great beauty, maybe she had felt inferior to Claire in some way. Maybe taking up with Knox was her only way out.

But then Claire stopped being sentimental. She thought of all the damage Jane had done to Deirdre. Then she was angry again.

Claire had to find a way to save her family—

Then another thought, one that brought a needed smile: comedian Paul Lydon's imitation of Matt and Knox. Lydon was so funny—

Footsteps.

Shadows.

She thought for a moment it might be Matt. His meeting over, he'd have gone upstairs looking for her. And not finding her there—

"Claire."

Dana Hopper, the agent who'd driven her to David Hart's all those times.

She reached over and turned on her desk lamp, a circle of light pushing back the darkness.

Dana smiled but she could see that he was concerned about her. Sitting in the shadows. Alone.

"Hadn't talked to you in a while; thought I'd say hello."

"Why don't you sit down?"

"I can't really. Just have a few minutes."

"You look good. That diet of yours is working."

The smile again. "It's called learning to love carrots."

She could tell that he'd come to say something specific. He seemed reluctant to bring it up.

"How's Deirdre?"

"Getting better I think. We met this great nurse who's helping her a lot. Even gotten her to smile a little bit."

Dana took a deep breath, stood up very straight and said, "There's something I need to say, Claire."

"All right."

"I consider a lot of this my fault."

"Oh, Dana, that's crazy."

"I do. You've been a lot better friend to me than I've been to you."

"Dana, please—"

"I should've told you not to go over there. To Hart's. You were going through— Well, you know how the press was about the President and that woman."

She smiled sadly. "Yes, I guess I remember that."

"Well, anyway, you weren't thinking clearly. So I should have done some clear thinking for you. I should have told you not to go over there."

"Dana, listen—"

"That's what I came to say. I knew you'd argue with me and say I was being ridiculous but that's the way I feel—and I'll always feel that way. I let you down."

"The trouble is, I know you're serious. But it's so crazy to blame—"

He held up his hand like a crossing-guard's "stop" signal. "And there's one more thing I want to say."

"All right. I don't think I can stop you anyway."

"Anything I can do, any way I can help— I'm here for you, Claire. And for the President."

"I appreciate that, Dana."

He shot the right cuff of his jacket and glanced at his watch. "I need to be getting back."

"I'm glad you stopped by."

"You hang in there, Claire. This is all going to come out all right. I just have that feeling."

She went to him then and gave him a sisterly hug. Every once in awhile you met somebody so decent, so selfless—like Nurse Ellen Katz—that it reassured you that most people were good and decent after all.

"I couldn't ask for a better friend than you," she said.

"Me, either," Dana said.

She was awake when Matt came to bed. She listened to him undress—jingle of change in pocket, snap of suspenders as he undid them, drops of shoes as he took his loafers off—only speaking when he slid into bed next to her.

"I'm so damned tired," he said. "We both need a good night's sleep." His voice was disembodied in the shadows.

"I know. I'm hoping."

She rolled over and faced him. "I want to tell you something."

"Oh?"

"You're a damned good man."

"What brought that on?"

"I was thinking that I don't tell you that enough."

"Well, you're a damned good woman."

"I wasn't fishing for a compliment."

"I know, but I thought I'd be gallant about it."

"Thanks."

"If I wasn't so tired I'd ask you to make love."

"And if I wasn't so tired," Claire said, "I'd accept."

"Just don't jump my bones in my sleep."

"I'll hold out as long as I can."

Then he kissed her and it was great. "God, I love you so damned much, Claire."

She slid her arms completely around him, and held him silently until she heard his first snoring sounds ten minutes later.

She went to sleep soon after.

67

★ ★ ★ Disorientation.

Images of a nightmare.

She was in a prison cell, screaming frantically for help, screaming frantically that she was innocent.

But no one came.

No one helped.

Disorientation.

Then—

Snoring. Not her own.

Matt's.

What time was it, anyway?

Then she realized that her left arm was asleep. Still under Matt's shoulder.

She slipped it free, the whole of it tingling.

Something had awakened her—

The nightmare.

Prison.

She saw herself again in the tiny cell, saw her terrified face gleaming with sweat. Heard her own cries for help and mercy.

But no.

Not the nightmare.

That wasn't what had awakened her.

Something else.

Something—

Then Claire came full awake, glanced at the glowing numbers on her nightstand clock: 3:14.

And then she remembered what had awakened her.

An idea.

A plan, really.

Then she rolled over and started shaking Matt.

"Matt! Wake up! Wake up!"

68

★ ★ ★ "I'd like to speak to Dan Rather, please."

"Who may I say is calling?"

"Claire Hutton. President Hutton's wife."

"I see." Pause. "Ma'am, I'm afraid I can't just take your word for it."

"About me being the First Lady?"

"Yes."

"How about if I let you speak to the President?"

"This is a put-on, isn't it?"

"Here, Matt. Tell the woman who I am."

Matt took the phone. "This is President Hutton speaking."

"Is this a put-on?"

"No, it isn't."

"When somebody important calls for Mr. Rather they don't usually go through the front office this way—"

"We're in kind of a hurry and—"

"Wait," Claire said.

She gestured for the phone. Matt handed it back.

Claire said, "Ask Mr. Rather if he enjoyed the Shrimp Louis he had the last time we had dinner together. And tell him that my husband really enjoyed his joke about Adlai Stevenson and Bill Clinton."

"Shrimp Louis?"

"Yes. And Adlai Stevenson."

"I'll be right back."

"Thank you."

While they waited, Matt said, "This is really crazy, darling. The whole thing. If it doesn't—"

"Do you have any better ideas?"

"Well—"

"I didn't think so."

The secretary came back on. "He said he loved the Shrimp Louis." She laughed. "I'm sorry I gave you so much trouble."

"No trouble at all. Thank you for your help."

There was a pause.

Then: "Hello, Mrs. Hutton."

"I thought we were Claire and Dan."

"Claire and Dan, then."

"I wondered if you might be interested in an exclusive story."

"Sure."

"As soon as I hang up here, I'm going to call Knox Stansfield and dare him to put me on his radio show this afternoon. I have a cassette tape that is going to shock an awful lot of people when they hear it."

"Do you think he'll put you on the air?"

"I can guarantee him the biggest ratings he's ever had."

"Can you tell me anything about the tape?"

"Only that Knox isn't going to be very happy if I play it. It could implicate him in the Hart murder."

"God. Are you saying that Stansfield had something to do with the murder?"

"I'm saying you'll find out this afternoon if Stansfield agrees to put me on the air. But I need your help."

"Oh? How can I help you?"

Twenty-eight minutes later, CBS interrupted one of its morning programs to announce: "We interrupt this program to bring you a special news announcement."

Cut to: Dan Rather in dark suit jacket, white shirt, red tie behind the CBS news desk.

"This is Dan Rather in New York. Less than half an hour ago, embattled First Lady Claire Hutton called me to ask if I would go on the air and tell America that she is challenging Knox Stansfield to put her on his radio show this afternoon. She says that she has an audio cassette tape that might well implicate Knox Stansfield in the murder of David Hart— the man the First Lady is presently accused of murdering. She says if Stansfield has nothing to hide, then he'll invite her on his show today."

"Hey, Knox!" the program director shouted as he ran into Knox Stansfield's office. "Turn on CBS!"

✳ ○ ✳

"In conclusion," Dan Rather said, "the First Lady assured me that this wasn't any kind of publicity stunt—or a bid for sympathy. She says that she has in her possession—in the form of an audio cassette—proof that Knox Stansfield was behind the death of David Hart. Beyond that, she wouldn't elaborate. But she did ask me to ask Knox Stansfield right now—on the air—to invite her on his show this afternoon."

"What the hell is she doing?" Knox Stansfield screamed at his TV set.

"We've got to have her on, Knox. There's no way you can say no," the program director said. "Think of the ratings. I'm going to go call the White House right now and tell her she can come on. O.K., Knox?"

But Knox was strangely silent.

"O.K., Knox?"

Only after a long time, and then in no more than a sullen whisper, did Knox Stansfield say, "All right. Tell her she can come on the show."

69

★ ★ ★ As soon as she heard from Knox Stansfield's representative, Claire called agent Dana Hopper. She'd already spoken to him once earlier this morning. "It's all set, Dana. You know what to do, right?"

"Know exactly what to do, Claire. I contacted him and he said he'd be glad to help."

"Oh, God," Claire said, "I sure hope this works."

"So do I," Dana Hopper said.

70

★ ★ ★ Deirdre said, "I wonder if I could have a radio for my room."

She wished Ellen Katz were here. There'd be no problem, then.

"I'll check with the doctor," the male nurse said. He was blond and beefy and dressed in a white polyester shirt and trousers.

"I'd really appreciate it," Deirdre said.

He looked at her and smiled. "You heard about your mother, huh, going on Knox Stansfield's show?"

Deirdre nodded. "Yeah. One of the patients told me. She'll tear him apart."

The male nurse winked. "Between you and me, I hope she does, too."

He paused at the door. "I'll get you that radio, kiddo."

"Thanks."

71

★ ★ ★ Jane called Knox immediately after Dan Rather went off the air.

"What's she up to?" Jane said.

"That's what I was going to ask you. What the hell tape is she talking about? You told me that LaFontaine didn't make any copies."

"That's what he told me."

"Then he must've lied."

"Or," Jane said, "Claire's lying."

"Meaning what exactly?"

"Meaning maybe she's just trying to scare you into something."

"You know, you could be right. That could be exactly what's going on here. A little grandstanding."

For the first time since watching Rather, Knox Stansfield felt some of his usual self-confidence.

"I'll bet that's exactly what that bitch is up to," he said.

"You just need to stay cool, Knox. You know, the way you usually are. You can't afford to act scared."

"You're right."

"If you can get through this, then everything will be fine. This is her last hope—trying to rattle you on the air."

Knox bunched his jaw muscles. "Well, that bitch is going to get a little surprise, believe me."

"Good, Knox. That's the attitude you need. I'll talk to you afterward. Love you."

"Love you, too," he said, but his mind was already on the radio show that would be starting in less than two hours.

72

★ ★ ★ On this particular afternoon, on the planet Earth, on the North American continent, in the country of the United States, in the city of Washington, D.C., a broadcast booth is transformed into an electronic arena that the Romans of the Empire days would have well understood and appreciated.

12:31 P.M. The presidential limousine reaches the studio parking lot.

12:36 P.M. Secret Service agents lead the First Lady inside, where she is met by the corporate president and his two most important vice presidents. They gush and exult. She appreciates their efforts, but nothing can calm her down. Her entire body is trembling, her mouth is dry and she is vaguely worried that she is going to vomit.

12:41 P.M. The First Lady goes to the bathroom, where she uses a stall briefly, comes out to the sink, where she runs a comb through her lustrous hair, and then washes her face with icy cold water. She takes several deep breaths and stands up straight. She knows she must look tough and ready when she finally encounters Knox.

12:49 P.M. The First Lady is shown into the broadcast booth. Her first impression is one of surprise. Knox Stansfield is such a powerful figure in American communications—and the booth is so small and old-fashioned, not unlike the many radio booths Matt was interviewed in as he rose from mayoral candidate to congressional candidate to senatorial candidate. Microphone, papers neatly stacked, two comfortable but unremarkable office chairs.

12:53 P.M. He's making her sweat it out. Mind games. Knox was always good at them. She thinks: There's seven minutes to air time and he's going to come flying into the studio with just a few minutes to go, trying to make me as nervous as possible. She must keep in tight control of herself. Absolutely must.

12:56 P.M. The white-haired audio engineer on the other side of the glass says, "Mrs. Hutton, we need a mike check. Could you just start speaking?" She's seen hundreds of mike checks and gives him just what he wants. He gets her audio level to just where he wants it and says, "Thank you very much, Mrs. Hutton."

12:58 P.M. The door opens and Knox is there. A little too much cologne, a little too much practiced smile. "I probably shouldn't tell you this, Claire, but you look absolutely great." He's even bold enough to lean down and give her a little peck on the cheek. "You really do look great. Honest." He nods to the wall clock. "There's still a minute to go. In case you want to back out, I mean. There's still time." She says: "I'm fine, Knox. But you're sweating a lot all of a sudden. It must be hotter in here than I realize." He looks at her and says: "Bitch, you're going to regret ever coming here. Believe me."

12:59:43 P.M. Knox sits down behind his mike and waits for the engineer to give the cue. And then the cue comes:

1:00 P.M. Knox says: "We're on *America Speaks.* With the only show that dares tell you the truth about our government."

Both contestants are now in the arena.

The battle has begun.

73

★ ★ ★ 1:01 P.M.

"So I'd like to take the opportunity to welcome the First Lady to our show today. It's a real pleasure."

"Thank you, Knox."

"As many of you know, Claire and her husband and I were very good friends back in our college days. And I like to think we still are."

She could be just as supercilious as he was. "Of course, Knox. It's great to see you again."

Knox nodded. "I just want that understood. Up front, I mean. That I still consider you and Matt good friends of mine. I've been a little rough on you from time to time—but that's just doing my duty as a political commentator."

"I understand, Knox."

"So I want everybody to keep that in mind as they're listening to the show today. Everything is meant in the best of spirits."

"Absolutely."

1:06 P.M.

"You'd think that jerk would choke on all those lies," McElroy said.

"No kidding," said the President.

✳ ✳ ✳

1:08 P.M.

"So you want to go through it step by step so that America will understand correctly, is that right?" Knox Stansfield asked.

"Right, Knox," Claire said. "The first thing I want to deal with is my marriage and all those rumors that my husband was having an affair."

"You're saying he wasn't having an affair?"

"That's exactly what I'm saying."

1:16 P.M.

"So you're saying that Matt—the President, I mean—never had any sort of physical relationship with the young woman?"

"Correct."

"And he was the one who told you that?"

"Right."

"And you believe him?"

"Yes. Yes, I do. He's my husband and I love him and I believe him."

1:27 P.M.

"She's doing well, isn't she?" Deirdre said to the male nurse.

"She sure is. In fact, if this was a prizefight, I'd say she's ahead three rounds to two."

Deirdre picked up the boxing parlance. "Now if she can only get a knockout."

1:28 P.M.

Bobby LaFontaine was listening to the radio as he packed. That broad was really giving it to Stansfield. When the truth about everything came out, Bobby might find himself implicated. That was why he was hurrying to get out of town.

A parolee like himself did not want to start answering police questions about murder and attempted blackmail.

Bobby hurried with his packing, and when he was done he took a last look at his nice, new apartment. This was the kind of place ex-cons like Bobby LaFontaine always dreamed of. But very few ever actually succeeded the way Bobby had.

Oh, well. Maybe he'd try Australia. It was a place pretty much like America herself, he'd been told. A land of milk and honey—and suckers.

Bobby hurried from his apartment, eager to start his new life.

1:34 P.M.

"So those times you visited David Hart—"

"Completely innocent," Claire said.

"I guess the operative word here is completely."

"That's what it was. Completely."

"You're a very attractive woman."

"Thank you."

"And David—well, he was certainly experienced with women."

"Yes, he was."

"So—"

"Completely innocent."

"You're repeating that for us?"

"Indeed I am, because it's true."

Claire tried real hard not to lean over to the wastebasket and throw up. She was terrified.

1:43 P.M.

The program director said, "You know how we could never get General Motors because of Knox's politics?"

The CEO of the Patriot Broadcasting Company nodded.

"They'll be begging us to get on the show now."

"I just wish Knox would rough her up a little," the CEO said.

"Yeah. At least make her admit that Hart got a little bare tit off her, if nothing else."

The CEO smiled. "'Bare tit.' There's an expression I haven't heard since 1961."

1:52 P.M.

"So Matt—I mean, the President—didn't have an affair. Right?"

"Right."

"And you and David Hart—"

"—didn't have an affair, either."

"All right. Let's say I accept both those statements."

She forced a laugh. "That's very nice of you."

"Let's say that I accept both of those statements—but still have to wonder about David Hart's murder. If you didn't kill him, who did?"

She knew she needed to be bold. "You did, Knox."

This time he forced a laugh. "I did? And just why would *I* have done it?"

Bold again. "Because you hate Matt and me. You never forgave me for dumping you and you've always wanted to pay us back."

He was sweating now and she could see his jaw muscles begin to clench and unclench.

"This gets better all the time."

"And I'm just starting," she said.

⁎ ⁎ ⁎

1:59 P.M.

Clemmons went over to the phone and dialed.

The receptionist said, "Shannon, Fine and Peyton law offices."

"Mr. Fine, please."

"Who may I say is calling?"

"My name is Clemmons. I work for Knox Stansfield."

"One moment please."

2:01 P.M.

Detective Michael Henderson listened to the Knox Stansfield show in a bar.

He was in a back booth by himself.

He was scared.

If it turned out that the First Lady wasn't the real killer—and that therefore Henderson had arrested the wrong person—well, who the hell was going to pay for a book or TV movie like that?

He'd go from hero to hotdog in minutes.

He'd gulped down three quick whiskeys in the last half hour. Now he was about to order another one.

2:04 P.M.

"You had Dan Rather tell America that you had a tape that would implicate me in the murder."

"Yes. I do."

"You brought it with you, I assume?"

"I most certainly did. But I'd like to hold off on that a little."

"Oh," Stansfield said, "and why would that be?"

"Because I have a question I want to ask you first."

"Yes, and what's that?"

"Does Reverend Goodhew know that you're sleeping with his daughter?"

2:04 P.M.

"Was that a knockout punch?" Deirdre said.

Before the male nurse could answer, Ellen Katz came through the door and said, "If it wasn't, it sure did a lot of damage."

She rushed to Deirdre's bedside. She smelled wonderfully of spring. "I just had to come here early and be with you, Deirdre."

Deirdre squeezed Ellen's hand. "I really appreciate it."

2:05 P.M.

"His daughter?"

"Yes. Jenny is her name."

"I know who she is but that's about it. Sleeping with her is a ridiculous allegation."

2:05 P.M.

In her apartment, Jane said, starting to cry, "You bastard. You bastard."

2:06 P.M.

McElroy said, "She's doing great!"

2:06 P.M.

Stansfield said, "Now it's my turn to ask *you* a question."

"All right."

"If you didn't kill him, how was it you got videotaped standing next to the body with the murder weapon in your hand."

Be bold. Strong. "That's how you set it up."

"Back to me again?"

"Absolutely. You killed him, then knocked me out and made it look as if I killed him."

"So I was in the town house while you were there?"

"Long enough to knock me out and set everything up."

2:07 P.M.

The CEO said, "You don't think Knox actually had anything to do with killing that guy, do you?"

"Knox? Are you kidding? Hell no he didn't."

2:10 P.M.

"So I guess we're kind of at a standstill here, aren't we?" Knox said. "You say I did it; I say you did it. But there's one difference. The police have a videotape of you standing by the body with a gun and you have—squat. Excuse the inelegant word but you don't have a damned thing."

"Don't I?"

"You mean the tape?"

"I mean the tape, Knox, yes."

"You really want me to play it?"

"I really do."

She noticed that his right hand was trembling.

"I really do," she repeated.

2:12 P.M.

"God, I'm sorry I'm squeezing your hand so hard," Deirdre said, sitting on the edge of her hospital bed in robe and slippers.

"That's all right," Ellen Katz said. "I'm just as nervous as you are."

2:13 P.M.

Detective Michael Henderson came back from the john and picked up a fresh drink on his way to the booth.

Things were disintegrating fast.

It sounded as if the First Lady was going to nail Stansfield to the cross.

Without a big-bucks media deal, there was no way Henderson could ever lure his wife Maggie back.

Not ever.

2:14 P.M.

"Here goes," McElroy said.

"You think it's going to work?"

"He's a smart sonofabitch."

"He's also a killer. Maybe his guilt'll do him in."

McElroy said, "I think that only happens in Lassie movies."

2:16 P.M.

"Ah, the legendary cassette tape that will prove conclusively that Knox Stansfield is a murderer."

Stansfield said this as she took the cassette from the pocket of her brown tweed suit. "The tape," she said.

And then held it up in the air and waved it in front of his face.

"I wish we had television, folks. I wish you could see the way Knox is sweating."

And he was indeed sweating.

2:17 P.M.

"Give it to him, honey," said the President of the United States. "Kick his ass around the block."

2:18 P.M.

"Why don't you take it, Knox? You look like you're afraid to touch it."

"Don't be ridiculous."

"Here. Then take it. Touch it."

She pushed it even closer to him.

She could see that he was in fact afraid to touch it.

His hand got close but he couldn't quite make it actually touch the cassette.

"He won't take it, folks. He's afraid of it."

* * *

2:19 P.M.

The CEO said, "What the hell's wrong with him, anyway?"

"I don't know. It's weird, though."

"You sure he didn't have anything to do with that murder?"

2:19 P.M.

"So that's what I'm asking you for, Mr. Fine. Your advice, I mean."

2:20 P.M.

McElroy said, "She's killing him! She's absolutely killing the sonofa-bitch!"

2:21 P.M.

He took the tape, Stansfield did.

"There. Does that satisfy you?"

"Took you a while."

"I can't play the tape in here, anyway. We'll have to give it to the engineer. We'll do that while we break for a commercial."

The engineer cued him that they were going into a commercial.

Claire said, "I wonder if your mother's listening."

"Is that supposed to be sarcastic?"

"Not especially. She never liked me anyway. After today I'm sure she'll absolutely hate me."

"You're making a fool of yourself on the air. I hope you realize that."

"We'll see who looks like a fool, Knox," she said. "We'll see."

2:26 P.M.

"Man," Deirdre said. "How many commercials are they gonna run, anyway?"

2:27 P.M.

The President said, "There should be a law against this—running so many commercials at one time."

2:28 P.M.

"This is Knox Stansfield, and we're back in the studio with First Lady Claire Hutton, who is about to prove—or so she says—that I'm a cold-blooded murderer. Or am I putting words in your mouth, Claire?"

"No. That's exactly what I'm going to prove. Are you sure you want your engineer to play the tape, Knox? What if you're wrong—"

Bold now. Very bold. "What if Bobby LaFontaine actually made a copy of it? And what if that's what your engineer is about to play?

Once your listeners hear that, Knox—well, they'll probably never want to hear you again."

She paused. "I really do wish we had TV, folks. Knox is getting very very pale!"

2:31 P.M.

Deirdre shouted, "Go, Mom, go go go!" as if she were leading a football cheer.

Ellen Katz put both thumbs up in the air.

2:32 P.M.

"Don't you think it's about time to run the tape, Knox?"

"I guess I don't see any reason why not."

"Then why don't you tell your engineer to do it?"

Another forced laugh. "You always did love drama, didn't you, Claire?"

"You're stalling, aren't you, Knox? Ever since I raised the possibility that Bobby LaFontaine made a copy of the tape—"

"I want to but it's time for another commercial break."

"Saved by the bell, Knox? Is that it?" Claire smiled sweetly.

2:35 P.M.

"Oh, man, she's gonna kill him now," McElroy said. "I can feel it."

2:36 P.M.

"Put him away, Mom! Destroy that jerk!"

"Well," Ellen Katz said, "it's good to see that you're still learning new words."

2:38:52 P.M.

Claire said, just before they went back on the air, "Will you try to kill me right in the booth, Knox, or will you wait till later?"

"You whore," Knox said, with all the contempt he felt for women.

2:40 P.M.

Clemmons hung up.

He was three blocks from the studio.

2:42 P.M.

Knox Stansfield knew he had to get it over with. He had to play the frigging tape and prove that she was bluffing.

But what if she wasn't bluffing?

What if Bobby LaFontaine really had made a duplicate?

Stansfield wanted to lean over the wastecan and puke his guts out.

Bitch. Rotten bitch.

His mother had been right about her. Absolutely right.

The engineer cued him, and Stansfield said, "Knox Stansfield again, my friends, sitting here with the very charming First Lady of the United States who insists that I'm afraid to play the cassette audiotape she brought along to the studio today. Well, fair lady, I am about to disabuse you of that notion. Sam—if you please. The tape."

Stansfield could feel his bowels start to loosen. A chill ran the entire length of his body. He felt his sphincter muscle start to loosen and—

God, he was literally starting to crap his—

And then his own voice, recorded, filled the studio:

"Even if I did kill Hart, no jury in the world would convict me. You don't seem to know just who the hell I am. I matter and you don't buddy, and you better goddamn keep that in mind."

The tape stopped.

Studio silence.

"Well, Knox, do you have anything to say to that?" Claire said softly.

"That's not a confession."

"No, it's not. But it's not something an innocent man would say, either."

"It doesn't prove anything."

"I think it does," she said, "and I'll bet you a lot of other people do, too."

2:47 P.M.

The CEO said, "What were you telling me about GM, you stupid little idiot? It sounds like our biggest star is a goddamned murderer!"

2:48 P.M.

"I didn't murder him, Knox. You did."

Stansfield heard her—but she sounded distant. Everything sounded distant—and felt distant. He glanced around the small booth. Everything looked so *alien* now. It was no longer his special province.

"Why don't you have him play it one more time?" Claire said.

She knew she had him, now.

Now she had to move in for the final assault.

All she could think of was how happy her daughter and husband would be when this whole nightmare was over.

"How about playing it one more time, Knox?"

And then he turned to her and snapped, "One more time? Sure, why not? You've taken over the show anyway! You may as well call all the shots! One more time—play it!"

* * *

He was undone.

He wanted his mother.

He wanted the sweet suffocating reassurance of her fleshy arms, that mixture of smells—cologne and Arrid cream deodorant (she hated roll-ons, considered them vulgar) and her beloved English Ovals, the very classy imported cigarettes—in which he had so often drowned so pleasantly.

The tape was played again, and he sat there miserably.

He was undone.

He wanted his mother.

Claire had him now.

There was no doubt.

She watched as he struggled to keep his composure as the tape played.

In just a few moments, it was all going to be over for him, and he would be exposed for the liar and killer he was.

And then, suddenly, he was laughing.

Laughing!

And when she looked over at him, she realized that he had discovered her secret.

"Paul Lydon!" he said. "That comic who imitates politicians! That's *him*—that's not me! He always drags out his syllables too long! I didn't catch it the first time—but the second time—"

2:53 P.M.

Deirdre said, "Oh, God, then it really wasn't Knox Stansfield on the tape?"

2:54 P.M.

McElroy said, "It didn't work. He figured it out before he confessed."

"And now he's never going to confess," the President said. "Never."

2:55 P.M.

Now she was the ashen, trembling, sweaty one.

"Are you going to tell the people what you did?"

"You've already told them, Knox."

"Trying to deceive them is what you were doing. Trying to deceive them just the way your husband and his entire administration has. Trying to pervert all the values of honesty and integrity that the American people cherish so deeply."

He was completely himself again, that sneer in his voice, that mockery in his eyes.

"No doubt you and the President cooked this up together—didn't you?"

She could barely find her voice. "He didn't have anything to do with it. It was my idea."

She'd called Paul Lydon, written out what she wanted him to say in the voice of Knox Stansfield, and asked her friend Secret Service agent Dana Hopper to take it over to Lydon. He'd brought her the cassette just as she was going into the studio.

But it was all over now.

Everything.

"Since the truth is coming out here, Mrs. Hutton, why don't you tell us about how you killed David Hart?"

She felt sick, dazed.

2:56:14 P.M.

Detective Michael Henderson slammed a celebratory fist on the table in his booth.

All right!

So she was faking all along.

His big-bucks media deal was back on!

2:57 P.M.

Deirdre buried her head in Ellen's shoulder and said, "Oh, Mom. I feel so sorry for her!"

Ellen stroked Deirdre's head.

2:57 P.M.

"We're going off the air here in less than three minutes," Knox Stansfield said. "There's still time for you to tell all our listeners the truth." He laughed. "Why don't you start by telling us about the sex you had with him? You've always liked sex, Claire. I'm sure you weren't any different with Hart."

2:58 P.M.

The President of the United States said, "I'm going to kill that sonofabitch!"

2:58 P.M.

"I didn't have sex with him and I didn't kill him."

"Now's the time for truth, Claire. Purging the soul. It's good for you."

"I didn't have sex with him and I didn't kill him."

"You're just making it worse with these lies, Claire. The American people are very forgiving when people tell the truth."

"I didn't—"

And then she heard the studio door open behind her.

She saw Knox's head jerk upwards and then frown. He waved the intruder off then returned to his microphone.

"Less than a minute now, Claire. Less than a minute to tell the truth. You killed David Hart, didn't you?"

"No, sir, she didn't," Clemmons said, and walked into the booth.

He leaned over to Claire's microphone and said, "You killed him, Mr. Stansfield. And when you did it, you got a little bit of his blood on your shirt. And I've got that shirt right here with me."

Claire watched as the handsome older black man reached inside his sport jacket and pulled out a white shirt.

"I'm going to turn this over to the police now," Clemmons said. "And then I'm going to tell them everything I know about the matter. And then you're going to be charged with murder."

Knox Stansfield jumped up from his seat and grabbed for the shirt but Claire threw herself between the two men.

"You dirty black sonofabitch!" Knox Stansfield was screaming to his millions and millions of listeners. "You dirty black sonofabitch!"

2:59:27 P.M.

Detective Michael Henderson slammed his drink so hard against the table that he smashed it into three nasty chunks.

One of the chunks sliced a deep wound into his right hand.

He didn't even notice.

He just kept thinking about his wife Maggie.

His soon to be ex-wife Maggie.

He thought all the way back to his youth—Maggie had always been there, his guide, his inspiration. But she was gone now, or would be soon enough, and gone forever.

He fought back his hot, bitter tears. But it did no good. The tears came anyway.

74

★ ★ ★ "I'm just so glad he came forward," Deirdre said. "Mr. Clemmons, I mean."

Deirdre and her parents sat in a small alcove overlooking a stand of pines. Deirdre would have to stay in the hospital for a few more weeks, but this afternoon's events had worked wondrous effects on her. Not that her ordeal would be over when she was released. She'd have to go to court and face punishment for what she did. Both her parents believed in each person taking full responsibility for his or her actions. Likely there would be probation and reporting to a probation officer regularly and continuing in psychotherapy. However good her intentions, Deirdre had been wrong to do what she'd done.

"He was worried about his nephew," Claire said, then explained how Clemmons had hired a good lawyer for the teenager—a lawyer who felt he could get the boy off with probation—and how Clemmons had then convinced his sister to let him come to the studio with the shirt.

Deirdre shook her head. "I got so scared when Stansfield figured out that you'd had that comedian do that imitation—"

Claire laughed. "Well, it almost worked."

Matt said, "I'm with Deirdre. When Knox figured it out, I thought, It's all over now. I believe I even used a few naughty words at the time."

Claire smiled. "In front of McElroy? I'll bet he was embarrassed."

"Oh, yes," Deirdre said, picking up the joke, "those virgin ears of his and all." Then her pretty face got somber. "I shouldn't have done what I did. Gone into his studio with a gun and all. That's not what this country is supposed to be about. I'm really sorry."

Claire took her hand and said, "I guess we've all done things we're sorry for, honey. Now we'll just have to live with them."

"I can't wait to get home," Deirdre said.

"It won't be long," Matt said.

And then Deirdre drew them together and kissed them both gently on their cheeks and said, "I really want to be a family again. We started drifting apart there, and we shouldn't have."

"No," Claire said, "no, we shouldn't have."

On the way back to the White House, Matt said, "We'll never be the same again, will we?"

"No. I doubt we will."

"It's like we've lost our innocence or something. The press—and all the people who turned on us—"

She leaned against him and put her hand on his. "That's not what we need now, Matt. We need to go on, and forget as much as we can."

"I know," he said. "But it won't be easy. It won't be easy at all." Then he was the old, joking Matt. "Believe it or not, some of those people really pissed me off."

"Really? I hadn't noticed."

Laughing, he leaned over and kissed her.

The limousine pulled up to the gate.

The MP, recognizing the vehicle, saluted.

Inside, the President waved good evening to the guard. The First Lady smiled as she glimpsed the magnificent lighted façade of the White House ahead of them in the night.

For the first time in more than three weeks, the splendid building looked not like a prison—but like her home. The home she'd missed so much.

A few weeks later, the White House had a very special guest, one who had the rare opportunity to see the upstairs where the President and his family lived.

Clemmons wore a dark suit, a white shirt, and a dark tie for the occasion. Dignity was so much a part of his demeanor that Claire noted the fact that Mr. Clemmons was far more impressive than many of the world leaders they met. And they owed him so much—he'd called Claire before she'd gone to Stansfield's radio show and told her about Stansfield and Reverend Goodhew's daughter. That's all he'd intended to say. But then, after hanging up and thinking about it, he'd brought the shirt to the studio.

At first, the conversation was somewhat stilted. Even given the fact that Clemmons's courage had saved this family, they were all a little uneasy as they struggled to keep the dinner conversation going.

Clemmons talked about his new job working for a public relations firm as its private driver; the President discussed his upcoming summit trip to Europe; and Claire talked about the story on the evening news that Reverend Goodhew's daughter—now that the Reverend had learned she'd been sleeping with Knox Stansfield—was entering a private girl's college. Reverend Goodhew himself would be going on a month-long "retreat" to his Ozarks cabin to "hear again God's true message."

Clemmons smiled. "Did that TV story mention that the Reverend's Ozarks cabin cost 1.9 million dollars?"

Claire smiled. "I guess I didn't hear that part of it."

Clemmons shook his head. "Maybe I'm just getting cynical. Maybe this is a real retreat for him."

The President nodded. "Even rich people need spiritual comforting." He laughed. "Hell, even *congressmen* need spiritual comforting from time to time."

"I don't know if I'd go that far," Clemmons said. "About congressmen, I mean."

Gradually, they all got a lot more comfortable with one another, so much so that by dessert Claire had already invited Clemmons back for a White House party five weeks away.

Then Deirdre said, "You seem like a very bright, reasonable man, Mr. Clemmons. How do you feel about girls my age having tattoos?"

"Oh, God," the President said. "Not the tattoo argument again."

"No, maybe Deirdre's right. Maybe that's what we need. Somebody who's really objective."

"I'll bet you think they're pretty cool, huh, Mr. Clemmons?" Deirdre said.

He looked at her a long moment and said, "You know, Deirdre, you're a very pretty girl."

"Thank you."

"And why you'd want to cover up even a little bit of the beauty God gave you, I'll never know."

Deirdre looked at her mother and said, "I guess he doesn't like tattoos, huh?"

Claire smiled. "I guess not."

"Then that settles it," Deirdre said. "No tattoo."

"Are you serious?" the President said. "The subject is really closed?"

"Yes, Dad," Deirdre said, "The subject is really closed." Then she smiled. "Finally."

"How'd you do that, anyway?" the President said to Clemmons, and they all laughed.

Late that night, Claire found herself awake in the darkness. She slipped out of bed and went to stand at the window, to look out at the White House lawn.

Only very recently had she even tried to sort out all the terrible things that had happened these past four months.

Washington, D.C., was a beautiful city at night, and she let herself enjoy the beauty for a few moments.

Just then, her husband started snoring loudly, and she looked back at him.

When his hair was tousled this way, he looked just like a ten-year-old boy.

Overwhelmed by sentimentality, she went back to bed and lay down next to him. She took his hand and placed it gently across her ribs, so that it rose and fell with the soft rhythm of her breathing.

And then she started crying softly, without quite knowing why, just crying there in the darkness of the White House, thankful that the three of them were alive and safe, thankful that the long nightmare with Knox Stansfield was finally over.